STRANGE CREATURES

Also by Phoebe North

Starglass

Starbreak

STRANGE CREATURES

PHOEBE NORTH

BALZER + BRAY
An Imprint of HarperCollins*Publishers*

Balzer + Bray is an imprint of HarperCollins Publishers.

ISBN 978-0-06-284115-5

Typography by Chris Kwon
21 22 23 24 25   PC/LSCH   10 9 8 7 6 5 4 3 2 1
❖
First Edition

I couldn't decide whose book this was
And then I realized I wrote it for

The girl I never was,
The boy I almost wasn't,
And the person who survived them both.

I dedicate this book to myself.

(Does that seem bold to you? Vain?
Do you wish I'd given it to you instead?

Fine. Here. Take it.

I wrote it for you, too.

To show you that if you live through this,
Then someday *you* can tell the story
You'd hoped your whole life to find
Every time you turned a page.

Bring it to me then. So I might tuck myself in
With your book. *Yours.*

My story's been told. I'm done with it—

But the world can always use

More books that are honest, strange

And true.)

❧

I knew he was in danger
because he was both the egg
and the one who cracked it —

—Jessica Fisher

EPILOGUE

EVERY MORNING ANNIT woke at dawn, while the two moons were still low against the horizon. Alone, she built her fire from the wood she'd gathered the evening before. Alone, she ate her meager breakfast, scraped her plates clean, dressed. There had been a time when she'd worn steel, a time when twin swords had dangled from her leather belt. If her men had doubted she had the strength to don her surcoat and arms, they never mentioned it. *Speak ill of the Emperata*, they whispered to one another, *and she'll cut off your tongue.*

She had never cut off a man's tongue. That had been petty gossip. But she'd cut off other things.

Now, no more armor. No more swords. The only weapon she carried was a small stone she'd found the evening before in the creek bed out back, tucked now into her pocket. The only armor she wore? An old tunic, secondhand and patched. A pair of men's trousers she'd found in someone's trash bin and her old familiar dragonscale boots. They were her only finery, and they'd been a gift from her brother, a long, long time ago.

She walked through the village, as she did every day. Today she was alone again, as usual—until she wasn't. A small boy walked quietly beside her.

The boy's hair was a disaster of black snarls. He kept his eyes down as he walked, although on occasion his gaze would dart up to ascertain that the old woman hadn't gone far. But in fact, the old woman kept pace with the child, matching stride to barefoot stride.

"I shouldn't take you past the village edge," the old woman said at last, as they neared the squalid row of mud-and-thatch houses at the end. "Your mother wouldn't like it."

Annit had been here for fifteen years, at least. She knew every face, had lived here long enough to see some of the babies grow up to have babies of their own. She'd even made a friend or two, like Ijah, the silversmith's only son, who occasionally traded her a spell for a cookpot or a spoon or some other useful trinket. But she didn't recognize the wide set of this boy's eyes or the growl that graced his lips when he replied, "Y'ain't taking me anywhere. I take myself."

The corner of the old woman's mouth quirked upward in a smile. "You do," she agreed. "Can't argue that."

And so, Annit began to climb a zigzag path up the side of the mountain, and as she went, she let the boy follow behind.

Had she ever been so young, so determined? Must have been, once. Her body bore the scars of it. But now she had only shadows of feelings, and none of them mattered. Now she lived a quiet life—a life without hurt or insult. There was no crying. But there was no hot passion, either.

And once, she had lived a life full of passions. Those vicious arguments with her brother. The spilled blood of a battle, and the celebration that came after. The music of a beautiful girl on a summer's day. The taste of wild mead on their lips as they joined their bodies together, their lives together, in the days before Annit had made an exile of herself. It had been inevitable. One cannot remove so many body parts without consequences. She knew that, and so she had accepted her fate willingly, and without hesitation.

And yet she found it pleasant now, after all these years, to have company. The boy's breath was a steady pulse, joining hers as the air grew thin and they drew close to the top of the mountain. It was on the far side that the old woman found it, her cairn, swaying against the cliff's edge.

The pile of stones was enormous—standing nearly twice her height, stacked narrowly at first, and then growing wider, like an enormous egg. And like an egg, it had one smooth side. No instrument in *this* world could cut a rock or carve a piece of lime with such intention. Now Annit walked to the object's far edge, feeling over the cliff face for the hole she knew would be there. This close to the structure, she could hear a faint hum on the air—could taste the metallic twang of electricity. It was magic. Hers. But not only hers. Reaching out, she slipped the small stone into the gap. It fit as if it had been carved precisely for this purpose, though she knew it had been shaped by the river. By the water. By the inevitability of time. She stepped away, joining the boy on the path's edge, crouching low beside him in the grass there, looking at the cairn. Her head was cocked to one side as she considered.

"No," she said softly. "It's still not right."

"What izzit, anyway?" he asked. She laughed a little, a dry, rattly laugh, and shook her head.

"You might call it a beacon," she said. She stood. She was looking at it from every angle now, her eyes tracing the smooth edges. There were no holes left in the cairn. Every stone had found its place. "It calls out to other beacons across the world. There are two others. They're meant to work together. My first love built one, on the shore of the Crystal Sea."

"And the third?" asked the boy, wrinkling his nose. She turned to look at him, at the serious face beneath so much dirt.

"My brother," she said.

The two of them were quiet for a moment. Perhaps the boy was thinking about his own brother, if he had one—which he probably did; these village girls whelped children like they were puppies. But if that was the case, the boy said nothing about it. His face was merely a mud-stained, determined mask.

"D'theirs look the same as yours?" he asked. Annit let out a scoff.

"No," she said, a little too sharply. She wasn't used to speaking to children. She wasn't used to talking to *people*, really—but especially children. "Magic isn't like a knife or a spoon, where one design works best. Their beacons would be of their own making. I have no idea what *theirs* look like." She fell silent, realizing, perhaps, that she'd been too harsh with him. When he answered, it was in a hard voice, too.

"And wot d'they do?" he demanded, standing now, as she had. "These beacons?" He came closer to the cairn, closer to the cliff's edge. That wild hair had begun to stand on end in the presence of so much magic. He lifted a hand. Almost, but not quite, touching the beacon's smooth wall.

"Oh," Annit said, and she let out a sigh. "It's supposed to crack open the eternal truth, and then rip a hole in the universe."

The boy turned, his hand still raised, and looked at her—eyes like the dots on the bottom of a pair of wide, wild exclamation points.

"Don't worry," she said grimly. Now she reached out, too, and put her hand against the cairn. She closed her eyes so she could better feel the hum of their music. Her own music. Her lover's. Her brother's. The three songs were almost, but not quite, a chorus. The notes were off-kilter, off-key, and worse—something was still hidden there. Some truth was still occluded. She said, "I built it wrong. It was meant to be magic, but there's no magic here."

That was a lie. There was magic everywhere, in every cell. In the stones, the cliff, the grass, the path. In this boy and his illiterate brain. In the girl who had taught her how to build beacons, stack stones, make art—so long ago that she'd been practically an illiterate child herself. In her brother, in some distant prison of his own making, a continent or two away from here.

There was especially magic *there*. It had been there from the beginning—undeniable. It was still there, through the miles that stretched between them. The magic that bound them. The magic that had set them, years and years ago, out on this adventure. And yet it wasn't the magic she had *wanted*. She had wanted to capture something, to destroy something, to make something new. And she hadn't, not yet. When she put her hand against the cairn, she felt how feeble it was. She could sense, though she could not see, small gaps between the stones. Imperfections. The truth was invisible to her. The door was closed. The door would never open, unless she made a choice.

She opened her eyes.

"Tell me, child, what do you want with me? Some spell to bring your mother back from the dead?"

"Mother ain't dead, either. Not yet, anyway." He finally dropped his hand to his side. And then he looked back down at his bare toes, and how they wormed through the sun-warmed dirt.

"I could teach you how to heal her," the old woman said. The boy's eyes didn't brighten. And why should they? Who should blame him for not wanting to carry the burden of his mother's life—or death? But something still sparked inside that stormy gaze. Hunger. "Or I could show you something else."

"Wot?" the boy demanded, looking up then. Looking hard. He was so starved for it. She was, too.

Annit considered what it might cost. She would have to squander this meager, peaceful existence. Still, there had been time enough for peace already. Magic seared through her, and had from the very beginning—no matter how long she'd tried to deny it. She only had to build something better this time. Something right. Something true.

Her hand was still against the beacon. The metallic taste of magic was in her mouth. And then, just like that, she swallowed it down. She pushed her weight against the cairn's wall. It sounded almost like the start of rain at first—one small stone dropping, then the next. *Plop plop plop.* But then suddenly there was a crash and rumble of rock down the mountain. That zap of magic went silent, like a candle going out.

The look on the child's face made it all worth it: wide-eyed horror.

"What'dya do?!" he cried out.

Annit just laughed. "Child," she said, "it's only stone. We'll build another beacon. One that works properly this time."

"An' your brother? An' your first love?"

Annit shrugged her thin, elderly shoulders.

"If there's any magic in them—and I think there is—then they've got work ahead of them, too."

"But how will they know?" he whimpered, his chin shaking. "They're so far away! And 'snot like you *told* them you was gonna do that!"

Her brow lowered. Well, the child had a point there. Still, they'd never needed words before. She particularly had never had to tell her *brother* a thing. When they'd been children, they'd spoken without speaking, traded secrets with a glance. Surely now, after all these years, their magic would be sufficient. Annit shrugged her age-worn shoulders, ignoring the doubts that the child had made creep in.

"They'll manage," she said simply. But the boy wasn't comforted by this at all.

"Wot's the point?" he whispered, and she could see that he was on the verge of tears. So soft, so easily defeated. "All those years, all those stones, only to have to build it over?"

Annit sighed. She held out her hand to him. He wiped his nose against his sleeve, snuffled. Took her hand in his.

"Child," she said. "I've learned so much since I've come here. Now, maybe I can tell the whole story, from beginning to end, or near to it. Now, maybe . . ." She trailed off, unable to finish the thought. Because it wasn't only up to her, was it? It would take all three of them—three different perspectives, three different stories, three different cairns. No, no. Her math was wrong. They would need six altogether, if they managed to build them again. But if they did it right, then the three of them, together, would be able to reveal something new. Something magical.

The truth.

"And then?" the boy demanded. She turned away from the heap of rock, from the dust that swirled in the air, no magic in it at all.

"And then we'll open up the gate and get ourselves out of this muddy shithole," she said in a singsong. He looked at her, his eyes back to two pools of surprise again, but there was something new there this time. The hint of a wicked grin.

"Come, child," she said, leading him down the path. "You have much to learn. And I have work to do."

Together, his small hand in her age-spotted hand, the old woman and the boy began to walk down the mountain.

I

People often ask me how I got my start. They lick their lips, lean forward in their chairs, adjust the microphones that are pinned to their lapels. I'm old enough now to understand the score: what they really want to know is how magic works, and if there is a tiny bit of it that they can steal.

What they don't realize is that they're asking the wrong question. They shouldn't be asking about me at all. If they really want to understand beginnings—if they really want to understand magic—then they need to be asking about Jamie. James Michael **[Redacted]**. My brother.

He's the one who started it all.

1

EMPERATA ANNIT WASN'T BORN, AND she was never truly an infant. At least not that she could recall. To Annit, the first memory was this: coming to life in the mudluscious bottom of the River Endless, as all Feral Children do, gasping and getting a mouthful of sludge and water, green.

The mermaids had wanted her for themselves, but Annit never belonged to anybody except herself. Still, she felt desperate hands grasping at her shoulders and toes and ears. Annit thrashed against them, fighting to reach the pale light of the surface. When she landed on the sodden shore, there were still the marks of nails over her bare belly, like a dozen long, hungry mouths.

The children came to greet her. They'd been waiting, aimless and empty without her. The days, the endless, listless summer days, had piled up like a cairn on the shore. But here she was, perfect: a girl, her hair a tangled mane of algae and mud.

"What are you looking at?" she asked, scowling.

❖

Torn apart. That's what my brother called it. He believed in our magic right from the start. According to Jamie, we weren't two identical souls, but one soul housed in two bodies. We could only be our true selves when we were together; and because we were inherently together on the inside, in the places that mattered, we could never really be alone.

September 26 was Jamie's first birthday. It was also the day that I was born. Jamie always claimed he remembered it with crystal clarity. In the moment before, Aunt Jennifer turned out the light in the dining room, and Jamie, in his high chair, in the momentary darkness, was filled with a yawning sense of dread. He said he always felt that way back then—but this was sharper. Even as Gram and Poppy began to sing and the candle on his cupcake flickered, he felt the blackness encroach on him. A squeezing nothing. He worried, as someone blew the candle out for him, that the doom might swallow him whole.

But then the light came on, and in the second that it took for our dining room to return to its ordinary sallow color, something inside my brother shifted. Snapped into place. Exploded, too. In that moment, he was abruptly made right.

Because in that moment, he knew, I was born. A sister. Annie—the name he'd helped Mom and Dad pick from their baby name book by waving his chubby hands at exactly the right moment that Mom's hand alighted on exactly the right name. It meant *gracious*, he later told me. *Merciful.* Most important, in Hebrew, it meant *prayer*.

Back then, when Mom sang prayers to him at bedtime, he'd prayed for me. I was the sibling who would make everything right. The other half that made him whole. He knew I was born before the phone started to ring, before Aunt Jennifer could share the news. He knew it the same way he knew the color red, that Grover was furry, or the special way the crack in the ceiling over his crib formed the shape of a lucky hare. I hadn't been there, and now I was, and he would never be alone again. The only injustice, he later said, was that he'd been born first. That the rest of the world would never know how we were secretly twins, or how we had been torn apart.

For me, there was no life before Jamie. He was older, and so his presence shaped everything that came after. And everything came after Jamie. In all things—walking, talking, weaving stories—he came first and, while he was patient with me, in the beginning I could only do my best to keep up with him. I wasn't merely following in his footsteps. I was tracing those footsteps perfectly, and often in his hand-me-down shoes.

But Jamie claimed he could remember a time before me. One long, empty year when there was a hole inside him he could not fill. Now, from a rational standpoint, it seems absurd, as absurd as the idea that he remembers all those details from his first birthday. Before I was born, he was an infant who could barely wrap his lips around a small handful of words, much less the idea of a deeper emptiness inside him.

Still, at home, when it was just the two of us, Jamie was brilliant—a shining gem. He knew the scientific names for all kinds of animals, knew every type of gemstone, knew every knot that could be tied. On the rare occasions that he was ignorant about something, he would press forward with dogged determination until he unlocked that knowledge or skill. One day, when we were very young, Dad brought home a yo-yo. I was hopeless at it, much to my father's disappointment. But my brother kept at it while I watched him from our back steps, winding and unwinding the string over and over again, until the night was thin and buggy, until our mother beckoned us inside for dinner.

"Just a minute!" he called, slapping away mosquitoes, his brow furrowed. Jamie, a knot around his middle finger, made the emerald cabochon of plastic spin and glow. By the time we went inside, he not only understood how to make his yo-yo bounce; he knew how to walk the dog and go around the world, too.

"It's almost like a superpower, Annie," he told me later. "If you try hard enough, you can learn to do anything. To *be* anything."

My brother was a genius. I understood that better than anyone, so when he told me that he remembered my birthday, remembered even a time before I was alive, I believed him. Back then, I believed every word he ever said.

We grew up in Wiltwyck, a sleepy Hudson Valley town wedged between the feet of the Catskills and the roaring Wallkill, two hours north of New York City on days when the traffic was light on the Thru-way. There were hippie apothecaries and twisting apple orchards and college students from the university in the next town over, on the hunt for cheap rent. It felt like a place where magic might happen even in the beginning. Perhaps that's why it did.

Because as soon as Mom brought me home from the hospital, Jamie and I were always together. Jamie pulled me to my feet for my first steps. He sang me songs in his own secret tongue. In turn, I stole his clothes and toys and laughter. He never seemed to mind that I was his shadow. We were one person, after all, not two.

On some afternoons, in the gray-gold light of our early childhoods, we would sit together, crisscross applesauce, on Jamie's bed. I faced him like a mirror, clasping his hands in mine. He would say "Annie Annie Annie," and I'd drone back "Jamie Jamie Jamie," until our names were a strange, creaky chorus of meaningless syllables. I studied his trembling chin, his bark-brown eyelashes, the gold flecks in his brown eyes, until, in the dim light, his features would seem to blur and his skin seemed to disappear completely. I could see shadows in his eye sockets, the grown-up teeth waiting in his sinuses, his nasal bones, thin and delicate and just like mine. We were more like each other than we were anyone else, more than Mom or Dad or Poppy or Gram or Grandma or Aunt Jennifer or any of the kids on our street.

On those afternoons, we'd tumble from his bedroom together, dizzy and exhilarated, half-numb from what we'd done. Dad would see us, and he'd laugh. This was back when his laugh was real, not studied like the laughter of those sitcom dads on TV.

"What have you two been up to?" he'd ask.

And we'd answer back together, "Nothing!" and hide our giggles behind our identical sun-browned hands.

2

THE BOY WHO WASHED UP on the westerly shore of the Island of Feral Children was different from the others. His body was bruised and battered. There were purple shadows beneath his eyes. Though other children had shown up scratched from mermaid claws before, this boy looked as though his flesh had been through several wars. He bore scars like sidewalk cracks, which had healed poorly and pinkened and bled and wept. Now his skin was gnarled as a baseball mitt. He was a boy, but he did not look like one. There was mourning in his gaze.

❖

We were lucky, my father always said. Our neighborhood was full of children. When the weather was warm and the light optimistic, the sounds of their voices provided a constant soundtrack. My father said that it was the kind of neighborhood he'd grown up in back in New Jersey, where children wandered in and out of screen doors, stealing snacks from different refrigerators, borrowing each other's bicycles, waging war on one another across their cul-de-sac.

In the summer when I was young and our bedtime was early, I'd sit up by my window, watching for fuzzy movement in the yards around us. There were a few girls with swingy ponytails among the older children, but otherwise it was mostly boys who played in the sunset space below. I'd study them as they put together pickup games of Wiffle ball or dodgeball, and then, after dark, watch them disappear together into the woods that bordered the backyards of all the houses on our side of the street. Inside my room, inside my body, I would be filled with an inexplicable hunger. Dad would come by, command me to go back to bed, and I would. But once I was tucked inside my sheets, my mind refused to go quiet. I wanted to understand who they were and where they were going. In my imagination, those teenagers were packs of wandering heroes, off on incredible adventures in the waning summer light.

My brother didn't share my fascination. If he was up late, it was with a flashlight, reading books under the covers after our parents went to bed. He learned to read early, and by the summer after first grade was already into Percy Jackson. On warm days, he'd sit in the corner of the sofa, making himself as small as possible, and read and read and read. I couldn't stand it. I needed to be outside, running under the sprinkler, catching fireflies in our backyard. I spent most of the summer sunburned and bug bitten, while Jamie's eyes got more and more sunken, his face wan.

On one August Friday, Dad came home early from work. He saw Jamie there, licking his fingers, turning pages. In a booming voice, Dad commanded my brother to put down his book and get himself some fresh air. I had been alone with my games that summer, utterly ignored by the other neighborhood kids. But Jamie's presence shifted everything. Even if he was pale and bookish, he was still taller, older, more handsome. Most important, a boy. It didn't take long for some neighbor kid who was in his grade to wander over to where we sat on the front steps and ask if Jamie wanted to come play football with him.

My brother hesitated, chewing on his lip. During the school year, I'd heard my parents' whispered concerns already, that Jamie was having trouble *connecting*.

"He's gifted," his teachers had said, and Mom had repeated this to us, though Dad had given her a warning glance, as though she wasn't supposed to tell us that. "But his social skills need work."

Was this what his teachers had meant? I watched my brother staring at this boy, and something about the way that their gazes were locked made me feel small. Invisible. The other boy was not my brother, but he had a face full of freckles and eyes that were a sparkly chestnut brown. His features were pinched and cunning, and he was at home in his body in that way that boys usually are.

Go with him, I thought. *Play. I would, if he wanted me. Go!*

My brother glanced at me as though I'd spoken aloud and had not merely thought those words. "Okay," he said, and sighed. "But Annie's going to come, too."

The other boy looked at me, his lips tightening into a frown. It was clear already that I would never be one of the swingy ponytail girls who the boys in the neighborhood tolerated as friends. My differences were obvious to them and to me, though I couldn't say how we all knew this. Still, my brother was wanted. And so the boy conceded, and waved me along, too.

"Fine, but she can't play," he said. "She's too little. I guess she can keep score."

A grin cracked my face. I pounded one fist into my other palm. "Great," I told him. "I can count real high."

The boy sighed, rolling his eyes. Jamie glanced back at me as we crossed the street, uncertainty bubbling under the surface of his gaze.

Their backyard was spare—the lawn cut short and emerald green whereas ours was always shaggy and dotted with weeds. There was a privacy fence around it, and inside, a trampoline, a tree house, a soccer net. Big-kid accoutrements. Our yard, on the other hand, was mostly cluttered with sun-bleached preschool toys and a kiddie pool full of mosquitoes that Mom always forgot to drain. But there was one other important difference: this yard was full of big kids. This boy's older brother and his friends were here, and they were nearing the edge of childhood already.

"Who's that?" one of the big boys asked. He had a football tucked under his arm like someone out of a soup commercial. My brother hesitated, stubbing his sneaker on the grass. He didn't speak, so I spoke for both of us.

"That's Jamie. I'm Annie."

The big boy looked at us, and then at the little brother who had led us here like a pied piper.

"Are you sure?"

"We need another player, don't we?"

The older boy snorted, nodded. He gestured first to himself, then to his brother next to him. "Fine. I'm Calvin. This is Neal. C'mon, Jamie."

Calvin didn't invite me to play, but I hadn't expected him to. I climbed up onto the trampoline and dangled my legs off to watch.

I knew the rules of their game already, or vaguely did, from watching through the window. And I knew that Jamie didn't. He didn't care about football at all. He was already lost. But I couldn't help him here, in this world of boys. I knew somehow, instinctively, that it would only make things worse for him if I told him about the rules. So I watched the big boys kneel over the football, listened to Neal shout something at his brother, watched the ball go sailing into his waiting hands and then watched as Neal pitched the ball toward Jamie.

The problem was that my brother hadn't been watching. Jamie had been staring, instead, somewhere off into the middle distance, following a pair of monarch butterflies with his eyes. When he turned and noticed the football careening toward him, he let out a scream and ducked. The ball bounced on the lawn several feet away from him, and my brother just crouched there as the other boys tumbled past him. Even from the trampoline, I could feel the fear rising up off him. These boys were wild animals, growling, snarling, their fingernails sharp as claws and twice as dirty.

When the play was over, Neal looked at Jamie, who was still crouched on the ground, and he spat on it, somewhere between the two of them. "Crybaby," he said.

A few minutes later, my brother and I were walking home together. His steps were trembling, uncertain. He rubbed his pink-rimmed eyes and his snotty nose against the back of his hand.

"It's okay," I told him, putting my arm over his shoulders. "You'll do better next time."

My brother didn't answer. His body was rigid beside mine. He only let out a tiny, wordless nod.

Jamie's sensitivity, and his brilliance—in those early days they were two sides of the same coin, in much the same way that Jamie and I were two sides of a bigger, different coin. At temple, he would sing the words of the prayers along with Mom, right out of the prayer book. He sang in Hebrew, his voice clear and angelic. But then on Purim, he'd throw his hands over his ears every time Haman's name was mentioned, wincing at the cacophony of groggers and shouts. Eventually, he would start crying, and Mom would take him out to the hall where she'd dance with him, or slip him a book from her purse and let him read to her aloud. Leaving me and Dad alone with strangers to hear the rest of the whole megillah.

Back then, Mom and Dad didn't fight much. But on the ride home from synagogue, when they thought we were asleep, I heard them talk in low voices. As always, they talked about Jamie. Never about anything else.

"You coddle him too much," Dad said.

Mom sighed. "He's sensitive. We don't want to snuff that out of him, do we? The world will do it soon enough."

Dad let out a grunt, his eyes searching the dark Woodstock roads as our car wound down the mountain. "You're the one who insisted we join the synagogue," he muttered. "It's so expensive. And you don't even stay for the services."

Mom didn't answer. She only switched on the radio and scanned through the stations without settling on anything.

When we got home, they carried us inside to our respective rooms, Jamie tucked inside Mom's arms, me in my father's. When he set me down in my bed, I kicked off the plastic heels that were supposed to make me look beautiful, like Esther, but had just made my feet hurt.

"You're awake," he said.

I nodded, grabbing the blanket and pulling it up so that it covered my whole body. "Is there something wrong with Jamie?" I asked.

He shook his head. "Your brother is different," he said. He didn't have to tell me that. I knew. I was different, too. "But different isn't wrong. Just—we have to make sure that we're there for him, to help him when he needs us. Okay, Annie?"

I nodded, settling lower under the blankets. I could help Jamie. It's all I ever wanted. To help him. Even then, I could feel him somewhere, past the edge of my awareness. Like a dream I hadn't quite forgotten upon waking. Pleasant and warm and loved. Precious. And he needed me, which meant I was precious, too.

"Okay, Daddy," I said.

My father didn't kiss me, but I saw the light of his smile in the darkness as he flicked off my bedroom light.

3

IT WAS IJAH WHO FOUND the boy, a sopping bundle between two cairns, waterlogged and just waking to life. When Ijah offered his hand, the boy refused to take it. He wouldn't touch anyone, not with those toughened, thick fingers. When Ijah led him to the sacred pool, the boy simply stripped down naked, crouched low, and poured the water over himself.

"What's your name?" Ijah asked, expecting the triumphant declaration that usually accompanied a soak in the pool.

The boy simply squinted and pulled himself from the water. "What's a name?" he asked.

❦

So Jamie was different from the other kids we knew. I was, too, of course, but it mattered less for me. I didn't mind being strange, and no one was really paying any attention to me, anyway. But everyone had their eyes on Jamie. Mom thought he might someday become a great artist—a poet, or maybe a painter, even though his drawings were terrible and the watercolors he did at school, even worse. She wanted to sign him up for ballet classes, or maybe take him to lectures at the local Buddhist temple. She wanted to teach him how to knit, just like her grandma Pearl had taught her.

But Dad wanted him to play soccer on Saturday mornings. Dad wanted to sign him up for Cub Scouts. Dad had learned certain things in boyhood, and he wanted my brother to learn them, too.

"It's why we moved here," we heard Dad remind our mother. "You wanted to raise free-range children. You wanted them to have a chance to *play*."

In the end, my father won. He knew what it was to be a man, after all. There was no ballet. My brother's knitting was abandoned between the sofa cushions. And though sometimes I suspected that my brother *wanted* to go to the Buddhist temple with my mother, before long he'd come to spend his weekend afternoons throwing and catching a ball in the backyard with Dad instead.

"I'll do it," I told him one day, watching while my brother carefully tied his shoelaces into bows. "*I* already know how to catch. Maybe Dad will show me how to throw a fastball."

My brother looked at me with eyes that were flat, clear mirrors of my own. He didn't bother sighing. He didn't need to. We both knew that Dad had no interest in teaching me anything.

"It's okay, Annie," he told me, though his voice sounded studied when he spoke—careful, like he didn't want to show how he *really* felt. "Dad wants me to go out for Little League when I'm older. It's something I need to learn."

I waited for them in the gray solemnity of my bedroom while I drew pictures of fairies and knights and a dragon who wrapped her long tail around the naked body of a girl. I colored in the girl's bruisey skin with the pencils Mom had bought for Jamie and Jamie had given to me. The window was open, and I could hear the sound of the baseball hitting Dad's old mitt. *Thwack, thwack*, over and over again, for what felt like hours.

And then a sound that was different from the others, sharper and more percussive. I saw it in my mind's eye: a flash of red, then white, like an explosion on TV. I pressed the tip of my pencil too hard into the paper, and it broke, but I hardly noticed. Instead, I was on my feet instantly, rushing down the stairs and outside.

Mom was already there—heavily pregnant by then with what would be our youngest sibling. She was taking up too much space in the sliding door, letting out an anguished cry. Outside was Dad, kneeling in front of Jamie, whose face was an explosion of blood. Jamie wasn't crying, though. Jamie was only nodding calmly, listening to our father.

"This is why you need to pay attention," he said. "You're not going to be an infielder if you can't react."

"Marc!" Mom was exclaiming as she rushed down the steps. "He's *hurt!*"

"He's fine," my father said. Jamie turned to us, squinting, and I saw how his right brow had been split by the ball, and how much it was bleeding, directly into his eye.

"I'm fine," he agreed, but Mom grabbed him by the hand and whisked him away to the downstairs bathroom, where she could properly fret over his wounds.

Later, we sat in his bedroom together, Jamie paging through my drawings like he was studying some ancient book. He turned to the one with a naked girl and stared at it for what felt like a long time. I think if it weren't for the Pokémon Band-Aid on his eyebrow, he would have lifted it, like Mr. Spock.

"This is really beautiful," he told me, his voice full of a familiar gentleness.

"Thanks," I said, shrugging off his compliment like I always did. "But you still haven't told me how you stopped yourself from crying today."

When we were little, almost anything could make Jamie cry. Not just boys like Neal. It might be skinned knees or sappy commercials about dogs. Someone would sling a small insult and then he'd run into Mom's arms and bury his face in the crook of her neck and she would rock him like a much younger boy.

At my question, Jamie set down the drawing. The corner of his mouth lifted, but it was a mysterious kind of smile.

"It's something that Mom told me," he said. "A trick. I'll show you later."

"Show me now," I said. But Jamie only shook his head.

"No, later."

I sat back in his bed, frowning. A secret, then. But my frown wasn't very deep. Jamie never kept his secrets for very long. Not from me.

Once, our backyard had been kingdom enough for me. But by the time Jamie made shortstop, we'd outgrown it. At the far edge of our property was a drainage creek, and beyond it, a few miles of over-grown, tangled forest. The woods out back were full of litter, mostly refuse from the teenagers who idled back there, too. Crushed beer cans. Crumpled wrappers. Wormy condoms, though I didn't know what they were at the time. But lately we only ever saw their garbage, never the teenagers themselves. When we went back there, it was a universe that belonged to the two of us alone.

Jamie had named this space Gumlea. It was a baby name. Meaningless. Embarrassing. But so familiar that we were never quite embarrassed by it. The day after Jamie's accident, we hopped off the school bus and headed back there together, not even bothering to check in with Mom.

We dumped our backpacks by the side of the drainage creek and launched ourselves over it, one after the other. Then we began to walk back.

"Today, I'm a pirate!" I exclaimed, grabbing a nearby branch from the ground and brandishing it in one hand like a cutlass. Jamie had filched the idea of pirates from an old copy of *Treasure Island* that Dad had given him on our last birthday. We always played games that were variations of what we'd seen on TV or read in books. It didn't feel like stealing back then, to say that lost children lived in Gumlea, just like they did in Neverland, or that there were hobbit holes in the ground, though we called them by other names. What did it matter if we pillaged other people's stories when we told our own? We were only children, playing games.

But not on that day. Jamie looked back over his shoulder at me and let out a wicked grin.

"Do you want to learn the trick Mom taught me?"

I stopped, resting my stick in the muddy ground. "Sure."

Then he did something odd. He gave a strange backward twist of his body, a bizarre flourish of his hands. Later, we'd refine this ritual. We'd make rules about it—the precise way you had to move your body over the drainage creek to open the portal to Gumlea and then, later, how you would reverse the movement to close it again. Right now, though? It was only the world's strangest and most awkwardly choreographed dance.

I giggled. Jamie didn't.

Because in that moment, the whole forest—full of litter and graffiti, mosquitoes and poison ivy and ticks—seemed to fill up with a gilded light. Just like that, it was transformed. The trash was gone, replaced by storybook toadstools and half-buried gold doubloons. The branches, shifting overhead, were no longer full of autumn's browning leaves. They were tipped in bronze and copper, with tinkling jewels for cherries, dangling overhead.

I looked at my brother, eyes wide. And in that moment, he wasn't only my brother. He was a prince, ermine draping his shoulders, ruby rings weighing his fingertips down. He was as beautiful and fine as ever, and when he spoke, bells seemed to ring through the underbrush. Or maybe it was a chorus of fairies calling out to us like peepers on a summer's night. I couldn't be sure.

"Mom told me that I'm different than the other kids," he said to me. "Because I have an *imagination*. When something is hard or weird—when it hurts so bad you think you're going to puke—you just need to go inside it. To the other place."

"Gumlea?" I asked. I was still holding the stick in my hand, and though part of me was willing it and willing it to become a cutlass, it was simply a half-rotten stick with a bunch of ants crawling on it.

But then my brother took it from me and held it in his hands. I saw then that it wasn't a stick, or even a cutlass. It was a dagger, with a scalloped blade and a fiery stone embedded in the hilt. Images were carved into it, but he was flashing it so swiftly in the light that I couldn't catch what they were.

"Yeah," he said. "Sure. Gumlea. C'mon. Let's find the princess. I think a dragon's got her."

He turned and walked deeper into the sparkling forest. I did the only thing I could. I followed.

4

EMPERATA ANNIT'S ROUNDHOUSE WAS BIGGER than the rest, full of gifts from adoring children: real slingshots made of rubber bands and forked sticks, a bow and quiver that someone had brought with them from home, eyeless dolls and hairless dolls. The boy kicked his way through the cruft. Sitting in the middle of it all was Annit, perched on a throne of harpy bones.

"What have you brought me, Ijah?" she asked. Her most faithful soldier knelt low in front of her, indicating the boy.

"A new arrival. He says he has no name."

"No name?" The boy's expression remained even. "Well, we have to call you something. We'll call you . . . Boy."

He didn't answer.

❖

It was all Gumlea after that, for both of us. Jamie was the one who told the stories; because I was the better artist, I was the one who drew the maps. But it was both of us, working magic together, who created the world, and all the creatures in it. There was a vast, salty ocean that covered the entire planet, and a ring of continents that punctured it. In the middle was the Island of the Feral Children, shaped like a hand spread out into the water. Against its southern palm was the mermaids' lagoon, a ragged heart between two fingers. To the north was the land of the Winter Mountains, which sparkled white even in summer, hunched up like an old woman's back. If you traveled eastward, you'd find the King's domain, where towns and cities of ordinary people—grown-ups, families—were ensconced behind endless walls.

I drew these places over and over again on Dad's computer paper and in the fairy notebook Mom got me at the Dollar Tree and on the back of my standardized test booklets and in the margins of my language arts reader. Then Jamie helped me make copies on Dad's scanner so we could have two of each page. One for the walls of his room, one for mine. At night, as the sharp edges of my vision faded and my mind filled up with something cottony and gray, I watched the rivers move, the mountains tremble, the walls crumble like teeth and the mirror over my dresser open, like a mouth gaping, waiting, welcoming me.

After school, and on breaks, we'd climb into the woods together, hungry for its magic. We were alone, but we were never alone. We were chased by harpies, harassed by mermaids. Clever foxes and delicate fawns moved through the woods beside us, calling out to us in low tones. We called back.

Deep in the heart of Gumlea, past the tree houses of the Feral Children, beyond the mermaids' lagoon, we always came to rest in the same place. The King's tower. It was a gray rectangle of unassuming stone that stood with its door open in a sunny glen. The space inside was a chilly black that makes me shiver, even now, to remember it. Older and braver, Jamie always went in first. I'd hesitate on the precipice just a moment before I pulled myself inside, too.

The air inside was cool, ever-fragrant with incense. Not the kind our mother burned when she sometimes overcooked dinner, but something sweeter. Jasmine, maybe, or freesia, and a damp smell beneath that. Hidden, sacred magic. A red carpet pooled in the shadows at the base of a very long, winding staircase. My footsteps echoed on the stairs.

As I climbed, the world got brighter. Clearer, too. At last, at the top, I'd find my brother, his body silhouetted against an enormous stained-glass window. It would take a moment for my eyes to adjust to the sight. Jamie, on a tarnished throne set with a thousand opals. Jamie, with a bronze ring on every finger, a scepter in his hand. Jamie, who loved beautiful things, who was a beautiful thing himself, his long velvet robe like silver moonlight, trailing on the steps below. I would kneel before him, touching my forehead to my knee. Sometimes I would peek at the embroidery inside his open gown, which told a thousand stories. There were birds. Kings. Queens. Traps. Blood tithes and flesh tithes and flowers growing up through bone.

"Sister," he'd say softly. I found myself blushing at his voice. At myself. Here I was, my freckled face smeared with mud and cookie crumbs. If I were anything, it was a wild creature. In our first expeditions into Gumlea and every trip thereafter, I never wore velvet or silver but rather the hides of animals I'd killed and sometimes scavenged. My dirty shoelaces bloated like a clot of earthworms. But none of this bothered Jamie. His voice was gentle. The voice of a poet-sage, a true prince. "Why have you come?"

"Only to see you," I'd tell him, then add, blushing more, "Sire."

It was true. I looked up and saw my own face, twinned there. My perfect opposite. Fine where I was coarse. Polished where I was gnarled. But the same freckles. The same earlobes, detached. The same heart beating inside. Our bodies had different shapes, but those differences didn't matter. We would always understand each other, the way the ocean understands the moon.

He'd come close. Link his fingers in mine. Jamie saw me as no one else saw me, and not just that. He found me worthy, too.

"If I'm a prince today, then you rule us all," he'd say. My brother pressed a kiss to my forehead, and I breathed in his perfumed scent. He smelled like sacred oil. Still, we giggled, both of us. At the exact same time.

I remember all of this. Our hiccuping laughter; our sticky children's hands; the light scattered through the dust motes; the light in all its myriad colors, coming in through the stained glass. I remember it just as clearly as I can recall the crow's-feet at the corners of my mother's eyes, or the steady, tuneless way he hummed when he raked the lawn. It felt real to me at the time, and it feels real now.

Did it happen? I couldn't tell you. Not while I lived inside it, nor years later, either. There are days when I tell myself that there is a line in childhood, one we hadn't crossed yet, where a million absurd possibilities might as well be true. Flying reindeer. Tooth-stealing fae. Universal peace. A future without death or loneliness or despair.

There are other days when I remember the way the afternoon sunshine came through the bubbled stained glass, pink as hibiscus tea, and I know that Gumlea is out there, somewhere, still. That somewhere, if I could just figure out how to open the doorway, there is a world where no one could touch us, where there are dragons, harpies, and walls of stone. And that inside it, a brother and a sister are linked and precious, safe in their secret world.

We discovered Gumlea just in time. Because the next year would be a hard one, as I turned six and Jamie seven. That was the first year we *needed* Gumlea. The first year we needed the escape.

That was the year the boys in the neighborhood took an interest in Jamie again, and not just for an afternoon. There was Neal Harriman from across the street, the one who owned a skateboard and a slingshot and a paintball gun—all the proper accoutrements of boyhood. And also Neal's older brother, Calvin, who was unspeakably cool and who therefore rarely tolerated the gaggle of younger boys who followed him and his buddies around. There was Geoff Ryman, whose parents were divorced. And Asher Kent, who had a palate expander and subsequent lisp, and introduced "jizz face" as a general term of endearment to the neighborhood pack.

And there was Jamie, my brother, in the middle of it all, charming and smooth. Learning not to cry, learning not to show his fear—that had been the golden ticket that he'd needed to join their club. He'd become the kind of boy who would make friends for the day at the playground or the county pool, and now he slipped in with the rest of them as if he really, truly belonged.

We both knew better. But I kept his secrets as well as I kept my own.

In the forest that was also Gumlea, the boys would play manhunt, or capture the flag. Jamie was skilled at their games—slick and confident. Never invited, I'd watch from a far-off cluster of trees to see how my brother performed. With them, he was always a winner. Easygoing. Unperturbed. He never cried when he got hurt now like Geoff still did. He never got angry and broke things or called the other kids names. If anything, he was *too* good—too calm, too. When in the normal course of a game he tackled Neal to the ground for the fourth or fifth time and Neal turned red like a turnip and shoved Jamie away, howling, "Get off me, you faggot!" my brother only rolled away from him, frowning at the insult.

He'd learned from our parents to turn his feelings off, to go some-where else—but his pain had to come out eventually. And it always did. With me.

Later, after dinner, in my bedroom, while I was preoccupied draw-ing maps, my brother came through my half-open door, interrupting me from my cartography. "Did you hear what Neal said to me today?" he asked, wringing his hands. He'd been holding this in for hours, and I could see how it was wearing on him—how close he already was to tears.

I shook my head, even though I remembered.

"He called me a faggot," he said, and he winced at the word. "I'm *not* a faggot."

I stared at my brother, who was sniffling, wiping his eyes on the back of his hand. Then I got up and went to my desk, getting out one of our notebooks.

"What are you going to do about it?" I asked, because we'd done this before, dozens of times. Some variation of this. Something would hurt Jamie, and he'd squish his feelings down just long enough to get me alone with a notebook and a pen.

"I've—I've decided," Jamie began uncertainly, "that in Gumlea, I don't have *any* name. I'm not the prince anymore. I'm going to be the Nameless Boy. And the Feral Children *think* the Nameless Boy is like them, but he's not. He's—he's different. Do you understand, Annie?"

I bit my lip. I didn't understand, not completely. But one thing was clear: Jamie needed me. Instead of asking questions, I began to scribble frantically. I drew my brother, clad in the animal skins and ragged clothes of the Feral Children. It looked just like him, but one of his eyes was missing. In its place, a gemstone. I drew beams of light ricocheting out of it, jagged lightning bolts in three different colors.

Magic. It was meant to be magic. Pouring out of my brother. Shining and delicate and powerful and strange.

When I was finished, he sat down next to me on the bed. Surveyed my work. Nodded, satisfied—and exhausted, too. He put his head on my shoulder, and I felt a sort of warmth flicker inside me. This was how it always worked between us. He'd save the feelings for me, for a story, for Gumlea. I'd write it down, or I'd draw it. I'd give him a way out.

That year, I needed an escape, too.

It was the year our mother had a baby. Before it happened, while she was still pregnant, I could pretend our lives would proceed unchanged. Even though most nights, Dad would rest his ear on Mom's belly on the sofa and sing "Goodnight, Irene" to the child who they hoped would be a girl, it was still only me and Jamie then, together, in the silence of our house. Telling stories. Building magic. Untouched by outside intrusions.

Mom had wanted another daughter. Someone of her own, who belonged to her. My brother and I mostly belonged only to each other, no matter how much attention she'd tried to heap on Jamie. And even in the moments when I was alone with Mom, when she tried to show me how her grandmother's sewing machine worked or take me shopping or demonstrate how to fold Dad's work shirts, when she tried to share stories with me of her great-grandfather's crossing to Ellis Island, I was always distractible. Squirmy. Somewhere else. Someone else. Not the mirror she had hoped a daughter would always be.

Mom had no one. It was me and Jamie, and then Mom and Dad, separate, even when they were together. They loved one another, of course. I knew that from the way that they'd flirt and giggle on the way out to their dates, while Gram, who'd come by to babysit, rolled her eyes at them. I knew from the way that they kissed after Jamie's parent-teacher conferences, when Mom was alive and glowing from the praise his teachers gave him. The way that their hips smashed together, their hands roving—obvious and mortifying. But Mom and Dad were nothing alike, really. They loved each other, but it never felt like they were friends, even then.

Our father was ordinary, hiding the things that made him special—the banjo he'd played in college, the book of dirty limericks he worked on sometimes after he'd had a beer with dinner—away in his office, presenting the perfect front of a healthy, normal American dad. Mom, on the other hand, had her own wild magic. She was funny and weird and hard and mean, and she followed new music even when the other grown-ups seemed to have given up on it, and her jeans were always cut to the latest style, and she wanted us to be like her—me and Jamie—but we weren't. So, she decided she needed to try again, with another kid.

She thought that the new baby would be different. Someone who was *hers*, and like her. Outwardly. Inwardly.

But then Elijah was born, red-faced, with a full shock of dark hair—practically a Xerox of my father's baby photos. The delicate peace my mother had imagined was broken by the baby's colicky squalls, and the home we'd known was shattered completely.

Jamie didn't mind the baby. In fact, he was the only one who could comfort him. He'd lie all night on the sofa with Elijah on his chest, even on school nights, letting the baby suck on a finger when he stirred. Sometimes he would sing to him in sweet, low tones—the same songs he'd sung to me when I was a baby.

I didn't feel jealous of their relationship. But seeing them together did make me feel . . . strange. Because I didn't experience *any* of the warmth or wonder that Jamie did. While Jamie would count Elijah's tiny peanut toes, or blow raspberries against his belly, I'd hang back, watching with owl eyes. I was scared to touch the baby. I worried he might bite me with his toothless gums, or poop on me, or worse. Elijah revealed unimaginable horrors: how babies have two huge eyeballs in two huge sockets, how they wrinkle their thin, pinkish eyelids closed in some perverse impression of a human being.

I felt these things. Numbness, disgust, fear. Of course, I didn't dare speak them. I knew how they'd hurt my parents' feelings. I knew that we were supposed to love Elijah, even when he was crying all the time. And he was. If he couldn't be with Jamie, he was screeching his head off. I'd ball up the pillow over my ears and try and try to sleep, but it never worked. On school days, I moved through the halls in a fog. Gumlea was my only respite. If I could get my brother away from the milky, dark living room, where Mom half slept beside the Rock 'n Play, and if it wasn't one of the days when he was playing basketball or video games over at someone's house down the block, then we could be in our kingdom, where the only babies were immediately sacrificed to harpies. The moment Jamie and I had turned backward and passed through the portal, he drew a breath and changed back into the brother I knew. Once it happened, we could pretend that the world still belonged to just the two of us. The Emperata and the Nameless Boy. The only creatures who mattered.

Sometimes it worked. But sometimes Jamie would stay behind to help Mom, distracting Elijah during a diaper change. I'd watch them and feel all the ways that I was inadequate. Girls were supposed to *like* babies, but in a secret place only me and Jamie knew about, I wished my little brother had never been born.

There are pictures from that time. My family, in rumpled dress clothes, at the reform synagogue in Woodstock at Elijah's naming. Jamie holds little Elijah tight. Beside them, my eyes are wide and sleepless. There's only one word for my expression: shell-shocked.

5

ONE AFTERNOON, JUST AFTER HER arrival, Annit had called the children from their tree houses. They all climbed a crooked path together, up and up the mountain. The air was swirled with gray clouds, and they met in a point there at the apex, then parted to allow the yellow sunlight through.

"Harpies, take me!" Annit cried, and she threw back her arms. For a moment, there was nothing, not even birdsong. But soon, the sky darkened, until the sunlight was nothing more than a razor-thin disk in the center of her forehead. A target. The shadows took on form, black and jagged. The children crouched low. Soon the world was full of wings.

The First Law of the Island of Feral Children states that a child must make one blood tithe to the King to stay there. Just one. The children who hid in the bushes had all done their service. They'd netted mermaids, strung up Winter Watchers, laid traps for pirates. They'd skinned those bodies and burned them at the mountaintop in a steaming pyre. They'd paid for their time.

But Annit didn't pay only once. When the sky had cleared of feathers and dust, when the blood—hers, theirs—was washed from her face, when the bodies were tallied and the bones burned, the truth was apparent to all.

She had killed every single harpy.

I wasn't like the other girls. That's not to say that there was anything *wrong* with the other girls. In fact, I thought that they were lovely creatures—like hollow-boned birds who called to one another from across the schoolyard. Jamie and I agreed about this. So often, our games were predicated upon saving some fictional maiden, who, we'd decided, was always discovered in some titillating state of undress. When I say that I was different—at least from any girl I'd met up until that point in my brief life—I mean exactly that. My presence among them always felt like an anomaly, to them, and to me.

Jamie understood, but no one else did. The teachers at school kept pairing me with other girls for school projects, and I was left to wonder if they hoped some of their softness might rub off on me—make me stop shouting the answer during class or doodling in my notebook margins when I should have been listening. And Mom kept arranging playdates between me and Nina Westervelt, the only other girl my age on our street. It would have made life easy for my mother; she was sometimes-friends with Nina's mother. I assume that she wanted me to be more like Nina: pretty and put together and a little snooty. But those drab afternoons were awful, and my mother could never convince me otherwise.

Nina had three older sisters, and so she'd learned how to be a girl. Or maybe it came naturally to her, the same way that drawing came to me. In either case, the room she shared with one of her sisters was nothing like mine. It contained a pair of white enamel beds with trundles for the sleepovers I'd never be invited to. Pink walls, lace coverlets. I hated Nina's room. It wasn't all the pink, necessarily, or all the fuss. I could ignore fuss. It was the dolls: the porcelain ones in the glass case in the corner who watched with shining eyes. Still. Waiting.

"You can't play with them," Nina told me, the first time I ever set foot in her room. I'd had no interest in playing with them, but she felt it necessary to warn me anyway. "My grandmother gets one for each of us on our birthday. They're going to be worth something someday." Then she paused. "You'll just break them, you know. You're such a baby."

I blinked a few times but didn't say anything. Even at eight years old, I knew that someone like Nina didn't matter. She needed to cut me down to make herself feel better, but what harm could come to me from what she'd said? It didn't change my body or the way that I worked inside it.

"Fine," I said, tearing my eyes away from those creepy glass eyes with their creepy spidery lashes. "But I don't see what the point is of dolls you never play with."

The look on her face told me that it was the wrong thing to say, but I was used to saying the wrong thing by then. Nina stuck her nose in the air like my answer confirmed some suspicion she'd been carrying with her all along.

"Whatever," she said. "Weirdo. Do you want to play Uno or not?"

We climbed up on top of her lace coverlets and, without another word, proceeded to play.

After, Jamie would ask how it went at Nina's house. I always figured he wanted to help me figure out how to escape her, the same way I'd helped him. I'd told him everything: the names she called me, the organic foods her mother would cook, the magazines full of makeup and sex tips she'd stolen from her older sisters. On those afternoons, standing in the doorway to my bedroom, Jamie would roll his eyes.

"Emperata Annit doesn't wear makeup," he declared. I let out a wicked grin.

"Sure she does," I told him. "Only it makes her look like an African wildcat, or maybe a fennec fox. All whiskers and fangs."

Jamie grinned back at me. I knew, in that moment, that we understood one another completely. That we were still the same.

And for a long time, that's how it was. One day, in the fall of fourth grade, Jamie and I wandered deeper into the woods than we ever had before, chased by invisible Winter Watchers, and we found a picnic table, flipped over, to which someone had taken a Sharpie. There, all along the splintering, peeled-paint surface, were obscene images, wedged between pot leaves and pentacles.

"Don't look," Jamie said, and shoved me in the other direction. But I saw enough to get the gist: Jagged marijuana leaves. Dozens and dozens of cocks of every shape and size. Testicles spiked with dark hairs, and women squatting low with their legs spread.

"Why would they do that?" I asked Jamie on the way home. The images were worse than anything I'd seen in Nina Westervelt's magazines. Worse than anything they showed us during the special assemblies we had in school, where they sent the boys away to learn of some other, unimaginable terrors. "Why would they draw those things?"

He looked over his shoulder, as if the invisible teenagers who had been there once and would visit again could hear him. His brow was furrowed, his mouth wrinkled, like he didn't want to talk about it.

"Something happens to you when you get to middle school, I think," he said. "You change."

"Just boys?" I couldn't imagine drawing those hairy, distended body parts, all dripping and slick. Just the memory of them gave me a strange sort of queasiness.

"I don't know," said Jamie. "I've never been a girl."

We both got quiet thinking about it. I could have promised to tell him what happened when I got to middle school, if what warped boys touched girls in the same way. But even that seemed wrong, as if I were admitting that I was going to change. I didn't want to. And Jamie was a year older than I was. For all we knew, he'd be lost to me by then, seduced by grown women and their dark, mysterious ways.

(If only I knew then what I know now about losing Jamie. But I was nine, and knew very little.)

So instead, I scrambled up the rock wall, using Jamie's hand-me-down sneakers to grip and climb. He laughed a little and reached out to me, but I was too fast for him.

"That's why I'm staying on the Island of Feral Children forever," I said, craning my arms open wide, as if I could soak up all of childhood through the mid-autumn air.

"You know the price of that," Jamie shouted back to me, and he pulled himself up on the wall, too. Precariously balanced, we walked together, one tottering foot in front of another in front of another. "There are rules."

It was true. My brother and I had whole notebooks full of rules. Rules for mermaids. Rules for pirates. Rules for ourselves. And we'd made promises to each other: that we would never tell a soul about Gumlea, that we'd never drink the sour wine our mother loved, that we'd never do drugs, that we would always love each other above all other people. In some ways, these promises were no different from the ones that other children made to themselves or their best friends. But because of Gumlea, ours were different. Every transgression would require a tithe to the King. Some sacrifice of flesh, or blood, or worse.

"Do you think I'm a coward?" I shot back at him.

When he smiled, I could see what teeth were missing, a couple of back ones that made him look a little like a rotten-toothed pirate. We never put our baby teeth under our pillows anymore. Dad was disappointed. He said we weren't too old for fairies.

If only he knew the half of it.

"Never, Annie," Jamie swore, his voice full of quiet awe. "You're the heart of all of Gumlea."

And then, just like that, he dive-bombed me, his chest hitting my shoulder, my elbows hitting the soggy ground below, and we fought and scrambled there until my hair was tangled with leaves and I pretended to forget all the things I'd seen, marker-drawn and spray-painted, like prophecies carved in stone.

6

IN THE SHALLOWS, THE BOYS and girls all tumbled and fought like their bodies would never be broken. The only one who didn't wade in was Emperata Annit. She stayed on the rocky shore stacking rocks upon rocks.

"What are you doing?" the Nameless Boy asked, wading in from the deepest part of the bay. He knelt in the water, covering his nakedness. Strange, he thought, how the other children didn't even seem to know that they were naked.

Annit was dressed in leather and fur, as always, and her mouth was a flat line of concentration, as always.

"I'm building cairns."

"What's a cairn?"

"They're markers. Some tell you about the people who have passed through a place. Others tell you about people who have died."

"This one?" Boy asked, gesturing to the stack of rocks that Annit was precariously balancing.

"A marker for the children who were drowned by mermaids."

"Mermaids." Boy turned toward the sea. In the distance, he saw figures in the water, black and murky. Sometimes a head would poke through the glassine surface. Boy would see a flash: blue or purple or golden or green hair, bright as a traffic light. But then, with a faint titter of bells, the blip of color would disappear.

We'd promised each other that life wouldn't change. But it was a promise we couldn't keep. The rules were shifting, just like my body had started to soften at the edges in preparation for what was to come—but I hadn't noticed yet.

That fateful day toward the start of fifth grade seemed like any other. Jamie and I went through our usual routine. He'd started middle school, while I was still at elementary, but while his bus came in ten minutes before mine, he always waited for me at the curb. That day, the squeaky yellow door folded shut behind me and we tumbled together into the house, leaving our backpacks in a heap by the front door. Then we raced straight out into the backyard. That day, Mom was somewhere in the house, but we weren't worried about her. It was a Friday, which meant that we had roughly an hour and forty minutes until Dad got home from the grocery store with our little brother, when he'd make us sit down to do our homework at the dining room table and then eat a proper dinner together, as a family. That meant we had an hour and forty minutes to be ourselves together, out in our little tangle of woods.

It all went well at first. We jumped over the creek. Turned around.

"The Feral Children are catching fairies today," I told my brother as we turned back around. I'd been thinking about it all day, all through a boring fundraising assembly at school. I thought that maybe whatever Feral Child got the most fairies would get a special award from Emperata Annit. Something better than an iTunes gift card and a rubber bracelet that said "WINNER." A necklace of bones, maybe.

But Jamie was walking fast today, his eyes half-hooded. Distracted.

I jogged to catch up with him.

"Hey, are you okay?" I asked. I reached out toward his arm, but he yanked it away.

"No," he said flatly. I knew he was hiding something from me, though he was doing it poorly, as usual. Walking faster than he had to, his eyes searching through the bramble beyond. "Everything is *fine.*" And then he broke out into a run.

"Hey, Nina!" he shouted, waving a hand.

I stopped. Out by the broken concrete stood Nina Westervelt, dressed in her usual uniform of brightly patterned leggings and an off-the-shoulder shirt. She looked unnatural in the woods, her ironed waterfall of hair standing in stark contrast to the frizzy poison ivy vines and sun-bleached soda cans and the saggy empty bladders of grocery bags that hung from the branches of nearby trees. She was our neighbor, but not one who usually spent her time in the forest. Her world stopped at the pickets that bordered the back of her yard.

"What's she doing here?" I asked, not even trying to disguise my disdain. We had a story we were working on in Gumlea, had been working on for a year. Nina Westervelt was *not* part of it.

She rolled her eyes at me. "James invited me," she said. "Hi to you, too, Annie."

"What the hell," I said. It wasn't even a question. I looked dumbly at my brother, who was sort of milling about the concrete girder's base, kicking stones around, not letting his gaze touch mine.

"There are girls in Gumlea, too, right?" he said, sort of vaguely, hooking his hands on to some rusted iron peg that was buried in the girder, pulling himself up. He sat there, close to Nina, and finally looked at me. Our eyes were the same, but I had *no* idea what was going on inside his head. When had he had time to invite her here? She wasn't even in his grade. "I thought it would be cool if we let Nina try. She can be a Feral Child, to start."

My eyes widened. I was glowering at Nina, my nostrils faintly flaring. But she just held her head high, like it was nothing that my brother had invited her into our secret kingdom.

"But . . . !" I whispered to my brother. He looked away from me, shrugging. He knew I didn't like Nina, knew how much I hated spending those afternoons in her room with her. Now she was here, in a place that was supposed to belong to me. I chewed the inside of my cheek.

Jamie's words came to me then. *You're the heart of all of Gumlea.* Well then, fine. I'd be the heart. We hadn't officially stepped through the portal and into Gumlea, but it wasn't as if it really mattered; Nina wouldn't know how to follow us in anyway. I pulled myself up on the girder, too, and set my hands on my hips.

"You should know, child," I declared, "that in Gumlea, I'm not Annie. I'm the Emperata, Annit."

Nina looked at Jamie for a second, doubt wrinkling her brow. She giggled. "Okay," she said.

"I rule the Feral Children," I told her. "And there are certain laws they must follow."

"G-d, you're so weird," Nina muttered. But then she forced her mouth into a smile. "What laws?"

"All Feral Children must pay a tithe."

Nina hesitated. Then she reached into her pocket and pulled out a wrinkled twenty. "Here," she said. "Don't tell my mom. I'm supposed to save that for horseback riding lessons."

She was holding out the money to me. But I didn't take it. I just grinned. "Foolish child," I said, still in my Annit voice. "Your tithe can't be *money*. Nameless Boy, tell her what she owes."

My brother's gaze was back on the forest floor. Only now, he wouldn't look at either of us. He'd started to blush a little, to chew his lip a little. He answered, but his voice was almost inaudible. I whacked him on the shoulder.

"Speak up, Boy," I told him. He laughed uneasily.

"It has to be a blood tithe. Like—like a person. Or an animal."

"Excuse me?" Nina was still holding out the money, but just then, she stuffed it back into her pocket. She laughed at us, incredulous. "You want me to kill an *animal*?"

"I mean, no . . . ," Jamie began, and I watched as he tried to explain the way we played, striking down imaginary foes with imaginary weapons.

Nina was still laughing, high-pitched, fake laughter. "G-d, you two are so *weird*," she said at last. Then she looked at my brother, a sour smile twisting her gloss-sticky lips. "Sorry, James. I'm out of here."

She spun around until she faced her house back through the woods, her hair spinning after her like a honey-brown cloak. And then she left us there, the two of us, alone.

We were silent for a minute. Jamie's hands were fisted at his sides. I'd seen my brother cry before, as a little boy and as an older boy, when it was just the two of us alone. But I don't think I'd ever seen him get *angry*. Especially not at me.

"Fuck" was all he said.

He stalked off toward our house, walking almost too fast for me to follow.

7

IJAH AND THE NAMELESS BOY went hunting one day, when the sun through the trees was green-golden and the wind had the scent of blood on it. They borrowed a pair of saw-toothed daggers from Annit, leaving a pile of stones in their stead. Ijah carried his on a holster in his coat. Boy buckled his knife to his thigh.

They weighted their trap with miniature Snickers bars and white bread smeared with peanut butter. Then they crouched in the bushes to wait. While they did, they spoke in low tones, first gossiping about the other children, then Annit, then the pirates whose ships had sailed too close to the island recently for either of their liking. At last, Boy fell silent.

There was a rustle. Then a *snap*. Then a scream, so raw that it made Boy's hair stand on end.

The boys bounded over to the trap. Ijah winced as blood splattered his face. Inside the iron jaws was a delicate body, small and girlish. Boy had the jumbled impression of filamentous wings, blue and green in the daylight, gossamer thin and broken.

I followed my brother in through the screen door. Mom was standing by the sink talking on her cell phone. Jamie opened the fridge and started rummaging through it, but before he could grab anything, Mom said, "Oh, here they are now. I'll talk to you later," and tapped the screen.

"You guys?" she asked, which was how she always spoke to us. Dad would say later that she was the reason we had so much trouble with Jamie, because Mom couldn't be counted on to be firm. "That was Dawn. She said Nina came home with the weirdest story."

I looked at Jamie, and my lip curled. He glanced over the edge of the fridge, arching an eyebrow back at me. His body looked tight with anger. It was a new sight, and terrifying. But I was used to standing as a shield between Jamie and the world. When he was sad, I took his sadness for him. Now I squared my shoulders.

"It's not our fault she can't follow the rules," I said simply.

That's when Jamie let out a noise that was halfway between a growl and a scream. "G-d, Annie!" he bellowed.

I flinched. Mom shouted Jamie's name. He didn't look back at me, his eyes full and wounded. He didn't look at Mom, either. He just looked at the kitchen tile.

She sighed. "Her mom said that you told her she had to kill a squirrel if she wanted to play with you."

"Not a squirrel," I said plainly. Nina was so dramatic. Besides, I'd only been trying to get rid of her, so that Jamie and I could be in Gumlea alone. Like always. "I just told her that she had to make a sacrifice of flesh—"

"Annie," Jamie growled. He was right. I was revealing too much. I shut my mouth, fast.

"Okay," Mom said, and she sighed again, lifting her hand to her face and pinching the bridge of her nose. "No killing squirrels. Or chipmunks. Or deer. Or each other. No killing anything, okay?"

We both looked back at her. My eyes felt big and guilty. But Jamie's were brick walls, cemented in anger. He didn't speak. I spoke for him.

"Okay."

"And play nicely with Nina. I don't want to get any more phone calls. You know I can't stand Dawn lately," Mom said, and she smiled a little, like it was a secret between us, so I smiled, too. I knew how to play this game.

"Okay," I said again, in a smiling smiling smiling tone. But Jamie wasn't smiling. He was leaning against the fridge door, his face bright red beneath his flop of dark hair, crushing Elijah's day-care art beneath his weight.

"Jamie?" Mom said.

It all happened in a flash. One moment, we were there in the kitchen, standing at a stalemate. The next, Jamie had slammed his hands on the refrigerator door behind him, sending the magnets rattling to the floor.

"No!" he roared, like an animal, one I'd never seen before. I knew my brother had big feelings inside him, but they'd never been this wild—this unpredictable. He took off down the hall, shouting, "I don't *want* to play with Nina! I don't *want* to *play* with anyone!"

His eyes went to me for just a split second. He saw my fear. But instead of acknowledging it, he tore his gaze away in disgust and stormed up the stairs. Like a moon, I continued to orbit him, drifting toward the foot of the steps, watching him stomp away from us.

"No no no no no!" he screamed. I took one step up, an almost-instinctual response. But Mom was behind me then and put her hand on my shoulder.

"Let him go," she said. She let out a third sigh, three sighs too many for me. She went back to the kitchen. I stood in the hallway, staring up into the angry dark.

❧

Dad got back from the supermarket with Eli, and when he saw Mom's expression, he plopped my little brother down next to me, in front of the TV. Over the rustle of grocery bags, their voices rose, terse and fretting.

"We should put him in therapy."

"Leave it alone, Marc. He's busy enough. And hand me the peas."

"There's no shame in it."

"He's just started middle school. It's normal to be moody—"

"Right. He's a normal eleven-year-old boy. And you've never been one. You don't know how hard it can be."

"He has *us*," she said, but it sounded insufficient, even to me. Because this was his constant refrain: Mom wasn't a boy, wasn't a man. Mom could never, ever know.

They went back and forth like that for a while. Finally, Dad convinced Mom that Jamie would be happier if he and Dad went running together every morning. Better to pound pavement than fists, Dad said, like it was a joke, but I had trouble seeing what was funny about it. I didn't think Jamie should have been pounding anything, anyone. But Dad knew best, so Dad decided.

Dad was still talking when I pushed out of the recliner and made my way upstairs. Nobody noticed I left, not even Eli. But if they weren't thinking about Jamie, then they certainly weren't thinking of me.

I knew Jamie. I knew how to talk to him. How to see him, even when Mom and Dad didn't. I pressed my face to his door. "Jamie?" I whispered.

His voice came back swiftly, like he'd been waiting for me.

"Leave me alone."

I closed my eyes and let my forehead rest on the hollow square of wood. I felt like I was broken inside, splintering. But I'd always been able to fix this before. Jamie needed Gumlea to feel better, to feel himself. So I wandered into my room. I stood in the dim light of twilight, watching the wallpaper go gray. I searched for something—a key, a talisman—that could unlock my brother.

My eye fell on the old drawing I'd done of him: Jamie with an eye missing. Jamie with magic streaming out. I could see now that the hands had been drawn poorly, that the likeness was vague. But that picture had once meant the world to him. We'd told so many stories about Gumlea, but now, as we careened toward adolescence, the epic saga of the Nameless Boy had become his favorite. With every passing day, the mythology had become more elaborate. Shadowed by his familiar, a wise old hare, the Nameless Boy walked through Gumlea's wilds searching for a home. He wasn't a Feral Child, although he'd lived under the Emperata's care for a time. He wasn't a Winter Watcher, either. He wasn't a pirate, and he certainly was no mermaid, though both the mermaids and pirates had tried to claim him for themselves. He was a traveler, an itinerant, and he belonged to only himself.

And yet according to our prophecies, this anonymous boy was heir to all of Gumlea's riches, the greatest protector of her magic, and the one who would somehow, someday, kill the King. And once that happened, he'd use his knife—his trusty old scalloped blade with a ruby set in its hilt—to open the Veil between the worlds. That's when Emperata Annit would lead her armies into our universe and kill everyone who had ever hurt us.

It was a satisfying revenge fantasy.

We hadn't gotten there yet in our stories. Right now, the Nameless Boy was still sojourning with the Feral Children. But soon, he would leave them. We were dancing closer to the climax of our story, day by day by day.

That picture was a promise to my brother, in a way. A promise that Emperata Annit would keep him safe. A promise that she—that I—understood him. So I plucked it down from the wall.

I went to Jamie's door again and pushed the single flat sheet below the gap. I was going to knock, but I didn't have to. The door swung open. There stood my brother, paper in hand, his face puffy from crying. He didn't tell me to come in. He didn't need to tell me anything. He shut the door behind me, and we sat together on his bed in silence for a long time. He stared down at the page and cried.

I put my hand on his. Squeezed it. But there was something in me—an angry shard. You could hear the flinty edge when I spoke.

"You brought *Nina* into Gumlea. You didn't even *think* about how that would make me feel."

He was quiet for a long time. When he answered me, he sounded like a little boy. "I thought she would understand."

Well, of course she didn't. It was weirder to me that this was news to Jamie than it had been that he'd brought her at all. "What do you care about Nina all of a sudden, anyhow?" I asked, and if I'd tried to make my voice sound neutral, I failed miserably.

He looked up at me, his eyes empty vessels, and my heart sank down into my gut.

"You *like* her?"

"I thought if we showed her Gumlea, she'd—I, I don't know what I thought."

"She's ridiculous. She's always been ridiculous, Jamie—"

"No." My brother drew in a shaking breath. "I want to go by James now. Jamie's a little kid's name. And this stuff, Gumlea. I— You're right. I made a mistake. It has to be a secret. We can't tell *anyone*. Nobody."

"Okay," I said, not really sure why I was agreeing to something so obvious. It's not as if there was anyone I wanted to tell; Gumlea belonged to me and Jamie alone—no one else. If I was honest with myself, though, the word felt bitter on my tongue, because I suspected Jamie's reasons for saying it were not the same as mine for agreeing. I wasn't *embarrassed* by what Nina had said. Why should Jamie be?

"Dad's going to make you start running, you know," I said, changing the subject.

"Cool," my brother replied faintly. My stomach squeezed painfully. But then he looked right at me. His eyes weren't empty hollows. They were my eyes, and they were grateful. "Thanks, Annie," he whispered.

I didn't answer. There were no words for what I was feeling. Instead, I got up and left my brother alone in his room.

8

HE UNSHEATHED HIS BLADE AND crept closer to the creature. His hand still shook, but less now. He was making plans: first, he'd sink the blade into her throat, just a nick, then draw it across the thin flesh there. It would be easy. She'd bleed out fast. He'd have to skin her later, but he knew that Ijah would show him how to arrange the parts for proper ceremony and burning.

But when he got there, the fairy's breathing had stopped. Her chest was still. Her eyes, between rivers of now-still blood, had a dull, waxy look.

Ijah, sensing Boy's dejection, raced to his side. "She's gone," he said, as if it weren't obvious. "You were too slow. You missed your tithe."

Boy let out a roar of frustration. He turned to a tree beside them and hurled the knife into it, striking true and deep. Years later, when the Nameless Boy was just a legend, the children would gather at this tree to tell stories about him, leaving offerings tangled in the roots.

⁂

We may have felt like the woods out back were ours alone, but they belonged to everybody in the neighborhood. Even if the other kids couldn't penetrate the Veil between our world and Gumlea, there was no keeping the other kids out of the tangle of forest that bordered *their* yards, too. After what happened with Nina, Jamie was worried we'd be discovered, and so we learned how to slip out of Gumlea more quickly, the way we peeled off our synagogue clothes as soon as we got home. One moment, we'd be storming the King's tower, demanding a ransom for our captured familiars; the next, we would be sitting on a log, pretending to play rock paper scissors for the right to pick a family movie that night. We'd pretend to be totally normal kids, for the benefit of kids like Neal and his brother who had just wandered out to play with mine.

That year, around our parents, we began to deliberately mispronounce it as "Glumly" or "Gummy," as if that concealed what we'd been doing out in the woods every single day after school. Around the other kids and our teachers, we were silent. Jamie never admitted to them that he *read* fantasy novels, much less that he'd been working on a grand fantasy of his own. If someone asked him, he'd tell them that he liked books about sports. Nonfiction, mostly.

Somehow, Nina never told anyone except her mother about that day. So to strangers, my brother was still cool. Still functional. Still brilliant. And over the course of sixth grade, separated from me, he bloomed into a full-fledged popular kid. He was a sports star who won spelling bees and math contests, though he was smart enough to pretend that he didn't know how to write a poem or a story. Those were *gay*, he'd tell his friends in his woods, snorting. All the while, he was saving his poetry and his stories for me.

So of course I kept Gumlea a secret, too, for him. After what happened with Nina, he decided that there were only ever two people in Gumlea anyway: the storyteller and the archivist. He was the one who created our legends, and I was the one who wrote them down. And in the months after the Nina Incident, I even helped him chronicle the punishments that would befall either of us if one of us let the truth spill out. We'd bleed for the King to make up for our sins. We'd leave our own teeth or fingers or eyeballs inside his tower. We promised each other, signing our names at the back of the leather notebook I'd saved up to buy at the witch store downtown.

It seemed like a small price to pay to keep Gumlea alive, to keep going back there. I didn't have any reason to tell anyone, anyway. Not until Miranda.

It was an ordinary spring morning, until it wasn't. I got on the bus and my usual spot, right up front behind the bus driver next to the window, was taken. It was a girl I'd never seen before, about my age, with a pointy little nose and high cheekbones and eyes like drops of ink. She looked kind of like an elf, and she was even wearing this silver cuff over one ear. Swirling loops of metal. Like something a warrior might wear.

I sat down next to her. "That's my seat," I said. I wasn't angry. Confused, though, by this strange, sugar-spun creature who was suddenly occupying my world.

"Sorry," she said, and I thought maybe she was doing that apologizing thing that some girls do. But she didn't sound sorry.

I felt something new. A bright crack of dawn. I liked this girl.

"Where did you come from?" I asked.

She shrugged. "Here. Wiltwyck. I was going to Springtown Valley, but they kicked my family out because we watched too much television."

Springtown Valley was in Elting, the next town over, a hippie school that my mom liked but we couldn't afford.

"What's wrong with television?"

"I don't know. Something about our souls. Are you going to tell me your name?"

It was kind of like talking to myself—someone who didn't care about what others thought about her, or maybe did care and wanted others to think the worst.

"Annie **[Redacted]**," I told her, and I held out my hand. We shook firmly, like men might.

"Miranda Morganson," she answered.

"That's like a superhero name," I said.

"I know," she answered, and when she smiled, her nose wrinkled just a little.

Maybe it would have been love at first sight, if we'd been older than fifth graders. Instead, it was the first flash of friendship I'd ever felt. Our heartbeats weren't paired like mine and Jamie's were. We didn't share secret languages or secret mythologies. But on that day on the bus, and every day after, we began to turn over the rocks of one another's pasts. She told me about her parents' divorce, the summers she spent at her uncle's farm, the little sister her mother would be having soon with her new husband. I told her about Elijah, and how I'd hated him at first. I told her about drawing. About books. About Jamie.

But there were things I never spoke of, secrets I kept. I never said anything about Gumlea, of course. But as the weeks passed, the temptation kept rising up over and over again. Was this what had happened with Jamie, just a few months before, with Nina? But Miranda and Nina were nothing alike—Miranda would understand. Probably. And soon, I found I actually *wanted* to tell her.

It was weeks before I worked up the nerve to ask him about it, one evening when he was draped over the living room chair, reading a library copy of *The Wind Through the Keyhole*.

"Jamie?" I asked. Standing in the doorway, I saw how the evening light silhouetted him. He was like a shadow on a throne. More an absence of a thing than a thing itself.

"James," he said, not looking up, paging through his book. I nodded vaguely. Today, I'd call him James, even though I usually forgot.

"James. I've been talking to a new girl at school."

"I know," he said. Of course he did. Jamie knew everything about me. He added, "Miranda Morganson. She's Neal's second cousin or something."

"Well, yeah," I said. Miranda had mentioned that, but I'd forgotten. I drew in a breath. "I thought I might tell her about Gumlea."

At that, Jamie finally looked up at me. I couldn't really see his eyes, just two flashes of light. I began to talk more, nervous, trying to fill the silence.

"She's not like Nina. She'd understand. She's into that stuff! Fantasy and all of that. She likes books about dragons and everything. She wouldn't make fun of us, I don't think. She's different."

"Different," Jamie echoed. He put his book in his lap. "You can't tell her about Gumlea. Look at what happened with Nina. And what if Miranda tells Neal? If other people find out, it would be social suicide. Can you imagine what those guys would say?"

He sounded patient as he explained it. Not angry or exasperated. I only had the vaguest idea what the guys would say, because of Nina. They'd probably laugh, or call Jamie weird. I knew enough about normal kids to know that. There wasn't much risk for me, of course. Everyone knew I was weird already. But my brother . . .

Even in the dim light, I could feel Jamie studying my features, considering me. He sighed.

"It's against the Laws," he told me, which finally softened my heart a little. I didn't care about those guys. But I cared about the Laws. "Didn't we decide that, together? It wasn't that long ago. C'mon. You remember this. Gumlea only works if there are two: the storyteller and the archivist. Right? I'm the storyteller and you're the archivist. There's no room for Miranda there. And if you violate the Law and tell her . . ."

"Blood tithe?" I said. It had only been a few months ago that we'd typed up the contract on Dad's computer and printed the whole thing out and signed it. We'd promised fingers. Promised toes.

"*Death* tithe," Jamie said sharply. I blinked. Part of me wanted to say that I'd never agreed to that—but Jamie was older, and he always remembered better than I did. "Execution. I don't take my Vows lightly. Do you?"

"No, Jamie," I said. My throat felt tight. "Of course not."

The next morning, Miranda was waiting for me on the bus. I sat down next to her, feeling all the things that I wanted to say bubbling up inside me. Popping. Vanishing.

"Hey," she said.

"Hey," I replied. I fished for something in my pocket. "These are my dad's old Magic cards. I thought you'd want to see them."

She grabbed the deck swiftly, began flipping through. "These are awesome, Annie," she told me. I could practically feel her vibrating beside me. But was it enough?

It wasn't. It wasn't.

"Thank you."

"Welcome," I grunted, and turned my eyes out toward the woods.

9

THIS TIME, WHEN THE NAMELESS Boy set a trap, he was all alone. It was late into the golden evening, and the other children were all busy eating their feasts of stolen jelly beans and Kool-Aid and Hostess CupCakes. Perhaps Ijah looked for him as he slipped down beneath the lowest branches of the Great World Tree, but the child was soon distracted by laughter and conversation. And Boy was permitted his task.

The bait was a fish, which one of the other children had caught the night before and had been cleaned and left to dry on the shore. It was rainbow scaled and nearly as long as his arm. It would have been a fine dinner for someone, but sacrifices would have to be made if he was ever going to leave this place. He pried the jaws of the trap open and set the fish inside it. Then he tucked himself into the bushes to wait.

❧

Jamie started seventh grade, and our lives began to unravel. Though we now took the same bus together again, once we stepped on it, we might as well have been occupying different planets. His life, once so tightly wound around mine, had taken on a new, hidden form. There had been a time when we had promised each other that nothing would ever come between us. Now it felt like that promise was impossible to keep.

Even our mornings were different now. Once, we'd wandered from our rooms at the same time, jostling each other over the sink as we drowsily brushed our teeth. Now, in the blue-gray hours before dawn, I'd wake up to the sound of Dad and Jamie warming up in the driveway. With my eyes turned to the wall, I imagined it. Dad would clutch his travel mug of coffee in one hand and would let it fog up his glasses as he jogged in place. Jamie would stretch his legs, which were long and getting longer. He would double- and triple-check his shoelaces. Maybe he would spit a few times into the driveway stones. I don't know. I never saw it with my own eyes. I wasn't invited.

I heard them speak, but not their words. Mumbled bits of conversation. It sounded fake, like the dialogue from a Lifetime movie.

By the time I went downstairs for breakfast, Jamie had been awake for hours without me. His gaze was hale as he headed to the back of the bus, where the cool middle school and high school kids sat. Meanwhile, I sat next to Miranda, and we mostly talked about cartoons. Sometimes I'd catch her peeking at my notebook over my shoulder, glimpsing corners of maps and mechanical pencil drawings of the Nameless Boy, but I'd shut them tight before she'd ask me any questions. I'd promised Jamie I wouldn't talk about Gumlea to anyone. And I, I was learning, was the one who kept promises.

That fall, Dad dragged us all out to Jamie's cross-country meets. I'd watch my brother move easily among the other boys, wearing the exact same clothes. Watched him line up on the track with the other runners, flex his muscles, his bare shoulders warm golden in the sunlight. I'd watch him move like a knife through velvet, slicing his way through the pack. Mom and Dad would cheer, and Elijah, too, and everyone around us, and I'd just watch and remember ancient words. Jamie had been practically a baby then, but he wasn't anymore. *If you try hard enough, you can learn to do anything. To* be *anything.*

Had he finally done it? Become a normal kid? A sports star? The son our father had always dreamed about? It looked like that, but I knew better. I could still feel the real Jamie, trembling beneath the weight of all those medals. I knew, deep down, that he was still awkward in his skin, still scared of his own shadow. He could hide it from the other boys, but he couldn't hide it from me.

There were still some days when he'd come into the living room and invite me to the woods out back. I'd pull myself from the sofa, leaving Elijah in the puddle of blue light, and together we'd head out into the early spring chill. One day Jamie challenged me to a swordfight, brandishing a long stick. But the way he moved was too wild and theatrical, like he was a child actor in a badly produced local play. I hardly fought back. I moved listlessly.

"Come on!" he shouted, striking harder. I could feel his mounting rage reverberate through my forearm. "Fight me, Annie!"

Something broke. Not wood. Inside me. I raised my arm high. But instead of fighting him, I threw the splintered branch down into the mud.

"No," I said. The word came out as a whisper, delicate and trembling. "I don't want to. *James.*"

I couldn't keep the tears out of my voice when I said his name. That's when I realized how hurt I was. Jamie was ashamed of me, ashamed of Gumlea. Ashamed, even, of his name. But he still wanted that magic. It wasn't *fair.* My throat was tight, but I wouldn't let myself cry. Not in front of him.

But Jamie must have felt something, too. His nose wrinkled. He narrowed his eyes. And suddenly, he sprang on me, full up with rage—real, shaking, spitting anger. I should have seen it coming, but I didn't. When he jumped, it knocked the wind out of me. I lost my footing. Went flying, face against the mud, shoulders against long-buried stone. He hit me once, hard, in the sternum. I tasted red bubble up past my throat. My mouth was full of something acrid. Some poison, fantastic in origin.

"Fight me!" he screamed. He dug his hands into my scalp, tugging up a full rope of muddied hair. My heart pounded. My chest ached. Not because he was hurting me, though he was, but because I had realized something. This wasn't about me. He didn't care whether I played in Gumlea with him. He hadn't cared for over a year. Something must have gone wrong at school. Something terrible must have happened. Something with Neal, maybe? Or Nina? He wanted to hurt me, but only because somebody else had hurt him first.

He needed me. I knew it. I was supposed to help him. He wasn't Jamie right now. He was the Nameless Boy, and he was calling on the Emperata Annit to save him. Wasn't that her job? Wasn't she supposed to tear the sky open, and then punish everyone who had ever harmed him?

"G-d damn, Annie!" he screamed again. "Fight me!"

But I wouldn't. Gumlea wasn't a game we played only when it suited him. I wasn't *like* Jamie, couldn't learn to tuck my true self into my back pocket like she didn't matter and then parade her out only when he needed her. Maybe he could have it both ways, but I couldn't. It was either magic or emptiness, but never both. I couldn't conjure the magic now. I just stared at my brother. I think that scared him most of all.

He got off me. It took a few minutes to roll my aching body over and push up against the moldering leaves. My hands shook. My throat, when I swallowed, felt full of a thousand little pins.

"Get out of here, then," he said. He wasn't shouting anymore. He was sniffling, crying, though quietly. I should have put a hand on his shoulder. Should have taken the pain from him. But I didn't. I walked away.

That day, I didn't bother walking backward into our yard. Technically, I stayed in Gumlea. That was against the rules, to leave without leaving, to go inside the house without slipping between the Veil first. I would stay up late saying a devotion to the King, begging forgiveness for leaving that doorway open. But Jamie would never know.

I went inside. Before Mom or Dad or Eli could ask questions, I stepped into the shower, where no one could hear me cry. I stayed in there for a long time, watching the mud pool around my feet.

Sometimes Miranda came over after school. It didn't surprise me that she didn't care about iPads or video games any more than I did. We played Magic: The Gathering or dickered around with a Ouija board. I deliberately pushed the planchette across the board, inventing elaborate biographies of the ghosts in our town to entertain her, unsure if she ever caught on to my lie.

But mostly I was alone. I'd have felt that way even if Jamie had been around, probably, but I wouldn't know, because he never was. Not anymore. He had too many sports to play, or friends to hang out with. I was alone in the afternoon in the forest, playing games that felt solitary and hollow. I was alone when the weather turned cold, when, out of desperation or boredom, I don't know which, I started streaming old episodes of *The X-Files*. And I was alone when I sat in my room and drew maps that I kept to myself. I put them on the walls over my bed, though they had no story in them. When I stared at them late at night, they might as well have been road maps of New Jersey. Nothing magical. Nothing that meant anything to anyone. Just the same places, hollow, meaningless. Over and over again.

I definitely didn't share them with Jamie, though after that day in the woods, he stopped talking to me about Gumlea at all. Anyway, he was busy that year. After cross-country, he started playing basketball, and hanging out even more with Neal, who was on the team. The two of them became best friends, inseparable. There was an apartment in Neal's basement where his older brother, Calvin, lived. That's where Jamie started spending all his time.

"I don't like it," Mom said. "Calvin's in high school. What does he want with a bunch of seventh graders?"

"He's a good Christian boy," Dad said, which was supposed to be a tease, but from the way our mother glowered at him, it was clear she didn't find it funny. "When I called his dad, he just said the boys eat junk food and play video games."

"Dad, I *told* you that," Jamie said. Dad reached out and ruffled Jamie's hair, which he hadn't cut since the summer. It was coming in darker now, the curls almost black. Mine was still streaked with lighter brown even in the waning light of early winter.

I don't know what they did in Calvin Harriman's apartment. I told myself that I didn't want to know. Jamie was leaving me behind, and now, for revenge, I was studiously turning my back on him. What I did know about—too much about, more than I could stand, really— was Nina. Not from Jamie. Miranda was the one who told me. She was Neal's second cousin and she heard all about how Nina had been invited to Calvin's house one night with her stupid friends Elise and Shelby, and the girls and the boys all played Quarters together. I'd heard the kids on the bus talking about it; it sounded like some kind of drinking game.

"Jamie doesn't drink," I protested, then cast my gaze to the back of the bus, where my brother was busy stealing some other boy's hat and laughing, too false and too loud. Maybe he did drink. He'd been the one to suggest that the Winter Watchers tapped trees for wine, after all. He'd always had that curiosity in him, that edge.

But then Miranda explained what Quarters really was. "The girls wear sweatshirts and sweatpants and the boys drop quarters down them and then they turn the lights out and the boys have to find them."

"That's stupid," I snapped, my voice a box cutter's edge. I didn't want Miranda to know how much the idea rattled me, how it made my stomach feel knotty and squeezed. I could almost *see* it: Jamie groping around Nina's skinny thighs, touching the thin fabric of her underwear. Touching other things. The idea made me feel sick. "If they want to touch each other, why not just do it? Why do they need some excuse?"

Miranda's eyes went wide. She blushed faint pink, like a little kid.

"I don't know. I don't know why anyone would want to touch each other at all like that. Nina could get *pregnant*."

I rolled my eyes. I let out a scoffing sound. I did everything I could to register my disgust. But whether it was at Miranda or Nina or even at Jamie, I wasn't even sure.

10

THE NAMELESS BOY WAITED. AND waited. His body ached. He contemplated returning to his home. But he already had so much invested in this—his time, his hope. And so he waited longer still, until the sky began to go purple at the edges and even the larger moon began to fade.

At last, a snap. A wheeze. A cry.

❖

I was still going to Friday-night services with Mom then. Sometimes Dad or Elijah would come, but mostly it was just the two of us. I think we both knew that it should have been Jamie—he'd be bar mitzvah soon and was supposed to be studying for it. But he was usually too busy with Neal.

Sometimes, after services, Mom and I would go watch the rabbi light the candles and say the prayers over bread and a Dixie Cup of grape juice back in the meeting room near the kitchen. A few people would bring potluck, a strange mixture of homemade kosher foods and dishes from local restaurants. There would be kugel and pizza, brisket and California rolls.

"Let's nosh," Mom would say to me. She always treated Yiddish like it was some kind of secret joke between us, one of many jokes, like the faces she made when Neal's mom called or the complaints she'd lodge about Dad's parenting when she thought Elijah wasn't listening. But I didn't mind. Not on Friday nights. Friday nights were candles and prayers and some faint, beautiful peace blossoming inside me, untouched by Jamie.

That was the truth, the real, ugly truth. I was glad he wasn't there. Glad it was just me and Mom, for once.

At least, on most nights. Because one night, Cantor Liebowitz turned to Mom and said, "Your son should be here. He has the best voice in his b'nei mitzvah class, you know."

"No, I didn't know," Mom said. His voice had been sweet when he was younger, but I hardly ever heard him sing anymore. Singing was one of those things that he and Neal and the rest of them had dubbed *gay*.

"He doesn't study," Cantor Liebowitz went on. "He has the most beautiful voice but he doesn't study. Boys like him, we never see them after they become bar mitzvah."

The line across Mom's forehead, the one that had been growing over the past few years, got deeper now. There was even a pair of parentheses framing her mouth. "He told me he'd been studying," she said.

Cantor Liebowitz pounded his fist on the table. Everybody jumped, even Rabbi Shulman. "Kids have no sense of the importance of religion anymore—"

"Hiram," Rabbi Shulman interrupted, her voice firm. It was the same voice that rose from the pulpit on High Holy Days. Sometimes I felt that there were two sides of her: the G-d side, and the friend side. On this night, she spoke with command presence to Hiram Liebowitz. "You've had too much to drink."

Cantor Liebowitz scowled, fell silent.

In the absence of his words, Rabbi Shulman softened her voice. "Besides, some young people care. After all, Annie is right here, isn't she?"

Maybe I should have blushed from the attention. Maybe I should have glowed. But my eyes stayed on Cantor Liebowitz and stayed hard. It was easy to glean his feelings: I wasn't enough for him. I wasn't Jamie.

That night, as Mom pushed our car through the winding roads, past dark woods and broken branches, she shook her head, muttering to herself about how she was going to make sure Jamie studied—how she couldn't let him let down the family. I said nothing, instead glowering out the dark window, watching darker shadows streak past. My hands were balled into fists on my thighs. It didn't matter to her, either, that I was there, that I had always been there, davening with Dad while she distracted my brother in the hallway. Begging her to tell me about the meaning of those dense Hebrew letters when she returned. My brother was all she could talk about, all any of them could talk about.

For the first time, I was really, truly jealous of my older brother. There had been days before when I'd envied him, sure, when I wanted to share the things that made his life different and good and blessed. But that night I kind of wanted to murder him. We might have been the same in so many ways, but to other people, we never would be.

Because to them—to Mom, to Dad, to our rabbi, to our teachers—Jamie was the only one who mattered at all.

That summer, the checks started rolling in for Jamie's bar mitzvah. Dad insisted Jamie deposit each one, then sat with him to write thank-you cards. Mom just rolled her eyes.

"A few thousand dollars isn't going to make a dent in his college fund," she said one spring morning, when the porch doors were open and the warm air laced fragrant and sweet through our house. "He should be allowed to buy something fun. Jamie, what do you want?"

My brother tightened his fist over the ballpoint pen. Dad had given in and started calling him "James" like he'd asked, though even he misspoke sometimes. Mom flatly refused to give up the name she'd called him since he was a baby.

I didn't call him anything. Not anymore. I sat at the breakfast table silently, watching this all play out. I'd learned to move carefully around Jamie's anger, avoiding it. Even now, I braced myself.

"A drum kit," he answered at last. "I want to play the drums."

I wrinkled my brow. It made no sense. As far as I knew, Jamie didn't care at all about music, no matter what the cantor at synagogue said about his voice. He cared about sports, and Neal Harriman, and the things that Dad told him to care about. Homework or whatever. And sure, maybe Jamie cared about digging around in Nina Westervelt's pants. But he didn't care about the drums.

Moments like these made it clear that he was really a stranger now. I studied his face, the way he stared down our father, and I wondered who he was.

Mom fished around in her purse for a checkbook. "A drummer?" she mused, bending down to write him a check. "Girls like drummers. I bet Nina will be into that."

Jamie started blushing. I pushed my food around on my plate and contemplated vomiting up my eggs. But before I could, Dad rose from the table and looked my brother straight in the eye. "The basement isn't soundproof."

There was a terrible vein of tension that ran between them. It was the same old argument between them, always, and usually Jamie gave in to him. Usually he bent and went out for Little League, or took up jogging. But not today. Today, I could feel Jamie's frustration bubbling off him. I put down my fork, bracing for that moment of impact. Meanwhile, my brother sat up in his chair. His voice squeaked.

"We can put it in the garage."

"No . . ." Dad shook his head, slowly but firmly. "The neighbors will complain."

"It's my money!" Jamie screamed. Eli threw his hands over his ears. I sat there, feeling my hands tremble, staring at my plate.

Mom was just standing there, too, her pen frozen over the check, looking between Dad and Jamie like she didn't know what to do. We were all holding our breath together, waiting for it. And sure enough, Jamie picked up Dad's half-empty coffee cup and hurled it at the floor.

We all cringed, a familial cringe, a collective cringe. Coffee and creamer and ceramic shards went everywhere, on the fringe of Mom's vintage tablecloth and into the planter in the corner and even across the Italian tile in our kitchen. I just sat there, staring down at a flint of glazed blue clay. That was Dad's favorite mug, and it was ruined now. Ruined forever.

Dad lost it, in a way he never had before. He marched right up to Mom and snatched the check out of her hand. Then he tore it into a dozen pieces and let them float down around him.

But even when my father was livid, red-faced with rage, he spoke carefully.

"I'm certainly not going to reward *that* behavior," he said.

Jamie's eyes were big and boyish, black holes in the pale light of our dining room. He blinked tears away. He didn't storm off, not this time. I could feel how hard it was, how painful. Moving stiffly, as though every single millimeter of motion made his body ache, he sat back down in his chair, picked up his pen, and started writing.

"I'll get the broom," Mom said softly. When she passed me on the way to the kitchen, she gave my shoulder a squeeze. I knew that what she really wanted to do was to hug Jamie, but Jamie was busy, his head bent, his eyes downcast. If a few drops of tears dotted his thank-you card to Great-Aunt Dinah, her vision would be too bad for her to notice.

11

IT WAS A HARE, ITS coat blue velvet and scattered with gold. The creature was kicking violently, trying to shake its foot free of the trap. It was almost as tall as the Nameless Boy himself.

"A Winter Watcher's familiar," Boy said softly. The creature looked at him with terror in its eyes. "What are you doing here?"

The hare sniffed the air, then kicked its legs again. That's when boy sprang on it. He held on tight, his muscles resisting the creature's bucking motions. He held a poison-doused cloth over its mouth. At last, the creature collapsed on the ground beneath him. Boy was breathing hard when it was finally subdued.

❧

Everyone came to Jamie's bar mitzvah. Gram and Poppy and Grandma and all four aunts and uncles and about two hundred other relatives, acquaintances, and students from Jamie's class. The synagogue was packed full of snickering, snuffling teenagers who whispered through the rabbi's speech and cheered when Jamie stepped up to the bimah. I knew he was popular, but I'd never really known how *beloved*. I felt almost affronted when I saw Nina's expression as Jamie read, her beady eyes warm and full of adoration.

The theme for the reception was rock 'n' roll. The banquet hall was draped with silver garlands made up of musical notes. There were miniature electric guitars in every centerpiece. The theme had been Mom's idea, a few weeks after the fight over the drums. Jamie didn't look too excited about it, even as he helped Mom tie up little baggies of personalized sunglasses and guitar picks, but he didn't fight her on it, either. As I sat there at one of the family tables, I wasn't sure Jamie cared at all about his bar mitzvah, the reception, the guests, any of it.

But then during the reception, after we were all done dancing the hora and the electric slide, something happened.

The band slowed the music down a little. Dad asked me to dance. Reluctantly, feeling silly in my stiff party dress of blue silk and taffeta, I went to the dance floor with him. I felt *seen* for a split second; truthfully, it was a nice feeling. But then my attention was drawn away again, to Jamie. I watched him cross the room out of the corner of my eye, feeling starved for some glimpse at my brother, now supposedly a man. He was all sweaty, rings of dampness visible through his blue dress shirt. Even his lip, lightly hazed with the first hint of a mustache, was beaded with sweat. He was headed for a table, and as I danced with Dad, I watched Jamie hold out his hand. *He's going to dance with Nina*, I thought.

But the girl who rose from her chair to dance with him wasn't Nina. In fact, I didn't recognize her at all.

That wasn't *that* weird. Jamie had just started eighth grade. Our lives were circles in a Venn diagram that overlapped less and less. My life was the same as it ever was, the woods alone and Miranda and the same old school and the same old story.

But the girl who danced with Jamie was a stranger to me. And she was beautiful. Her hair was a long curtain of black velvet down her back, soft with flyaways. She was pale skinned, but with bronzey undertones. Her eyes were a pair of inky drops, a little too big for her face. Her mouth was just a bit too broad, too. But it worked. She was charming somehow, not despite her imperfections but because of them. She was dressed in all black—black pantyhose and a knee-length black skirt and a black blouse that was kind of clingy. I found it almost impossible to look away from her, so I didn't.

At a glance, she could have been Jewish. In a way, she looked more Jewish than I did. But there was something different about her from the other dark-haired girls at synagogue. When she danced with Jamie, her wide, made-up lips parted, showing the edges of gapped teeth, and something happened in my stomach, a wild kind of flip-flop.

I stepped on Dad's foot. He laughed, thinking I'd meant to tease him, and gave my body a spin. I tried to catch a glimpse of Jamie's face, but the entire room was a blur, the world inside me a frantic jumble, too. Out of the corner of my eye, I watched as she drifted back toward her table. There was a man sitting there. In a way, they looked so similar. Same gapped teeth. Same dimples. But in a way, they looked so different, too. She was a dark-haired shadow of him, and her skin was smooth and burnished where his was freckled. He must have been her father, but he wasn't one of the men who went to Friday-night services or the guys Dad had invited over for dinner from work.

What's happening? I thought. *Who is she?*

On the way to school that Monday, after Jamie had departed for his separate, popular life at the back of the bus and me for my lesser, smaller life at the front, Nina wedged herself beside me and Miranda. I had the window seat; my eyes were cast to the woods we passed, imagining Winter Watchers climbing through the leafless trees. But Miranda was stuck in the middle, and she whined as Nina sat on her coat.

"Hey! Watch it!" she cried.

"I'm not here to talk to you," said Nina. "I'm here to talk to Annie."

I turned. Nina and I had hardly spoken a word to each other since that day in the woods, more than two years ago now. "What?" I asked. I spoke to her like I always did, without any patience.

But then I saw how her lips parted and her eyebrows knitted up, how sad she looked when I spoke to her harshly. "James told me he doesn't want to hang out with me anymore. He's dating the girl with the weird name. Vidya. Since this summer, apparently."

Nina's news was like a punch to the gut. *Dating?* Like, a *girlfriend? Since this summer?!* But I didn't want her to know how bothered I was. My feelings were none of her business. *Jamie* was none of her business. We'd said Vows, pledged loyalty to one another above all else, and even if everything else had changed between us, that hadn't. I had to keep it under control. I couldn't tell her anything, not with my eyes, my face—much less my words.

"Sorry," I said quickly. It felt like there was a fist wedged in my throat. *Vidya*, I thought, wrapping my tongue around the new name. Not a Jewish name. Indian? And she was Jamie's *girlfriend?*

"I only went to his stupid Jew party because I thought he wanted to dance with *me*."

"Gosh, Nina," Miranda said, her voice thick with sarcasm. "That must have been really, really hard."

"Well." Nina turned her head the other way, across the aisle to where some sixth-grade girls were giggling over a magazine. "You tell him that

I don't care. Calvin Harriman asked me out, and I'm going to say yes."

I snorted. This was easier for me to talk about. I could look calm, even though my mind was still churning over this news about Jamie. "Isn't Calvin Harriman like seventeen?"

"So?"

"That's creepy. What would a seventeen-year-old boy want with *you*?"

Nina was still looking the other way. But I could see the coy, curling edge of her smile.

"I'm not going to explain it to you. *You* wouldn't understand, Annie."

That's when Miranda shuffled her hips in place, first swinging left, then right, hard. Nina sailed out of the seat and fell in the aisle on her butt. The girls across the way snickered. The bus driver glanced at her in his rearview mirror, then waggled his finger.

"Back in your seat," he said.

"G-d," said Nina. "Whatever."

She stood up and headed toward the back of the bus. Miranda looked at me, forcing a laugh. "Can you believe your brother is dating that girl Nina was talking about?" she asked.

I shook my head. I couldn't train the horror from my expression. "I can't believe he's dating *anyone*."

It was true. In my mind, no matter the gossip, he was always doomed to be the big brother who had told me to look away from the other kids' graffiti. Who was disgusted by it all, like I was. Once, we'd been Feral Children. Still innocent. Now he'd left me behind. Waltzing off with some girl who hid her eyes behind a curtain of smooth hair. It wasn't fair. It wasn't right.

Miranda studied me, her face long and serious. "Are you okay?" she asked.

I shrugged a little, tightening my coat around me. Jamie had an actual girlfriend. A girlfriend whose name I hadn't even known. He hadn't told me about it. I'd had to hear about it from *Nina*.

"Yeah, I'm fine," I lied, and pretended to go back to looking for Winter Watchers in the garbage-strewn woods.

12

HE HEFTED THE HARE OVER his shoulders and started up the side of the mountain. The breeze whistled through its night-dark coat. Once again, the Boy waited.

It wasn't long before he saw the feathers draw near. There was only one figure that shadowed the mountains, only one harpy left. So much for Amnit's plan to have him massacre a whole flock, Boy thought with a snort. But it didn't matter. He wasn't going to kill anyone—not this harpy, or any other.

She didn't see him there. She fixed her claws onto the heavy hare body and began to lift flagging wings through the air. Her rise was clumsy into the morning. She was focused on her meat, her prize. She didn't see Boy approach.

❦

I wasn't fine. I wasn't fine at all, and Jamie wasn't, either, and I was the only one who knew it. Oh, I think Dad suspected when Jamie said he didn't want to go running anymore. And maybe Mom knew, too, though she pushed the thought out of her mind through Hanukkah and Christmas and New Year's while Jamie sulked and stared at his new cell phone and the rest of us tried to drum up some kind of fake holiday cheer. If the grown-ups knew, they ignored it and gave Jamie his *space*, which was something he needed now, supposedly, since he'd turned thirteen and become a creature with new Laws, foreign and strange. I was the only one whose stomach hardened into an angry stone when I saw the bruises on my older brother's neck, purple blossoms like irises, or how he clamped his lips tight when Dad asked us how school was going over dinner.

I'd talk about the trouble I got into for doodling during history, or how Miranda had invited me to her uncle's farm this coming summer. Dad lifted his eyebrows. Mom shrugged. Eli said he thought it would be fun, that maybe I'd get to feed the llamas, but then everyone turned their focus expectantly to Jamie, waiting to hear what he thought of my summer plans, or about *his* day, or, well, anything.

"What?" he'd say, and roll his peas around his plate until Dad rose, sighed, and started clearing the dinner dishes.

He'd begun to put walls up. Even when he was home, he wasn't really present. The door to his room was shut, or he stared at his laptop or his phone. Even when he was home, I felt like half the soul I'd once been. We were divided now. Individuated. Alone.

One thing that hadn't changed was that he was still friends with Neal, and every Friday he still spent the night at Neal's house even though both of them had dropped out of basketball. They took the bus home together on Friday evenings, which meant that there was a long stretch between Friday afternoon and Saturday morning that my brother's shadow wouldn't darken our hallways. Sometimes when Jamie wasn't home, I'd sneak into his room late at night and shut the door behind me. The maps had all gone yellow on the walls, and now were joined by crude drawings of boys in animal pelts and dark-haired fairies who all looked like Vidya.

Vidya. I'd only seen her that once, but her image was seared into my memory. Jamie sucked at drawing, but he'd somehow captured her anyway. There was Gumlean print under each image. I didn't bother to decode it. I was too unmoored. Vidya, in Gumlea. That was worse than Nina. Okay, maybe not worse than Nina. But it unsettled me.

But at the same time, seeing those drawings, I felt relief. Jamie hadn't forgotten. He hadn't left it completely. Somewhere, deep inside him, he still ruled the feral kingdom. Or maybe the feral kingdom still ruled him.

I thought about Vidya more than I wanted to admit to myself. In class, when I was bored, doodling in the margins of my math notebook, I wondered how often they saw each other and where, whether it was only at school or at Neal's house, too. I wondered what Jamie saw in her, why he'd chosen *her* to be special. There had been something digestible in the thought of Jamie and Nina, though it had disgusted me from the very start. Nina was known, part of the story of our lives. She hated me and I hated her, but I could handle that hate. Somehow, though, I couldn't wrap my head around this girl. His *girlfriend*. I didn't know how I was supposed to feel about her. I didn't know why the thought of her made my stomach hurt.

In the margins of my notebooks, in the middle of class, I tried to draw her from memory. Art that would do her justice, better than Jamie's. I sketched that upturned nose. The broad lips. A gap between her teeth. Her fine hair, sticking to her lip gloss. I imagined her and Jamie together, doing the things I'd heard he'd done with Nina on the very same sofa in Neal's parents' basement. I drew fingers. Folds of cloth. Folds of skin. When I looked up, my blood pounding in my ears,

I saw Nina staring at me from the other side of the room. I turned my notebook page, glowering at her, trying to pretend like I couldn't feel the heat high on my cheeks. Looking away from her, I decided to tuck my thoughts away for later.

Later. After the bus ride home and an empty walk through the woods, after my favorite episode of *The X-Files*, "Jose Chung's *From Outer Space*." After the silence of dinner and the taut sound of Dad almost—but not quite—fighting with Jamie from the threshold of his bedroom door, demanding to know about his homework. After I brushed my teeth and put on my pajamas and tucked myself into bed and didn't kiss a single soul good night, I turned off the light and closed my eyes and thought my private thoughts. I imagined Jamie, peeling away layers of dark cotton. A sweater. A band T-shirt. A bra. Imagined his hesitation, his self-consciousness, his desire. Or was it my own desire? Once, our thoughts had been the same thoughts. Our fantasies the same fantasies. Fairies and mermaids. A shopkeep's daughter we'd saved from a dragon, together. But I couldn't be sure anymore. In Neal's brother's apartment, he'd moved past me, into foreign kingdoms. There were things I didn't know about already, huge gaps of black time in his life that I couldn't access. I needed to fill those spaces in. So I imagined what it would be like to be Jamie, moving against her. More of an animal than a prince, or even a Nameless Boy.

The sound of footsteps in the hallway intercepted my thoughts. Under my door, I saw a jagged bolt of light. *Jamie*, I thought, and huddled down deep under the covers. With my eyes closed, I envisioned him ambling through the bathroom in his pajamas, going from the toilet to the sink, where he didn't wash his hands but only sort of absently scratched at his skin until one of his pores was raw and weeping. He looked at himself, and he saw me there, with my shameful thoughts laid bare before him. Sighing, he only shook his head, turned off the bathroom light, and went back to his room.

I didn't dare think about Vidya again that night—not consciously. But as I squeezed my eyes shut and willed myself painfully to sleep, I couldn't help but remember the way her clavicle dipped at the base of her throat and the tender way her lips parted when she smiled. I knew then that her body wasn't all that he liked about her. It was something else. Her voice. A certain way of looking at the world. But those were mysteries to me. I'd never spoken to her. Never heard her speak. My brother's girlfriend was a stranger.

I knew she wasn't mine to think about. Of course, she didn't precisely belong to Jamie, either. She owned herself, in that way that most people own themselves. Except for Jamie and me, of course, even then. Sleeping in our separate bedrooms. Dreaming, though we never talked about it in the morning light, the exact same dreams, and of the exact same girl.

One Saturday morning in the gray space between winter and spring, after Jamie had spent the night at Neal's, I woke up early, pulled on boots and jeans and my shearling coat, skipped breakfast, and trudged outside without a word to Mom or Dad or anyone else. Not that it mattered. Not that they'd ever asked. They knew the woods were safe. Nothing had ever *happened* there.

But that day, feeble March, the frost still thickly encasing every budding branch, something did happen. I heard voices, low and dark and familiar. And then I smelled something. A new smell. It wasn't anything of Earth, that much was certain. I pressed deeper and deeper into the woods, past the wall, past the girders. I wasn't chased. I was compelled, right toward that old picnic table with the cocks and vulvas and sacred leaves scrawled on top. There was my brother, perched on top like a gargoyle, his back to me. Neal was sitting next to him. Their shoulders were touching. They were whispering, then coughing. There was a smoke cloud over them like a dark portent.

"I don't care what she tells you," Neal was saying. "She's a girl. She's never gonna understand."

"She's different."

Neal snorted. "Not likely."

I watched them, how their bodies nearly formed two halves of a heart, how the smoke swirled around them like a faint calligraphy. My hands curled into fists. That's when I decided that I'd watched them long enough.

"What are you doing?" I demanded. Both boys jumped, spewing mouthfuls of smoke as they turned. Their eyes were red-rimmed, like they hadn't slept. It was early, but it wasn't that early.

"Shit. Annie."

Those words from Jamie weren't talking *to* me; they were talking *about* me. He hopped off the picnic table and dropped something in the dirt and gravel, then stomped it out with his Skecher. But Neal was slower to turn, and when he did, he was still holding something in his hand, a lumpy little cigarette.

"Are you guys *smoking*?" I asked in disbelief. He pawed at the back of his neck.

"You. Can't. Tell. Anyone. Annie." He paused between every word.

"Why not? Where did you get those? Neal, did your brother buy you those cigarettes?"

Neal stared at the white little thing, squinting. "No," he said simply. And then he took a drag out of it. I sniffed at the air. It didn't smell like an ordinary cigarette. The scent was halfway between Gram's old hippie incense and a skunk's spray.

"That's pot, isn't it?" I asked, and if my stomach wasn't already somewhere down by my feet, I certainly felt it tumble over then. Drugs. Neal and Jamie were doing *drugs*. This was un-fucking-believable, as Jamie would say, if he said anything, but he didn't. He only kept squinting at me, like the early spring light was much too bright.

"We took a Vow!" I spat my words. My brother started to open his mouth to answer. But I wouldn't let him. I only shook my head. "I don't even know you anymore, *James*," I said. Between Vidya and this, I felt like he was standing on the deck of a ship, and I was left on the shore watching him drifting away. He held out his hands. They looked wrinkled and pale.

"You know me. I'm your brother. I'm the same as you. We're—"

"We're not anything," I said, gritting my teeth. "Don't talk to me anymore. I don't want to hear it."

I spun around and walked off through the woods, my steps brisk, breaking sticks beneath my feet as I left.

"Wait here," I heard my brother say to Neal, but I pretended I didn't hear anything as I ran through the forest, fleeing the kingdom we once shared. There used to be so many rules, and we'd negotiated each one together. Now there was no negotiating. Jamie lived his life. I lived mine.

I heard him chasing me. I heard but didn't care. *Let him smoke what he wants and kiss who he wants and live whatever damned fool lie he wants*, I said to myself. But when he fixed his hand on my arm and spun me around, my face erupted into tears.

"Annie, you won't—" he began, but then he saw how I was sobbing. I collapsed on the ground, hugging my own knees. He didn't hug me or touch me again. He just stood over me, his mouth open.

"Are you okay?"

"What do you care?" I spat, and wiped my nose on the back of my arm. He didn't say anything, so I pressed: "Don't pretend that you do!"

In one of the trees overhead, what seemed like a thousand sparrows were roosting, raising their voices all at once. They sounded frantic. But my brother looked calm. He started again. Quietly, this time: "I just need to know that you won't tell—"

"*I* know the Laws!" I screamed. Jamie flinched like I'd hit him where it hurt. I guess I had. But it was true. If anyone had been faithful to the agreements we'd made, it was me. Jamie was the one who needed to make absolutions. But we both knew that he wouldn't. We both knew how he'd sinned and would continue to sin.

"Okay," he said. "Good."

Then he turned and walked away. He went back to Neal and their experiments, their shaking laughter and crude boy jokes, and left me there in a bed of leaves and mud and feathers, crying until there were no tears left.

13

IN ONE SWIFT MOVEMENT, THE Nameless Boy grabbed on to the harpy's tail. She was so surprised that she dropped the hare on the rocks below. Boy noted how the hare's eyes bolted open, waking to life. Then he saw it take off through the bramble.

Return to your Watcher, Boy thought as he climbed the harpy's powerful body. She was thrashing beneath him, craning her head back. But then he whispered in her ear:

"I won't kill you. I won't harm you. I just need you to take me far away from here."

❖

That was the summer that I was supposed to go with Miranda to visit her uncle's farm. But it never happened. Instead, that spring, Miranda caught Lyme disease from a tiny deer tick that had buried itself behind her ear. She was on two different antibiotics, and when I visited her, laid up on her parents' couch, she looked pale and exhausted, like she hadn't slept in months. She said her skin was changed from the meds. That she'd burn instantly in the sun. Practically a vampire, she said with a grin, even though I don't think she thought it was funny. But I caught the drift. There would be no trip to her uncle's farm that summer, no escape.

Jamie was gone. Off with Vidya or Neal, I couldn't be sure. I tried to push thoughts of all of them from my mind, though questions about Vidya occasionally wafted through. I stomped them out as best I could. On the rare occasions I'd see my brother at dinner, he had a rumpled look. His eyes were watery and hooded. He smelled musky, like a skunk, like a piece of spoiled fruit. No one else seemed to notice or care. Sometimes I thought about chasing him down. Confronting him. Demanding he share himself with me, that he make everything right.

But the look on his face during dinner told me that it would get us both nowhere. Jamie wasn't *there* with us, even when he *was* there. He was somewhere else.

That summer was a bad one, long and bright and ugly. There is nothing else to say about it, or at least nothing good.

14

AS THE HARPY LIFTED HIM, the boy's stomach seemed to tumble down through the soles of his feet. He felt his body buck and sway, but he never quite seemed to achieve weightlessness. Instead, something dragged on him. His old life, perhaps? Emperata Annit? With his eyes still closed, he gave his head a shake. Annit would be fine without him. She had an entire kingdom to herself, followers. She had a moon. She had so much more than he'd ever owned. All he had were a few broken toys and some dirty furs. He was just a nameless scamp, an orphan. What was he to her, anyway? She would surely survive the loss of him.

❖

The first day of eighth grade. I had my backpack all ready, my notebook sorted by subject, my pencil box filled with mechanical pencils, the brand I liked, 7 mm leads.

This year would be different. This year I would be organized. This year, I wouldn't doodle in my notebooks. I wouldn't daydream. The teachers wouldn't send notes home: *bright, but unfocused*. This year, Dad wouldn't even have to institute homework time. I'd come home and go straight to my room, and my desk would be clean, and when I was finished and I went to watch TV after dinner, I would watch the same shows that all the other kids watched, the right shows, and I'd have something to talk to them about as we filed onto the bus in the morning.

I was almost thirteen, and my bat mitzvah was in a few weeks, and that *meant* something. I would be an adult in the eyes of G-d, and it was time for me to start acting like it. That day, the first day of eighth grade, I waited outside for the bus with Jamie, who was starting high school in the building adjoining the middle school. I was all hope and nervous energy. My brother was a dark cloud beside me. He was zitty and rumpled and I had trouble understanding what a girl like Vidya saw in him. He looked—what had Dad called it?—"troubled" lately, and when Rabbi Schulman asked me at synagogue where my brother had been, I could only shrug. In the back of my head, I knew the truth: the woods, sacred cigarettes. Neal. Vidya. But unlike Jamie, I kept my Vows and the Laws to heart. I told no one what I knew.

As part of my new, adult identity I vowed I would take every opportunity that came. Maybe it was because Jamie had begun to withdraw from school and home life. In return, I resolved to be the perfect, upstanding kid he no longer was. So in the first week of school, not only did I join art club, like I always did, but also debate team, chorus, and field hockey. Mom cringed at the cost of supplies, but Dad seemed pleased.

"You should take a cue from your sister," he told Jamie. Jamie just pushed the hood of his sweatshirt down over his eyes and sulked up the stairs, letting his door slam behind him and leaving all the pictures trembling on the walls.

Miranda didn't understand why I'd become such a joiner. My new schedule meant that I no longer sat next to her on the bus on the way home. Instead, I took the late bus with the other overachievers who were scattered throughout our town. To my surprise, Vidya was there, too, sitting in the back, her nose always stuck in a book. The sight of her made my pulse throb, though I was careful to make it look like I hadn't seen her. But when she wasn't looking, I peeked at the covers of the books she was reading. Fantasy novels. George R. R. Martin. Patrick Rothfuss. That kind of thing. I wanted to ask her about them, but I didn't. She belonged to Jamie. She was Jamie's girlfriend. I shouldn't have been staring at her. I told myself I shouldn't have cared.

But it was hard. Something about the way she smiled as she read drew my gaze magnetically toward her. I told myself that it was because she *knew* Jamie, in a way no one else did. Even me. She might have been the rune that would have let me decipher him. That's what I assured myself when I stared at her on the bus. It had nothing to do with how she held a hand against her throat, smiling at something she'd read. It was all only about Jamie.

She was in chorus with me, too, one of the only classes that was composed of both middle and high schoolers together. I was a soprano, part of the huge pack of girls who sang in high, reedy voices together. She stood on the other end of the risers, by the boys. She was a contralto, one of three.

I tried to pick her voice out. Usually I couldn't, but sometimes I heard a low, loping melody. The notes seemed to weave themselves around and around each one of my ribs, knotting them tightly. But why? The sound made my throat tight. I thought a thousand times about going to talk to her. I could ask her about Jamie, what they'd been doing all summer, *where he'd been*. I could ask her about the books she read, if she believed in alien abduction, something, anything. But there was something about her that made my mind feel all frazzled and wild. Usually, words came easily to me, even though I was someone who spent most her time avoiding people. Not now, though. Not when it came to her.

When the first chorus rehearsal of the new school year was over, I rushed to stuff my sheet music into my backpack, keeping my eyes down so that no one would see how my nostrils flared, my cheeks heated, my palms sweat.

"Hey, you're Annie, right?"

I turned around as quick as a crossbow's bolt. Improbable though it was, there she was, her messenger bag slung over one shoulder, her hair down like a gossamer canopy. Her features were big, dark, and perfect. She wore a velvet choker around her neck, some kind of coin that shone, stark silver, against her warm skin, right at the base of her throat. I thought of Jamie kissing that throat. I pushed the thought away.

"Yeah?" I answered, making myself stand up straighter.

"James told me about you," she said, and tucked a strand of hair behind her ear. I had the feeling that she was trying to sound casual, and failing. I hoped she didn't notice how my hands shook. *What else do you two talk about?* a voice at the back of my mind demanded, but I couldn't form those thoughts into words. I shoved my hands into the pockets of my jeans.

"Yeah?" I said again. I was desperate to know what she wanted with *me*. Since Jamie first left for middle school without me, his friends and mine were never the same. Even Neal refused to say hello to me now, though after my outburst in the woods, I'm not sure I blamed him.

Sometimes I wished I could obliterate my feelings. Maybe rebuild myself from cold metal and gears, one part at a time.

"Yeah," Vidya said, and she smiled nervously. When she smiled, I saw that gap between her front teeth. It was cute, a little chipmunky. "He told me that you write fantasy stories together."

In my pockets, my hands went still. They went cold. They went heavy. I started to grab my backpack and throw it over my shoulder.

"He's not supposed to talk about that—"

"Oh, don't worry. I wouldn't tell anyone. I think it's cool. James is a great writer. He mentioned you draw maps? I really like maps of imaginary places. I used to have one of Middle Earth on my bedroom wall."

I felt my lip tick up, almost of its own volition. I'd tried to read *The Lord of the Rings* last year but had only gotten halfway through *The Two Towers* before I got bored. That was a problem I always had with fantasy books. Who cared about other people's fantasies?

But she was looking at me, chipmunk smile and snub nose and that silver token rising and falling with each breath. I narrowed my eyes at her, still wary. Jamie had *told her*. Even though he'd sworn he wouldn't. "Cool," I said icily, wondering if she was going to let me leave. By then, the other kids had started filing out toward the hallway. I started walking. But for some reason, she just walked beside me. Like I wanted her there.

And honestly, part of me almost *did*. I could feel the heat of her hand beside mine as our strides matched. A thought drifted through my mind, treacherous. *You could hold her hand.* It was appalling. Mortifying. And it must have been why I kept talking, despite the hot coal of betrayal that was simmering in my belly.

"You like to sing?" I asked. Stupid words. Empty words. When what I really should have been asking her what Jamie had told her— interrogating her about how he'd broken his Vows.

"Oh yeah," she said quickly. Her skin darkened a shade, like it embarrassed her. "I'm thinking of joining Madrigals next year instead. You know, the medieval choir? It's only open to sophomores and upperclassmen. I hear they even wear costumes. My dad thinks I should do jazz band instead, but I don't like playing guitar and singing at the same time."

"You play guitar?" I was finding myself swept up into the current of conversation despite myself. She seemed so easygoing. So *normal*.

"Yeah, I've been taking lessons since I was six. I also play bass, clarinet, and some piano. Oh, and the banjo. Ukulele, here and there. We have all these instruments around. My dad's kind of a music nut."

My eyes went wide as we stepped into the bright blue light of the September afternoon. I wondered what Vidya had thought of Jamie's bar mitzvah theme. It must have seemed cheesy and fake to her, someone who *actually* knew about music.

"The only stuff my dad likes are work, jogging, and talk radio," I said, even though that wasn't entirely fair, and it wasn't exactly true, either. Dad also liked black coffee and filling out crossword puzzles and yard work and knowing the names of all the birds at our feeders. Those were the things that Mom loved about him, and I loved them about him, too. But Vidya didn't need to know all that.

She laughed a little, and the sound reminded me of the inside of a sweatshirt. "James told me. He sounds like a hard guy to live with."

I looked at her, my gaze sharpening to a laser intensity. "You mean Dad, or Jamie?"

Vidya opened her mouth, showing the inside where the lipstick had worn off. Then she closed it again and smiled. "There's my mom," she said, waving to an SUV in the distance. "It was nice talking to you,

Annie. You should think about Madrigals next year."

"Two years," I corrected her quickly. "I'm only an eighth grader."

"Oh," she said. "Sorry. I always forget you aren't twins. You seem a lot like him, you know."

I didn't know what to say to that. But I didn't have to. Vidya's mom leaned on her horn.

"See you," Vidya said, and ran off, just like that, her hair a trailing storm system behind her.

I found my brother in the bathroom, picking his acne in the fluorescent light of Mom's makeup mirror.

"You told," I said. Jamie's zit popped with a dramatic explosion of pus and blood. He didn't even cringe, just wiped everything up with a piece of toilet paper, then used rubbing alcohol to clean the wound.

"What are you talking about?" he said. "Get out of here. You're supposed to give me my privacy."

It was true. We were supposed to let him have as much time as he wanted in the bathroom, no matter how badly anyone needed to pee. "That's why we have two toilets," Mom had said, even though Dad had coughed awkwardly at the idea, saying, "Why can't he just do it in his room?"

I had asked what *it* was, but they pretended not to hear me. Apparently, *it* was popping zits. He was just digging into another when I repeated myself.

"You told. You told Vidya. You told Vidya about *Gumlea*."

Jamie glanced at me, annoyance sparking in his eyes. "Did not," he said, like it was even possible for us to lie to each other.

"Did too. She told me, James. I guess you're a good match for each other. Neither one of you can keep a secret."

My brother turned to face me now. His skin was red and splotchy and angry, but his brow was even, like he didn't feel a single thing. "I didn't tell her about *Gumlea*. I only told her we write stories together."

I squinted at him, not quite believing. It felt unlikely—or pointless. Gumlea had never been about me and Jamie. It had been about *magic*. About making a space where we could be ourselves, and not whatever everyone else thought we should be. What was there to say about our "writing stories together" that would be of any interest to someone like Vidya? She was just an ordinary girl, wasn't she? She was never going to understand. Still, it was a small comfort. A smaller betrayal, then. Not like the drugs I'd caught him smoking with Neal.

But Jamie was rolling his eyes, adding, "Or used to write them, I guess. Before you changed your mind about that."

My fists clenched. "*What?*"

"Anyway," Jamie went on, ignoring me. "Who cares if I tell her? She's my girlfriend."

My nostrils flared. G-d, I was angry. Perhaps mostly because, sure, part of me understood why it was happening. I thought of Vidya's long, velvety veil of hair, remembered the sweet smell of her, like incense and dryer sheets and piano dust. I'd wanted to give it all away for a girl before, for Miranda. I understood. But I hadn't done it. When it had counted, I'd been faithful.

"You can't do this," I said. "There are Laws. There will be a price to pay."

"Come off it," Jamie said. He closed the medicine cabinet, not hard, but quietly. Just a year ago, he'd been the kind of boy who had thrown things, broken things. Now he kept his temper in check. Now he felt nothing, or claimed to. These changes had taken place elsewhere, away from me. But I knew better than anyone how anger burned through his veins, all the G-d damned time. "I'm not playing that stupid game anymore."

He brushed by me on the way to his room, not even bothering to make eye contact. But he muttered something as he left.

"Let it go," he said.

He might as well have punched me. That's how much it hurt.

15

BENEATH THEM WAS ONLY SEA, endless and churning. The boy gripped the harpy's wing more tightly. That was his mistake. She let out a cry of displeasure, casting her head back, lifting her voice to the empty sky. Her wings hesitated. Her back arched. That's when she threw him, when, weightlessly, his body arced through the air.

I'm finally free, he thought. With eyes open, he waited for death to take him as his body barreled toward the sea.

❖

Through the first week of September, Jamie was always off with his friends, and I was always alone. After my activities got out and I came home on the late bus, I'd go out into the woods by myself. The days were getting shorter, rapidly tumbling toward the dark of winter, and it seemed like the neighborhood kids had abandoned this place in favor of warmer, brighter spaces. Calvin Harriman's apartment, I guess, or behind the bleachers at the high school, or the mall up in Kingston if they could bum a ride from one of their older friends, or a parent if they had to.

I hiked through the forest, my boots sticking in the mud. I climbed trees, letting the bark bite at my hands. In my head, I tried to conjure Gumlea, but it was getting hard to see it now. Sometimes I'd spot a Winter Watcher's hideout or the shape of the King's dragon, skulking through the underbrush, but mostly everything around me was normal. Spray-painted pot leaves. Crushed beer cans. Poison ivy trailing over the path.

There was a massive old oak tree up ahead, half rotted away and hollow, carved with the graffiti of a thousand boys and me, too. Its guts were always crawling with carpenter ants and termites. It had been one of my favorite places in Gumlea, the site of the King's tower if you were through the Veil, full of danger and packed with wild, unchecked magic.

"I'll save you, Princess," I said, with a flourish to hide how halfhearted my words felt when they rattled inside me. I pulled myself into the tree and hauled my body up. If I closed my eyes, I could smell the fungus and the moss and the mold, a dank, warm, familiar scent, and I could almost pretend it was just a few years ago—before the whole damned world went wrong.

I imagined voices. Shrill, girly screams. The King. The King was torturing her. I opened my eyes and pulled myself even higher into the hollow, my feet sinking into the rotting wood, my back braced against the oak's worm-eaten heart.

I fixed my hands on the bark, yanked myself up to where I knew there was a crack in the trunk. I peered over, expecting to see nothing. But instead, I saw a light up ahead. A flashlight's beam, bobbing with every step my brother took over the tangled ground.

He wasn't alone, of course. He never was lately. He was with Neal, walking forward, talking in low tones.

At least they're not smoking, I told myself as I watched them, invisible inside the oak tree. If he had been paying one iota of attention, he would have known I was there, waiting for him. But he was busy.

"I don't feel guilty about it," he said. There was more emotion in his voice in that single cryptic sentence than I'd heard from Jamie in the last year. "Any of it. I just don't understand why it has to change."

"You've got a girlfriend now."

"She doesn't have to know."

"Yeah, well, *I* know."

"Is this about church?"

My brother stopped walking in the middle of the path and turned his flashlight directly onto Neal. The other boy grinned for a moment in the white circle of light, but then that moment passed and he batted the flashlight's beam away. Toward me. I pressed my spine down, hoping to be invisible. Of course, I didn't need to worry. Jamie wasn't even thinking about me.

"No," Neal said humorlessly. But Jamie kept pressing.

"Because you know that's all a lie. Things people tell themselves to make themselves feel better. No one wants to admit there's nothing else out there. Just the real world, with nothing surprising in it." My brother kicked at a beer can as though to punctuate his thought. "And then death."

"You've been talking too much to Vidya," Neal said.

Jamie shrugged. Smiled. Blushed. "Talking. Yeah. Among other things," he said with a grin. I saw a flash of white as Neal rolled his eyes. I rolled my eyes, too.

Among other things.

I thought of my brother, his hands clutching at Vidya's back as they danced. I thought of them together, long afternoons in Calvin's apartment, and everyone else suddenly gone. I thought about him telling her about the stories we'd written together. About the two of us, building fantasy worlds in our bedrooms or the backyard or the woods. I imagined how they would press their skin together after talking about everything, their bodies intersecting at all the right points. Or all the wrong points. It made me feel sick to think about it, Jamie and Vidya. Talking about me. But it made me feel other things, too.

Inside that sacred tree, emotions burst open inside me. I couldn't tell what was lust and what was jealousy and what was pure white-hot rage.

"Anyway, I hope we can still start that band together . . . ," my brother was saying, but his voice sounded suddenly distant as I scrambled up over the top of the old oak tree, my ears instead filled with the roaring rush of blood.

"Yeah, if you can get that drum kit."

"I'm working on it. I've got a connection—"

In that moment, I thrust my body over the jagged top of the tree, letting myself fall toward the forest floor. And Jamie. I was aiming myself at Jamie. An ambush, like something out of a movie. I flew toward him, my broken nails bared.

"Aaaaauuuuuuugh!"

I screamed, and my brother yelped out "What the hell?" as his body broke the fall of my body and we went tumbling toward the hard ground.

I could hear the wind go out of him. We hit the ground next to one another, but soon, I scrambled back toward him. On top of him. Holding down his wrists.

"You betrayed me!" I yelled, finally letting my anger get the better of me. "You broke the *Laws!*"

"Annie, what the hell?" Neal was coming toward me, reaching his arms around my shoulders to pull me off. I wasn't stronger than he was, but I was angrier, and no matter how hard he pulled at me, he wouldn't distract me from my task. I wanted to punish my brother. To make him feel sorry for everything he'd done.

Jamie's eyes got wide. I didn't have a plan for what I would do— only rage, unchecked, at the growing space between us, the differences that hadn't been there before, the loss. I grabbed at his clothes and raised my open hands and watched as my brother flinched away from me, waiting. Neal was still trying to pull me away, but he was just a distraction. My brother and I were the only ones who mattered.

"Sorry!" he yelped. "I'm sorry!"

He squinted one eye open at me and I felt in that minuscule slip of time something shift. A vision, the way we used to see Gumlea. I was a harpy, claws outstretched, screaming, beating her wings. I was a harpy, dropping him into the open ocean. I was a harpy, flying away.

I scrambled back, and Neal fell back with me. We were all breathing hard, the three of us, as I looked at my brother and saw him in two places at once.

Here, in the forest behind the drainage creek. There, tumbled inside an ocean of swirling, endless blue.

"Sorry," Jamie said to me again, and I could hear how he meant it. I began to nod, to tell him it was all right. The King would soon forgive him. Everything would be okay.

That's when I felt something hard hit me at the edge of my cheek-bone, *thwack*. I winced, saw an explosion of light, watched a rock tumble into the roots of that old, broken oak tree. When I looked up, my brother was glowering at his friend.

"What the hell, Neal?" he said. Neal's hand was still up, raised from where he'd thrown the rock.

"I was only trying to help," he said.

16

WHEN HIS BODY WAS HAULED from the water, he protested at first. It was too much light, too much sound, the seagulls and the ocean waves roaring beneath him and the raucous cries of men among themselves. His tongue tasted salt—water? blood?—when it wanted to taste nothing. He should have been gone already. Instead his flesh was assaulted by what felt like a thousand dull-edged knives. Rope, cutting into his shoulders and back and legs, wet and swollen and splintery. This was like waking up on the first day of school after a long, languorous summer. This was wrong, all wrong, the Nameless Boy thought as the net opened and his body slammed into wooden boards and two lungs full of water came rushing out of him.

❧

Jamie chased me through the woods again, but by the time I reached the creek, he'd given up. Alone, I launched myself over and out of Gumlea and stormed through the screen door, leaving a trail of mud and soggy leaves behind.

It was nearly dinnertime. I could hear my father in the kitchen, cooking pasta while listening to a bombastic podcaster shout about investing. He didn't seem to notice me, and I was glad for it. I breezed by him and rushed toward the bathroom, hoping to examine my wound in private.

Though the cut was small, my cheek was split right on top of the bone, a small vein of brown blood crusted over it. My eyes looked bruisey already, though it was mostly from crying. My hair was a tangled, dirty mess. I looked like a wild animal. I riffled through the drawers of the vanity, searching for a Band-Aid that didn't have one of Elijah's cartoon characters on it.

"Can I help?" I heard Dad's voice in the door behind me and winced. When I turned, he was watching me expectantly. Maybe another father would have been shocked or upset at the way I looked, but my normal, boring father took my feral appearance in stride.

"I guess," I said thickly. My father gestured to the toilet; I sat down on the closed lid. The last time I was in here at the same time as him, my legs would have dangled, but that was a long time ago now. I sat with them splayed, like a man. Mom would have told me to sit differently, but Dad never did. I could never decide if that kind of thing was a relief or a curse. He didn't police me. But maybe he never really noticed me, either. Even now, as he dabbed the wound with rubbing alcohol on a cotton pad, I had the weird feeling like he was looking through me. His eyes were green like money, and even this close, I couldn't hook them. They avoided mine.

"I'm not going to ask you what happened," he said. "But you can tell me, if you want."

He turned his back to me again and went to get a plain Band-Aid out of a box on the top shelf, hidden behind some of Jamie's brand-new stinky aftershave. I looked at the staid, boring frame of his shoulders and considered saying nothing. My father wasn't a liar. He would have let me sit in silence. But my anger and confusion were still all boiling up inside me, tearing up my guts like some kind of sour soup.

"Me and Jamie got into a fight," I said. It didn't matter to me that Neal had been the one to throw the stone, or that it was somehow Neal and Vidya's fault, together. What mattered was me and my brother.

"James, you mean," my father said, gently correcting me. He was always careful to call Jamie that now, no matter how often they butted heads.

"Yes," I said tersely. "James."

"Well," my father said. He peeled the bandage off the backing and stuck it carefully to my cheek. "I'm sure the two of you will work it out."

"I don't know," I told him. As I reached up to touch my fingertips to the thin strip of plastic, my stomach felt squeezed. Uneasy. Sick. "He doesn't want to . . . to tell the stories we used to tell each other anymore. And he told some friends about it. He said he wouldn't, but he did."

"Gumlea?" Dad asked, like he'd always known.

I nodded. "Yeah." My stomach churned. I wondered if it was true. "They were *our* stories, Dad. They were private."

"It's his life, too, Annie. His story."

I studied my father's face, all the little wrinkles, the receding hairline. "You always take his side," I said, and it was immature and not at all true. If anything, Dad was harder on Jamie than he was on me. But I felt petty. Jealous.

Still, it didn't bother my father. He shrugged. "I honestly think it's better that he's found other friends. Better for you, too. I used to worry about both of you. You were always such interior creatures."

I felt my lips pucker out in a scowl. "What do you mean?"

"I worried that the two of you would have trouble when you got to school. Half the time it was like you were speaking a language no one else could understand. And that can't last forever. Someday, your brother will go away to college. You'll have to find something else."

"There's nothing else," I protested. "I *love* Gumlea. We need it. Me and Jamie—"

My dad gave me a withering look. "If you spend all your time immersed in fantasy, you'll miss out on real life. You won't even notice how much you've lost until it's already gone."

"It's not a fantasy," I said. It wasn't. Gumlea was real, by whatever definition mattered; Jamie and I had built it together out of our magic. How could something be an escape from reality if it *was* your reality? I held my hands over my eyes as though I could shield myself from what my dad was saying. I didn't want to hear it. Didn't want to even consider it.

"It's good to get out there," my dad was saying. "Experience the real world. Make friends. Feel things."

"I have friends," I said, my hands still over my eyes. "I feel things."

"Annie." My father put his hands on my hands and guided my fingers down. I couldn't remember the last time our fingers had touched. I'd probably been a little kid, rushing across the street with him, my small hand tucked in his. Now I was grown in my father's eyes. And in my father's eyes, it was time to put away childish things. His touch didn't linger. His hands were back in his pockets before I knew it, the expression on his face stern. "I know you had fun with the games you played with your brother, but they weren't real. They were never going to last forever. He's growing up now, and you are, too. Don't let yourself get distracted from the things that matter."

"Like Jamie?" I asked in confusion.

My father sighed. "James," he said. "Yes. But I really meant school."

With that, my dad turned around to leave, and when he did, he shut the light off out of habit. I sat in the dark, feeling like I wasn't even there.

I didn't want to hear what my dad had to say, but I'd heard it, anyway. All through dinner, while Jamie stared at his plate and my mom fussed over him and Elijah, I thought about Gumlea. How hard I had tried to hold on to it, and how quickly it had slipped through my fingertips. I still felt as tethered as I ever did to Jamie, but I had to admit that Gumlea was no longer what tied us together. When I looked at him, giving him our old, secret smile, the Band-Aid wrinkled up and pulled at my skin and hurt and he only looked away.

After dinner, I cleared my plate, told my mom I had homework, and shut the bedroom door behind me.

The walls were covered with my drawings. There were thousands of hours of work there, my entire blood supply poured out over every single page. There were the white cliffs and the beacons on the edges that Emperata Annit had built. There were the trade routes of the pirate ships, and the place that the Nameless Boy had been hauled on deck by pirates. I'd lived these stories once, knew them as well as I knew my own heartbeat. I had been the archivist, holding them all close. Caring for them.

Now they didn't matter. I was missing out, Dad said, on real life. *Let it go*, Jamie had said.

I didn't want them to be right. Dad. Jamie. I wanted to fight for it. To keep fighting. But . . .

I reached up and touched the Band-Aid and felt the throbbing split in my skin beneath it. I thought of Miranda, and everything we'd never said to each other. My lonely days in the forest, which had brought me nothing but misery. The things I felt when I thought about Vidya.

What would happen if I let that go? Would I have space in my life for something else, then? The idea tugged at me. I saw my future stretch out. Clean. New.

I knelt on my bed and began to take the pages down. The wallpaper was faded bunnies, brighter where the taped-up pages had protected the ink from sunlight. I put all of our maps in a stack, and then tucked the stack into a binder, and then wedged the binder into the bottom of my desk drawer, along with ancient yo-yos and toys from Chuck E. Cheese that I'd kept for reasons that were beyond even me. I didn't throw any of it out, but I told myself that Gumlea belonged with all of that. Childhood garbage, worth saving, maybe, but hidden somewhere dark and forgotten.

After, I lay on my bed and watched the sunlight set over the strange shadows in the colorful wallpaper. I told myself that it was good. Healthy. Normal. I told myself it was okay that there was no more magic left in the world.

17

THE PIRATES HAD FILMY EYES, red-rimmed at the edges. The pirates were missing hands, legs, fingers, teeth. When they walked toward the Nameless Boy, they smelled like urine and body odor, the stink that boy had scrubbed off himself at the end of the day, the sour perfume that none of the other children wore. He looked up at the pirates as he wheezed and panted and dripped down on the deck.

"Stay away from me," he growled. The pirates all looked at one another, bushy eyebrows lifted in surprise, and they laughed and laughed and laughed.

❧

It was a Thursday, an ordinary day. I ate a yogurt for breakfast. Jamie argued with Dad about whether he could have a cup of coffee, until Mom got tired of the yelling and made him a cup of black tea instead.

I went to the bathroom while Jamie stood over the kitchen table, texting someone. I wouldn't even remember this detail except that the police asked me about it over and over again later: *Did James often text his friends in the morning? Do you know who he was texting?*

But no, I didn't know. My brother stared down at his phone, his brow furrowed, and I left him there and went to pee and then, wordlessly, we headed out for the bus together.

It was September 13, but it still felt like summer. Blue sky, the leaves green but just starting to go gold at the edges. The morning was clear and beautiful, like something from a dream. We stood on the curb and waited for the bus, not speaking. But we never talked while we waited for the bus anyway. Jamie's phone buzzed in the pocket of his hoodie again. He took it out and began to answer. Nina wandered out of her house, her hands hooked into her backpack straps. She kept stealing glances at my brother, like she hoped he would speak to her. But he didn't.

The bus arrived. We trudged up the steps. If I'd known what I know now, I would have buried Jamie in a hug. I would have made it so my arms could keep him there, in our bubble of suburban safety. At the very least, I would have said goodbye.

But Jamie went to the back of the bus, where his friends sat making trouble, and I sat next to Miranda and said good morning, and turned my eyes to the road. When I tell this story, when I think about this moment, I think: *Turn around, stupid. Look at him. You're never going to see him again like this.*

But I didn't. I kept my eyes to the woods. And I've been told that I couldn't have known, that it wasn't my fault, but it's a weight I carried for a long time: the last time I saw my brother for certain, boarding the bus that morning of Thursday, boring stupid Thursday, September the unlucky thirteenth.

Sometimes Jamie was home after school. Most days, though, since last year, he wasn't, off smoking G-d knows what with Neal, or making out with Vidya, or whatever. I liked the days without him better. On those days, I'd have forty-five minutes to myself before Mom came home and

Elijah's bus arrived and then Dad finished with work, too, and Jamie finally came home, grumbling like an overworked motor. Forty-five minutes with the house empty and comfortable, when I could draw or write or imagine all to myself, when I could eat potato chips and stream *The X-Files* endlessly for the millionth time and be by myself, my full self, my true self. Once I'd been able to share her with Jamie. But now she was a secret, one that I told no one. Now she only lived when I was alone.

On that Thursday, no one was home. I went inside and locked the door behind me. I turned on the television, threw my bag down on the sofa, then went to the kitchen to make myself a snack. Crackers and cheese, carefully arranged. Apple slices. A jelly jar of diet soda. I was standing at the counter, pouring, when my gaze drifted out the kitchen window.

I still don't know if what I saw was real or some sort of delusion. All the evidence points to the latter, but in the moment, it seemed completely real, if unbelievable. There was Jamie, standing by the woods in the back of our yard. I thought, *He must be going to meet Neal.* I sipped some of the foam off my soda, cringing at the thought. Pot. It was so ridiculous. We'd once agreed that drugs were stupid, a waste of time. We'd promised each other we would never try them. Guess he'd changed his mind. Or lied about it, way back when. Neither would surprise me. Nothing did with Jamie, not anymore.

And then I saw something that made my breath catch. Jamie was stepping backward into the woods. He was walking into Gumlea, something he hadn't done in longer than I could remember. I saw him disappear between a thorny mess of bushes.

A small voice inside me said, *Go to him.* A small voice inside me said,

He needs you, Emperata Annit.

Instead, I put the lid on the bottle of soda, tucked it into the fridge, and wandered off to watch TV.

Mom came home, then Dad with Elijah in tow from their Tiger Scout meeting. Dad was going to make stir-fry for dinner. He was in a good mood. They all seemed to be. They were in the kitchen, laughing and cutting vegetables in the yellowing evening light. I was sprawled out on the sofa still with my homework. My *X-Files* episode, "Small Potatoes," ended, and Mom put on the news. The house was filled with the smells of garlic and soy sauce. Years later, every box of Chinese takeout I smell still turns my stomach.

The newscasters were talking about household cleaners that might kill you, and then the weatherman came on and predicted storms for the rest of the week. That's when Mom came in, a dish towel over her shoulder, and asked, "Hey, kiddo, have you heard from Jamie? He doesn't usually stay out this late."

18

ONE OF THE PIRATES HAD a young face, the kind that made it difficult to guess at an age. He could have been thirty or twenty-five or sixteen. He could have been forty-five or sixty-seven. He had a patch over one eye. The other shone like a blue marble. When he walked, he swaggered, and the sea wind whipped up his clothes.

"This one's my catch," he said, and before the boy could react, the pirate reached down and hefted the boy's soggy body over his shoulder.

The ship was a living creature. Though from afar, it looked as if her mouth was nothing more than paint on boards, now inside, he could see the light squinting between teeth, each one as big as he was.

When the pirate walked, his boots sank into something pink, viscous, alive. A tongue, the boy thought with horror as the pirate threw his body into one of the many beds that were nailed into the flesh of the ship's cheek.

❦

I told them that he was in the woods. I'd seen him, after all, or thought I had—strange though it seemed that Jamie would step backward through the Veil after all this time. But when Mom texted him, then called, he didn't answer.

Dad was plating up dinner. Elijah was setting the table. I sat down, my notebook still in hand. It was no big deal, I figured. Maybe he'd forgotten to charge his phone. He'd be through the door any minute. He'd let it slam behind him, and then would sit down at the table like an argumentative little storm cloud. Everything would be terrible, but normal.

Instead everything was terrible, but broken, too.

When Dad saw the look on Mom's face, he turned off the burners, grabbed his coat, and headed out into the backyard. Mom went into the kitchen to call Neal's mom. I heard her voice, low and worried. Elijah pulled himself up to the table beside me. He picked at the oily peppers but didn't eat.

"Is Jamie okay?" he asked at last.

I shrugged. "I'm sure he's fine," I said. And I was sure. He was in the woods. Dad would find him soon.

Mom came back and sat down across from me. She wore a strange expression on her face, like a question she couldn't quite bring herself to ask. "Andrea said Neal hasn't seen him. He wasn't in any of his classes after lunch, he said. The school should have called me."

"He was on the bus this morning," I said.

Mom shook her head. "It's not like him to cut class."

"He's fine. He's in the woods. I saw him."

When Mom looked at me, her eyebrows were all wrinkled like one of those curly brackets turned on end. Eli was glancing between Mom and me, and I had the feeling that I was supposed to say something, so I did.

"Maybe he's with his girlfriend."

"Girlfriend?" The curly bracket frown deepened.

He'd been hooking up with Vidya for a year; I knew she hadn't been over to our house or anything, but had Mom really not noticed?

"You know, that girl he danced with at his bar mitzvah? Vidya. She's in chorus with me. They hang out together at Neal's a lot. I bet she knows where he is."

Mom looked like she'd been hit by something heavy. I could almost hear her thoughts: *How could I not know Jamie was dating someone?* Suddenly, I regretted saying anything. I wondered if Jamie hadn't been the only one to keep his relationship with Vidya a secret. If our parents didn't know, maybe hers didn't, either. Mom didn't know a lot of things about Jamie. She stood up again.

"I'll have to call Andrea back, see if Neal has her number."

She disappeared into the kitchen just as Dad came in through the screen door. He was rubbing his thick hands over his eyes.

"It's getting dark out there. There was no sign of him."

Mom came back. She stood in the doorway, one hip on the doorjamb, her phone tucked against her cheek.

"Andrea's getting the number for me," she whispered.

Dad frowned. "What number?"

"Annie says he's dating someone. Vida—"

"Vidya," I corrected her, then offered, "Maybe her parents are hippies."

Dad shook his head like he didn't know what to say to that. "I'm calling the police," he said, and walked off to use the landline in the office, leaving the three of us alone there, our dinner getting cold on the table.

Two police officers came to the door, a young woman with breasts that looked smushed under her uniform and an older man with a smiling face that I didn't quite trust. The older man put his hand on my mom's hand and listened closely and nodded admiringly at the picture of Jamie that Mom handed him right off our wall, my brother in his bar mitzvah tallit, looking handsome and clean cut.

"When was this taken?" the female cop asked, and when Mom said, "Last year," she asked for a more recent picture. Mom hesitated a moment before she took out her phone and found a recent photograph. Jamie at Gram's house, wearing a too-big sweatshirt, his curly hair in his eyes, his mouth flat. You couldn't see his hands in that picture. They were tucked into his sweatshirt like he was trying to hide something. When the police looked at the photo, everything changed.

"You can put out an Amber Alert, can't you?" Dad asked.

The cop drummed her fingers on the tabletop. "Only if it's a confirmed abduction. Kids like these . . ." The way she said *these* was pointed, deliberate. Mom winced at the phrase. ". . . they run off sometimes. We'll talk to the girlfriend, put out a missing persons alert. Chances are, he'll be back within twenty-four hours. Kids end up at a bus station somewhere, realize their birthday money won't take them very far. Call a friend for a ride home."

"He's *not* at a bus station," I said. "He's in the woods. I *saw* him go into Gum . . ." I let the word trail off. "I saw him go into the woods."

"Your father checked, sweetie. He's not there," Mom said soothingly. It was strange. She never called me *sweetie*, not normally.

But the rest of them weren't even listening to me. Dad leaned forward on his chair, setting flat hands on the table. "I feel like you're not taking this seriously," he said. "He's only thirteen! He's a child."

"He's almost fourteen," the female cop said, as if that helped anything. The male cop set a hand on Dad's shoulder. It looked big and fleshy and useless, sitting there.

"We'll do everything we can, you have my personal word. This is the best number to reach you?"

Dad gave the cop his cell number, but from his expression I could almost read his thoughts. They weren't going to call, not tonight. They weren't going to do *anything*. They left us at the dinner table with our supper, cold and filmy. We hardly ate.

I went to bed early and didn't dream.

I woke before the dawn had even begun to crack. When I went into Jamie's room, it was still empty, filled only with autumn's chilly breath. The gently curled, yellow, ancient papers on his walls made it appear as if my brother had been gone for months, not only hours. I suppose, in a way, he had.

"You can't sleep, either, huh, sweetie?" came Mom's voice at the door. Sweetie, again. I looked at her, and before I even knew what was happening, I began to cry.

She held me in my dark room. She didn't tell me to be quiet, that I would wake my little brother down the hall. She didn't tell me it would all be okay. Instead she said only this:

"I hear you. I know."

When I finally pulled away, a lifetime later, I saw that her eyes were bloodshot. "I can't wait around all day," she said. "Every minute that passes is . . . It feels like a minute he gets farther away. What do you say we go out and find him?"

My mother smiled, strong for both of us. For a moment, I felt my body fill to the brim with that impossible, illogical, irrational emotion: hope. We went downstairs, and she wrote a note for Dad and Eli and hung it from the refrigerator with magnets. Then we grabbed our coats and trudged out into the dawn.

The sky was soon shot with streaks of purple and gold, then a blue so bright you almost couldn't believe it. It promised to be a beautiful day, more summer than autumn, still. We drove from bus stop to bus stop to train station to bus stop, looking for Jamie, showing his picture to all the bored clerks behind the Greyhound counters and every stern conductor, too. We had breakfast from McDonald's, greasy hash browns that made our chins and unwashed hair oily. It didn't matter. We were going to find Jamie.

The day wore on and on, brighter still. Mom called me out of school and fought with Dad over the phone about it while I sat on the hood of the car and pretended not to listen.

"I need to find him, Marc. Go to work. Pretend this isn't happening. I don't care."

Then she called the police for a third time, a fourth time. Asked what they'd heard, which was nothing again. The circle that Mom was driving in was tightening more and more around our house. We stopped at the mall and looked in Barnes & Noble and the food court and the Regal lobby. We drove to Kirky's, the convenience store where he and Neal had once been caught shoplifting. The clerk said he hadn't seen him, not since the day before yesterday, even though he usually stopped by every day after school.

Mom pressed her lips together, tried not to look worried—for my sake, I suppose—and said, "Thank you."

By this point, it was almost three in the afternoon. Mom drove into our neighborhood. But instead of pulling into our driveway, she went straight to Neal's house and went out and rang the doorbell three times while I waited by the car. No one answered, but when she went to ring it a fourth time, I saw Neal walking up the road, his shoulders hunched.

"Neal!" I called, and Mom whipped her head up, and we both pounded the pavement to get to him. He looked like roadkill right before impact. Like he'd been caught. For a fleeting moment, I wished Mom wasn't there. There was no way he'd tell us anything true or helpful, not if he thought he was going to get in trouble for it.

But Mom wasn't like that. She just wanted to find Jamie.

"The police called my parents last night," he said hastily, before we could even ask. "I don't know where he is. He cut last-period English yesterday. He's never done that before."

Mom and I chewed over this information together. But before we could respond, Neal added, with a fretful face, "He really hasn't come home?"

Mom drew Neal close in a hug. Mom was full of hugs that day. Neal looked embarrassed, his face pressed up against my mother's canvas jacket, while she hugged and hugged him anyway. "We'll find him," she said.

But we didn't. We went home after that. I sat next to Elijah on the sofa and we both watched television while Mom and Dad took turns screaming at each other and calling the cops. Nobody made dinner that night. It was as if they forgot we were supposed to be normal people. Elijah eventually asked me to give him a bath, and I sat there in the steamy bathroom, not talking, not even thinking. When I tucked Elijah in that night and then went to bed, too early to do anything but stare into the darkness, I knew in the pit of my stomach and the thorny place in my heart that my brother was never coming home.

19

THE PIRATE'S BED WAS NARROW, hardly big enough for both their bodies. When the pirate sat beside him, the Nameless Boy felt their hip bones press. He leaned away. He smelled the pirate's sour breath. He turned his head. When the pirate reached across him, he flinched back. But then he saw a length of something in the pirate's hand.

Rope.

❖

Dad insisted that Elijah and I both go to school on Monday even though I told my mother that there was no chance I'd be able to pay attention. When I said that, she thinned her lips and gave me a long, meaningful look.

"Dad and I will be doing everything we can to find him," she said; then she ushered me out the door after Elijah, where I watched him get on his bus, then waited with Nina until our own bus rolled up to the curb.

I sat down next to Miranda in silence. I suspected the news about Jamie had already spread through the school, and Miranda's bright tone confirmed it.

"Hey, I got a new Pokémon deck. Do you wanna see?"

I watched the trees roll by. No Winter Watchers in the woods. Nobody. Nothing. I could have been angry at her question, but instead, I felt a strange, burning sort of dullness inside.

"You don't have to try to talk to me. We don't have to talk today."

"Oh . . ." Miranda looked down at her cards. Her expression seemed to collapse from inside. "I thought maybe you'd want to talk about something besides Jamie. That you'd want to be distracted."

"I can't be distracted," I told her.

"Oh," she said again.

The bus rolled into the schoolyard.

Everyone looked at me at school that day, their eyes wide and owlish. There were whispers as the bodies parted like a sea around me. Before we walked into civics class, Miranda lowered her voice and pulled me aside. She wanted to warn me. She wanted me to know that Jamie's disappearance was all anybody could talk about on Friday, and that there were rumors. Something to do with Neal Harriman, drugs. I remembered the way the boys had looked at me that afternoon that I'd caught them in the woods. Like they wanted to murder me for being there, interfering with them.

I told myself that it was nothing. Jamie had just been trying out a new persona like a selkie might pull on a new skin. In a few months, if he returned, Jamie might decide he was a nerd, or a jock, or a surfer, even though we lived hundreds of miles from the water.

"He only smoked *pot*, Miranda," I told my friend. "This isn't *Breaking Bad*."

She winced when I said it, and I knew then how awkward that sentiment sounded, coming from me. I sat at my desk and ignored the look she'd just given me, the way that everyone's eyes were on me. Jamie might have liked becoming someone else, but I was always myself, even in that moment. I told myself that I could turn into an impenetrable pillar. There were no cracks in me. I was strong.

But as I squared my shoulders, I bit my lip. I wondered. Jamie had gone into the woods that day and not come out. Maybe he'd smoked too much. Maybe he'd tried some other drugs, something worse. I imagined him puking into the bushes. I imagined him stumbling, falling, smacking his head on a log, bleeding out on the forest floor. His body going limp, going soggy, going cold. I told myself that it was impossible. Dad had searched the woods that night. He wasn't there anymore.

He was alive somewhere. He was fine.

I didn't cry at school. I told myself that I was fine, too.

On Tuesday afternoon, there was a knock on our door. Elijah and I watched from his bedroom window as Mom and Dad went down to talk to the police. We held our breath together as the squad car door opened, but it was only the female cop with the squished boobs. And this time, her hardened expression had gone weak at the edges.

Lately, Mom and Dad hadn't been touching each other. But now they walked down the front steps, leaning into one another, Dad's hand on the small of Mom's back. As though, in that moment, they had one heart again, one pulse, one spine. Kneeling on the window seat in Elijah's bedroom, I found myself reaching out to touch my little brother, too. I wanted to protect him from whatever it was that had swallowed my other brother up. It was here, still. Lurking. Hungry. Waiting.

"Is James dead?" Eli asked in his innocent, boyish voice, as if those words weren't a knife's cut. He wasn't supposed to say them. If we didn't speak of it, it wouldn't happen. But he didn't know that. Eli had never really understood the rules—to Gumlea, to chess, to all sorts of games. Jamie always said it was because he was too young, but the look on his face now was hard. Intentional.

"No," I said. I saw that image in my head again. Jamie someplace dark, bleeding. Jamie too sick to even stand. But I pushed those thoughts away. "If he was dead, I would know. I would feel it."

"And you don't?"

I watched Mom and Dad. Nobody was crying. Neither one held the other. They just spoke softly to the cops, nodding their heads.

"I don't feel anything," I told Elijah, and convinced myself it was true.

The cops left. Mom and Dad stood outside talking for a moment, and then Mom looked up at us. She waved, a thin, shaky wave. Elijah and I waved back. Then we climbed down from the window seat together, and left his room, and went downstairs.

Mom and Dad were standing in our front entryway. There was a cloud of fresh autumn air all around them, and for a moment, it smelled like hope. But then I saw their faces. Not hopeful, but not crushed by grief, either. Dad kept flexing his jaw. Mom furrowed her brow. I didn't know what to make of either one. Elijah flung himself forward into Dad's arms, and Dad lifted him up, but I hung back. Nervous.

"What did they say?" I asked. "Have they found Jamie?"

I was asking Mom, but she only looked at my father, who sucked in a breath, then shook his head.

"No. They found his backpack."

"In the woods?" I asked quickly, remembering what the straps looked like on Jamie's shoulders as he faded into Gumlea.

Mom's frown deepened. "Annie, you know he's not out there. We told you—"

"Shira, stop," my dad said. Usually, Mom would have argued with Dad when he spoke to her in that tone. But not today. Today, she stopped.

Dad crouched down, so that he was eye level with Eli and even shorter than me. He looked at us calmly, thoughtfully. "They found his backpack in a rest stop bathroom in Pennsylvania. His phone was in there, and his wallet. All of his schoolbooks."

"Pennsylvania?" Elijah squeaked out. "What's he doing there?"

"We don't know, Eli," Mom said. "The police are going to find him, though. They've promised us that."

My little brother muttered something. I couldn't really hear it at first, not until Dad set a hand on his shoulder. "What, kiddo?"

"I want Jamie to come home," Eli said, and threw both arms around Dad. Dad picked him up like he was a baby and not a first grader.

"I do, too, kiddo," Dad said, and, sharing a glance with Mom, he carried Eli off toward the living room.

I stood there with Mom in the foyer for a minute, next to the shoe rack, still stinky from Jamie's sneakers.

"Are they going to give us his backpack back?"

Mom shook her head in an idle way, as if she almost wasn't listening. "No, honey. It's evidence."

I'm not sure why, but this news was what finally cut me, deep inside. These were my brother's *things*, the only thing I had left of him. They should have been mine.

But then, Jamie wasn't dead. Maybe it was only right that his phone (bricked, they would tell us later, having been dunked in the rest stop sink and then returned to the bottom of his bag) and his wallet and his crumpled school papers all went somewhere else.

Just like he had.

"Okay," I said, and turned to go upstairs, leaving Mom to stand alone by all those sandals and rain boots.

20

IT SEEMED TO HURT THE pirate to move. He winced with every hand's pass as he showed the Nameless Boy some knots. As the boy watched with round eyes, he felt how the sheets were damp beneath him. He wondered if he'd peed himself, or if the pirate's blankets were always wet. Like the boards around them, the sea beyond, the pirate's eye, his breath.

"Clove hitch. Bad in wet conditions. Slips."

The pirate let out a cough, his lungs rattling with phlegm. He wiped his mouth on the back of his hand. And then he said, "Wrists together. Hands out."

It took a moment for the boy to realize what the pirate meant. So the man, sitting beside him, their shared weight sagging the tiny bed, showed him. Held out his wrists, pressed together at the pulse points, the fingers meeting so that his hands formed a sort-of heart. Shaking, the boy did as he was told. Wrists together, hands out. The pirate bound him. Then he pulled the rope taut and rose, stringing the ends from the teeth above and tying them tight.

"Cat's paw knot," the pirate said. "Let's see you swim out of this one, minnow."

❧

Days passed. No one knew what to say to me at school, but everyone looked. Watching as I drifted between classes, tracking me out of the corners of their eyes like they were hunters and I was prey. Even worse were the smiles that the teachers gave me, close-mouthed and pitying.

"Be strong," Mrs. Kenner told me, a hand falling on my upper arm, heavy and wrinkled like a leather baseball mitt when I went up to hand in my makeup work. "They'll find him."

Jamie had been in Mrs. Kenner's class the year before. *I hate her* was what he'd muttered over his geography homework at night. *She gives us notebook checks like we're babies, and what does she care if our notebooks are messy so long as we learn the capital of stupid Lithuania?* But my notebook was always perfect and my grades were much better than Jamie's had been. When she touched me, I give a small, numb nod of my head and floated all the way back to my seat.

My only real comfort was Miranda. She never tried to talk to me about it, and in a way, deep down inside, that might have bothered me. But more than that, it was a relief. Some mornings on the bus, she talked to me about video games. Others, she told me about books she'd read. And on the bad days, the dark days, the days when I could hardly speak to myself, much less to her, she just sat beside me, her shoulder touching mine.

"Dykes," Nina said, and threw a wad of notebook paper at us. Miranda lowered her brow, looked at me, and rolled her eyes.

"I'd say it's like she never had a friend," Miranda said to me, "except the sad thing is, we both know it's true."

I put my head on her shoulder. The bus chugged endlessly along, spitting out black exhaust.

The days came and went. I turned thirteen alone, without my brother to share it. The night before my bat mitzvah, my mother and father had a fight. I heard their voices buzzing through the thin plaster of my bedroom wall. Dad thought that we should cancel it. The party part, at least. It wasn't right, celebrating without Jamie here, without knowing if he was hurt or whole, alive or—

Mom didn't let him finish his sentence.

"Of course you wouldn't understand, Marc," she said. "But it's not like we can postpone Annie *becoming a woman*."

I lay there in bed, my hands on my belly. It growled under my palms. I hadn't eaten dinner. No one had noticed.

But there was anger there, underneath the hunger, and it burned steadily. Not at them, for fighting, or because they forgot about me, but, in my darkest, most honest moments, at Jamie. That rage stayed inside me all through that night, while I dreamed of ships crashing against jagged rocks and red ocean waves seeping in through cracked boards. And it was with me over breakfast, when I picked at my bacon and eggs, and in the morning, when we arrived at the synagogue, too. I'd been assigned a much more difficult Torah portion than Jamie had. And yet I read it easily. Really, I was only half there. Instead, I was thinking of Jamie, hating Jamie, the rage burning and burning and burning. I looked up to see the sparsely populated pews, the cousins and aunts and uncles, and how they all looked distracted. They didn't care who I was or what I'd become. All that mattered was that Jamie was gone now. He eclipsed me, even in his absence.

But the anger was counterbalanced by another, equally hefty feeling. Guilt for hating him, for feeling anything but pain and loss and loneliness. This was not a time to be thinking of myself. This was a time to think of Jamie and his possible fates: dismembered or on drugs somewhere or starving to death on some street.

My party was smaller than Jamie's because I didn't have as many friends, though no one said so. There were only a few tables crowded together in the VFW hall, mostly filled with family. We danced the hora. We lit candles. We ate cake. Our smiles in the photographs were false and empty. People started streaming out early. Even Miranda left without taking a favor.

Later, alone in my room, I looked at myself, tallit draped over my shoulders. I liked the heavy, smooth feeling of the fabric, like a ceremonial robe. But other than a frank jolt of pleasure at that cool sensation, I felt hollow.

A knock came at my door.

"Come in."

It was Mom. She held a box in her hands, wrapped carefully. "I have something for you, sweetie." It seemed I would always be *sweetie*, now that my brother was gone. Mom sat down on my bed, then patted the bedsheets gently. I came and sat beside her. As I carefully removed the wrapping paper, I saw her eyes sweep the walls, where the maps of Gumlea once hung.

I opened her gift. A pair of tarnished bronze candleholders, wrapped in tissue paper.

"They were my mom's," she said, and her voice had a strange note in it. We never talked about my mother's parents. Her mother had died when she was a teenager. Her father, when I was a toddler. I hardly remembered him.

I touched the metal, which felt somehow warm in my hands. The surface was waxy.

"Why me?" I asked. "Why not *him*?"

I didn't want to speak his name, but it seemed I didn't have to tell her who I meant. She gave me a withering smile.

"Something the rabbi said a few years ago. Traditionally, women were the keepers of faith at home. Even though the men went to temple every day to pray, the women were the ones who kept the candles lit on the sabbath."

A faint wick of something lit inside me at her words. Mom understood. Maybe she always had. Jamie may have been gifted, but I was the faithful one.

I wanted to hug her, but for some reason I couldn't make myself move. Even my gaze remained fixed on the heavy candlesticks in my hands.

"Thank you," I said softly. She leaned forward and kissed my forehead. For just a split second, the whole world smelled like *Mom*. Sandalwood and the delicate detergent she used to wash her clothes. Then she stood up and turned to leave.

But before she did, she looked at my walls again. Bare now, though you could still see the shadows where the maps had been. She let out a long sigh and said exactly the wrong thing:

"You and your brother and those stories you used to tell."

Then she left me there, alone in the dark.

21

A FIGURE APPEARED AT THE top of the stairs. At first, he thought it was another man. But then he saw the smooth curve of her jaw, her slight breasts beneath her double-breasted coat. A lady pirate. He didn't know that those existed.

"Here," she said, and she offered him a cup, the lip spiked with terrifying splinters. But the Nameless Boy was so thirsty that he drank anyway. It tasted—it tasted like the color orange, like some overripe tropical jewel. It burned going down.

"What is that?" he finally panted. By the flickering light of her candle, he saw that her lips were chapped and badly peeling.

"Grog," she said. She held the cup to his lips again. He drank until it was empty.

"Why are you doing this?" he asked her when he was done.

"There will come a time," she said, "on some future day, when the walls of this ship will open, when your ropes will come loose. His back will be turned, and his passions elsewhere. That time is a door, and it's closed now, but when it opens, I need you to slip through. You must take it, Jack. You must."

Then she stood, slowly, carefully, ducking beneath the ceiling girders, and left again. The boy was once more alone in the dark.

And he wondered to himself: *Who the hell is Jack?*

❧

Vidya hadn't been in chorus the first week after Jamie's disappearance. Mom and Dad said that the police had already spoken to her, but they didn't seem satisfied by whatever it was she had said. Mom said she wanted the police to talk to Vidya again. She had to know *something*, my mother said. The thought tugged at me—how Jamie and Vidya had spent hours together, far from my awareness, right up until when he disappeared. A few days after my bat mitzvah, when she'd finally returned to school, I watched her on the late bus. At first, she wouldn't meet my eyes. I hesitated by my usual seat, wondering if I should go to her. From what Mom said, if she had answers about Jamie, she was keeping them locked away.

She'd lost him, too—I knew she felt that, looking at her and how she steadied her sad gaze out the foggy bus window. But her loss was nothing like mine. I had been trying hard to make myself strong—but my resolve was beginning to waver. As the days passed with no news, doubts had begun to seep in, sour and bitter as a lemon peel. Mom thought Vidya knew something. And we had been friendly, once. She'd been nice, even—telling me to join Madrigals. What harm would come from talking to her?

So I pressed forward through the aisle. When I sat down next to her, she didn't look at me, only kept her eyes cast out the window.

"What do you *want*?" she whispered, and I was surprised to find her voice had an edge to it. Her chin was already trembling, like she was wobbling right on the verge of tears.

"Jamie's still missing," I told her. I was surprised, too, by how it sounded like there was an accusation in my voice. Outside of my parents, I'd hardly spoken to anyone about Jamie, so I didn't have any practice at it. I didn't know how to talk about him without sounding angry, or mournful, or both.

"I know that," she said. She wiped the corner of her eye against her hand.

"Well," I pressed her, "don't you have any idea where he is? The two of you spend so much time together—"

"I don't know!" She was trying to keep her voice down and failing. A few kids glanced at us. The bus driver's eyes darted to meet mine in the rearview mirror. "I told the police already that I don't know!"

"Maybe he told you to keep it a secret. Or maybe you don't think it's safe to tell me. I'm his *sister*, Vidya. Please, you have to—"

"I don't have to tell you anything!" She finally turned to look at me, and I saw how angry she was, her hair a wild cloud around her, her mouth a bruisey pink.

She's beautiful. The ridiculous thought flashed through my mind. I could kiss her, right there on the bus, in front of the band nerds and everybody else. I'd never kissed anybody before, but I could imagine what it would feel like. Soft. Warm. Sweet. Still, I knew it was wrong. She didn't want to kiss me. She just wanted to be left alone. My shoulders slumped.

"Okay," I told her. "I get it." I waited until the next stop, grabbed my backpack, and stood. But as I started off toward my seat by the front of the bus, her voice called out to me. Stopping me.

"Annie, I swear, I really don't know where he is," she told me. "For all I know, he might as well be in Gumlea."

I turned to look at her.

"Take a seat," the bus driver said to me. I sat down, dismayed, then glanced back at her. But she'd sunk low in her own seat, out of sight.

Jamie had promised me he hadn't told her about *Gumlea*. Told her we'd just made up stories together—that was all. But the details, the geography, the *name*—those were supposed to be ours. How did she know that word? Had he lied to me? Or had the truth come out later, during some gray afternoon on Neal's sofa? Holding hands with her while the other kids drank and joked around, and maybe he had leaned in and whispered our secrets to her: *Annie and I called our kingdom Gumlea. I know it sounds babyish, but it was magical. . . .*

My heart was pounding. I clutched my backpack to my chest. What else did she know about us? Did she know I was the Emperata, and he the Nameless Boy? Did she know about our plans to open the Veil together? To let all that magic come tumbling out?

I glanced back toward her one last time as our bus pulled up to my curb. *He might as well be in Gumlea*, she'd said, like it was an absurd idea. But maybe she knew something that I didn't about my brother. She wouldn't look at me. Wouldn't confirm or deny anything I was thinking. I shook my head. At last, on shaky legs, I stood and stepped out onto the curb.

In Gumlea.

I thought of him stepping backward the day he'd disappeared. I'd *seen* him go into the woods. The police said that I had been mistaken. He was probably miles away by then, careening toward Pennsylvania.

But what if he wasn't?

I had a dream that night. I was walking slowly down a creaking set of stairs, ambling through the pitch-dark. In the distance, I heard a rustle. A whimper.

"Who's there?"

It was Jamie's voice. My brother, calling out to me through the darkness. As my feet hit the wooden boards, the ground beneath seemed to sway. I came closer. There was no candlelight in this space. The air tasted like salt, or blood, I wasn't sure which. Narrow strips of moonlight were cast through the ceiling. Shadows shifted around us. In skinny flashes, I saw the pale light of Jamie's naked body. And something rough and splintered. Rope. There was rope.

I realized I was holding something. A wooden chalice, the liquid almost spilling as the ground gave another lurch. I wanted to say something to my brother. Offer him some comfort. He was trapped here, in this ship's cabin beneath the ocean. But all I could do was hold out the cup.

"Here," I said, and as he frantically drank, his eyes met mine. We had the same eyes, as always. And we were both afraid.

I jerked myself awake, my heart pounding through the darkness. As I peeled the covers back from my sweating body, I could almost feel the bed still swaying under me.

The pirate, I thought. *The pirate has him.*

It was a ridiculous notion, more dream than reality. But I thought it with clarity. With absolute certainty. Maybe Vidya hadn't *known* where Jamie went. But on some level, she might have been right. We had exhausted all other possibilities. He wasn't here. They hadn't found him in Pennsylvania. He was trapped somewhere, unable to return to me.

What if he was trapped in Gumlea?

As I considered the possibility, I went to my desk and pulled my binder of maps from the bottom drawer. One by one, I hung the maps back up on the wall, fitting each sheet onto the darker rectangle of wallpaper like I was putting together a jigsaw puzzle. When I was done, I stood back and studied my work. In my mind, I was tracing a line across an ocean, one that led from the Island of Feral Children toward the King's dominion. But something happened in the middle. The path got murky, unclear. I shook my head. It was ridiculous. Jamie wasn't in Gumlea. Gumlea wasn't *real*. They'd found his backpack at a rest stop. But still . . .

The pirate has him, I thought. *The pirate has him and he can't escape.*

I'd seen him go into the woods. Stepping backward. Slipping into our kingdom. Gumlea was a real place: a fistful of forest behind our house, strewn with litter, full of kids. But if you let your eyes cross, just a little—if you knew how to walk, what words to say—it could almost become real, couldn't it? There had been a time when I believed that. A time when I'd seen Gumlea for everything it was.

I left the maps on the walls and tucked myself back into bed. But I couldn't sleep. Instead, I was haunted by the image of Jamie—no, of the Nameless Boy—tied up in that skinny bed in the bottom of a ship, his eyes wide open and full of terrors.

22

JACK WONDERED WHAT THE LADY Pirate had put in his drink.

First, he slept, strange dreams, thick dreams, about a naked glass eye examining his every movement and projecting distorted silhouettes to the creaking boards behind him.

Then he was sick all over the bed, not once, but again and again. Until he was empty. Until he was clean of everything he once had been. In snatches of thought between the murk in his brain, Jack wondered if this was what the sacred pool had done to the other children. Like an antiseptic, killing everything that was light inside him, filling him, instead, with inky black.

Sometimes, he sensed the pirate there with him, cleaning him, laying tender hands on him, putting him in fresh clothing, singing him sea shanties, whistling through the gaps in his teeth. But more often, he was alone.

❖

Eli and I clung to one another that autumn and into the winter, when Mom and Dad were preoccupied with police reports and lawyers and hating one another. Every evening, after Dad would heat up another casserole provided by some kind old lady at Gram and Poppy's church, my brother and I would tuck our bodies against each other on the sofa and pull Jamie's old nubby comforter, the one that had been on his bed the day he disappeared, up over ourselves and watch TV. The show didn't matter. Sometimes, we'd just watch HGTV all night long, our faces blank as some woman showed a couple pictures of the house they could have. What was important was that there was noise, and that it wasn't Mom and Dad's noise—arguing, again, about whether Vidya had anything to do with his disappearance—and that it wasn't the noise in either of our heads. The noise said that now, after weeks had passed, and months had passed, and Hanukkah and Christmas and New Year's came and went and with Valentine's Day fast approaching, our brother was never coming home.

Sometimes Eli slumped under the blankets and would start to cry. I'd take his soggy body and hold him against me. I wanted to cry, too, but I couldn't. I needed to be strong for him. G-d, someone had to be. The worst nights were punctuated by the noise of cabinet doors slamming, dishes slamming, Mom telling Dad she couldn't stand to look at him anymore and Dad telling Mom to keep her voice down, damn it, because the kids were right in the next room, as Eli's head was a heavy weight on my chest and his tears soaked through my T-shirt.

Saturdays, I woke up early, did my homework before the sun even touched the sky, and then went out walking in the woods that had once been Gumlea. I had to do something. I couldn't stay home. The trees were dusted with snow. Everything felt fresh and alive and promising. I kept waiting to find Jamie there, or some sign of him. His sneaker, maybe, trapped beneath a log. His sigil, carved into a tree. But there was nothing useful. Instead, only trash.

Once, after the snow had melted, I found a cardboard box, soaked through with rain. Inside were stacks of pornographic magazines. I knelt down in the mud and thumbed through them. They were old, the women's hair all blown out into copper clouds, the makeup on their lips pinky orange, their tans bright. Their breasts . . .

I looked around. There were black-winged birds above me, worms pulsing through the dirt, but no one else. I knelt down in the mud, behind the box, and slid my hand along the hot skin of my belly. In the cold forest behind my house, in late January, while life at home fell apart, I looked at ancient magazines and touched myself until shivering waves washed over me and there were a thousand stars exploding into broad daylight overhead. For a moment, there was nothing. Only my body, the heat of my skin, the clammy cold of my hands, and pleasure.

Then I took my hand out of my jeans, threw the magazine into the box, and trudged back to the hollow misery of home. I showered, whispering my gratitude to the King, and dressed, and microwaved some chicken nuggets for Eli for lunch. Then I sat down on the couch beside him and pretended to be a person again.

The next time I returned to the forest, the box was gone. There was no brother in the woods for me, and no joy, however fleeting, either.

I don't blame my parents. Dad was busy, with work and with fielding phone calls from the police, even though those came fewer and farther in between. Mom was busy, too. At first, her theory that Vidya had somehow led Jamie away from us kept her in a vise grip. Sometimes, I would stare at Vidya in chorus, watching her shift from foot to foot, her hair swaying like a waterfall behind her. I'd remember what she'd said, about how he might as well be in Gumlea. And I'd consider telling my mother that she'd said that. But deep down, I knew no good would come of it. Mom had never understood Gumlea. She'd only think it was some trick of Vidya's.

Eventually, though, my mom began to let that theory die. Instead, she disappeared into Dad's office every night, where she spent all night on some Facebook community for parents of missing and exploited children. Someone there told her to make a website for Jamie, so she did. www.wheresjames[redacted].com. The banner image on the top was Jamie's bar mitzvah picture, a false portrait of a boy who had been gone far longer than those thin, dark months. Under that was a space for guests to leave messages or information. As the text began flooding in from friends of Jamie's and family acquaintances and people from synagogue and Gram and Poppy's church, Mom spent more and more time in the office, reading and rereading them.

"What do you think of this one?" she'd ask me when I passed on my way to the kitchen, Jamie's blanket lumpy over my shoulders. Then, before I could answer, she'd rattled it off: "I hope you find news of your son soon. G-d bless. Kevin Monahan."

"What am I supposed to think?" I asked. Mom's face was blue, her eyes fixed on the screen.

"I think there might be a clue in it. 'Find news'? That's odd phrasing, don't you think?"

I sighed, rolled my eyes, and walked on. Mom didn't notice.

I didn't blame her then. She was devastated. We all were. And I don't blame her now. Something I'd learn years later was that our brains are good at putting together patterns from nothing. I did it, too. All those years searching for cairns in the woods, and swearing I'd found them in what was really just a pile of randomly toppled rocks. And that March, I was still casting my eyes out the bus and counting the Winter Watchers in the shadows. They were everywhere that spring, their dark curls limp and wet, piercings dangling from every naked knob of flesh. I saw them at the mall and in the trees and on television as Eli changed the channels. They stood there, their familiars at their sides, watching me with silent eyes. They were judging me, I was sure of it. Because I hadn't saved Jamie. Because I hadn't opened the Veil. Because I was still *here* and not there.

I wanted to go after him. Of course I did. But I didn't know how. We'd invented elaborate rituals that made the impossible real. We needed knives, salt, blood sacrifices, potions. All of this had existed only in our minds, only in fantasy. I needed them now *here*, with me, in my actual hands. I needed real, actual magic. But our world was ordinary and drab, without the least bit of magic in it.

Anyway, Eli needed me. That's what I told myself. No one else was watching out for him. Not Mom and not Dad. He was too little to understand, still. Almost eight. But still a half boy, who sometimes cried in his sleep and needed cups of milk warmed up in the microwave. I was the only one still paying enough attention to hear him, to sit by the bed while he sipped and slurped, to take the empty mug from him and tuck him in again.

I was needed here.

Until one Sunday, everything changed. Dad came into the living room, dressed in the same khaki pants and button-down he always wore, and declared that he was going to church. He said we were welcome to come, me and Eli. My little brother scrambled up from the sofa like we'd just been invited to Six Flags. But I stayed there, frozen.

It had been months since we'd been to synagogue. We'd kept going right up until my bat mitzvah, but that had been September. It was spring now, and that awful day had faded into memory. It hurt less now when I thought about it, even though I mostly tried not to remember. But I was still me. Still Jewish. Whether or not I went to synagogue didn't really change a thing.

"I don't think Mom would like that," I said, pulling the blanket up beneath my chin. She wasn't there. She was gone already, to a meetup of her Facebook friends, if you could call them that, where they would drink mimosas and talk about all the ways they'd gone wrong as parents and chased their children away.

Dad just looked at me and gave me a smile that wasn't really a smile, too wide at the corners. "How do *you* feel about it?"

"It's not really my thing," I said. I made my voice as flat as I could. I wasn't sure, really, how I felt about it. I was Jewish. Jesus sounded okay—for other people. For Dad, if he wanted him. Eli, too, I guess. But not for me.

Dad's fake face smiled for a moment longer. Then he nodded. "Suit yourself. You know the rules, then." He gave my foot a little squeeze through the blanket and headed upstairs to get Eli dressed.

Of course I knew the rules. Don't answer the door. Don't talk to strangers. Don't do anything Jamie might have done. Don't disappear.

But I wanted to. I pulled the blanket—which didn't smell like my brother anymore, only smelled like corn chip crumbs and my own body—over my head, and did my best to pretend that I was somewhere else.

23

HE THOUGHT OF ANNIT. HE thought of Ijah. He thought of the fairy he had watched bleed to death on the island's soil. Maybe this was his payment for every cruel and evil thing he'd ever done. Couldn't he have paid more attention to the Laws? Couldn't he have made reparations to the King? Couldn't he have made that damned tithe, like Annit had asked? He told himself that could have killed a million harpies, if only he'd wanted to.

Jack knew in his trembling, bound hands that he couldn't have. But that didn't stop him from feeling full of regret.

❧

I woke up to the sound of thunder. No, to the sound of the garage door thundering closed. Sitting up in the darkness, I blinked three times, waiting for my bedroom around me to take shape. I'd been dreaming of the Wide Salt Sea again, and Jamie trapped beneath it, waves tossing his lifeless body like a rag doll, trailing seaweed like streamers behind him. For a long time, I couldn't shake that image, or the cold, dead feeling of my hands, until voices outside pulled me to life.

I went to the window. Mom and Dad were standing on the front lawn, arguing in whispered tones. But my windows were thin; the curtains, thinner. I heard it all.

"How could you do that without asking me?"

"How could I? Where were you? What was I supposed to do?"

"They're *Jewish*, Marc. We decided that fourteen years ago. It's too late to change your mind."

"Look, I never converted—"

"It doesn't matter. That's not how it works."

"Well, tell me how it works, then?" In the shadows, Dad put his hands on his hips. I couldn't see his sneer, but I could imagine it.

"If the mother is Jewish—"

"Oh, come on. The boys weren't even circumcised."

"We had a brit shalom! You were there. You promised—"

"I only did it for you. You know that. It didn't mean anything to me."

"And church does?"

"Yeah, it does."

A long, chilly silence stretched between them.

"Eli wanted to go, Shira."

"He's a child. It's not up to him."

"Who's it up to, then?"

Mom sat down on the front steps in a huff. I couldn't see her anymore, but I could see the angular shape of her shadow cast in the porch light. It was moving erratically as she jiggled her knee.

"You don't know what it's like," she said, dodging the question. "Do you know I used to get invited to church groups all the time? Everyone was worried about my soul. Everyone wanted to save me. No one cared what I wanted."

"This isn't about you. Can you imagine what it's been like for him? Can you think about someone else for just a minute?"

"Oh, that's rich."

"They welcomed us, Shira. They've been nothing but welcoming to us."

"Good." Mom's shadow stood up. I heard the front door open. "You can sleep next to them, then."

The door slammed shut, leaving all the windows to tremble. Dad stood frozen on the lawn, an awkward statue. When I turned away, I saw someone behind me in the darkness. For a second, I could have sworn it was Jamie, hair mussed from sleep. But then the boy who stood in the hall light opened his mouth, and Elijah's voice came squeaking out.

"Are they mad at me?"

I went to him, picked up his cold, clammy hand, and brought him to bed with me.

"No, Eli, of course not," I said as I tucked in Jamie's blanket over us. My brother's body silently shook beside me. I hugged him, even though it was the wrong body, the wrong brother, all wrong.

24

THE PIRATE SANG TO HIM. The pirate stroked his hair when he was sick again. The pirate was gentle in all the wrong ways. He didn't want to be touched, no matter how gingerly. Not by this man. Not in this nightmare place.

Sometimes Jack felt something pressed to the small of his back. A sharp point. A knife's edge. Digging into his tailbone, piercing his flesh through the salt-stiff fabric of his clothes.

At nights, the tongue swelled, swallowing the salt water that rushed through the ship's teeth. Sometimes Jack thought blood seeped between them. Or maybe he had simply gone mad now. Alone. All day and all night, in the deep, groaning belly of the beast.

❖

When I came home from school the next day, Dad was back, quietly packing his belongings into boxes in the downstairs office. I stood and watched him for a long time without his realizing I was there. When at last I spoke, asking, "What are you doing, anyway?" he jumped.

"Annie, I—"

And then I saw that his eyes were watery, which was all wrong. My father never cried, because it was something men like him never did, not even when their sons called them names or slammed the door in their faces or disappeared into nothing.

I felt a heavy wave of emotion. Once my family had been okay, but they weren't anymore. Now Dad was crying. Now Dad was a hot mess.

Still, I held my chin high. If he was going to cry, I needed to do the opposite, make it so that every cell of my being was made out of granite. I needed to be strong for him—for *us*.

"Mom asked you to leave. She wants you to go to Gram and Poppy's. And then . . ."

Dad gave his broad shoulders, cloaked in pressed cotton, a shrug. He didn't know what came next. Nobody did.

"This isn't about you," he told me, even though he didn't have to. I *knew* it wasn't about me. It was about Mom and Dad, and his stupid church. It was about Jamie missing, and everything we couldn't talk about. It was kind of about the secrets I kept—the dreams I had about Jamie trapped somewhere, and the theories I built, wild and impossible and above all, true.

But it was never about *me*. That was the point. I was invisible.

"It's not that we don't love you," he continued. "We love you and Elijah very much."

"Yeah," I agreed. It sounded like something he'd gotten from a Very Special Episode of a '90s sitcom. Only on TV, everything usually went back to normal at the end of thirty minutes. And on TV, people's children didn't just disappear like the writers had forgotten them, leaving a bleeding hole in the middle of the story.

Dad crouched down over the file box of taxes, dripping pitiful tears into it. Then he drew in a breath.

"You don't have to decide now," he began, not meeting my eyes.

"But at some point, your mother might ask you where you want to live. I'll get an apartment, something . . ."

His voice went shaky. My father was trying to find a script for a story for which there was no script. And he was failing.

"You're asking me if I want to live with her or with you?" I said.

My father laughed a little, even though it wasn't funny. "I suppose I am, Annie," he said.

I saw the future stretching out in front of me, and it looked like a long braid of time. One strand was my life with Dad. Dependable, respectable Dad, who wore khakis even on his days off and went to church and had a firm handshake and kept the whirligigs from sprouting in the gutter. Dad, who sometimes got mad at you for the wrong thing, who thought you were embarrassing. Who wanted you to be normal, even though you could never be normal. Who was too hard on you. Too hard on Jamie.

The other strand was Mom, and her sometimes mean laughter, and sometimes remembering to light the candles on Friday nights but forgetting more often than not, and tucking yourself onto the sofa beside her and falling asleep with the TV on.

On the one hand, rules, stability, boring days marching on and on and on. On the other, a deep well of joy, but loneliness, too, gossiping together, but just as often fading into the already-faded wallpaper. I was the third strand, drawn between them, pulling them together even as they were pulling apart.

But there was no choice, not really. It wasn't about Mom, or Dad, or me, or even Eli. It was about the wild woods out back past the drainage creek, and my brother trapped inside them. I dreamed about him all the time. I saw him with his hands bound up in Boy Scout knots, struggling and sick and weeping. I called out to him: *I'm waiting for you. Come home. Come home.*

But if he heard me, he didn't understand, or couldn't. He was stuck, and I didn't know how to help him, so I was stuck, too. In this house, waiting.

I couldn't leave. Not for Dad. Not for anyone.

My father took my silence for uncertainty. "You don't have to decide anything now," he said, and came close, pressing my face to his button-front shirt.

My father cried, but I didn't. I was strong for Jamie. I could be strong for all of us.

By the time Dad found an apartment, I'd started to spend every spare moment I could in Gumlea. Alone in the woods those weeks, I tried every spell I could remember. I'd stand on one foot, hum, chant. I climbed inside the King's tree and said a million prayers. I pricked my fingertips with Mom's straight pins, let them bleed down onto the wormy earth. It didn't work. But I kept trying. I was the only one trying anymore.

When the kids at school whispered about me, when the grocery clerk at ShopRite asked Mom if she'd heard anything and she just hung her head—that's when I was most determined. The idea that Jamie was trapped in our kingdom wasn't just a comfort in those days. It was a shield, an armor. No one else knew the truth, but I did. And only I could see how badly my brother, trapped by a pirate with a child's face and hooks for hands, truly wanted to come home.

In retrospect, I'm not sure why I did it, except that home was awful and school was awful and even though the world around us was bursting into spring, blossoms and throat-sticky pollen everywhere, birds singing in a cappella waves, I felt awful, too. I'd made Vows to the King and Jamie and myself and I'd always, always kept them, even when Miranda had been desperate to know everything about the stories in my notebooks, even when Jamie had told Nina and Vidya, too. But before Jamie left, I'd kept it all under lockdown.

Now Gumlea seemed all too eager to go spilling out.

On the bus one morning, I sat down beside Miranda and, without preamble, started speaking.

"I saw him slip away."

"Hi, too," Miranda said, and looked up from her paperback. "What?"

"Jamie. I saw him go. I think he's in the middle kingdom."

"Where?" she asked. When I didn't answer, her brow pressed low over her eyes.

"You . . . saw him. Maybe you should tell your mom."

Once, Miranda would have said *Mom and Dad*, but she knew about their separation. I couldn't hide it; Eli no longer waited for me at the bus, not since he'd asked to go live with our father during the week. Mom had been livid at first, of course, but Dad convinced her, somehow, that it was best to let Eli choose where to spend his days—just like I was allowed to choose where to spend mine.

"I tried. They searched the woods. Anyway, he's not in *those* woods, not anymore. He went through the Veil. He's on a ship now. Here."

I pulled out my notebook, the pages all overstuffed with homework assignments and maps. Paging through, I found the drawing I'd been searching for. It was done on college-lined paper. The ship's sails billowed over the waves.

"Wow," Miranda said. She put her finger against something I'd drawn on the mast, smudging the pencil. She touched the mermaid's breasts. Maybe I should have been embarrassed, but I wasn't. That drawing wasn't telling Miranda anything she didn't already know. "This is really nicely drawn."

I wasn't expecting that. I felt my cheeks heat just a little, felt my mouth go dry.

"Thank you," I said, even though my art wasn't the point. The point was Jamie. Trapped. In Gumlea.

"But Annie . . ." Now Miranda's brow was going all furrowed. She spoke quickly, like she didn't want to hurt my feelings. "This stuff about Jamie—it's just, like, a game, right? A coping mechanism or something?"

I didn't want to hurt her feelings, either. And I could see in her eyes that she was scared for me. Of me.

"Of course it is," I told her, and closed my notebook quickly. Then I brightened my eyes, trying to look cheerful, curious, interested. "What are you reading, anyway?"

25

JACK WATCHED THE SUNLIGHT GLINT between teeth. He listened to the seagulls overhead and heard the shouts of men. He felt the ship lull him to sleep over and over again. Jack lost himself to easy sleep, and dreamed of Annit, and Ijah, and wondered if they missed him.

Sometimes when Jack's eyes closed he saw the lady pirate. Sometimes she became someone else. Dark hair knotted into a loose ponytail, freckles scattered across the bridge of her nose. Eyes like his, but somehow different. Younger. More free. She was saying something to him, her mouth forming soundless words. In the gray stretch of boredom, the cradle rock of the ocean churning endlessly on and on. The language was different, lost to him. But somehow Jack was able to suss out their meaning:

The knife. He has a knife. Take his knife.

❖

Our family had fallen apart, but I was distracted. Maybe it was easier to focus on Jamie, stuck in Gumlea. Now, most nights, there were only two of us at our house. At *Mom's* house. Sometimes, when she worked late or went out with her friends, I was alone there. It was a rattling skeleton of emptiness, and even Dana Scully couldn't fill it. But if I

159

missed Elijah or Dad, I told myself they didn't matter. Not until Jamie was home and could fix everything. And I had to figure out how to get him home.

One night, I dreamed about a knife, shining up from the carpet on my bedroom floor. It was practically a dagger, the same length as my forearm. The blade was carved into a wave, then scalloped, the kind of blade you'd never have to sharpen. The hilt was made out of some kind of well-worn bone, with images carved into it in scratchy black. It was the same knife Jamie had shown me in Gumlea on that very first day, the one he'd conjured out of nothing but his own shining magic. The one that we'd decided would open up the Veil between worlds, back when we were children and full of ideas. Only now, for the first time, I could see the images on the blade: there was an ancient man, his beard all long and pointed. There was a girl with flowers in her hair. There was a boy between them. On the other side, there was just one figure. A wild hare.

The knife waited for me. Silver. White hilt. A gemstone buried in the center of the silver surface, a throbbing ruby.

Strange, what that dream did to me. I woke up agitated, my heart racing. I touched myself until my brain went quiet, then I threw my covers back and stalked down the steps and straight outside.

If Mom knew I was up, she'd be pissed. It was a school night. She had work in the morning. Even though I didn't have a bedtime, she was still my parent, a rational creature who, like everyone else in this lonely world, thought nighttime was for sleeping.

But if nighttime was for sleeping, she slept too deeply those days. Sleeping pills, though she thought I didn't know. Ever since Jamie, then Dad, then Elijah left, she took two every night with a tall glass of water from the kitchen sink. She would never know that I was up, much less that I'd gone outside. I was a good kid, after all. She didn't have to worry about me.

The ground, still cool in the late-spring dawn, was soggy beneath my feet. Dew dotted every blue-black blade of grass. There was no wind. No crickets, not yet. Not even a moon. But there were a million billion stars that night, puked up into the sky so that the whole universe seemed sick with them. I sat down on the back steps and stared out into the woods.

He was out there somewhere, but I couldn't reach him. Maybe it was because of puberty. Maybe I'd lost the ability to slip away between worlds, to reach out for him, to bring him back.

Maybe it was up to Jamie to come home.

But for some reason, he wouldn't. No, couldn't. I closed my eyes, seeing the gently curved handle of that knife. Somehow, it was key to his escape. If he had the knife, then he could come back to me, and we could fix this. Or maybe I needed the knife. I needed to find it *here* and pierce the Veil. Jamie could come home, and then Dad, and Eli. We could figure out how to repair our family once and for all.

I heard a voice call my name. In the dark cold yard, I stiffened. But then I realized it wasn't Jamie. The voice didn't come from the woods. It came from the house. Mom. I rushed inside, drawing my hooded sweatshirt around me like it might shield me from whatever might come next.

There she was, looking tired in the kitchen. "There you are. What are you doing up, sweetie?"

I shrugged. "I just couldn't sleep."

"Me neither," she said. She went to the tap and turned it on, catching a glass of water inside one of our colored glass tumblers. Then she got a pill out of the cabinet and handed both to me.

"This should help," she said. "Don't tell your dad." Then she winked at me, like it was a secret joke between us.

I didn't know what to say. I nodded, then swallowed back water and pill, both. My eyes were on Mom. Her smile was so faint, so small.

But my mind, my mind was on the knife.

26

THE PIRATE HAD A KNIFE had a knife had a knife and Jack could not stop thinking about the shape of the knife and the edge of the knife pressed up against his back that knife could be his escape his salvation but he could not show that he was thinking of the knife when he obediently drank down his grog and let his skeletal hands hang limp because if he let his smile show at the pressure of the knife pressed up against his back while the boat heaved and the pirate heaved beside him then maybe the pirate would grow more careful with his knife would not let it flash so freely in the dark deep night of the sea.

The pirate had a knife and Jack learned the shape of it without ever seeing it the carved blade the ragged blade the bone handle and the gemstones pressed inside it the pirate had a knife and Jack could not stop thinking about it maybe it was the knife that was named Jack maybe the boy was wrong and it was his name but it didn't matter because the pirate had a knife and Jack could not stop thinking about it and the blade was the sort that never needed sharpening and usually it was warm from the pirate's grip but one night one fateful night that faithful knife was forgotten in the sheets and Jack did not even know it was there until the ship tossed his body in a wild growing storm and his bare leg touched something cold.

The knife.

Saturdays and Sundays that summer I spent at Dad's apartment. That's what Mom and Dad had worked out with a mediator. They weren't divorced, not yet, but that day was bound to come soon, and with it, lawyers and custodial agreements. Right now, they were keeping things casual and tersely friendly. I wanted to try to stay friendly with them, too, so when my father asked me if I'd like to spend weekends with him and Eli—days after they'd already decided—I shrugged and said, "Sure."

Saturdays we ate pizza and played board games. Then Dad would make a big show of tucking Eli in on the pullout sofa, and I'd do my homework by a little clip-on reading light that looked like an alligator. If I wanted to do something, anything else—draw or read or touch myself or call Miranda—I couldn't. The apartment was only four rooms, and only the bathroom had a door and there was no place I could hide if I didn't want Dad to come knocking.

I missed my room on those Saturday nights, the carpet a little crusty from long-dried Play-Doh and the maps on the walls shivering in the spring breeze, the sense that my brother could come home at any moment, the bed that had been my bed since I was three years old and was supposed to be my bed until college. Who knew *what* would happen now, though.

On Sunday mornings, Dad and Eli would leave for church and I'd be alone in the apartment. I'd make myself tea in Dad's electric kettle, the one that used to be in his office, and grab his laptop and curl up under a blanket on the couch with it, the TV droning in the background. And I searched and searched and searched.

For knives.

I could not stop thinking about knives. No, that's not true. I could not stop thinking about *that* knife, the hare knife, the one my brother could use to split the Veil. The gently curved handle. The firm hilt. The red ruby, shining within it, bright as fresh-spilled blood. I needed that knife. He needed that knife. I combed Amazon and eBay and Etsy and a lot of extremely dorky fantasy websites and extremely unsettling weapon websites for anything resembling that G-d damned knife.

We'd once been obsessed with knives. The two of us. Jamie had a penknife that Dad had given him, and when I was a little kid he'd sometimes lend it to me to open up a box or tear open an envelope or just stand there with it in my fisted hand, feeling tough. We'd looked at knives at the local renaissance festival and Jamie had talked about getting a sword once, before Dad said no.

But this was different. This knife was a dream knife, a magic knife. The knife that would bring Jamie back to me.

I found some with scrimshaw handles. Some with curved blades. But as I scrolled and scrolled and scrolled and scrolled, searching until my eyes went dull and my hands numb and all the knives blurred into one knife, the ur-knife, the knife against which all other knives could be judged, I came up empty. At last, I'd clear my browser history and toss the laptop aside and try to sleep until Dad and Eli came home from church.

When they did, all laughter and glee, every single week, talking about the sermon they'd heard or the people whose hands they shook at the end of the service, Dad would give me a small, knowing look. I suppose he thought I was looking at porn on his laptop. But that wasn't the case at all. The truth was so much darker, so much worse.

27

JACK'S HEART RACED. HE FELT a knife's edge of pressure at the small of his back. But it wasn't a knife. The knife was tangled in the sheets, pulsing, shining, the ruby in the blade as red as the sky on an unlucky night was red as his heart was red as his flesh was red and his anger, so much anger, was bright, bright red.

How did Jack do it? He'll never be able to explain. Except on that night, the ship tossed by waves, the pillow sand-damp beneath him, Jack used his anger to reach outside himself. He felt for the knife in the blankets like one might look for a light switch in a dark bathroom. He wrapped his thoughts around that carved hilt and hefted that knife through the air. His hands were waiting, bound, clutching the sheets. But they would be empty for a while longer still until he used his mind to plunge that knife's blade into the pirate, not once, not twice, but a dozen times, until blood poured out over both of them, coating the ship's groaning belly.

As the blood rushed in, so did the water, brackish and dark between the ship's teeth.

Soaked up to his knees, Jack withdrew the knife.

❧

In the past, my brother had paved the way for me. I'd known what to expect in middle school because Jamie had done it all first—the orientation and the locker assignments and the mandatory assemblies on bullying. I'd felt like an expert compared to the other kids, and I liked it that way.

Ninth grade meant new, open waters. Shark infested, with no brother to guide me. He was gone now, and I would have to muddle through it myself. The problem was that I was caring less and less lately about the real world, the one that was in front of me. Maybe it was because the real world was awful. Reams of homework, and Mom and Dad fighting every time they spoke. My brother still gone, and maybe never coming back. The kids at school ignoring me, or snickering when I gave an answer in class, or whispering when I passed by them. Or maybe it was because I was sure, in my heart, that I could *do* something about Jamie. I'd split open the sky, let all the creatures of Gumlea come tumbling out, and then what would school matter? It wouldn't. Not anymore.

But our high school teachers tried to convince us that it would, that this academic year meant more than any before it. It was time to take ourselves and our futures seriously. In high school, every choice we made would make a ripple out into our adult lives. The days stretched on, each one indistinguishable from the one before. But these days were important, they said. That's what Mr. McKavity told us, at least, at freshman orientation. It was the first day of school. It was still warmish, but the sky was gray, bleak and empty. We were sitting in the auditorium, supposedly going over the schedules we'd selected at the end of eighth grade, as we started to solidify our adult lives. But I didn't care. I was only half listening. Hunched over my notebook. Drawing knives.

"Do you think it's really true?" Miranda asked me, watching the wild motion of my hands. I felt irritated at her, at the whole world. I felt like that a lot these days. I wanted to be somewhere else. Out in the woods, in Gumlea, working to get my brother home. I'd managed to keep my grades up and my head down through the end of middle school, staying out of trouble. But it took more and more work lately to pretend like I was normal.

"I don't know," I said irritably. "I kind of think it's all a load of bullshit."

I was trying to draw the handle right, but it wasn't coming out exactly as I imagined it. It looked lumpy. Weird.

"Good," Miranda said, but she sounded uncertain as the kids started standing up around us. "I think it's bullshit, too."

She flashed a smile at me. I think we were supposed to feel like we were on the same team in that moment, but I knew the truth. I wasn't on the same team as anyone.

We filed out of the auditorium with the rest of them and into the high school wing of the building. The hallways smelled like floor polish, like locker dust, like any other school. I clutched my notebook to my chest and tried to imagine how my life would change in the next year, but I couldn't. If I couldn't get Jamie back, it would be more of the same. The same old awfulness. The same old loneliness.

"Follow me," Mr. McKavity was saying. "I'll show you the cafeteria."

Someone behind us was gushing about how there was a snack machine in the high school cafeteria, how we could eat whatever we wanted. Someone else was telling them not to be stupid, that it wasn't like we'd be allowed to eat *candy* in school. Miranda looked at me pointedly, rolled her eyes. I could have smiled back at her then, but I didn't. I looked down at my notebook instead.

"What's that?" she asked me as we shuffled forward with the group down the hall.

I shrugged. "A knife. The one I need to get Jamie back. But I can't draw it right. It's just not working."

Miranda was looking at me, not saying anything. So I looked away.

"Hey," she asked me after a minute, as we were wedged through the cafeteria doors with the rest of them, "isn't that your brother's girlfriend?"

"Where?" I asked, whipping my head around, searching for Vidya. It felt like a lifetime since we'd last spoken, though it had only been a few months. Once, she'd said my brother *might as well be in Gumlea*, and in that moment, I had a feeling that it had been much more than a joke.

Could I talk to her? Ask her about the knife? If she knew where it had gone, where I could find it? Ask her if she knew how Jamie did it—crossing through the Veil? I once thought that nothing could have been worse than him breaking the Vows, telling Vidya about Gumlea, but now, if he had . . .

But by the time I turned, she was gone. Mr. McKavity was talking about our meal plan cards. I crossed my arms over my chest tight, holding those drawings of the knife against my heart. I told myself it didn't matter, anyway.

A few days later, during third-period study hall, Mr. McKavity called me to his desk. In a low voice, he said that Dr. Katzenberger wanted to see me. I heard snickers from the students who had heard. Dr. Katzenberger was the school psychologist. Not the guidance counselor, but the one who spoke to kids with *problems*.

I had avoided this fate so far. I'd kept my grades up, maintained my friendship with Miranda, done well in extracurriculars. I didn't act out in class or crack jokes or even laugh at the wrong moments. I was careful, and for a reason. If anyone found out what was really happening—where Jamie had gone, and how I knew—then they would have thought I was nuts.

I'd told myself I wouldn't let that happen. But somehow, anyway, it had. I walked down the hallways, watching the kids move like Feral Children in the classrooms. Boys flirting. Girls making fart jokes.

Dr. Katzenberger's office had his name on the door. I knocked once. When a voice called back, "Come in," I opened it and slipped inside, hoping that no one saw me.

But then the sight of my parents, sitting in a pair of chairs in front of the psychologist's desk, washed all of that away.

"What are you guys doing here?" I asked, and the unspoken word was: *both*. What are you *both* doing here, and why are you conspiring together against me?

Neither of them answered. They only looked at Dr. Katzenberger. He was a large man, mustachioed, suspender-clad, and tall. His chair was the oaken kind that could tip back on its hinges.

"Take a seat, Anne," he said.

It was Mom who spoke up for me, which was nice, I guess. "We call her Annie."

"Oh, yes, of course," Dr. Katzenberger said as I sat down. But it sounded like he wasn't listening at all. He leafed through a manila folder, reading something. "Your friend Miranda Morganson came to me. She was concerned."

"Miranda," I said, and winced. I'd been too real with Miranda. Too open. Too *me*.

"She said you've been talking about a knife, honey," Dad said. He never called me that, not normally. But now he reached out from his chair and touched his hand to my back, just between the shoulder blades.

I shrank back. "She shouldn't have told you that," I said darkly. Of course, Miranda didn't know the Laws. I could make a sacrifice in her name. An insect, maybe, something I would find in the woods . . .

Dr. Katzenberger was looking at me, grimacing. He nudged something forward along the desk. A piece of paper.

"What's that?" I asked.

He angled his chin up, indicating that I could take the paper, so I did. It was my first geometry quiz. I'd gotten 100 percent on it.

"What?" I asked.

"Turn it over," he said, and I swear, he was repressing an eye roll at my expense. I flipped the page.

I'd drawn knives, dozens of knives. Only they were all one knife. The same knife. Jamie's knife. Over and over again, until I got the handle right. Eventually, my hand had gone kind of crazy. I'd started to draw the knives so close together that the page was packed with ink, overflowing, dark as blood.

"You don't understand—" I began, but Mom, leaning forward in her seat, interrupted me.

"Annie, were you planning on hurting yourself?"

The question felt almost like an insult. I steeled myself inside, trying not to look incredulous, which is precisely how I felt. "Of course not. Don't be stupid."

"Don't call your mother stupid, honey," Dad said. Though I knew he'd said much worse about her, under his breath and in his black heart.

"I would never hurt myself," I said, clearly and precisely, with no name-calling at all. Dr. Katzenberger nodded.

"Good. You know, Anne—"

"Annie," said Mom.

"Yes, Annie," Dr. Katzenberger began again. He was sitting up straighter in his seat now. "You've been through a lot in the past year.

Your mother and father told me they separated. And then there's the issue of your brother's death—"

"Jamie's not dead," I said, my words coming swiftly as any knife. Out of the corner of my eye, I could see tears shining on Mom's face. But it was Dad who spoke, firmly and with conviction.

"Annie, we have to face the possibility—"

"Are you *serious* right now?" I said firmly. I sat back in my seat. I guess I sounded like kind of a brat. But I needed them to know that I knew Jamie was out there. I couldn't explain how I knew, not to them, but I did.

Dr. Katzenberger sighed. "This isn't an interrogation. What you're going through is serious, Annie. I've recommended a counselor to your parents. Kit Hendricks is her name. She's wonderful. You'll like her."

"It doesn't matter if I like her or not, though, does it?" I asked.

Dr. Katzenberger stared at me. His eyes were small and black in his broad, pale face. "Of course it does," he said, his eyebrows wrinkling in concern.

I looked to Mom, and then to Dad, and then back to Mom. They had the same wrinkles, the same concern.

"Fine," I said tersely.

Because it was fine. I'd jump through any hoops they gave me. I'd be good. I always was. I needed to stay in the King's favor if Jamie was going to return to me. My parents were both watching me. Dad, his anger smothered in a smile, not for me, but for the school counselor. Mom couldn't even fake it. The edges of her mouth were all wobbly, like this was some kind of personal defeat.

28

THE NIGHT WAS STARLESS, THE moons only hazy smudges beneath a Veil of gray. When Jack reached the upper deck, he was surprised to find the ship empty. A lonely wind whipped through the torn sails, tousling his hair. Ahead of him was the mermaid, but she no longer sang. Her body was slack and blue, her hair forming a lacy net over her face. Jack sighed and went to her, cutting her body down. It was the least he could do.

It was just as he went to free her from her bindings that he heard it, rising up over the sound of her body slipping into the water. It was a whisper, a murmur, a susurration. It seemed to vibrate his whole body like wind in whispery autumn leaves.

{Jamie.}

Jack turned in shock. There was no one else here. No mermaids. No pirate women. And no men. But there behind him, still as a gargoyle, sat a creature. Its ears were long and trembling. Its whiskers picked up the salt on the breeze. It was a hare, its coat a dappled gray that looked almost blue in the moonless night.

{Jamie,} she said. He drew closer. She was nearly as big as he was. {Jamie, come home.}

He didn't move. He watched himself, mirrored in two globes of endless, formless black.

❖

Two weeks later, on a Thursday afternoon at the beginning of ninth grade, I started counseling.

II

ONE

JAMES **[REDACTED]** WALKED OUT OF my life in the second week of ninth grade. Really, not only my life, but his own life, too. He disappeared. Nobody knows where he went, or why, not even me. That's what I told the cops because it's the truth. And afterward, I did what any freshman girl would do. I spent six months wearing black and too much eyeliner and writing lyrics in gel pens on the back of my book bag, and then I tried to move on.

I hate to say it, but in a way, his disappearance saved me. Not emotionally, but from, like, bodily harm. Because I hadn't told my parents I was dating James. Up until the minute the police called our house, they thought I was a good, upstanding daughter. A nerd, really, who loved the local renaissance festival and who got decent grades when she worked at it and who had been taking mandolin lessons since sixth grade. The whole time I was dating James—almost a year! A lifetime in middle school—they thought I was hanging out at Harper Walton's house studying, when we were all really in James's friend Neil's basement, getting stoned and getting kissed and other things that, still, my mom only knows the half of.

She would have murdered me under normal circumstances. But you see, James was *gone*. It was a *tragedy*. And where she comes from, there's nothing more important than your epic first love. She never loved a guy before or after my dad, you know? They met at a basement show in college and, just like that, the shape of her entire life changed. So even though my relationship with James hadn't been perfect—even though his sadness was too much for me sometimes, despite the fact that I thought the way his hair fell in his eyes was hella cute—she seemed to understand that I'd really lost something. She went easy on me, even though she took away my phone for a year and made me take the early bus straight home. In her culture, widows aren't even people anymore—not "she"s but "it"s and I think—since James was gone and no one knew where he went—she expected me to be more a vision of a living, breathing heartbreak than a real, actual *girl*.

And for a long time, I was. He understood me, once, like nobody else had and I'd given up hope that anyone would look at me the same way he did ever again. But eventually, you have to move on, right? By the end of ninth grade I'd started to give up on the idea that James was ever coming back. And I didn't *want* to be a woman in mourning for the rest of my life. Not at fifteen, and not now, either. I let my mom believe what she wanted. It made life easier for me. But in my heart, I started to tell myself that what James and I had hadn't been love, anyway. After all, we were only stupid kids. Him and me, both.

Anyway, I started dating Keira in tenth grade when James was just a memory, a story I'd tell at parties when I didn't want to really talk about myself. When I wanted to seem poetic and interesting. It usually worked. Like, that was the first thing Keira ever asked me about over texts. Not Mr. Reickert's geometry class, which is where we met, or my secret love of the local renaissance festival or the Godzilla movies I watch with my dad, but James Fucking [**Redacted**]. And she ate that shit up. We dated for two months and in a new attempt at radical honesty, I brought her home to meet my parents, and things were pretty good with the two of us, or so I thought. We'd trade playlists and she said all the right things about all the right songs and she made me laugh a lot. It's kind of stupid, but we had nicknames for people. Like Mr. Reickert was "the baker" and Anita Devlin was "Ms. Powerwasher" and Keira was "shopping cart." I told you, it's stupid. I was "Gemini," even though that's not my sign (I'm a Taurus). It was from a poem Keira wrote and then I wrote the music for, about how I have gems in my eyes. It feels embarrassing writing it out like that, but at the time, it was the most romantic thing that had ever happened to me. Forget stupid old eighth-grade James. When it came to Keira, I told myself I was really, truly smitten.

And then I found out that she'd been cheating on me the whole time. Or that, actually, *I* was the person she was cheating on her boyfriend *with*, which felt even shittier, because I didn't even come first, not chronologically, and not in her heart, either. I should have known something was up when she refused to tell her parents I was anything more than a friend, and when she made a thousand excuses about my parents meeting hers, but I thought that was just a gay thing, not an our-whole-romance-is-a-lie thing. (Later, I found out that the Gemini poem was about him. She *sang* it to him, using the melody *I* wrote. Of course Theo was an actual, real-life Gemini. I mean, fuck me, you know?)

So I'm alone again, all the way into the end of tenth grade, but I don't mind. That summer, my parents send me to rock camp and I don't make out with anybody and I don't really mind that, either. I hide inside my music, which comes naturally to me, because I've been doing it for years. At least here, I'm not the only one. At that point, I've almost entirely forgotten about James, unless someone asks. And at rock camp, nobody knows me as The Girl Whose Boyfriend Disappeared, so no one asks at all. I'm just Vee, master of a thousand string instruments, lover of J.R.R. Tolkien and Brian Wilson. You know. *Me.*

Then comes eleventh grade. The week before it starts, when I haven't even unpacked my bag from rock camp, Dad comes into my room without knocking.

"Privacy!" I shout, out of habit, but he talks right over me.

"I have something for you," he says, and I look up from my phone and see that he's holding a shoebox between his hands like it's sacred.

"Why?" I ask, grinning, and he grins back at me, because, like, *why not?* Nanaji and Naniji are always going on about how spoiled I am because I'm an only child, and maybe they're right. I scooch so Dad can sit down next to me on the bed.

"Eleventh grade was a special time for me," he says.

I roll my eyes. Here we go.

"What!" he says. "It was. That was the year I went from a total dork to totally cool."

"You're still a dork," I tell him, but I'm grinning when I say it so he just kind of blushes. I mean, it's true. My dad *is* a dork. But a cool dork. The kind of dork who can tell you everything about John Peel, and it sounds boring at first but then you realize that it's all totally fucking magical because John Peel was one of the most important people in music *ever.*

"Fair," he says. "But, you know, that's when I dropped out of marching band and started a *real* band. The Plastic Elastics. And that's—"

"How you met Mom," I say, finishing the sentence for him. This isn't the first time I've heard the story. How her roommate dragged her to his show because she said my mom didn't get out enough, how Mom couldn't stand their music but couldn't take her eyes off the bassist. The Plastic Elastics only lasted another couple years, but their relationship has lasted fucking forever. It's *epic*. To them, at least.

"That's right," he says. He leans over and presses a kiss into my temple. He smells like slightly stale coffee, like he always does. "That was the beginning of the whole dang story."

"Dang," I say softly, giggling.

It's Dad's turn to roll his eyes. He shoves the box into my hands. "Here," he says, faux-offended. "You're welcome."

"*Thank* you," I tell him, opening it up. There's a pair of purple Converse All Stars inside. High-tops. Not the low-tops. They're perfect. I don't know how Dad knew they would be perfect—it's not like I would have *asked* him for a pair of purple Chucks—but they *are*.

I'm just kind of looking at them, quiet, because they're gorgeous and I can't wait to wear them on the first day of school.

"You hate them?"

"Oh!" I say, and I look at my dad and realize he's actually kind of nervous about this. "No! They're great. Really great."

Dad looks like he's about to cry, and I die a little bit inside—mostly because I feel like I'm about to cry, too. "Try them on," he says.

So I do. After they're all laced up, I stand in front of the mirror on my closet door, turning my feet this way and that way. And they're perfect. Magic shoes.

"I had a pair just like them," he says. "In eleventh grade. When the whole dang story began."

"Purple?" I say in surprise, turning to look at dopey old wonderful Dad, who is still sitting on my unmade bed.

"Yeah, purple," he says with a laugh. "I'm comfortable with *my* masculinity."

He laughs, and I laugh, too, and it's a magic moment. That's when I know that eleventh grade is going to be fan-fucking-tastic. The start of the whole dang story.

TWO

I WEAR THOSE SNEAKERS FOR the first time on the first day, and even though they're stiff and the backs rub my heels a little, I like how the laces look—all white and perfect. The weather is gross still and so I wear a pair of shorts—knee length is as short as my mom will let me get away with—and a sloppy purple T-shirt with it. I am the total opposite of eighth-grade Vidya. These days, the only black I wear is my bra, hidden beneath all that cotton.

As I climb onto the bus, a memory of him comes back to me. The first day of ninth grade, how he found me at my locker and pressed a note into my hand, his smile small and secret. He was always the kind of guy who would slip you a note folded into a fortune-teller or an origami frog. It almost didn't matter what the words inside said. It was more about the fact that he'd written something down with a pen, in his own hand, and then made the paper itself into something beautiful. Like, art. Sure, we texted and all that. But I lost those when my parents confiscated my phone. All those notes folded into tiny animals? They're still in a shoebox in the back of my closet. I saved every one.

Ugh. Not that it means anything. Because I didn't really *love* James, right? What fourteen-year-old understands a thing about love? No, no, we were just dumb kids, and it was over before high school really began. Not even worth thinking about anymore. It hurts, but I push the memory away. Instead, on the bus with my earbuds in, I listen to Jan and Dean, and I think about what's to come. Maybe this year, I'll finally join jazz band to make my dad shut up about it, or to find other kids for the band I've wanted to start for years, because the girls I'm friends with are all too shy and the boys are too scared to play with a girl who is better than they are, and maybe this year, I'll finally make honor roll, and maybe this year, I'll finally fall in love for real.

It seems like everything is a possibility. Lunch with the emo kids, cracking jokes, the boys looking at me like I'm casting some sort of spell over them. The new textbooks in Honors Trig, and the way the spine cracks when I open mine and write my name inside the cover. And then I add my secret symbol in Tengwar after it: *vilya esse*, for Vidya Emerson, like I always do.

Okay, so, there's probably something you should know about me. Way back in the day, in fifth and sixth grade and even a little into seventh, I was totally obsessed with *The Lord of the Rings*. At first it was all about the movies, and I spent my spare time writing fanfic about Orlando Bloom and Viggo Mortensen, but then I discovered Dad's copies of the books in his office and it kind of spiraled out from there. Like, I begged my parents for a mandolin, and dragged Harper to the ren fest, and every night before bed I'd look up at the poster of Middle Earth that used to hang on the wall and recite Elven poetry. I don't even know *why* liked it so much, except it made my world feel more exciting and beautiful and rich, and I guess there's a part of me that will *always* want magic to be real, even though I know it isn't.

And I know it's not. I'm not like those kids who LARP or boff or whatever. I'm not a witch. And I've moved on from my ren fest obsession (mostly). I'm into music these days. Sixties and '70s underground rock. I saved up my allowance for a used powder-blue Fender Jazzmaster that I play every moment I'm not at school, until I see chord charts in my sleep. I learned to talk about *that* instead, and about records, which the kids at school think is a little weird but also cool—respectable. It's not like I'm ashamed, exactly, about loving all that fantasy stuff I used to love, but I learned pretty quickly that most people don't want to hear about it, or will think you're weird for talking about it. And I like having friends and being able to get along with everybody. Don't get me wrong—my close friends were always cool. Harper liked wearing a bodice at the ren fest and eating turkey legs and shouting "Huzzah!" But she made it clear that it was *my* thing, not hers, and that it always would be. But now, for the most part, I understand that magic belongs in the *margins* of my notebooks. It's not something I can share with other kids, like music. It's just for me.

I guess in retrospect, that's kind of half of what I liked about James back in the day. Because he was a secret dork, too, when you got down to it, and an even bigger one than me—not just reading fantasy but writing it. And he'd learned to cover it up even better than I had, because you know that the stoner guys he spent his time with, Neal Harriman and all of them, *definitely* wouldn't understand. But I did, and he understood me, and it was kind of a relief sometimes to be a pair of secret dorks together.

Anyway, at least I have Madrigals. That always scratches that sparkly-robes-and-castles itch for me even if the rest of my life is pretty ordinary. I've been in it for over a year now—Harper, too, because she figured out that the competitions are mostly just an excuse to hook up and party—and it feels like one place that I can actually be myself.

After school, I'm sitting on the risers in the music room we use for Madrigals rehearsal with Harper, paging together through the sheet music and making plans for our first competition in October. She whispers that she's going to bring vodka. Her brother can get it for us, and she can hide it inside a water bottle. No one will know. And at first, I don't even notice the girl at the other side of the stands, watching me with owl eyes.

It's actually Harper who elbows me in the ribs and angles her chin that way. "Vee," she says, "look who it is."

As Mrs. Kepler hands out the schedule, I sneak a glance. It's the eyes that hook me first. I *know* those eyes. I've spent hours staring into eyes just like those. They're James **[Redacted]**'s eyes. Only they're not.

"Annie," I blurt out, and Harper elbows me again, so I put a hand up over my mouth. But a couple of the guys who are hanging around us glance over.

"Smooth," Harper says with a snicker. I look down fast at the schedule and pretend that it's *fascinating* that we have practice every Tuesday and Thursday, just like we did last year.

"She's been watching you for like ten minutes," Harper whispers.

"Shut up," I say, but when I look up, I see that it's true. Annie **[Redacted]** is staring at me and she doesn't break her gaze even when our eyes lock. It's weird and I kind of feel like I have to puke. It's not like I haven't seen James's sister around school here and there since he disappeared, but she gave me a wide berth, for the most part, and I gave her one, too. I mean, the last time we spoke it didn't go so well. She asked where James had gone, as if I had some information and was keeping it from her for . . . what? The world's worst fucking prank? I told her I didn't know, and to leave me alone—and she did. It was a relief, after the way her asshole parents had acted toward me. And when I dropped out of chorus last year to join Madrigals, I'd figured it was gonna keep going like that for the rest of high school. Annie living her life. Me living mine. It was for the best.

So why is she staring at me?

The bell for the late bus rings and me and Harper get up to gather our stuff. I'm looking down, and my cheeks are burning red hot. I don't want to glance over to see if Annie is still watching me or not. I want to pretend that this whole thing isn't happening.

"She's still looking at you," Harper murmurs. "Like she wants to come talk to you and doesn't know how."

"Oh God," I say, cringing. I glance down at my beautiful new Converses with their bright white laces. And notice with a flash of relief that one of them has come undone.

"Just act normal," I whisper to Harper as I bend over to tie my shoes. So Harper starts talking to me a little too loudly about how she's not sure if vodka is the right choice, actually, because of how much I puked last time. I laugh, and it's loud and fake, but it works. When I stand up and glance over toward Annie, she's not only stopped staring at me—but she's scurrying from the room, dragging her worn-out backpack behind her.

"Well, that's a relief," Harper says. "You okay?"

My best friend reaches out and brushes my hair away from my eyes. I laugh a little, shaky, and nod.

"Sure," I say.

"So I guess she's joining Madrigals?"

"I have no idea," I say. "Let's get outta here."

It's funny, though. When I leave the music room, chatting with Harper about guys and booze and all of our usual, ordinary stuff, I don't really feel relieved. For some insane reason, I only feel disappointed.

THREE

FUCK.

I can't stop thinking about Annie **[Redacted]**.

Why was she staring at me? What did she *want* from me? Why was she even coming out for Madrigals? I think I told her she should join up way back when I was in ninth grade—she'd had a perfectly fine voice, and it seemed like it would be her thing—but that was before the world went to shit. When James was still alive, when me and James were still together, when I thought that being nice to my boyfriend's sister might be the Right Thing to Do. But I thought my last conversation with her sealed it, that she knew better than to bother me, especially after everything her parents had put me through. I've been happy to ignore her for the last few years—to ignore the thought of James, of eighth grade in general—and, I thought, she'd been happy to ignore me.

But now, here she was. In Madrigals. Staring at me. With those eyes.

All through the next two days, I think of Annie and nothing else. I think about her when I'm fucking around on my guitar and I think about her when I'm eating dinner. I *should* be settling into the new year, organizing my notebooks, practicing piano for my lessons, and avoiding Geoff Ryman, who Harper thinks is going to ask me out. But I'm so spacey and out of it that I accidentally let him sit next to me at lunch on Thursday. When he talks at me about Jack Antonoff, I'm hardly listening. Instead, I'm tapping my fork against the Styrofoam plate, thinking about the way it felt to look into Annie **[Redacted]**'s eyes.

"God, she doesn't *care*, Geoff," Harper says as she pulls a chair up with her foot and squishes herself into an almost-too-small space between us. "Vee, what's *up*? Where are you?"

I glance over my shoulder. Annie's in my lunch. I saw her on the first day in the lunch line, taking too long to pick, holding everything up. But I can't see her right now. The cafeteria is too crowded. "I'm right here."

"Sure," she says, then adds, "Yeah right."

I sigh. "Fine. I'm just wondering if Annie's going to be in Madrigals again today."

"Wait," Geoff says. "James **[Redacted]**'s little sister?"

I nod, and it kind of hurts, because everybody here—at our table and in our school and in our whole damned town—knows all the dirt about me and James. How I acted so utterly, *hopelessly* hooked on him, and what a hot mess I was after his disappearance, for months. At the time I didn't care, but I hate feeling like this *now*—like a side plot in his story.

Sure enough, Geoff just lets out a low whistle between his teeth.

"Oh, shut up, Geoff," Harper says, and I lean my shoulder into hers, thankful as I always am to have her here for me.

"Even if she is in Madrigals," Harper tells me in a low voice that's meant just for me and not for Geoff and the rest of them, even though they've started their own conversation now, "you don't need to *talk* to her."

"But," I say slowly, and my stomach kind of squeezes when I say it, "what if I *want* to talk to her?"

A pause. Harper's looking at me, frowning. My cheeks are burning up.

"What?" I say.

"I mean," Harper begins carefully, picking at the wilted iceberg lettuce and shredded carrots that make up her gross school lunch salad, "if you need, like, closure or something, sure."

"But?" I ask.

"I just wonder," she says, taking a bite. Tucking it into her cheek. "If you really, truly want to do that to yourself?"

I stare down at my own tray, and the remnants of the grilled cheese there. I don't know how to answer Harper's question. Because what if I do?

By last period, I've completely convinced myself that letting Annie talk to me about whatever it is that she wants to talk about is totally the right thing to do. Have you ever convinced yourself to do something that is obviously a terrible idea? Shoplift just to prove you can, smoke something even though you know your parents will lose their minds if they ever find out, kiss someone who you know is bad for you? I mean, I tell myself, it's not like I'm *kissing* Annie. I'm just going to be nice to her for five minutes and put an end to whatever this is—this weird tension that's totally wrecking what should be the beginning of an awesome school year.

Madrigals. Warm-up exercises and "Ah, Robin, Gentle Robin." And Annie standing there across from me and Harper on the risers in a cluster with the rest of the sopranos. I'm pretty sure she's not friends with any of them from the way that they all turn away from her to talk to each other between songs. And I can't really blame them. She sticks out like a sore thumb here, but then, she kind of sticks out everywhere. She's got bangs, and a bowl cut like a Victorian child laborer that's gotten a little overgrown, just touching her shoulders, and she's wearing dark blue jeans and a gray T-shirt, and she's got ordinary freckles and she's not super short or super tall or super skinny or super fat. But still, there's something *off* about Annie. James stood out, too, but it was a different sort of off. A good sort. He'd give you a crooked smile and you suddenly felt like you lived at the center of a whole new solar system. Annie's the opposite of that. Some people might call it resting bitch face, but even that isn't quite right. When she's looking at the sheet music or singing or glancing over at me for a split second like she doesn't want to lose track of me in this little half-full room of people, she looks *pissed*. Like she might burn down the school or something. She's Goth as fuck, without even trying.

When the bell rings for the bus, I slide my sheet music into my folder and tuck it into my backpack. I'm watching Annie do the same thing, and I'm mulling it over. Mulling *her* over.

"Well?" Harper says.

I nod a little, shaky. "I'm going to go say hi."

Beside me, Harper rolls her eyes. But she follows me anyway. "What?" she says when I glance over at her. "I can't let you go talk to her alone."

Annie's zipping up her backpack, and when she looks up she kind of startles. Like a frightened animal in a trap.

"Vidya," she says. It's not a question. Her voice is a little deeper than the last time we spoke. What was it, two years ago now?

"Hey," I say. "So, you're doing Madrigals?"

Annie stands up a little taller, hiking her backpack over one shoulder. She glances at Harper, then quickly away, like she doesn't quite know what to do with her.

"Um," she says. "Yeah, well, you told me to join. So here I am—"

"Annie," I tell her, "that was *years* ago."

She's looking at me, all owlish and round-eyed again. Under those freckles, she's blushing furiously. And, Christ. It's kind of cute, and cute in a way that I have to admit has nothing to do with James. She has a *dimple* in her left cheek. Just the left one. I remember in that moment that I always kind of liked Annie, or the idea of her, anyway. The stories that James used to tell about her made her sound like magic—like Peter Pan or something. But, you know, a girl. A magical fairy who was always on the verge of sweeping you up into an adventure.

"Well, uh," she says. She glances at Harper again, who makes a soft scoffing noise behind me. "I figured it sounded cool. And that, uh, it'd also be a good way to talk to you."

I arch an eyebrow. "Talk?"

"Um," Annie says. She looks at Harper one last time, and finally, I sigh.

"Go catch the bus, Harp," I tell her. "I'll find you in a few."

"You sure?" Harper asks. I give her a nod, and she angles her chin back. Not toward me, really, but more toward Annie. There's a glare in her eyes, like some kind of tough girl warning, which is hilarious if you know Harper, who is a total wimp and has never been in a fight in her life. But, after a moment, she leaves.

"Go ahead," I tell Annie.

She sighs. Her face is still pink and mottled, like the blood is taking a long time to return to where it's supposed to be. "Well," she begins, "my parents have decided that we're having a funeral. For Jamie. And, like . . . okay, they didn't want to invite you? But I thought it was the right thing to do."

I blink. "A . . . funeral?"

"Yeah. My therapist told them to do it. They said it would give me closure. It's ridiculous. I *have* closure. I know he's not coming back," she says quickly. "But I guess this is as good a time as any. And I was thinking you should be there. You guys were important to each other, right?"

There's a spiky ball in my stomach. A hedgehog curled up tight, maybe. I let myself think, for just a narrow flash of a moment, about James. About the weight of his hands on my belly. About his eyes under his shaggy mop of hair. And how they look like Annie's eyes, right now, burning with the same kind of intensity. But how that intensity was all directed at *me*.

"Yeah." I hate how my voice cracks just a little when I say it. "Yeah, we were."

"I thought so," she said. "Sorry. I know it's stupid, to drag this whole thing out again. You probably don't want to. I mean, I wouldn't, if I were in your position. "

Do I want to? I can't even be sure. Harper would tell me it was a terrible idea, and she wouldn't be wrong. But somehow, no matter what Harper thinks, it feels like the right thing to do. Even if his parents don't want me there, James and I *did* care about each other. Once.

"I'll go," I say finally. "When is it?"

"Sunday," she says. "Ten in the morning at Oakwood Cemetery. This is all so stupid. It's not like we have a body to bury. But. You know. 'Closure.'"

Part of me wants to reach over and squeeze her hand. Part of me worries that she'll go supernova if I touch her. So I just smile, gently, kindly.

"I'll see you then," I say.

And then, before I can think better of it, I give her a little wave and head off toward the bus.

FOUR

SEPTEMBER 13. TWO YEARS TO the day since I last saw James. A Sunday, and I usually sleep in on Sundays, but I've hardly slept at all in the nights leading up to this and today I'm up with the dawn. The light through my bedroom curtains is bright and wild, right away. It's the perfect day for a funeral, clear skies and birds singing and the world overflowing with joy. James would like a day like this, I tell myself. But what do I know about what James really liked? It was ages ago. And now he's dead.

And what do you even wear to your dead boyfriend's funeral, anyway? I go through my closet and find a dress that I used to wear a lot back then. It's stretchy crushed velvet, black, but kind of gray where the light hits it. I'm not sure it's going to fit until I pull it on over my head and give myself a glance in the mirror. Maybe a little tighter around my curves than it used to be, but not so bad that it's off-limits for a funeral. Anyway, James would have liked it, I tell myself, and then I laugh a little, because sometimes it seemed like James didn't like anything. His feelings were always so dark and stormy, which is what I liked about him then, the drama of it all.

"You don't have to do this," Mom says to me over breakfast as I reach for another pancake. "I don't trust his parents after how they treated you.

Acting like it was your fault."

"Mom—" I begin, because I know what's coming next and I'm not sure I want to hear it.

"You were a *good girl* until that boy came along. And they treated you like you were some criminal."

It's true, that I was good until James, but only technically. I *wanted* to kiss him. Wanted to hang out in Neal's basement, watching stupid old movies and playing drinking games. I wanted to be like the other kids. Hard and strange and wild like they were. And for a minute, it felt like I was, but—

"They're racist, Vidya. You need to watch out for them."

I press my lips together. Suddenly I'm trying not to cry. Years ago, I'd defended them. *James* hadn't been racist, and I cared about him, and that's what mattered. But I don't know if I have it in me right now.

"Mom, I—"

"My mother tried to warn me," she's saying, stabbing her pancake hard enough that the plate rings out under the fork tines, "when I got involved with your father. 'You'll never be one of them.' I hated to hear it. She was wrong, then. I was lucky with his parents, but you—"

"Mommy, *stop*," I say, loud enough that my words surprise me. For once, she does. She looks at me, at the tears trembling in my eyes.

"I lost James," I tell her, "and they did, too. Going there is the right thing to do."

She doesn't say anything to that. She can't. Deep down, my mom has this big, generous heart. She's a caretaker—of me, of Dad, of the old folks who live down the road, everybody. She shovels their walk and brings them groceries when it snows. She cooks for everyone, for every occasion. I always thought I wasn't much like her, but maybe I am. Because when I say it, I mean it. It is the right thing to do, no matter how *I* feel about his parents or the way they treated me. She says softly, "You know, Vidya, I'm so proud of the woman you've become."

I feel guilt tug at my stomach, because I'm not sure I'm much to be proud of, even now. But I hide it. Instead, I just wrinkle my nose. She laughs at me a little, so I force a laugh, too. Thankfully, we don't talk about James anymore, or his parents, which is good. I don't know if I have it in me.

I don't have my license yet. After everything I went through with James—all that hiding, so many secrets—my parents thought it would be better if we waited until senior year for the test, when I could finally prove I was mature enough. Luckily, Dad offers to drive me to the funeral. We don't talk about James. Instead he rambles to me about the day John Lennon died when my dad was eight and thought that rock stars lived forever. That's my father for you. He sees everything as a metaphor for his own life, which has mostly been lived out between vinyl record grooves. I look at him, nodding. I wonder if he's ever lost anybody. As far as I know, he didn't have any girlfriends at all before Mom. He's such an enormous geek, even for a dad. When he talks about Mark David Chapman, his voice cracks, and he wipes away a tear. It makes me want to give him a giant hug. I guess it's that kind of day—when everything is tender and painful and right on the surface. "Anyway," he finally concludes, in a wheezy voice, "I hope you'll call me if you need me. If his family says anything to you—"

"Thanks, Dad," I say quickly, and, not wanting him to finish his sentence, I press a kiss to his scratchy cheek to show him that I appreciate the sentiment and hop out of the car before he can say another word.

God, this day is so freaking gorgeous. It feels like fall will never come, like summer will stretch on and on and on. I walk through the cemetery alone, numb, at first. I don't expect the wall of feeling that slams into me the moment I reach the small crowd gathered around the **[Redacted]** family plot.

Fuck. This is happening. Fuck. James is really, truly dead.

I think about all those nights the last couple of years when I'd hoped he'd call me, out of the blue. That he'd show up on my doorstep and start talking to me like no time had passed at all. Somehow, I guess, I had never given up hope.

Suddenly I'm thirteen again and I realize that I've only met his parents once, at James's bar mitzvah. They didn't know who I was back then. Didn't know that I would matter. And I'd only just met James in those first couple days of middle school, and even though I'd thought he was cute and hoped he would find me cute, too, I had no idea that he—or they—would matter. Now I know how important they are. Part of his story, too.

They're standing far apart, but I recognize them immediately. His mom, in a black cotton dress, gauzy and thin, down to her ankles, and a pair of big sunglasses. She's pretty, but tired. Kind of like a washed-up celebrity. His dad is in a black suit. Freshly shaved. Thinning hair slicked back. James hated his dad, *hated* him. And I did, too. Every time the cops dragged me down to the police station and I'd have to recount the whole damned story about my and James's entire romance, I felt my hatred harden a little bit more. Harper used to offer to egg their house, and it helped, in the moment, but not much. Because what they'd really been saying about me, all along, was that it was somehow my fault. When I was just as much a victim of James as the rest of them.

But now, looking at them, they almost don't look that bad. Middle-aged, like my parents, but more exhausted. Lines showing on their faces in this bright sunlight as they give grim smiles to their older relatives. It's hard not to feel bad for someone, I guess, at their kid's funeral.

At James's funeral.

Right now, Mr. **[Redacted]** is talking in a low voice to a boy who's standing in front of him. He claps the kid on the shoulder, gives his arm a squeeze. I recognize Elijah. James's youngest sibling. The baby of the family, everybody's favorite. You can see it now, in the way that Mr. [Redacted]'s eyes shine when he looks at him. It's that *love*—open and generous—that James probably always wanted, but never got.

Meanwhile, Annie's standing alone beside the headstone. She's wearing a black shift dress, which would be shapeless if it weren't for the shape of her body. Her pale brown hair is brushed neatly back and tied at the nape of her neck. She looks pretty standing there, like the world's saddest song. She's got a handful of rocks in her hand and she's stacking them up on the headstone in a little tower, until her mom goes over to her, puts a hand on her shoulder, and whispers something.

Annie's eyes go wide. Her nostrils flare, like she's super offended. But she tosses the rocks away and goes to stand by her mom.

A priest gets up there. A rabbi, too. I can hear my dad, cracking jokes in my head. They talk about James, and the priest says a prayer, and the rabbi sings something in Hebrew. Then the mom comes forward and starts talking about what James was like as a baby. She starts crying, so we all do. I didn't expect to cry, not on a day as pretty as today. I'm dabbing at my eyes, wishing I hadn't put on so much eyeliner. Thinking about James as a little baby, pink and new and clean, and all that hope that his mother must have felt about him. How he'd go to college someday, get married someday, have kids of his own. Not with me, probably. I never thought he was my one true love, like my dad was for my mom. But, like, someday I figured he'd have babies. With someone. My stomach feels like an open wound at the thought. I swallow, hard, tearing my eyes away from his mom.

That's when I look at Annie and realize that she's not crying at all.

She looks so, so pissed, like she might go charging off at any moment. Like she might break something. Someone. Her fist is curled beside her body, and I can see the muscles sticking out of her lean arm. But instead of punching or stomping or kicking, when her mom is finished, she gets up there and unrolls a wrinkled notebook page. She reads a poem in this soft little voice, like a bird's voice. I can only pick out a few words.

". . . cairn . . . and then he said . . . for the king."

Everyone's nodding along, like they understand it, but I don't. Still, I lean forward, straining to listen. It sounds like something out of Tolkien. Like, a beautiful fantasy. I think about the stories James told me they used to write together, and I wonder if it's something like that. Part of their shared mythology. I only ever got scraps and pieces from him. I'd always wanted to know more, but he barely told me anything. Holding it close to his heart.

It seems like Annie holds it close, too. She barely speaks loud enough for anyone to hear her. Someone coughs, and it's enough to swallow up the sound.

And that's it. Like Annie said, there's no body to bury. Other people go to the headstone and stack up rocks on it, too. Then they start to wander off toward their cars. But Annie's still standing there, her head hanging down, holding her wrinkled notebook page in one hand. I do the only thing I can think of. I go to her.

I think about putting my hand on her shoulder, but I don't think she wants me to touch her, so I don't. Still, I can't help but be curious about what she read to us. The fantasy, and the mystery of it.

"What's a cairn?" I ask gently.

She whips her head up. Her eyes—James's eyes—have a wild quality to them, like she's a feral creature. Maybe that's why, when she speaks, she doesn't answer my question.

"We're supposed to go back to my house to, like, eat sandwiches or bagels or something. But I can't yet. Will you go for a walk with me?"

God, what am I getting myself into? I can practically *see* James inside her. The soft part of him. The part that was fucked-up and hurting. A complicated, beautiful boy who had magic inside him, even if I barely got to see it for myself.

"Sure," I say.

FIVE

WE WIND OUR WAY DOWN through the headstones and footstones and monuments toward the old part of the cemetery where you can't even read the names. Sparrows are calling to each other and worms are turning over fresh dirt. It feels more like spring than almost-fall. But Annie's expression is hard. She just tucked the memory of her brother into the ground, even if there was no body to bury beside it.

I'm not sure what to say. My mother is good at moments like these, but I have a feeling that any comfort I can offer will sound hollow or fake.

So instead, I offer the only true comfort I can. I sing.

It's an old song, one we sang in Madrigals last year, "The Water Is Wide." My dad played the Pete Seeger version for me once, but I liked the one we sang in school better. It seemed more, I don't know, ancient. My voice is low and velvety and seems to echo even in the soft branches and green grass.

The water is wide, I cannot get o'er
Neither have I wings to fly
Give me a boat that can carry two
And both shall row, my love and I

A ship there is and she sails the sea
She's loaded deep as deep can be
But not so deep as the love I'm in
I know not if I sink or swim

I leaned my back against an oak
Thinking it was a trusty tree
But first it bent and then it broke
So did my love prove false to me

I reached my finger into some soft bush
Thinking the fairest flower to find
I pricked my finger to the bone
And left the fairest flower behind

Oh love be handsome and love be kind
Gay as a jewel when first it is new
But love grows old and waxes cold
And fades away like the morning dew

Must I go bound while you go free
Must I love a man who doesn't love me
Must I be born with so little art
As to love a man who'll break my heart

When cockle shells turn silver bells
Then will my love come back to me

When roses bloom in winter's gloom
Then will my love return to me

We're at the edge of the cemetery, where a bunch of scrubby brush rises into tangled wildness, as I finish the last verse. Annie doesn't say anything at first. That doesn't surprise me. She's always seemed so quiet at school. Shy, I guess. Even when I used to see her with her one weird friend at lunch, the two of them hardly spoke. Now she just sits down on a nearby footstone, her feet crossed beneath her, those familiar eyes of hers hard as marbles. And then she speaks, and I can't even be sure that she was listening to me sing at all.

"He's not dead. I'm not saying that because I'm delusional or in denial. I'm saying that because I know."

I blink. "But, when you invited me to the funeral, you said—"

"I know what I said, but I'm telling you now. He's not dead."

I don't know what to say to this. I have no idea whether it's the truth or not, whether it's some stage of grief I don't know about. How could I have any clue what she's going through? And honestly? I don't want to have this conversation. We *buried* James today, finally. I need to move on, too.

But even so, something makes me lean forward. "How do you know?" I ask her. "Are you in touch with him?"

Her eyebrows wrinkle. She picks up her hands and rubs her palms over her face, against the sockets of her eyes and then through her hair like the question is incredibly painful for her.

"It's hard to explain."

I lean forward even more and let my mouth smile, the smallest smile I can manage, like my mom would. "I'm here for you."

Annie looks at me. Her lips, which are wide and full and just a little bit chapped, pucker for a second. Then she draws in a breath, nostrils flaring.

"Fine. But you can't laugh."

"I won't," I tell her. "I'm listening."

"Okay," she says, and then she says it again. "Okay, fine. You know about the—the stories we used to tell?"

She's kind of shaky when she asks it, and her cheeks are pink, like she's embarrassed. Or maybe scared. And I remember James's face when he first spoke to me of them. *Hey*, he'd said, his voice a little husky with excitement. *You like fantasy books? Me too.*

It hadn't come out all at once. If it had, he probably would have scared me off, the same way other people got weird when I told them that I could recite poems in Elvish or that I know everything there is to know about Brian Wilson. But bit by bit, I'd learned tiny scraps of information about James's kingdom in the woods. The one he'd spent his childhood building. The one with the Island of Feral Children, all dressed in furs and speaking in animal tongues. The one with the mermaids' cove. The one with the king they talked about killing—a story I always figured was secretly about their dad.

"Gumlea," I say. And Annie winces when I say it.

"What?" I ask. She's still cringing, her eyes half closed, as she shakes her head.

"It's just . . . weird to hear you talk about it. He wasn't supposed to tell you about it. I'm not supposed to tell you about it, even now."

"Sorry," I tell her softly. "I didn't mean to upset you. If it helps any, I've never told anyone about it. Not even Harper Walton, and we've been best friends forever."

Slowly, she opens her eyes and lets out a long, low sigh. "That—that docs help. A little. Yeah."

We're quiet for a moment, the two of us. I'm not sure what to say next, so impulsively, I reach out my hand and put it over hers. Her skin is warm and dry. "Go ahead," I tell her. "Tell me about Gumlea."

She's looking down at my hands. Really staring at them. When she speaks again, she doesn't move her eyes at all. Just keeps them down there, still, on both of our hands.

"I don't know how to explain it," she says in a low voice. "It was real to us, in a way. Not just make-believe."

That's not what James told me. Stories, he said. He always called them stories. I always figured it had been kind of like having an imaginary friend, only it had been an imaginary *place* instead. But I don't want to scare her off. I keep my hand where it is and give her fingers a little squeeze. "Okay," I tell her.

She exhales, hard. "He's—he's there. He's in Gumlea, right now. There's a sort of wall, or more like a curtain, between this world and that one. It's called the Veil, and he's stuck on the other side of it. There's a ritual I can do. To pierce—pierce the Veil. Pull him out of Gumlea. But I can't . . . I couldn't figure it out. So he's stuck. He's not coming home. And it's my fault."

God. Jesus. She's got to be kidding. And at the same time, I know she isn't.

She pulls her hand away from mine and cradles her face in both hands again. "Augh," she says, a little too loudly. Then she pulls her hands down, sniffling. And laughs at herself. "It sounds insane. I know that." And she looks right at me then, and there's an accusation in her eyes.

"I mean," I begin slowly, and pause. I don't want to make her any more upset, but I also don't want to lie. "It's kind of hard to swallow."

She doesn't fight me on that. James said she was always spoiling for a fight with him, but right now, it seems like all the energy has drained out of her. In fact, she laughs again, a little wildly. I find myself laughing a tiny bit, too.

"Yeah," she agrees, and quickly looks down at her feet. She's so tense, she's pulled up a bunch of grass in her fists. She's scattering the blades down on her bare legs, green against pale white. "It sounds crazy. That's why I don't tell anyone. Not even my shrink." Then she lets a smile curl her mouth and adds, "Especially not my shrink."

I don't know what to say to that. We're quiet for a long minute. In the distance, I see the black limousines pulling away, Annie's friends and family tucked inside them. I guess she's walking home today. It's probably time for me to leave, too. Dad's waiting for my call. And I should get away from here—from this bizarre story and this even more bizarre girl. But before I can do anything, Annie wrinkles her nose, looks up.

"I could show you Gumlea," she says. "It would be a lot easier than just talking about it. You'd believe me, if you could see it."

"I . . . What?"

"I've never showed anyone else," she tells me quickly. "I wanted to show Miranda, but Jamie wouldn't let me. But—I think he'd be okay with you seeing it. You said you haven't told anyone, right?"

I already told her I didn't, but she seems desperate to hear it again. Slowly, I nod.

This conversation is *bananas*. I know it is, and Annie's got to know it is, too. It's so weird that my brain can't even quite catch up to what's happening. I think if it did, it would tell me to stay away from Annie **[Redacted]** and her crazy family and her even crazier ideas.

But.

I study her face. Pug nose. Freckles. Brown eyes, veined gold. Eyelashes thick and dark even in the golden sunlight. I want to believe her.

Hell, I want to go with her, and not just because she reminds me of James. There's something about her that's magnetic, like a queen or a rock star. Wild and otherworldly. Vulnerable, and, yeah, pretty, too.

"Okay," I tell her, holding my chin high and sure. "Gumlea. Sure. This week?"

"After school," she says. "Not Monday. I have therapy. It'll have to be Tuesday or Wednesday or Friday. Mom's in class late those days. You could come over—"

"Tuesday is Madrigals," I remind her. I can't quite believe that I'm saying it. But I am. "We could take the late bus to your place. I mean, if that works for you."

Annie stands up. She brushes the grass off her legs. In that moment, she looks happy. Her grin is crooked, like a little kid's, and I see that dimple again on her left cheek. Something inside me tugs and twists. A part of me that has been fast asleep since Keira. Or maybe since James.

"Sure," she says. "Okay."

"It's a date," I agree. And I don't mean it like that, except maybe I do.

SIX

ANNIE RAISES QUESTIONS I DON'T know how to answer. Questions about her sanity—and mine. Wardrobe questions, too, apparently. On Tuesday, summer's finally left us, and the weather's gone cool again, even though the leaves are still mostly green with only the slightest brown tinge. In the morning, I stand in my closet, stumped. What do you wear, anyway, before you go to a magical kingdom? With your dead ex-boyfriend's sister? Who swears he isn't dead at all, but trapped in said magical kingdom?

In the closet, my hand lingers on my ren fest dress, which I haven't worn in a couple of years. It's not like I could ever wear it at school, anyway. Our Madrigal robes are bad enough. So I pull on some dark skinny jeans and a boxy T-shirt and the hiking boots Mom got me last year before rock camp that I never really wore, because no one hikes at rock camp, but she didn't know that.

During lunch, and then later at Madrigals, I mostly act like everything is normal. I catch Annie staring at me a few times, but don't stare back.

When Mrs. Kepler lets us go and I head down the risers to meet Annie, Harper gives me a pointed look. "Do you want a ride?" she asks me, and there's another question there. She wants to ask me what I'm doing hanging around James **[Redacted]**'s little sister. Again. But I don't know what to tell her. Hell, I don't really know what I'm doing hanging around Annie **[Redacted]**.

"No, I have plans," I say to Harper, full of breeze and springtime and sparkles, so happy and definitive that Harper closes her gabby mouth fast, but there's still a question in her eyes and I know that my phone will be full of texts before I even get to the bus:

Harper: Vee, what's up????
Harper: You can tell me. I won't tell anyone! Is
this about James? You went to his funeral this
weekend, right? Did something happen??
Harper: Veeeeeeeeeeeeeeeeeeeeeeeeee
eeeeeeeeeeeeee!!!!!!!!!!!!!!!

Sure enough, in my backpack, my phone buzzes and buzzes. I ignore it. If Annie hears it, she ignores it, too. She walks like an old-school cartoon of a schoolgirl, her books over her chest, shyly pushing her hair behind her ear. We walk up the stairs of the bus together. She's silent as we take a seat. For a minute, I kind of regret doing this. I have no idea what to say to her. We have nothing in common except James, and he's gone, even if she says he isn't.

I glance over. She's staring out the window as the bus pulls out of the empty parking lot. And then, without looking back at me, she starts talking.

"Do you ever get bored, and look at things, and imagine them some other, more interesting way?"

"Like daydreaming? I guess. Doesn't everyone?"

"I don't know. I'm not everyone. It feels like, if it's something that everyone else does, it's different than the way I do it. Like they're thinking about, I don't know, school dances and homework and who said what to who and who is fucking everyone else and I never think about any of that."

I'm smiling at her. She's just said more than I've heard her say *ever*. I remember James once texted me to complain about his sister.

She just won't stop talking about all this Gumlea stuff. It's mortifying.

Wait, I'd said, *are we talking about the same Annie? I've met her. She barely talks.*

That's because you don't KNOW her, he said. *Believe me. Once she's got something in her head, she'll never shut up about it.*

I'm looking at her now, and almost grinning because I can see it. The blabbermouth little kid who always got on James's nerves.

And you know what? She's not wrong about how it works for most people. Most of the time I *do* think about school dances and homework and who is fucking everyone else.

"What do you think about?" I ask her.

"Ways my life could be more interesting. Like, look. Do you see those woods on the highway?"

I see them streaming by the window, green and brown and overgrown and a little soggy, clinging to the guard rail and in some places overtaking it. There's garbage and there's mud and muck and maybe a bird or two.

"Yeah," I say.

Annie lets out a short, joyless laugh. "I used to always wonder, why do we have these spaces in between shopping malls and behind schools and in between subdivisions that no one even notices? They're like null spaces. But they're real places. Woods and meadows. Once, the whole world would have looked like that. When we were cave people or something. But now we pretend that we're not animals anymore. That woods and nature are just spaces between our houses and roads and stuff, not the other way around."

"Well, we're not animals," I say. "We wear clothes, have jobs . . ."

"It just seems wrong to me," she says quickly, like what I said doesn't matter. "So Jamie and I came up with a better way. We decided that there would be people, called the Winter Watchers, who live in the woods. They have animals—familiars. They ride the backs of silver-furred ten-point deer and stuff. His was a hare. You know, a rabbit? And the Winter Watchers, they record what it's like to live, I don't know, in the margins of our world. They're observers. Mostly you see them in the forest, but sometimes, if you're at the library and there's a pretty girl with a pencil behind her ear who keeps doodling in her notebook, she's probably one of them."

I stare at her. Pretty girl. And it's absurd, but my stomach feels good and warm at the thought that Annie might find a girl pretty. Might find *me* pretty. That we might have something in common—that we see the prettiness of girls. That we might be able to bridge a gap, and not just a gap between worlds, like she claims. But a smaller one. More human, but more important, too.

James's. Sister, I remind myself. And I stuff those thoughts down.

"So Gumlea," I begin, very carefully. Annie still winces when I say the name of her magical kingdom. "It's a story you guys dreamed up when you were bored, kind of."

"It's a story we dream all the time," she says. "I look out the window, and I can see the Winter Watchers there, looking back at me. I go for a walk and I hear Feral Children playing on the playground. It's not like I think it's real.

Rationally, I know it's not. I know that ordinary people don't see airplanes fly over them and look up and tell themselves, well, that's just about the same length as a dragon. But I do. And honestly? I can't even imagine what it's like not to have that. It seems so boring."

I study her face again. What I don't tell Annie is that I know what she means. I don't tell myself stories, but when I stare out the window during Advanced Chemistry, I hear music. Surf music, sometimes, mostly. My own and other people's. I doodle notes in my notebook margins. When I walk down the road to get the mail for my dad, it's usually in 3/4 time. Once, when I was a kid, my daydreams were Lothlórien all the time, but since eighth grade, it's mostly been the Beach Boys. Now, I listen to Annie talk about Gumlea, and I imagine a life without song, and she's right. I almost can't imagine it at all.

But I don't tell Annie that. Instead, I give her a wry smile and say: "Am I boring to you?"

She laughs a little. "No, you're fine," she says. "You like Tolkien and play the ukulele and aren't named, like, Olivia. You're different. Interesting. Even if you don't know the Laws of Gumlea."

Different. Interesting. I know that she really means geeky, but for some reason, in that moment, I don't mind. I stretch out my legs in front of me and smile down toward the toes of my purple Chucks. I'll take it. Compliment's a compliment. Even from Annie.

Maybe especially from Annie.

Beside me, she sighs. "I know I should have given this all up a long time ago. Jamie thought so, starting when he was, like, eleven. He thought it was embarrassing."

"If it makes you happy, who cares?" It's something my mother would say. A small kindness.

Annie laughs again. "You sound like my shrink," she says, but she isn't mad about it.

Soon, the bus lets us off in front of her house.

The [**Redacted**] home is a two-story white colonial with green shutters. There are bushes, neatly trimmed, all the way up the walk. I'm not sure what I was expecting. In the back of my mind, I think I always assumed James lived in a rotting old Victorian covered with vines. But their house looks pretty ordinary. Annie turns over a fake rock under one of the front windows and fishes out a key.

"You said your mom has classes?" I ask as she lets us inside.

"Yeah, she's studying to be a school psychologist," she says, throwing her bag down in a front entryway that's littered with mail and shoes and winter coats that probably haven't been worn in a long time. "She says it's because my therapist has made such a difference with me, but I really think it's because of Jamie."

"How do you mean?" I ask carefully. I want to hear about James but I also don't want to hear about James. There's a part of me that would love to forget that he's the thread that's tying us together, Annie and me. But I can't forget, and she can't, either. We have that in common, too.

"She thinks she can stop it from happening to other kids. Because he was, you know, 'troubled.'" She moves her fingers in air quotes.

I peer at the photos on the wall by the front entryway. James is in them, younger than when I knew him, grinning and sunburned on vacations, sitting next to his sister's car seat, wearing an ugly blazer in a school photo, his dark hair slicked down.

"Does your family talk about him often?" I ask.

Annie snorts. "No, never. Well, that's not true. Dad talks to people at church about him, and Mom talks about him with her internet friends, but we never talk about him together. I mean, they don't talk much together at all since Dad moved out. But we don't even mention anything that might remind them of him. Running, or synagogue, or whatever."

"The funeral must have been weird. I mean, it was weird for me. But it must have been super weird for you."

"Yeah," Annie agrees grimly. She's standing next to the interior door, her head cast to one side and hair trailing down her shoulder. She looks pretty, young, sad. I want to tell her that I've been there, thinking of James in an endless, useless way but totally unable to speak his name to anyone. The other girls didn't get it. Not even Harper. The only person I was even remotely friendly with who really knew James really was Neal Harriman, and he transferred to private school last year.

But before I can tell her that, she turns away. "Want a snack?" she asks.

I tell her, "Sure."

As we walk through her house, Annie turns every single light on, until everything is sickly yellow inside. We stand in the kitchen, our weight against the counters, eating string cheese and glasses of iced tea made from a powdered mix. I have a weird feeling, like we're little kids on a playdate or something, and our parents might come in at any second and tell us to be sure to share nicely. But we're alone in Annie's house. There are no grown-ups here.

She wads up the plastic wrapper from her cheese in her palm and tosses it in the trash can. Then she grins at me. "Are you ready?"

I'm not sure what to expect. Magic. Or nothing. Or everything. James, returned from the dead. A forest full of ghosts. Nervously, I nod.

Annie leads me out the back door.

"This is it," she says as we stand on the edge of a creek that is hardly even a creek. It's totally dried up in spots, just a muddy bog.

But on the other side is their magical kingdom. The epic, fantastical land of Gumlea. I remember how James used to blush at the babyish name, and I can imagine him blushing now. It's not much to look at. There's some kind of plastic ride-on toy stuck in the mud a few feet away. The woods ahead are tangled with underbrush and litter. It's nothing more than a narrow strip of land. You can even make out the traffic from Route 32 on the other side through the tree line. I see poison ivy, broken bottles, crows. But no knights or princesses or whatever.

The house is like four car lengths behind us. I glance over my shoulder.

"And your parents don't care if we go out there, even after what happened?"

"Mom doesn't care what I do. Dad would probably kill me, but he doesn't have to know, right?"

Before I can answer, she launches herself over the creek in one swift movement, landing with her sneakers heavy and thick in the mud. Then she does something strange. She stands straight, squaring her shoulders, and takes one step backward. Then she turns around.

"Your turn," she says, and her whole face lights up. Her eyeteeth stick out a little when she smiles, I realize. It's different from James's smile, which was all straight and perfect after years of braces.

Plus there's that dimple. *God*.

I bumble over the creek, my steps uncertain. When I make it to the other side, Annie elbows me.

"Step backward," she says. "That's how you enter Gumlea."

I hesitate. "This feels . . ."

"Ridiculous, I know. But come on, you must have had tea parties as a kid. Played house, whatever. You get up there and sing in medieval robes in front of the whole school and no one cares. Who's watching you? Just me, and I'm crazy. I won't judge."

She's looking at me with James's eyes, and a smile all her own. More flip-flops. More hope sparking in my brain. Maybe we could share something. So I draw in a deep breath, hold it for a moment, and exhale.

Then I step backward, too.

SEVEN

I'M NO IDIOT. I'M NEARLY seventeen years old. I never believed in Santa Claus or the tooth fairy. My mother always said she didn't want me to be surprised when I got older, like she was, so she started teaching me about the birds and the bees out of old anatomy textbooks back in elementary school. I never believed in the stork, and I knew that Bloody Mary wasn't going to appear in our elementary school bathroom no matter how many times Harper said her name. But still, when I step back into Gumlea, I find myself hoping that something will happen. Lightning will split the sky. A beam of light will lift me off the ground. I'll see a doorway open in the line of trees and find myself barreling toward it, pushed by the wind and the farts of unicorns. It's a crazy, stupid hope, and yet I can't help but cling to it. Funny thing is, I had no idea I was unhappy *here* until *there* fails to materialize.

Because when I step backward, I'm still in the woods, my clean new hiking boots sinking into the mud.

Annie's grinning at me, a toothy, wild grin, even though we haven't really entered a magical kingdom. Even though we're nothing more than a couple of ridiculous kids playing make-believe in the scrubby woods behind her house. Even though we're too old for make-believe, for any of it. It doesn't seem to bother her at all. She waves me forward.

"Come on," she says. "Let's go."

There's nothing else to do but shrug and follow her. The woods smell like dirt and moss. We tromp a rhythm over the broken glass that's shattered like diamonds and buried in the mud. Annie talks to me in a low, excited voice as we walk. It's like she's waited her whole life to have someone to tell this stuff. And I know that feeling. There's been so much I haven't shared with anybody, not since James disappeared. Music and stories. Absurd dreams. Brian Wilson.

"Do you come out here much?" I ask, looking around at the garbage—at the rotting boards someone's nailed to a maple tree. She touches them, frowning.

"Not often enough, I guess. I should fix that. That's the fortress of the Emperata Annit. Or at least it used to be. Oh, hey, look! This is the Castle of the Solitary King!"

The "castle" is a massive tree, half-rotted through, carved with the initials of what I'm assuming were a million boys long since grown: CH, NH, GR, JK, AK. We're walking deeper and deeper into the gray tangle of underbrush. I can tell we're not the only ones who have made this trip. Beneath my feet, I can see the tracks of mountain bikes and big-footed dogs. Annie tells me they're wolf tracks, signs of a Winter Watcher.

We walk past a picnic table that's all bent and caked with spray paint. Annie tells me that this is a pirate ship. She rambles something about feeding the ship mermaid flesh, waving her hands wildly through the air. The thing is, I'm sure she used to share these stories with James. They must have meant something to both of them. I know that's why she's telling me now. I'm connected to him, maybe more than anyone else. I knew him, kissed him. I remember what it was like to whisper low words into his ear. But James and I hardly ever talked about any of this. We talked about thick doorstop fantasy novels, the ones I stole off my dad's bookshelves and traded with him. We talked about God—my lack of belief, his massive question mark. We talked about the next time we could get each other alone. The handful of times he told me anything about Gumlea, he blushed, embarrassed. Or else expressed annoyance at his weird, obsessive little sister who wouldn't let her fantasies go. We were in middle school, after all. Too old to have an imagination.

Annie doesn't blush anymore. When I first mentioned Gumlea to her, it was like I was slinging arrows into her private heart. But now that I've uncorked her, Annie has no shame. She's decided to share Gumlea with me—so I guess that means she's going to share every rock, every stone, every single myth. James let it all go, but it's clear, even though it's been a while since she's been out here in these woods, that Annie never has.

I don't notice we're walking uphill until Annie's words catch in her throat for a second and then she gets quiet, all at once. I'm breathing harder, too, and as our shoes grip the surface of the hard rock, carved into a mountain face by polar ice thousands of years ago, the sound of our progress is almost like a chorus. This is better, I tell myself, the silence. She's no longer saying anything weird, anything scary. I'm relieved. Honestly, part of me feels like I've just slipped into the woods with a madwoman. Even while another part of me is undeniably crushing on her.

She parts a thick wall of brush with her hand. Turning back, she grins at me. "You'll like this," she says. "Winter Watcher's mountain."

I follow her through the door of gold-tipped leaves, and suck in a breath. We've reached some sort of rocky outcropping where the rock face falls away into nothing. The wind whips, cool and biting, all around us, but the sun is warm and perfect. Annie sits on the rock, squinting into the distance. You can see everything here, our whole world. There's the high school, hollow school buses lined up outside. There's Kirky's Deli, the supermarket, the bank, the library, the massive river that curls through downtown, a chain of garden apartments. There's the Thruway in the distance, the cars shivering down it. I perch beside Annie.

"It's beautiful," I say, because it is. Funny to see it like this. It looks almost like a scale model of our lives instead of the real deal. Truth is, I spend a lot of my time looking ahead. College, semesters abroad, maybe internships in New York City. Bands I might join, like the one my dad joined. Boys and girls I might kiss when I finally get out of this boring town. I spend a lot of time fantasizing about the music I'll write and the adventures I'll have. I spend a lot of time fantasizing about just getting . . . away. But here's my whole life, sunlit and perfect, and for a second, I can almost remember what it felt like to be a little kid and be happy with it. I glance at Annie.

She's not happy anymore, though. In fact, her expression is sour again. There's heat in her voice. "I hate it. All of it. Every fucking apple on every fucking tree. School and our parents and fucking Nina. I'm trapped here, though, until Jamie comes back."

I have no idea who Nina is. Does she mean Nina Westervelt? But before I can ask, something darkens behind her eyes. "I was so pissed when Jamie didn't want to come out here anymore. It's the only good thing about our whole world, and he shit on it. Even before he disappeared. First with sports, and Neal. Then there was the pot. And you."

She looks directly at me. My hands are cold. On the one hand, what she's saying is ridiculous. *The* pot, like she's some grandpa who's not quite down with the ways of *kids these days*. I want to defend myself, tell her it wasn't like that. We were innocent, James and me, only kids. But that wasn't true, was it? I remember the afternoons in Neal's basement, Neal gone God knows where. I remember the pipe smoldering on the coffee table, and the weight of James's body on mine. It felt like we spent a lifetime in that basement. Talking about books and poetry and music. Any time away from it, in the real world, was time we were starved to get back. Part of it was just lust, adolescent and basic. But I think there was a sort of communion in the time we spent together. Something sacred, silent and beautiful.

I see you, he used to say to me. *You're not like anyone else.*

That's not true, I'd tell him quickly. *I'm just like you.*

I wanted it to be true. I wanted to be made out of magic, like James was made out of magic. Like we were a pair of ancient elves, married to one another, and not just a couple of middle school kids. But really, I know— I've always known—that it's not true. I'm not magic. I'm just an ordinary girl. I was nothing like James, not really. And looking at Annie, I know that I'm nothing like *her*, either.

It hurts to look at her. Hurts to think it. So instead, I look over to the town. Sunlight is coming in through the clouds in slanted rays like a picture from some kind of Jesus calendar. That's when I realize something. I stand, shading my eyes with my hand, and look back the way we came.

"It doesn't make sense," I say.

"What, you stealing my brother?" Annie asks.

I shake my head. "No, not that. This place. We could see the road from your yard. There's no room for a mountain here."

I hear Annie let out a small laugh behind me.

"Gumlean geography," she says. "It works differently than your Earth geography."

"That's nuts. That doesn't . . ."

I let my words fade. Because honestly? I want to believe this mountain is real. So I glance back at Annie. She's still sitting on the rock, watching me, dressed in blue jeans and a too-big men's T-shirt that shows her pale collarbones and a little too much of her bony chest. Her bare lips are pursed. She's angry at me, still, for taking her brother away—even though I never meant to take anything from anyone. But she's half something else, too. Amused. Laughing at me in her own silent way, golden sunlight illuminating her black eyelashes. Her legs are all akimbo on the rock. Her fingers are slightly curled into a bed of moss.

An image flashes through my head. It's fantastic, absurd as her stories. In my mind's eye, I see myself going to her. I'd sit beside her and brush the hair back from her shoulder and out of her face so I could see her better. Then I'd kiss her. I'd touch her throat, her small breasts, wrap my legs around her waist, feel the whole world tilt around me.

Damn. I shouldn't be thinking this way. Annie is watching me still, and her anger's fading, but now she's just confused. I'm staring too much, and for too long.

"I miss your brother," I tell her, because that's the only explanation for it, isn't it? I was always drawn to James. My body was an instrument, tuned to his. They're similar, almost like twins. I'm lying to myself, and I know it, but I choose to believe it anyway.

Annie looks down at her dirty fingernails. "I do, too. I've tried to bring him back. I've had dreams about it. The Nameless Boy—that's Jamie in our stories—he killed the pirate already. He should have come home. I think he's waiting for me to do something. Work a spell or find his knife or just open the damned door. The ritual. We have to do it, both of us. But I can't. I've failed him." Her voice cracks then, and finally she adds, "He's never coming back, and it's all because of me."

"You know it's not your fault, right?" I ask her, ignoring her fantasy talk.

She rubs her forehead with the tips of her fingers. "Yeah. Rationally, I know that. But sometimes it still feels like it is."

The wind whips up around us. Her hair is a brown cloud around her face. She lets out a sniffle, but it's lost in the chorus of air, distant traffic, and stirring leaves. When it dies down again, she wipes her eyes on the back of her hand. She's still sniffling, but less now. I go and sit beside her.

"You know, I haven't been able to listen to the Beach Boys since he left."

"The Beach Boys?"

"We were supposed to have a date that Friday. He was going to come over, and I was going to play my dad's Beach Boys bootlegs."

"Like . . . 'Surfin' U.S.A.'?" she asks, a wry smile brightening her crooked mouth.

"Not all of their stuff is like that. Some of it's amazing. James thought it was silly, too. I wanted to show him that it wasn't. Sometimes, I feel like I'm still waiting for that Friday to come. I wanted to share something with him. I thought, out of anyone, James would understand."

Annie tucks her hair behind her ears. "You could play it for me," she says.

"What?"

"Jamie and I are practically the same person. I know it doesn't look like it. But if he's out there somewhere, and I think he is, then you could play it for me. Somehow, he'll hear it."

"That sounds like more of your stories. Fairy magic. Kids' stuff."

She shrugs. "Maybe. But I know you wanted to show him. So why not try? Everyone goes around acting like there isn't any magic. What if there is? Isn't it better to believe me than to believe *that*?"

There is no magic in the world. That's what I've always told myself. What I've always believed. For a few minutes in middle school, when I loved Tolkien and James, I hoped I might be wrong. But that dried up when he disappeared. Now I pretend I'm an ordinary girl and pretend that makes me happy. But it never does.

"Okay," I say softly.

Annie's smile gets a little wider. Then she stands, fishes her phone from her pocket, and looks down at it. "We should head back. My mom will be home soon."

"Okay," I agree, because I don't want to see Annie's mom at all. I take one last look down at the town below, the people like tiny plastic figurines, the cars like die-cast toys, the shape of the mountain impossible. This mountain shouldn't be here. I shouldn't, either. But we both are. Together.

I turn and follow her down the path, my heart beating gently in my throat.

We giggle together when we step away from Gumlea like a pair of kids who have had too much candy to eat. Maybe it's the sun fading through the trees and maybe it's the prospect of listening to Brian Wilson with her, but I feel good and peaceful now. So, the girl's got an overactive imagination. Maybe I would, too, if I'd gone through what she has, brother gone and parents divorcing and all that.

I text my mom, and Annie and I sit on the front steps together to wait. We don't talk about Gumlea anymore. We talk about Madrigals. I tell her all about the trips we'll be taking this year, how people always smuggle booze in their bags and then hide it in the tanks of the motel toilets. "My parents would freak if they knew. I'm allowed to have a glass of wine here and there at home, but I'm not supposed to do it out of the house," I tell her. Then I catch her expression out of the corner of my eye. Not disapproving, but shocked, like she's seeing some other side of me. I sigh, remembering what she said about her brother smoking, and add, "I don't even like to drink that much. I mixed vodka and wine last year and couldn't stop puking."

"Oh," she says, like she's relieved, and it's kinda adorable. "I've only ever had wine at Passover."

My mom rolls up then in our SUV, which looks black in the waning sunlight. I stand, clutching at my backpack straps.

Annie squints up at me.

"So you'll come over this weekend?" I say, adding quickly, "To listen to records," in case she's forgotten.

"It would have to be Saturday morning, earlyish. I go to my dad's Saturday nights into Sundays and he's weird about losing his time."

"Oh, okay. Um, ten?" That's going to be a stretch for me. Usually, I'm hardly out of bed at ten on Saturdays. But I guess Annie's a morning person. Seems like she would be. Up with the dawn or something.

"Sure, sounds good."

My mom lightly beeps the horn. I cock my thumb that way.

Annie just laughs. "See you," she says.

I rush down her front walk, hop into the car, and close the door behind me. My mom is giving me a significant look, but I ignore it until we're at the end of the road.

"New friend?" she finally asks pointedly.

I can't wait until I get my full license so I don't have to get the third degree every time I go somewhere. "Yeah," I say. "Her name is Annie. She's a sophomore."

I'm hoping my mom doesn't remember that James **[Redacted]** had a little sister. It would just be too weird to explain now. Luckily, she only nods. "A sophomore," she says as she signals around the corner. Her tone is curious, probing, nosy. I shrink down in my seat, waiting for it. "Is she a friend-friend or a girlfriend?"

There it is. I hold my hands over my face. Sometimes I think it would be easier if I'd just stayed in the closet. "Mom!"

But my mom is great about these things. She always is. I should be grateful, really, that she wants to talk about them, that she wants to know about my life and that she never, ever judges me for it.

"Sorry! I just can't help but wonder—"

"She's a friend, okay? Just a friend."

"Okay," my mom says, but something about her smile is twisted at the corners, like she knows something I don't. She says again, "Okay."

I hate that smile. I hate the feeling that's tossing my stomach right now, a perfect mix of excitement and embarrassment. I hate the fact that my mother always knows me way better than I know myself.

EIGHT

IF MY MOM DIDN'T SUSPECT anything before, then she definitely does now, Saturday morning, when my alarm goes off at eight a.m. I take a long shower, combing out my hair and braiding it down my back. Then I go into my room and stand there, in only a towel, trying to figure out what to wear. Again. Years ago, with James, it would have been easy. I was all about dresses then, heavy swoopy makeup caked on. But I've changed. I'm not the same person anymore. And Annie isn't James, anyway. She's always dressed like she's hardly put any thought into it. She's not a total slob, but her shirts and jeans and sneakers seem just slightly out of style, like her mom grabbed whatever was on sale at Target because Annie was going to wear it no matter what.

I've managed to put on underwear, and nothing else, when my mom walks by my open bedroom door.

"Your friend is coming over, isn't she?" she asks, like we didn't talk about it at dinner last night. "What was her name? Hannah?"

"Annie," I say smoothly, like I don't care that she's asking.

Mom leans against the doorjamb, looking at me. "What are you guys going to do?"

"Listen to records. Daddy said we could hang out in his office."

"How retro," Mom says, grinning at me. She's teasing. She didn't even listen to records as a teenager. It was all cassette tapes for her, until my dad showed her the rich, pure sound of vinyl. Dad's ridiculous about that stuff, but he's not wrong, either.

"You know me. I'm totally eighties fabulous," I say.

"Bodacious," my mom says. She comes over and pushes a strand of damp hair behind my ear. "I think you should wear something comfortable."

"Because I'm gorgeous no matter what I'm wearing?"

"Well, that," Mom says, nodding slowly. "But also, if you're hanging out listening to records, I think it's best to project an air of effortless beauty. Casual confidence. Unpretentious ease."

I can't help it. I giggle a little bit at that. Mom throws her arms around my shoulders and smushes my face in a kiss. Then she leaves me to it.

I put on a camisole top in deep purple, and a pair of stripy pajama pants. Nice ones, though. Then I head downstairs for breakfast, ready to face the day.

Ready to face her.

I climb the steps to Dad's attic office, Annie trailing next to me. She's staring at the album covers framed on the hallway walls, pausing at each one just a little too long. I want to get her into his office before Mom starts asking us questions, but Annie's in no hurry. She points to one of the many George Harrison albums, one where he looks a little bit like a serial killer, long hair and a beard.

"Your dad must really have the hots for this guy," she says, chuckling to herself at her joke. But it's practically not a joke.

"Yeah, that's his favorite Beatle. He was going through this whole

George Harrison Hare Krishna thing when he met my mom. That must have been disappointing."

"What do you mean?"

I slump my weight against the wall, smothering a few David Bowies behind me in the process. "He probably thought she'd help him find enlightenment. You know, he started yoga, picked up the sitar, started dating a Desi woman. But Mom's an accountant."

"They get along, though, right?"

Annie's tone is worried. I remember that her parents don't get along. From what James used to tell me, they never really did, except in a highly fucked-up, dysfunctional way. I want to reassure her. I smile weakly.

"Yeah, they do. It works for some reason. Maybe because Dad gave up the whole cultural appropriation nirvana thing and went back to being an atheist. They've been crazy about each other since the day they met."

"Good," Annie says. She hustles up the stairs past me, her shoulder brushing my chest. As she passes, I hear her say, "I'm glad they get along. My parents hate each other's guts."

I don't know what to say to that. I follow her up the stairs.

My father's record collection takes up an entire floor-to-ceiling wall of Ikea storage. When I was a kid, he kept it all in our living room. But Mom eventually got annoyed with it. She said that the records were sucking in all the psychic energy of our house. She's kind of superstitious about that sort of thing in a way that Dad never is, so we disassembled the Expedit and spent a weekend putting it back together and hefting hundreds of records up the stairs and realphabetizing them. Sometimes I miss it, the way my parents used to put on Duke Ellington and dance together after dinner. But usually these days Mom will ask me to play some piano for them to dance to instead, so I really don't mind. It's the dancing that matters. Not the soundtrack.

"Wow," Annie says, running her fingertip along a row of albums, "your dad really loves music."

Her gaze sweeps the finished attic space. There are guitars hanging from the walls, a keyboard in one corner. The sofa bed has framed sheet music hanging over it. All my dad's favorite songs. I think I know how Annie is feeling. When I was a kid, I felt the same way up here. Kind of in quiet awe. It's almost like a holy space. My dad's church.

"He should. He's a professor of music history. He's teaching at State today, actually. History of Rock and Roll, his favorite."

"I'll bet," Annie says. Then she looks over her shoulder at me. She's smirking, but it's more out of embarrassment than anything else. "Is it weird if I admit that music doesn't do much for me? I only started taking chorus because I wanted to do something without Jamie."

My eyes widen. The truth is, I can't imagine it, not being moved by music. It's the fabric of my life, from my earliest memories to my most distant future. It's a language I've been speaking since I was a baby, and I wonder how muted the world would sound without it.

"Only a little," I lie.

She winces. "Sorry. It's nothing personal. I see it means the world to you."

"Yeah," I say softly. I don't know why I feel so shy about it. Mom is always telling me that there's no shame in loving something. But things are *different* in high school for me than they were for her. I know that to the other kids only certain types of love are acceptable. It's much easier to be cool, calm, unaffected. Easier not to care about anything, even the super-important stuff. That's why I took down my Tolkien pictures, why I mostly keep my love of ancient rock stars a secret from everybody but Harper.

Maybe that's why I've been trying to forget how much James meant to me. Because he did, didn't he? No matter what I say to my friends at the lunch table. I loved him once. A lot. I mean, and crap, my hands are shaking as I pull the bootleg Beach Boys record out of Dad's shelving unit. I waited so long to share this with him, and never got to. Now I'll share it with his sister, who doesn't even care. It's not the same, but it's all I've got.

Annie sits down on the sofa, watching as I open up the record player, lift the arm, and set the record down. But Annie's not really listening as the record pops and fizzles and then starts up. She's squinting at me, a question in her eyes.

"What?" I ask.

"How did you and Jamie meet, anyway?"

My stomach drops. I turn away from the record, where the Beach Boys are starting and stopping "God Only Knows" over and over again.

"What?" I say again, even though I heard her fine the first time. I didn't expect her to ask me this. I don't know why, but I didn't expect to ever have to answer this question.

"Where did you guys meet?" Then she adds, "I always thought it was weird, because he was kind of with someone when you guys got together. Nina Westervelt. And that didn't seem like him. To like two girls at once."

No, I guess it wouldn't have. James was a little bit of a rebel, but he'd always had a noble heart. I take a breath.

"At GSA," I tell her. I don't have to tell her what that acronym means. Everyone in our middle school knew about GSA. There were posters on the walls, announcements at morning meeting. Part of the principal's anti-bullying measures. Gay-Straight Alliance. Except straight kids never really joined. The Queer Kids Club was what we called ourselves. We met in Mr. McKavity's office. Talked about our parents and whether or not they

231

accepted us. Talked about marching in the pride parade in Elting, even though we never did. That kind of thing.

". . . Oh." Annie says. She's staring at me, and I'm nervous as hell. One of the Beach Boys coughs, and Annie starts talking, but I do, too, at the exact same time.

"He was questioning a lot of things back then, you know?" I say. "Religion and sexuality—"

I guess it was the wrong thing to say, because Annie says firmly, "Jamie isn't gay."

Oh, fuck. I didn't mean to out him to her. It doesn't feel right, even now. It's *his* business, or it was. Not hers. But then, he's dead now, and maybe it would help her to hear it.

"Not gay," I say. "He thought maybe bi, like I am. You know, questioning—"

"But Jamie doesn't like boys," she says. "I know he doesn't."

"You can't know that."

"No," she says quickly, "I can. Because we're the same, and *I* don't like boys."

Just then, the Beach Boys are all murmuring together, and Annie's mouth shuts tight. A dappled pink color seems to appear out of nowhere on her neck and chin and cheeks. I realize: she's never said that before. She might drop tantalizing references to "pretty girls," but it's thoughtless, breezy. She's never come out. This is her first time. I go and sit down next to her.

"How's it feel to say that?" I ask her. I remember how it felt my first time, terrifying and exhilarating. Like I was kind of a superhero. I wonder if I should take her hand, but she just cringes.

"Unnecessary" is all she says. She's still bright pink, but the color is fading now. She won't look at me.

"Your brother wasn't sure," I say gently. "He was still figuring things out. He said something had happened with—"

"Can we not talk about Jamie right now?" she asks. Then she buries her face in her hands and speaks into the creases of her palms. "Sorry I brought it up."

"It's okay," I tell her. And it is. Or it will be soon, even if she doesn't know it. I lie back on the sofa bed, staring up at the high vaulted ceiling. Remembering my first time. I'd been nine when I told my parents I thought I might marry a girl someday. They took it in stride—like they take everything in stride. Of course, not everyone in my family was so accepting. Naniji and Nanaji still pretend like it's not true. But eventually, saying it became easier, most of the time. I know it will someday for her, too.

But right now, Annie is still sitting there, rubbing her eyes. The record crackles. And then it starts. "Help Me, Rhonda." The reason I'd invited James here that Friday.

"Listen," I tell her. She drops her hands, tilting her ear toward the speakers. It's the same old familiar song, the one that plays on whatever classic rock Spotify playlist and over the tubes at the supermarket. No music, just vocals, but then the Boys stop singing and another voice, soft and angry and urgent, comes in.

"Who is that?" she asks. The man in the background is saying that the song sounds horrible. But it doesn't sound horrible. It sounds like magic.

"Brian Wilson's dad."

Annie is quiet for a moment longer, listening. The Boys keep trying to sing, but they can't. They keep getting interrupted. "What's his problem?" she asks.

I shake my head. "I don't know. My dad says that Brian Wilson is deaf in one ear because his father hit him when he was a little kid. But in his biographies, he's not even angry about it. He says that his father being so hard on him is what made him good at music."

Annie lies back in bed beside me. She closes her eyes, listening. Murry Wilson is saying over and over again, "Loosen up. Be happy. Be happy." Her hands are resting on her belly, rising and falling with her breath. She licks her lips before she speaks but doesn't open her eyes.

"Funny how you can tell someone is yelling even if they don't raise their voice at all."

It's true. The sound of Murry Wilson's voice makes my pulse race. I've listened to this album probably a thousand times but it still makes me feel kind of nauseous. And *my* dad would never talk to me that way.

"I know why you wanted to play this for Jamie," Annie says, eyes still shut, even though we're not supposed to talk about him. "His whole life used to be like this song, I think. Trying and trying, and disappointing Dad, no matter what he did."

My stomach clenches. She understands. She gets it. Sees something special in these grooves, which is almost as good as understanding me. I'm looking at the wet spot in the middle of her lower lip.

"Is it like that for you?" I ask. "With your dad, I mean?"

Annie snorts a little.

"What?" I say.

She opens her eyes, staring straight into mine. I've been watching her so closely that I feel untethered. Brian Wilson is talking, anger mounting in his voice, but I can't hear him.

"Dad doesn't worry about me. He used to, because I was weird, but he doesn't anymore. I don't know if it's because I'm a girl or what. I mean, he and Elijah are thick as thieves. But I might as well be invisible."

I look at her, hair fanned out across the ancient plaid sheets, crackly bolts of light in her eyes, those vampire teeth showing beneath her lips as she breathes deeply, like the air in my dad's office might somehow cleanse her whole body. She's got freckles and a small faint line in between her eyebrows, which are just a little wild, like she's never plucked them.

"I see you," I tell her. Echoes of James's words. I'm stealing them from him, and that's wrong, but in the moment, it feels right, too.

She draws in another breath, shrugging. "I'm just the sister left behind."

In this light, I can see the nearly invisible hairs on her earlobes and all along her thin, bare arms. The Beach Boys are finally singing again. They've kicked out Brian Wilson's dad at last, and it's only their voices, swelling toward the ceiling of the attic room, full of light.

"No, you're not," I tell her, smiling. I'm not sure if I'm teasing her or not when I say, "You're Annie, Queen of Gumlea."

She wrinkles her nose at that. But then she sits up anyway, leaning her weight on her elbows. She looks down, her eyelashes trembling. Then she looks up again, and she's kissing me, or I'm kissing her, I'm not sure which.

NINE

WHATEVER WAY YOU WANT TO look at it, Annie's body is soft and warm
beneath mine. Her mouth is all wet and slippery, tongue and lips, and her
hands don't stop at all as they trace my curves from throat to chest to belly
to hip. My back arches, and I feel my body melt into hers. At some point
the record crackles over to the next track, an outtake version of "Good
Vibrations." Spaceship sounds are all around us, and we're kissing without
ever coming up for air. In that moment, that endless moment, wrinkling the
sheets beneath our bodies, dozens of dead rock stars smiling down at us,
we're not two girls brought together by the tragedy of James M. **[Redacted]**.
We're just two girls, our bodies on fire, notes humming through every cell,
just two girls kissing in an attic, our bodies singing the very same tune. I
think, as I slide my hand up her shirt and feel the warm skin of her belly,
that this song has been sung for a thousand years. Someday, when the sun
goes supernova, two girls will be kissing one another while music written
by robots fades out behind them, their bodies burning away together to
nothing but dust.

The record's over and the needle back in place by the time we pull our
bodies apart. Annie's hair is all askew as she puts her bra back on. Her eyes

are wide and full of laughter.

"Wow," she says at last, biting her lip. Then her smile grows. "But you know, I'm not actually a queen in Gumlea."

"No?"

"No. *Emperata* is the term Jamie came up with."

I'm not sure, but I think her smile flags a little at the mention of him. Honestly, I don't really want to think about him, either. Not anymore today. This world is for me and Annie. Not for James.

But we can't escape him, can we? After all, he'll always be her brother, even dead and buried. And he'll always be my first love, too.

"Anyway," Annie says, stomping her feet down into her sneakers, which somehow came off at some point, "thanks for playing the record for me. You know, the Beach Boys. I don't think I'll ever look at them the same way again."

She grins at that. I grin back. "No problem," I tell her, then, stepping close, I brush the hair from her eyes and kiss her deeply once again. When she pulls away, she's giggling, her fingers enveloping mine.

"Jamie's girlfriend," she says, and giggles again.

I wince. "I haven't been his girlfriend in a long time."

"I guess that's true," she says. "But I'll always be his sister. And this is weird."

"Does it *feel* weird?" I ask her.

She bites her lip. I want to taste it. I want to taste her. "Mmm, no," she says. "Not really. Not unless I think about it."

"Don't think about it. You should let yourself be happy sometimes. You deserve it." I mean it. When she's happy, Annie is like a jewel, sparkling with light from the inside.

But somehow, my words don't work. Because that light inside her flickers, then shuts off. Her eyelids flutter down. The edges of her mouth sag. "I can't," she says.

"Because James is dead?" I ask gently.

And then, just like that, the door that was open inside her slams shut. She steps away from me, running a shaking hand through her unruly hair.

"No, he's not . . . I thought you understood." Her voice is low and muttered, full of vocal fry.

"Sorry?" I offer. It comes out as more of a question.

"I don't know," she says. Which scares me maybe more than it should, because if Annie [**Redacted**] is anything, it's always completely certain. "I should call my mom. My dad is waiting for me. I should go. My phone's downstairs. Eli . . ."

She's talking too much as she starts down the steps, away from my dad's attic office, that magical space, that magical light. I follow, because it's all I can do.

Annie waits outside for her mom. She doesn't want me to wait with her. Somehow, I screwed it all up. My mom senses the change in the air. She sits with me in the living room with her laptop, her hip against mine, steady and reassuring.

"Sorry it didn't go well. If she doesn't want to be friends, she doesn't know what she's missing."

I watch Annie run for her mom's car, a lightweight autumn jacket streaming behind her.

"Yeah," I say, but I'm not entirely convinced, even though it helps to hear my mom say it, I guess.

TEN

LOOK, MAYBE I WOULD HAVE forgotten all about her if it wasn't for the dream I had about her that night. I've kissed plenty of people before, not just James and Keira, but also Lucas Bower, and Jill Wainwright when we were nine on the bus. Plus all those people I kissed playing spin the bottle at rock camp. Does that count? I never counted it before. Which is telling you something, I think, about how many people I've kissed and how it doesn't matter to me, not usually. It's only lips. Bodies. Spit and skin and all of that.

But that Saturday night, while Annie is sleeping at her dad's apartment, I dream about her. We're sitting together in a shelter made of cardboard and wire fence. There are bombs going off in the distance, and I want to kiss her and the whole world shakes with it. I pull her close, tangling my hand through her hair, and her mouth opens and her lips are pink and her tongue inside is bright red, like a ruby, like blood. We're kissing and flowers are opening inside me and it's like she's my whole heart and then—

We're not alone. James is with us, behind me, brushing my hair from my face, touching me with his soft hands. I pull away from Annie and look at him. He's sad. Silent. Knowing. But then he smiles and touches Annie's temple with the back of his hand. I almost see a star light up there, like a freckle, right where he touched her.

He's giving her to me, I think. He's telling me it's okay.

Did Annie see him? I can't tell as he gets up and walks off into the war-torn suburb, into the endless afternoon.

On the bus on Monday, I listen to "Life During Wartime." All day, I look for Annie in the hall. But there's no sign of that bark-colored ponytail. At lunch, Harper catches me darting my gaze all over the cafeteria.

"Vee," she says, and when I don't answer her, she adds, "Vee. VIDYA?"

I spot Annie then, sitting down at the table with her skinny pixie friend. If she even remembers what happened on Saturday in my dad's office, she sure isn't showing it. She's laughing and smiling and acting like life has just rolled on, as usual. Meanwhile, all I can think about is the taste of her mouth, how it felt to have her breasts against mine.

Harper hates to be ignored. She studies my expression, then follows the line of my eyes, and her mouth forms a perfect O. "Oh shit."

"What?" I say, finally breaking my gaze and stabbing at my taco pie.

Harper nudges me a little. "You know what. What's up with you and Annie **[Redacted]**?"

"Nothingsky!" I protest, trying to pretend like I'm playing with their name. But Harper won't accept that. She knows it's not a joke. Her mouth is a screwy line. So I sigh, and add, "We just kissed, is all."

"You *just* kissed?"

"Yeah. So?"

"You just kissed your dead ex-boyfriend's little sister."

"We don't know he's dead," I say faintly. Because it was thinking that James was dead and gone that got me into this mess. Maybe if let myself believe Annie . . .

"Yeah, well, that would be even weirder."

"Yeah," I agree, and continue to watch Annie from across the crowded cafeteria. She doesn't notice.

She's not at Madrigals on Tuesday. Fuck my life.

Vee: So I think I have it figured out.

Harper: What figured out?

Vee: How to win Annie [Redacted]'s heart.

Harper: Looooooooord.

Vee: What? I had a dream about her last night, you know.

Harper: Was her dead brother there?

Vee: Harp, u jealous?

Harper: I just think this whole thing is weird as hell.
Harper: But whatever, tell me about your dream.

Vee: I can't. It's too raunchy. But good!

Harper: I bet. You were
always a sucker for that
boy. Why would it be any
different with his sister?

Vee: This has nothing
to do with James.
She's really cute!!!
Vee: And a good kisser.
Vee: And interesting, too.
Did you see that painting
she did in the art show?

Harper: No, do tell.

Vee: Oils, all layered
thick. A skull with a
daisy in the eye socket.

Harper: Dark.

Vee: I know. I love it. She's
super weird. And tortured.
Very Brian Wilson. Anyway,
her birthday is coming up.
Vee: (I remember cause she
and James had the same
birthday and he was always
complaining about how
much it sucked to share it.)

Harper: Cool, you gonna
get her something?

Vee: I thought I'd go to
that witch store downtown.
Get her a wand.

Harper: A WAND???

Vee: It sounds kind of dorky
but she loves that stuff.
Fantasy and all of that.
Vee: And so do I.

Harper: Sometimes I feel
like I don't even know you.

Vee: What's that
supposed to mean?

Harper: I'm just kidding.
Mostly. I just think it's not
going to really work out
between the two of you.

Vee: Why, because
of James?

Harper: No, because of Annie.

Vee: What do you mean?

Harper: She's not like her
brother. He was cool, in his
way. But Annie's a goody-
goody. Straight As and
straight edge and everything.
Everybody knows that.

Vee: That's fine. I can live with that.

Harper: Can you?

Vee: YES. I like her, okay?

Harper: Ok, but don't say I didn't warn you.

Vee: Do you want to come with me to the witch store tomorrow or not?

Harper: Sure, I could use some more sage.

Downtown is a stretch of storefronts wedged between Main Street and the deep cavern that is the Wallkill. There are restaurants run by former Brooklynites, a yoga studio that changes hands every few years, an art supply store that Harp and I used to shoplift from when we were bored. And there, smushed between a vintage shop owned by a gay couple and a bagel place that's always closed, is the witch store, the Faerie Realm. James and I used to go there, just the two of us. I always thought he was humoring me, since no one else would go. But maybe he liked it, too. I know it'll be the perfect place to find something for Annie.

Thursday after Madrigals, Harper and I walk there together, even though the weather is getting bad. We wear the hoods of our sweatshirts up over our eyes and tuck the legs of our jeans into our rain boots and try to act like we don't want to splash in the puddles like little kids.

I've known Harper since we were little kids, actually, and she's always been like that. Trying to pretend that she doesn't know how to be silly. She barely tolerated my weird fantasy geek stage and would never have joined Madrigals if it weren't for me. So far, all of the above has been true for Harper. Look, I don't mind it. It's who she is, and she gives good romantic advice and always passes to the left without having to be nagged.

But watching her drip her way through the witch store is funny as hell. When James and I used to come here, we always got really quiet, like the whole place was sacred. Not Harper. She doesn't belong here. She's like a dark rainstorm surrounded by a thousand crystal doodads, and she keeps picking up geodes and ugly sterling silver necklaces and waggling her eyebrows at me. When the store owner, a thick-bellied dude with a long scraggly beard, comes by to ask if we need any help, Harper starts outright flirting with him, stroking his age-spotted hand and cooing about his aura. I roll my eyes, slipping away.

There's a fat golden cat sitting on the bookshelf in the back. I curl my fingers and offer them to her, and she sniffs at me, then rubs her teeth against my hand. I feel myself smile. I've always liked cats, but Dad's allergic and Mom doesn't like dealing with animal fur. I knock my knuckles against the cat's spine, watching her arch her body into me. In a strange way, it reminds me of Annie. It's getting all mixed up in my head now, what parts of our encounter I dreamed, and what was real. But I do know this: her body answered my body like she'd been waiting for me. Like an animal, starved for someone to touch her fur. Like there was a connection between us. Real.

I wander away, but the cat follows me, tangling around my ankles.

"Is Demeter bothering you?" the shop owner asks.

Harper starts to crack a joke, but I say, "No, it's fine," just as I almost trip over the cat. I reach for a nearby counter to steady myself. That's when I see something inside. It's just a glint of silver under the lights at first. I have to bend low to see it, nestled there with a bunch of wands with crystals hot glued to their handles.

It's a knife, about the size of my forearm. It has a swooping, scalloped blade and a white hilt made out of some kind of resin. I guess it's supposed to look like ivory or even whalebone. *Scrimshaw.* That's what they call this stuff. There's a red stone at the bottom, and an image carved into the surface. It's a rabbit, leaping toward a crescent moon.

A hare, I say to myself. Didn't Annie say something about a hare? I'm searching my mind but coming up empty. I swear there was something about a hare in Gumlea. Her familiar. I think that's what she said. . . .

If I asked Harper, I know she'd say that the knife was cheesy. And it *looks* cheesy, glinting under the fluorescent lights. But not really. Because if you squint, you can almost imagine it tucked into a girl's hand as she stalks through the forest. In Annie's hand. Harper would laugh at it, but Annie Annie would understand.

"Can I see this knife?" I ask. Demeter is still braiding herself between my ankles but I don't even care. The bearded dude comes over and unlocks the glass case. He sets it on top.

"It's not a proper athame," he tells me. "The hilt should be black. If you're going to cast a circle—"

"Oh, she's not going to cast anything," Harper says, rolling her eyes. The bearded guy looks a little embarrassed.

Ignoring them, I pick up the knife. It's got a nice weight. It feels good in my hand. I imagine it tucked against Annie's palm. Her hands were small and cold against my body, surprisingly smooth considering all the time she spends outside. I think the knife will feel warm against her skin. I imagine her squeezing the hilt. In my mind's eye, the red stone glows. I know then that this is it. She's going to love it.

I feel a thrill when I correct myself: she's going to love that *I* gave it to her.

"It's really more of a dagger than a knife," the guy says.

I ignore him. "How much?"

A long pause. Demeter mewls and wraps her fluffy ginger tail around my calf.

"Are you eighteen?" the guy asks.

I'm a good liar. I look at him like there was never any other answer. "Yeah," I say.

He doesn't even ask me for my ID. "Seventy-nine ninety-nine." I do my best not to wince. Mom would kill me if she knew I was spending that much on a birthday present for a girl. But I earned that money myself— stocking shelves in the music store in Elting all summer, rearranging the picks, sorting guitar strings, just about dying of boredom. It's mine. And she's worth it.

"Will you take seventy?" I ask, because somehow it feels more worth it to spend that much if I know I'm getting a deal.

He watches me for a long moment. Then a reluctant smile warms his furry face. "Sure," he says, "Any friend of Demeter's is a friend of mine."

I fish my wallet out of my bag.

ELEVEN

I CAN'T BRING THE KNIFE to school. Zero tolerance and all of that. So that Friday, the day before Annie's fifteenth birthday, I write her a note.

I'm sorry I was a jerk,

it says.

I believe you about James. If you say he's alive, then he's alive. I know it doesn't make up for what I said, but I have a present for you. I thought we could maybe meet in the cemetery after school today? At the empty grave. I think you know what I mean. No pressure. I know it's your birthday tomorrow. Maybe you already have plans. But it would be nice to see you, and it won't take long.

I'm not brave enough to put it in her hands myself. I squeeze it through the vents in her locker between classes and brace myself for rejection, telling myself, well, at least I tried.

I don't expect her to be there. I take my time walking west across town after the bus drops me off at home. The leaves have started to change now, going bright and flaming against the clear blue sky. I should feel fucking great, but I don't. I'm just kind of heavy and resigned as I walk, trucks rushing by me, the knife a solemn, gift-wrapped weight at the bottom of my bag.

I walk through the wrought-iron gate, thinking about James. The truth is, I'm *not* sure if I believe that James isn't dead. But I guess it doesn't matter. Annie believes that he's out there somewhere in their magical kingdom, past the veil, whatever that means. Stuck. And if I want to support her, to kiss her, to hold her, well, I need to believe her.

Or at least I need to keep my big mouth shut about whatever it is that I believe.

I climb the hill leading to his grave. To my surprise, there's Annie waiting for me. Or not strictly waiting, really. She's building another stone tower on top of the grassy earth. Her hair is down in her face as she works the soil beneath it. When I come close, she shields the sun from her eyes with one dirty hand.

"Hey," she says.

I crouch down in front of her. "What are you doing?"

She smiles a little, like she's been waiting her whole life to tell someone this. "It's a cairn. An ancient trail marker. I'm trying to tell Jamie how to find his way home."

I remember the word *cairn*, and the rocks she stacked on top of James's grave at the funeral. "If he's in Gumlea," I begin slowly, "then how can he see it *here*?"

She looks at me with hard eyes, not answering. The sunlight is bright and the freckles are bright across the wrinkled bridge of her nose. I imagine tilting her head back and kissing her. Instead, I just sit back on my heels. And I only have one thought then: *God, she's pretty.*

"It's almost your birthday," I say awkwardly. "Happy happy."

Her eyes are still hard when she says, "I'm never happy."

"I know. But you will be."

Without hesitating, I put my bag on the ground in front of us and unzip it, digging through until my hand hits the wrapped box. I've put some silver curling ribbon around it, but I'm terrible at wrapping things. The seams show. There's tape everywhere. Annie takes it, sitting cross-legged in front of her cairn, and starts to tear the paper.

I'm holding my breath as she opens it. It's only after the wind rustles through the trees above us that I realize that she's holding her breath, too. She's staring down at the knife, not moving, one hand over her mouth.

It's only when her shoulders begin to shake that I realize that she's crying. I wonder if I should hold her. I wonder what it's all about.

"Do—" I begin hesitantly. "Do you hate it?"

She sort of snorts through her tears. Laughs a little, but it isn't a funny laugh.

"No," she says, wiping the tears on the back of her hand. "It's perfect. Where did you even *get* this? For years, I've been searching . . ." She trails off, but looks up at me, her eyes wide and wet and bright.

"That witch store downtown," I tell her, feeling suddenly awkward. "I hope you like it. I don't know why, but it made me think of you. Something about the rabbit—"

"Hare," she says. Even though her eyes are still wet, the corner of her mouth edges up a little.

"Are you happy now?" I ask her. *Kiss her kiss her*, I'm thinking, watching the way she bites at her lip. But the moment isn't right. Not quite. Not yet.

"I will be," she tells me. "This knife is the key to everything. You saved him, Vidya. You saved him."

The way she's talking scares me a little, but it doesn't matter, because Annie puts the knife down on the ground beside her cairn and crawls over to me across the warm, never-turned earth. She plants her mouth on mine, and we're kissing and laughing and kissing again, our bodies bright, our hearts furiously beating, and as a thousand bones are turned to dust beneath us, we are the only things alive.

I hold her hand and walk her home. Birds are singing and she has the knife tucked into the waistband of her jeans like some kind of fucking pirate and she looks so, so happy that I almost expect her to take off, flying above the sidewalk, still holding my hand in hers.

To be honest, I could fly a little, too.

She hasn't stopped talking since we left the cemetery. She has big plans for that knife, a whole ceremony plotted out. There will be singing and prayers and offerings to the king. Nothing weird, she says, in case I was scared she was going to sacrifice a small animal or something—just some drawings she's done. She says that Jamie will have to do his part on the other side, but she has faith in him. He's been trying to get back to her, she says. She's sure of it.

Do I believe her? Do I think this whole weirdo ceremony will work? Hell, probably not. But I'm watching her as she talks, and it's like her whole body is sparkling. She's so damned animated, waving her free hand through the air. I wonder how she comes up with this stuff, and if it makes her feel better about . . . you know, everything.

I wish I could believe. That I could work magic like this, too. The thing is, the more time I spend around Annie, the more I feel like it's really, truly, ridiculously possible.

But then, as we cross the street to her house, she gets quiet all of a sudden, biting her lip. "We'll have to wait until the winter solstice," she says. "It'll be cold to be out in the woods, but the veil is thinner then. There's no way it'll work now."

I feel relieved. Part of me wondered if she was going to ask me to pull

James between worlds now, while we wait for my dad to pick me up. "That's fine," I say, and squeeze her hand. "I'm not going anywhere."

We stop in the middle of the road to kiss. Someone could hit us with their minivan. I don't care. Her body is pressed up against mine at all the right points.

When she pulls away she says, "Spend the night? Please. It's my birthday tomorrow, right?"

That knife worked better than I thought. I say, "I'll have to ask my parents."

But that doesn't faze her. Nothing does, I think. "Cool," she says, breaking away from me, racing toward her house.

I rush after.

TWELVE

DAD'S NOT HAPPY TO HEAR I'm staying over Annie's. "You're supposed to go with your mom to see Naniji and Nanaji tomorrow," he says, and he sounds worried when he says it—probably because he knows *he's* going to be in for it when he tells Mom. I feel bad. I twist my mouth. I'd forgotten. Or maybe I hadn't exactly forgotten but had wanted to forget.

We're not close, my grandparents and me. They love me in their way, but they don't understand me at all. They always make it clear, though, that it's a problem with Mom—not with me. If only she'd married the boy they wanted her to marry, if only she'd raised me the way that *she* had been raised. If only I'd been taught to cover myself up like a good Indian girl, to stay away from white boys . . . they never even mention that I've dated white *girls*. That's a kind of crime they can't even imagine.

And I guess I love them in their way, too, but it's hard being around them sometimes, when I hear Mom fighting with them on the phone late at night because they don't like the outfit I'm wearing in my school photos and they don't approve of my grades, which are pretty good, I think, but never spectacular in anything except music. Mom always sticks up for me, but it breaks my heart a little bit that she has to stand up for me at all. We could all get along, I think, if they took even a moment to stop trying to make me—and my mother—into the daughters they think a daughter should be.

"Can she go without me just this once, please?" I say. Then I lower my voice, hoping that Annie can't hear me speak from where I'm sitting in their living room, even though she's only one thin wall away, talking to her own mother. "It's a girl."

There's a long pause. It's been a long time since I told him about anyone. Not since Keira.

"Crap," he says. And it's one of those weird minutes where talking to Dad almost feels more like talking to a brother than a father. "You know your mother's going to kill me if she finds out I'm covering for you."

"Pleeeeease, Daddy?" I ask, and I hear him sigh.

"Is she at least *nice*?" he asks. "Nicer than the last one?"

I glance over my shoulder to where I know Annie is waiting, and probably listening, too. "Yes," I tell him. "She's super nice. An artist. You'd like her."

He *would* like her. They could talk about Led Zeppelin together or something. It's not a lie.

"You know that if this is serious, then we're going to have to meet her parents."

I nod my head a little. I knew that. I just didn't want to think about it. "It might be hard. They're, like, going through a divorce right now."

"Her mother, then. We'll have her over for dinner soon. Your mother will be thrilled."

Mom tried this with Keira, too, the whole respectable meeting-your-girlfriend's-parents thing. Of course, it never happened. Didn't matter how many times I asked for her mom's number or told her my mom wanted to friend hers on Facebook. Wasn't going to happen.

I don't really want it to happen with Annie, either. It's too much, too weird. How would I ever explain that this was James's mother, too? But I know that this time I have to throw Mom a bone. Especially if I want my father to cover for me. And he probably will. He's a total sucker for some light teenage rebellion.

"Sure, I'd like that," I say with a summer breeze in my voice, and then add, "I'll call you tomorrow afternoon when I need a ride home."

I don't mention Nanaji and Naniji again, and he doesn't, either. I know there'll be fallout from that for him—but that he'll weather it just for me. Sitting on the sofa at Uncle Jovan's house, listening to my grandparents pick my mother apart. He sighs one last time.

"Don't get into any trouble," he tells me. "I love you."

I tell him that I love him, too. Then the line goes quiet.

"Everything okay with your parents?" Annie says as she saunters into the living room, then sprawls out across the sofa like she owns the place. I guess she does.

"Yeah," I say simply, even if it's half a lie. "Yours?"

Annie shrugs. "She won't be back until, like, eleven. She has night classes on Fridays. When I said that a friend was sleeping over, she just figured I meant Miranda and I didn't correct her."

I look at her for a long time. Her pale face, moonish in the daylight that's fading behind the curtains, doesn't show any emotion. Not happiness, or even pain.

"But tomorrow is your birthday," I say. "Don't you have anything planned?"

Annie shrugs again. "Yeah, she'll make disgusting pancakes or something, but that's usually it. Honestly, I think she'd rather forget," she says, so matter-of-factly that my teeth grit a little bit to hear it. My mom would *never* forget my birthday, not for a minute. But I understand a little better when she adds, "You know, because it's his birthday, too."

Her brother comes home a while after that. Well, her other brother. Elijah. He's got a face that's a little likes James's but fatter, and big hands and feet and a skinny body. He's nine and looks kind of like a disheveled puppy. He barely makes eye contact when she introduces us, then sits at the dining room table to wait for his dinner while Annie makes it for him.

I get up and help because that's what you do in my family—and that's why it bothers me so much that he just sits there. He's old enough, I think, to microwave his own plate of leftovers. But without skipping a beat, she does it for him. I plate us up some leftover pasta, too, and before I know it I'm sitting at the table with both of them, about to dig in.

But just as Annie picks up her fork, she sets it down again.

"The candles! I almost forgot!"

I'm not sure what I'm expecting. Some kind of Wiccan stuff, I guess? A bunch of tapers carved with runes? But Annie gets a pair of brass candlesticks out from under the sink instead, plus two of those white emergency candles. She lights them, covers her face, and murmurs a prayer into her hands. I guess it's Hebrew. Elijah rolls his eyes and digs into dinner before she's even done.

"What was that about?" I ask her carefully, making sure to sound curious and gentle as Annie sits down in the seat across from me. It's weird, how normal this feels, a family dinner without any parents.

"Shabbat prayers," she says. "We don't go to synagogue anymore. But I've been reading about what makes someone Jewish, and if you participate in rituals, that's enough. Well, according to some people, it's enough if your mother is. I don't know. It just feels important to me. I think Eli should hear the prayers, too."

More eye rolling from Eli. "I don't care about that stuff," he says, like it's an old argument. "I'm Christian now, anyway."

"I don't think you can choose like that."

"I just did. But thanks, Mom." He flings food at her with his fork, but she's not offended. She only giggles, then looks down, guiltily, at her plate.

"You probably think it's stupid," she says to me. "You're, like, Hindu, right?"

My hands feel a little tingly and cold at the assumption. "No. I'm an atheist. Born and raised."

"Oh. Sorry. You probably think I'm doubly stupid, then."

Both she and Eli are looking at me. His eyes are nothing like his siblings' eyes. They're pale, like algae in a lake. Hers are sunlight through autumn leaves. But the message is the same in both of them. I've seen it before, a million times from the kids at school.

Have you accepted God into your heart? it says.

God only knows, I want to tell them, *I've tried.*

"No. It would make my grandparents happy, I guess. They're pretty religious. But my parents don't believe, and I've never really seen the need. You can be an ethical, happy person without all of that."

"Oh," says Annie, picking up her fork.

We eat the rest of the meal in silence.

After we eat, we load up the dishwasher while Elijah flops out on the couch in front of the TV. Then, like we agreed to it beforehand, we trudge up the stairs together in silence. I figure we're heading for her room, but Annie stops in front of a closed bedroom door. She stands there for a moment, staring.

"What's up?" I whisper, because it feels right to whisper, touching the thin skin just above her elbow.

The hall light is dim, yellowing her face like old paper. "This is Jamie's room. Do you want to see it?"

His room. How many times did I imagine it, on secret nights when I was alone in mine? I never saw it. He didn't want me to meet his dad, which was understandable, I guess. In my mind, it was the coolest room in the world, lit by black lights and string lights and tiny cones of burning incense. I nod, bracing myself. Annie opens the door.

At first, only darkness and the smell of dust. But then she turns on the light, revealing a space that's pretty damned ordinary. There's a messy desk, scattered with paper, with stickers half peeled off all along the sides. A twin bed, neatly made, in the corner. Baseball wallpaper, mostly covered by band posters. But over his bed, you can't see a single silk-screened baseball. Because there's wide-ruled notebook paper taped over it instead, a whole notebook's worth. It's scribbled with blue pen and pencil, maps and poems and stories. The maps are even better than I imagined, more detailed, with towering mountains and rushing rivers and cities, all hard angles, invading the wild lands.

"You drew these," I say, kneeling on the bed so I can see better. Annie is standing behind me, not saying anything even though I can hear her breathe. "James told me. He loved your maps."

"They're nothing special," she says, but I can practically hear how she's blushing, something about the thickness of her voice.

"Don't be ridiculous. They're beautiful." I reach out and touch one of them. The paper is as delicate as a butterfly's wing. It looks like a real place. I try to imagine James, lost in those twisting mountain roads. Here in this room, with the air full and trembling, it's easier than I expected.

"Hey," Annie says suddenly, grabbing a page from the wall and tearing it off. I cringe at that. This feels almost like a temple, a sacred space. But she seems eager to change the air. "Look at this. I think it's about you."

I sit on the edge of the bed, taking the sheet from her. It's his handwriting. Tiny. Tight. You know whose. I would have recognized it anywhere. I used to read his notes over and over again, wondering if they held some kind of clue about where he went.

> In the Obsidian Tower,
> the Lady lies in wait.
> Her hair is an Ebony Rope.
> Her eyes are Smoldering Embers . . .

I cringe.

"What?" Annie asks.

"An Ebony Rope. I don't know. It's kind of embarrassing."

She smiles at me. Her crooked teeth suddenly remind me of fangs. "He loved you. He probably still does."

I'm holding the page against my chest, almost hugging it, crushing it in my hands. I'm looking at Annie. I loved James once. Part of me still does, too. But another part of me is falling into her eyes, wanting to kiss her again, and for what? For reminding me what it felt like to be with him? To be seen, to be understood?

I look down at the page again. "He wrote me other songs, you know. That's what this is. It's not a poem, it's a song." I say it with certainty, even though I shouldn't be sure about anything when it comes to James. "Not as cheesy as this one. We were going to start a band. I'd do vocals and play the bass, and he'd play the drums. Neal Harriman was going to play guitar, even though he sucked. I kept telling them I should play lead guitar instead."

"Dad wouldn't let him get a drum kit," Annie says, and her eyes are full of tragedy.

"I know. He said he was working on it, though. He had a plan, I think. Saving up his money or something."

"I bet he would have done it. I bet he would have been a great drummer."

To Annie, no one is as amazing as James could have been. "Yeah," I agree. I look down at the song one last time. "Can I keep this?"

"Sure. No one will notice it's gone. This place is worse than a tomb. I'm the only one who comes in here."

I fold up the page very carefully. Then I slip it down inside my pocket. It's Annie's birthday, and yet she's giving me a gift.

Two gifts, actually. Because then she offers me her hand. For some reason, my legs are shaking a little when I take it and rise from James's bed.

"Thank you," I say softly. But Annie doesn't say anything. She just leads me into her room, leaving the memory of her brother crashing against invisible rocks behind us.

We go into her room, and Annie closes the door behind her. It's nothing like her brother's room. There's no kiddie wallpaper. Instead, the walls are painted a rich yellow, like ground mustard seed. The carpet's been pulled up, revealing the paint-splattered wood floors beneath. Her desk is clean, piled high with books. The whole place smells lived in—like unwashed clothing, rather than ancient, perfectly preserved dust.

The only thing that links the two places are the maps on the walls over the bed, the same maps, drawn by Annie herself, maps of Gumlea.

I'm looking at them again, but this time, I'm not brave enough to crawl up into her bed. That's moving fast even for me. I'm looking at the maps very carefully, as though I haven't seen them before.

"You're a great artist," I say again. "I remember your painting in the last art show. The skull. It was beautiful."

"Thanks," she says. She's doing something behind me. Closing curtains. Opening drawers. Getting undressed and dressed again. I'm pretending not to listen. "I've thought about art school, but I dunno. Jamie's trying to get back here. I can't *leave* when he's trying to come back."

It makes me want to cringe again to think about her setting aside her plans for a boy who just had a funeral. *But it's what she believes*, I tell myself. "You have plenty of time to decide" is what I say. "But if you ask me, you should go for it. This stuff doesn't look like it was drawn by some kid. And you drew it a few years ago, right?"

"Most of it. The portraits are newer."

My eyes drift from the taped-up maps to the images beside them. There's a self-portrait, half of her face rotted away to a skull. There's a picture of her friend Miranda, antlers curling from her pixie-cut hair. There's . . . there's me, half my face obscured by my hair, the other half of me smiling.

"There's something behind these drawings," I tell her. "They're deep. I can tell just by looking at them that you've been through a lot in your life."

"Oh yeah?"

Annie sits on the bed beside me. She's wearing a pair of boxer shorts now, her legs pale beneath them. I can see the fine fuzz of short blond hairs all along her thighs. I want to put my hand on her skin, to see if it's cool to the touch, or as warm as I'm imagining. But I don't. Not yet.

"Yeah. It's like Brian Wilson's music. Trauma does something to art, I think. It's why I'll never be a great musician. My life's too good."

As soon as I've said it, I regret it. It sounds stupid and ignorant. Annie's expression is strange, too. She shakes her head. "Whatever I've lived through, it's nothing compared to Jamie. However great an artist I am, it's nothing compared to him."

"Annie . . . ," I begin. I want to tell her that he's gone. I want to tell her that she needs to live for herself. I want to tell her that she could be so fucking fantastic that it hurts to even think about it, like it makes my stomach clench and the air feel thin in my lungs.

But she doesn't let me. She shakes her head again. "Can we just lie down?" she asks, and tucks herself under the covers on the far side of her twin bed. Then, hesitating only a moment, she reaches up to turn off the light.

I hesitate, too. I'm still wearing my jeans, my hoodie, my bra. In the darkness, where Annie can't see how big my belly is, or the fact that I haven't shaved in a few days, I shimmy out of my jeans. Then I leave my hoodie and my bra in a pile on the floor, too, and slide under the covers beside her.

My heart is beating so loud I swear she must hear it. Her breathing is light and quick. She lets out a giggle. I do, too. I'm so nervous to touch her, and to be touched. It's never been like this with anyone, really. I feel like a kid with her, until I scooch closer, and our legs touch, and electricity shoots through me.

Annie, too, I think. She jumps a little.

"Are you okay?" I ask.

She giggles again. "Okay" is her answer.

I put my hands around her slender waist and pull her close to me. We're kissing and we're kissing, tangling our bodies tight.

Sometime after, I see a thin light through the window, and hear the garage door open. We're still all stuck together, sore and sweet, but I turn at the sound of the car rattling up the driveway.

"Just Mom," Annie says, her voice full of sleep. Then she pushes her lips against my neck, not so much kissing me as breathing me in. I'm not sure what to do, what the script is. Should we be scrambling for our clothes, rushing for cover, like Keira and I used to? But Annie doesn't seem bothered. She's frozen and calm against me, her hands heavy against my naked skin.

"Okay," I say, and relax back into her, because really, it's all I want, too, to just be here with her, our hearts slow and syrupy and beating together. I feel her lips at my throat again. This time, she is kissing me, and then she says something soft and I almost don't hear it at first.

"What?" I whisper into the darkness.

She lets out a low chuckle. "You're amazing," she says. I feel myself grinning, feel a thousand feathers dance in my belly. *You, too,* I think, but before I can say it, she adds: "I can't believe we're going to get him back. I've missed him so bad, Vidya, you have no idea."

I have some idea. I've missed him, too. But at the same time, it's different for her, and I know it. Because I've never had a brother. And I've never lost one, either.

So I don't pull away from her. I just let her hold me, her hands warm and steady, even though my heart's gone to ice in my chest.

THIRTEEN

WHEN I WAKE UP, THE room's hot with autumn late-morning sunlight through the curtains, and Annie's gone. But I hear movement downstairs, the sound of dishes and water. I smell coffee, too. So I get up and pull on my dirty jeans, then my bra and my hoodie. I start toward the door, stop, find deodorant on Annie's desk and smear some on to mask my smell, like sex and sweat, now hidden under baby-powder sweetness. Then I head downstairs.

I stand in the hallway for a minute, listening. Annie's talking to her mom.

"Birthday breakfast," her mom is saying. "What do you want, sweetie?"

"Not pancakes. They always make me feel kind of sick."

"Bacon? Or is Miranda still vegetarian?"

"She is, but she's not here."

There's a long pause, filled only with a clattering of dishes. I realize I'm holding my breath, waiting for Annie to say it.

"Oh," her mom asks. "Did she decide not to stay last night?"

Annie takes her time in answering. It's funny to hear her like this. She's been so open with me. But things are different with her mom, I guess. At least when it comes to me.

So I decide it's up to me to help her. I walk into the kitchen, my smile broad, like I belong there.

"Hi, Mrs. **[Redacted]**."

"Hello." Annie's mom is frowning, like she doesn't quite understand, and why should she? But Annie's grinning. I resist the urge to go to her and press a kiss to her cheek. It should be up to her, how much she shows to her mom. Up to her how much she reveals about herself.

"Mom, you remember Vidya," Annie says. "Right?"

I put my hands on the center island, waiting for a response. Annie's mom is chewing this over. In the late-morning light, I can see a thousand lines in her face. She's older than I thought she was at the funeral, even more tired. And confused now, too.

"Jamie's girlfriend?" she asks.

That's the question that I knew was coming, and it's like a punch in the gut. But I keep my smile steady. I'm not his girlfriend, not anymore.

And Annie agrees. "No," she says, and she walks over to me and puts her hand over mine on the counter. "She's mine."

Annie's mom is staring at us. The water is still running, but she finally goes and turns it off. With her hand on the cold water faucet, she looks at us. I can see how her brain is churning over this, putting the pieces together.

"Oh," she says at first, flatly and without emotion. And then she adds, with dawning realization: "Oh."

She turns back to the sink. There's a window there, looking out to the yard, and the woods beyond. She's distant when she speaks next.

"Vidya, do you eat bacon?"

Breakfast is the worst, like the most awkward possible, because no one is talking about the big stinking pile of shit in the middle of the table, as my dad might say, which is the fact that I dated James and now I'm dating

Annie and that's weird as hell. Like, instead their mom is asking me about Madrigals and Elijah inhales most of the plate of bacon and no one else really eats anything except Annie, who keeps tearing the crusts off her toast to dip them in raspberry jam and eating only those.

Awkward.

I'm telling Mrs. **[Redacted]** all about our Madrigals trips, but giving her the most sanitized version, without Kings or Quarters or David Henley's massive purple bong. These are things I might share with my own parents, because they're safe, but I don't know what she's like, not at all, except right now it seems like she's being careful and I am, too. I don't want to get Annie in trouble. And I'm also not talking about the boy in all those pictures on the wall, the boy with the haunted eyes, and how I knew his lips and the way his hips dipped into the waistband of his pants and how it's nothing like the way his sister's hips dip into the waistband of her pants even though it's all I can think about. I'm sure it's all written in my face anyway, a big blinking sign over my head:

Bad news bad news this girl is bad news and she has hooked up with two-thirds of your children and everyone at this table knows it bad news bears

After breakfast, Annie clears the table without being asked. She's so damned responsible, and I want to kiss her for it, but I can't, not in front of her mom and little brother. It's just too much. So instead, I scrape the plates for her, and when her mom leaves the room, she comes over and puts her hand on the back of my neck.

"That went so well," she says, and from the way her eyes are glowing I can tell that she means it even though my stomach is a hard burnt pile of bacon and anxiety.

But I kiss her temple anyway. "I'm glad," I lie, even though I'm anything but glad right now. "I should call my mom for a ride soon," I add. I just need to get out of there, even though my parents are probably getting ready to go to my uncle's and they aren't expecting me for hours still. "I'm supposed to visit my grandparents today. Mom usually leaves by ten."

"Oh." Annie's face looks a little sucked in. "Is it something I did?"

Her freckles are bright in the white light of the kitchen. A few of them disappear as she wrinkles her nose in worry. She's not the problem, not at all. It's her mom, and this space, and her brothers, both of them, the ghost and the strange sullen almost-teenager. It's the way the police treated me the last time they dragged me to the station —asking me questions that I knew came from James's mother. With Keira, all I wanted was to meet her family and be accepted as one of them. But right now, I just want to get out of here.

Still, it's not Annie's fault. I lean over and kiss her deeply. "It's fine. I'll see you Monday, promise."

Annie licks the spit off her lips, letting her mouth curl up at the edges. Before she can say anything, I hear her mom clear her throat behind us.

"Vidya, do you need a ride? I can give you one."

"No, that's fine—" I start, but Annie's mom shakes her head.

"No, I insist. I'll get my keys."

"I'll come, Mom!" Annie calls out, starting to follow, but her mother shuts that down fast.

"Stay here and watch Elijah," she says.

I look at Annie, shrugging. But inside, my heart's a frantic bird's wing, wildly fluttering in my chest.

FOURTEEN

MRS. **[REDACTED]'S CAR LOOKS LIKE** it hasn't been cleaned since Elijah was a baby. The seats are crunchy with crumbs. There are fossilized French fries scattered over the floor mats. As I buckle myself up, she puts on the radio, and it plays one of those '90s alternative bands that my dad calls a "pale imitation of real music."

"What's your address?" she asks. I tell her, and she makes a face, like where I live says something about me. And I guess it does, even though I've never really thought about it. Even though Annie's family lives in one of the bigger houses in their neighborhood, theirs is mostly blue collar and working class. The kids on her bus are just as likely to be in 4-H and Gun Club as they are in GSA, whereas there are only a few teenagers on my street, and we're all the artsy sons and daughters of professors.

Mrs. **[Redacted]** rolls down the driveway, not looking at me, and I know for sure she's got something on her mind that goes beyond the neighborhood where I live.

"Nice weather . . . ," I say softly, desperately, because I can't even begin to channel my mom right now. I don't have it in me to be polite. I wonder if Annie's mom is going to tell me that I can't see Annie anymore, that I shouldn't be corrupting her little girl with the sex and the drinking and the touching like I did with her son. That I shouldn't *ruin* her like I did with her son. That I'm dangerous. That I might make her disappear. I'm sure she can see it all, what kind of person she thinks I am, written in huge letters across my forehead.

But when her mom speaks, it's not about Annie at all. It's like she said. She's invisible in this family.

"Do you know about wheresjames[**redacted**].com?" she asks.

I feel my stomach clench. "Me and my friend Harper looked at it a few times right after he disappeared." I pause. The word is hanging between us like one of those dangly air fresheners, which, honestly, this car could use. "After he died, I mean. Sorry."

My cheeks turn hot. I don't know which way Mrs. [**Redacted**] wants to look at it. To Annie, he's alive. But her parents paid for that funeral and everything. Their mom is hardly listening to me anyway, just drumming nervous hands on the steering wheel, not quite on the beat.

"There was a comment there about a year ago that I can't stop thinking about. I thought maybe you left it."

"No, I never left a comment!" I say, maybe a little too quickly. But I *didn't*. And I'm so, so *sick* of them treating me like I've committed some kind of crime. Like I was the one who *made* James disappear. Like it was all my fucking fault. Not that leaving a comment on some website is a crime, anyway. But I didn't even do that, and still I get blamed. I do *not* want to talk to her about this. It's one thing to talk about it with Annie. But *this* conversation brings back bad memories, how his parents kept sending the police to talk to me and I'd have to sit there, under humming fluorescent lights, next to Dad's lawyer in my nicest clothes so that they'd think I was wholesome and normal, explaining again and again that I had no idea where he went. Honestly, I wish I *had* known what happened to James. Then I could have told them, and made the whole thing stop.

But none of us could stop it. It was a hell we had all been trapped in. Me, Neal, Annie, their whole family. And apparently, I'm trapped in it still.

"There was no email," his mom goes on, like she doesn't even notice my discomfort. "I sent the comment to the police, but they couldn't trace it. The person said their name was Jack."

I don't say anything. That name means nothing to me.

"Stop looking, it said. Your son is dead and gone. There is no more James **[Redacted]**."

A shiver runs up my spine. We're on my street now, pulling slooooooooowly up to my house. It's a beautiful autumn day, leaves all gold-tipped and perfect. But my hands are cold. I hate this. I hate her. I want to get out of here. But the child safety lock is on, and she's looking at me, waiting for me to answer.

"I'm sorry," I said. "That sucks, but . . . it wasn't me."

Mrs. **[Redacted]** looks at me for a long time. Her eyes are circled and circled again by wrinkles and bags, like she hasn't slept in years, and I bet she hasn't.

"I believe you," she says finally. "I never thought you were the enemy, you know. Not like my husband does."

I bite my lip. What can I say to that? Nothing.

"He's kind of racist," she adds, and then laughs, even though I'm not laughing and it's not funny. Then she holds a hand up over her eyes and shields them. I'm afraid she's going to cry, but she doesn't. She just shakes her head. "Anyway, I'd hoped it was just you and your friends, fucking around. I remember what it's like to be a teenaged girl, you know."

For a second, my anger weakens, and I can almost see it. She would have been nothing like Annie, I think. More like Harper. Saucy and brave, but more as an act than a real identity. Mrs. [Redacted] would have been the kind of girl who would egg someone's house for you in a minute. The kind of girl who would leave a mean comment on someone's web page for their dead, missing kid, just for a laugh. Just to fuck with them.

"I'm sorry. I wish I could tell you who left it."

"It's okay," she says. "I really need to let it go, anyway."

Neither of us says anything. We both know she can't.

"My mom's waiting for me," I eventually say. Mrs. [Redacted] unlocks the car door for me. I hop outside, kind of vaguely waving, because she's a grown-up, because it feels like the right thing to do.

"I'm glad we had this talk," she says, before I slam the car door and she drives away. I race up my front steps and burst through the door.

"Mo-om?" I call, and run straight into her, coming down the stairs. She's got her purse over her shoulders.

"Vidya?" she says, laughing as I bury her in a hug. "How was Harper's?"

I feel a deep tug of guilt. My mom raised me to be better than this, didn't she? But somehow, I never am any better. I keep making the same mistakes with the same people. The freaking [Redacted]s.

When I don't answer, she laughs more. "I didn't expect you back so early. Naniji and Nanaji will be so pleased to see you today."

"Mmmf" is all I say, giving my mother a squeeze. She squeezes me back. She's warm and safe and predictable. Not like Annie's mom—who's going to be stuck for the rest of her life hunting down ghosts.

"Everything okay?"

"Yeah, fine," I say quickly. "I'll go get changed."

I run up the stairs to my room, sure that when I come down, my old, familiar mom will be waiting for me.

FIFTEEN

ANNIE IS EVERYWHERE ON MONDAY. I see her in the parking lot as I hustle off the bus and in the hall between classes, bumbling through the crowd, pushing her hair out of those dark, boyish eyes. And half of me is thrilled to see her. I feel a jolt of electricity run down my spine and straight into my belly when her eyes seek me out through the crowd.

But I pretend I haven't seen her. I look away.

I haven't told anyone about my conversation with Annie's mother. All through the car ride with my own mom, I sat with my feet up on the dash, fiddling with the playlist, talking too loudly about the Velvet Underground. I acted so sunny and centered at my uncle's house that I think Naniji even suspected something was up.

"Vidya, what's gotten into you?" she asked, giving my mother a pointed look. That look said *drugs*. It's one she's given me before. The two of them started bickering then, taking the pressure off me. And thank God, because I don't think I could explain if I tried.

I was a fool to get involved with Annie. I see that now. I shouldn't have done it, and that conversation with Annie's mom is just the price I had to pay for being so damned stupid.

Harper notices something's weird with me. Lunch rolls around, and I'm not looking at anyone as I unroll the crinkly ends of my paper lunch bag to pull out a yogurt and a sandwich and a seltzer, peeling the foil off my sandwich like my life depends on it. She lowers her voice so the emo boys can't hear.

"You hung out with Annie this weekend, right? I tried texting you but you didn't answer. How'd it go? Vee, did something happen?"

I know that Harper texted me—eight or nine times. I didn't know how to explain any of it then, and I don't know, so I just pretended not to see them. But I guess I don't have to explain anything to her. Because when I lift my eyes to look at Harper, Annie is standing right behind her, clutching a lunch tray in hand.

Shit, Harper mouths when she follows the line of my eye up and spots Annie. And then: *Should I take care of this?*

I shake my head.

"What's up, Annie?" I say, loudly and firmly.

Annie cuts right to the chase. I should expect nothing less from her, I guess. "Why are you avoiding me? Did I do something wrong?"

I shrug, peeling the lid off my yogurt and skimming the top off with a plastic spoon. The truth is, she didn't do anything wrong. It's not her fault. It's the whole damned situation. It's James and her mom and her maybe-racist dad. It's the hollow silence of their house at night. It's James's empty room, and his even emptier poetry, with all of those Empty but Important Capital Letters. It's the whole situation. Harper was right, I know that now. It's too, too weird.

"It's fine. I'm just busy—"

"Damn it!" Annie exclaims, loud enough that everyone at the table turns, and the next table over, too. Her hands are shaking. The plates on her tray jitter and jangle. Of course, she's not just eating fries and a slice of pizza like a normal teenager. She's got a whole school lunch feast there, salad and a slice of quiche, and a glass of orange juice, and they're doing the electric slide over the plastic tray. "You can't just pretend like nothing happened. I know it did, Vidya. And you do, too."

She looks at me, and I see that her eyes, so bright and so familiar, are full of tears. I cringe. I know how other kids can be, what fucking assholes they'll be about her if she cries in front of the whole cafeteria. And I care, unlike Annie. I can't let her humiliate herself.

I jump out of my seat and pull the tray from her hands, setting it on the table. Then I lead her toward the door.

"Where are you going, missy?" Mr. Macklin calls out.

I sigh and turn around. "Can we have a bathroom pass?"

Mr. Macklin is glaring, and I can tell he's about to say no, so I add: "She's got her period. I need to get a tampon out of my bag."

He rolls his eyes at that. "Just go."

Annie's still sniffling as we head down the hall, but I hear her let out a little snort of laughter. "Nice. Brave."

For some reason this annoys me. "It's not the first time I've cut class," I tell her, even though it's something I haven't made a habit of doing since James. Mr. Macklin is still peering at us from the doorway, so I make a big show of heading toward the bathroom, but the minute his back is turned we rush into the northwest stairwell instead.

Annie's still holding my hand, hers limp and warm in mine. But then she squeezes it tighter as I duck under the stairs, out of the view of pretty much anyone. The light from the windows is slanted and blue, and her tear-streaked face is wan. But still pretty. With her rumpled hair, and the way the light dances through the naked trees outside, she looks almost like a mermaid.

I squeeze her hand back.

"We need to talk," I tell her.

She winces, and at last, pulls her hand away. She shields her eyes with it instead, like she can't stand to look at me. "What did I do?"

"Nothing," I tell her, which is true. It's *not* Annie. "I like you. A lot. But it's your family and . . . this whole situation. James. It's too much for me. Your mom grilled me about some internet comment about James on the car ride home."

"Oh," Annie says. She rolls her eyes. "Wheresjames**[Redacted]**.com. She's obsessed with that whole stupid site."

"Yeah. That. And she acted like it was somehow my fault that some rando left some creepy comment, and you know what they *did* to me after James disappeared? Your mom and dad? Do you know how many times they insisted the police talk to me?"

Annie's staring at me, hard. And then she looks down, her hair veiling her eyes. "I knew you had to go in a few times," she says softly.

"Eight. Eight times. That's how many times they questioned me. Twice, they made me leave school in the middle of the day. No one said sorry to me or anything, you know that? No one even acknowledged that I lost him, too."

My voice cracks when I say it. I let it. My gaze is fierce, even as my eyes are filling up with tears.

Annie's still looking down at her feet. Guilty, maybe. Or sad.

"I'm sorry you lost him, too, Vidya," she says. "He loved you and it shouldn't have happened and it sucks."

She looks up at me, and her eyes are like a bright, clear morning, and I feel my heart break in two all over again. The tears are streaming down my face now, flowing hard.

"Thank you," I say, and my words are practically whispered.

She reaches into her pocket and pulls out a clump of cafeteria napkins.

God, she's weird. But I take one, laughing a little despite myself, and wipe my face.

"Thank you," I say again.

Annie swallows hard, nodding. "I'm sorry," she says. "They shouldn't have made you feel that way. You matter, too. But in my family, it's like . . . if you're not Jamie, then you might as well be—"

"Invisible?" I offer. My heart feels squeezed. I know in that moment that we're in this together. Because no matter how bad it's been for me, it's been so, so much worse for her. "Your family is so fucked up," I tell her.

She laughs a little, weakly, at that, even though her eyes are shiny with tears, too. "Isn't everybody's?"

I want to tell her that no, everybody's isn't. My mom would never do what her family did to me. She would never talk to Annie the way her mother did to me, too close and too weird and too raw. She's always my *mom*. My dad isn't some hazy figure I only see twice a week but a constant, steady presence, giving me mixtapes and guitar lessons and brand-new pairs of perfect purple shoes. I don't have any brothers, gone or otherwise. My parents wanted to be able to travel, they always said. That's why they had one kid. All their attention is focused on me, not split in a hundred different directions. If anything, there have been times when I felt like I was *too* visible, when all their love was laser focused on helping me with a problem or making sure I did the right thing and I'd wished, secretly, that I could have had more space.

But we're not perfect. I think about Naniji and Nanaji, and the things that I don't tell them, and the way that I dress when I go over to their house—like I'm a different person altogether. I think about the way that I feel when I'm there, under scrutiny, and how my mom has it even worse, how she always puts too much sugar in her own tea just because she's so nervous, like a bird in a cage that can't stop pulling out its own feathers.

My life isn't like Annie's life. But that doesn't mean it's perfect, either.

"Yeah, I guess," I tell her.

She wipes away the last bit of tears with that weird wad of napkins. "I really, really like you," she says, and she steps closer. I can feel the heat off her body, there in the echoing space under the stairs.

But still. I think of her brother. I think of everything I once shared with him—how he'll always be the ghost standing between us. Or not even a ghost for her, because to Annie, he's *alive*. I consider protesting, but then I look at her, the fawn-colored hair hanging in her face, the fine line of her eyelashes. She's pretty. So so so so pretty. And in that moment, contemplating her freckles, I'm not thinking about James at all. I'm stepping forward to meet her, brushing back her hair, and crushing her in a long, deep kiss. In a moment, our mouths are open and our bellies are squished together and she's pinning me up against the wall and I'm only thinking of her as I kiss her fiercely and my body is warm and wet and Slip 'N Slide slick.

She pulls away, suddenly stern and serious. "I want you to know that the way I feel about you has nothing to do with my brother," she says. "Except that from the moment I first saw you, I thought you should be with me. Not with him."

God, what a line. But I'm smiling, and my face is hot, and my heart is beating fast. "I thought you were the same person or something," I tell her.

It's at that, of all things, that she blushes. "There are doors I kept closed from him," she says, then lowers her voice to a whisper. "Even in Gumlea."

I'm not sure what that means. I'm not sure that I want to know what it means, either. But there's one thing I'm certain of: I want to kiss her again. So I hook my finger into her belt loop and pull her close.

I kiss her and kiss her. At some point, when I take a breath, she wrinkles her freckled nose at me.

"So this isn't too weird for you, then?"

I want to laugh, but I'm too breathless. Because it is, and it isn't. It is, but it doesn't matter to me, not right now.

We kiss more. The light is slanted and green through the trees. Then there's a sound, and a beam of harsh yellow light from the hall.

"What are you girls doing?" Mr. Macklin calls. I take Annie's hand and lead her, red-cheeked and giddy, out of our hiding place.

"Nothing," I say, in a voice so firm, even Mr. Macklin doesn't question it.

We head back to the cafeteria, together.

SIXTEEN

WE'RE TOGETHER ALL THE TIME after that. No one questions it, not Harper or my mom or the emo boys or Mrs. Kepler. We sit next to one another on the risers between songs, her head on my shoulder. We walk down the hall together, our fingers intertwined. I bring my ukulele to school sometimes and during study hall, I serenade her, while she draws the action of my hands, the line of my lips. We always take the late bus home together after Madrigals, snuggled up on the plastic seat together, the whole world streaming by our window. At home, if she's not with me, she's tucked against my cheek on the other end of my phone. We talk about everything and nothing. Her family. My family. Madrigals, and the first competition that's coming up. Harper and her boyfriends. Her best friend, Miranda, who is transferring to vo-tech next year. We talk about music, and the guys in the music store downtown who always ignore me even though I play better than most of the dudes who go in there. About art, and the fact that she's always been good at it, without even thinking about it. About Gumlea.

Tangled together on my parents' sofa together after school, she tells me how we'll open the veil. The way she talks about it isn't much different from the way a regular kid would plan a party. She rattles off all the things we'll need: sage and dark red wine and the ashes of animal bone. When I ask her where we'll get that, she only smirks at me, like it's a stupid question.

Then she gets the knife out of her backpack.

"I wish you wouldn't bring that thing to school," I tell her. "You're going to get caught. And then what?"

"I'm not," Annie says firmly, like there can be no arguing. Then she turns the knife over. I see that she's drawn something there in Sharpie.

"Let me see that," I say, holding out my hand.

The knife has a decent weight. The hilt feels good tucked against my palm. There, on the white artificial bone, Annie's drawn faces in ultrafine black pen. It's a man, his beard long and scraggly, and a girl and a boy, facing him down together.

"That's the pirate," Annie says softly. "He's the one holding Jamie on the other side."

I look at the faces she's drawn. They look just like the two of them, with their strong profiles, messy hair, and glaring eyes. Seeing James makes my stomach shift. It always does.

"How do you know that he'll do his part in the ritual?" I ask her, holding my thumb over James's face so I don't have to look at him.

Annie lets out a long sigh. "I don't. But every night, just before I drift off to sleep, I ask him. Jamie once said that Gumlea was a dream realm. We're born from it, and we return to it each night, over and over again, until we die and stay there for good. So I figure if there's any truth to what he said, the veil is thinnest right before I fall asleep. I should be able to speak to him through it even though I'm stuck here now."

Like a brand, James's face feels like it's searing itself into my thumbprint. "I hope so," I lie.

Sometimes, I like hearing Annie talk about Gumlea. It makes my life feel a little more starlit and strange, a little less ordinary. But I don't like talking about our "ritual." I might *want* magic to be real, sometimes, but I'm old enough to know better. And even if it was, I'm not entirely sure I want James to come back, either. Of course I want him to be okay, to come back to his family, where he belongs. But I can barely imagine what it would be like if he did, and in the meantime, the situation between me and Annie is complicated enough without her brother standing between us.

Before Annie can say anything else, my mom comes in. I tuck the knife underneath a throw pillow before she can see.

"Are you staying for dinner, Annie?" she asks, because Annie's been staying for dinner a lot lately. My mom doesn't know about the knife, warm and sticky in my throbbing hand. When Annie says she is, my innocent mother only smiles.

SEVENTEEN

A FEW DAYS LATER, WE'RE in her bed together as the sun goes down. It feels like her mother is never home, and since her little brother is with her dad during the week, we're alone in her house all the time. I love it.

It's a gray day, but the leaves outside are red and gold and fiery and make the dusky sunset seem brighter. She's playing a mix I made her from the laptop on her floor. The Modern Lovers and the Silvertones and of course the Beach Boys. The music is weaving its way through us, gently humming in our bones and our brains. Maybe that's why everything feels so amazing. Or maybe it's just the way I feel when she's curled up next to me, her head on my shoulder, her hand clutching mine.

"You know what I like about you, Annie?" I'm asking her. I hold up her hand, kiss her knuckles, feel the smooth rich texture of her skin. *Tell her it's okay*, Jonathan Richman is singing. *Tell her it's all right.*

She doesn't even open her eyes. "What?" she asks sleepily.

"You are really and truly yourself. You say what's on your mind and don't mince words with anyone. You're so brave."

She lets out a small, snorted breath at that, which surprises me.

"What?"

"I'm a fucking liar," she says, which makes my back stiffen even in the cradle of her soft mattress. Keira was a liar. And look how that ended up. But Annie must feel the way my body's changed beside her, because she adds, "Not to you. Never to you."

"To who, then?"

"The rest of the freaking world. I get perfect grades and keep our house clean even though it makes me want to blow my brains out and I never say anything when Dad goes on and on about his new girlfriend from his church even though the whole thing makes me sick. I'm such a coward. I'm not like you."

"I'm not brave," I tell her, but she's suddenly squeezing my hand so tightly that it starts to tingle.

"Lies."

"What? I'm not. Look at the way I lie to my grandparents." I've told her all about how Naniji and Nanaji disowned my mom for a few years after she married my dad. Because of that, I'm happy letting them believe that I'm the perfect granddaughter. They don't know a thing about Annie. We just don't talk about it. We pretend like that part of my life doesn't exist. That I'm a good girl. Even though I'm not. "Plus, I let Harper boss me around all the time. The drinking and stuff."

"That's nothing. That's normal."

"You're normal, too," I tell her.

That's when she sits up and looks at me and we both start laughing.

She tucks her head down against my neck, laughing a moment longer. And then she looks up at me, her eyes burning with a steady light. "I lie to my therapist," she says. "She's just there to help me and I lie to her. I'm terrified of what would happen if she knew the truth about Gumlea."

I'm not laughing anymore. My throat feels a little dry. "What do you tell her?"

"She knows it's something I thought about once. I let her believe that it's a coping mechanism for losing Jamie. A paracosm, she calls it. She told me that Charlotte Brontë and her sisters had one, too."

Annie rolls her eyes, as though the idea of sharing something with the long-dead writer is absurd, just absurd. It doesn't sound absurd to me. None of it does.

"But you don't really think that?" I ask her, because it sounds pretty good. The idea that Gumlea is a story that Annie tells herself to make life easier is comforting. Neat. Normal. Maybe someday she'll grow up to be a writer, too, and it will all make sense.

But right now, she shrugs. "Gumlea was there before he disappeared. Before we even discovered it. He was always the Nameless Boy. And I was Emperata Annit, eyes like water, hair like fire. Fists of fury."

She punches me lightly in the arm. I punch her back. Then we're kissing for a while, her knees up between my legs and everything warm and right.

After, I tangle my hands through her brown hair. Her cheek is pressed against my collarbone. The playlist has ended, and now I can hear how our breathing matches.

"Hair like fire, huh?" I ask, looking at hers in the fading sunset. Even in this ruddy light, it's brown. Just brown.

Annie shrugs. "I always wanted to be a redhead," she says.

I look at her hair a moment longer. "Why not just do it?"

She sits up, staring at me for a long time, silhouetted against the window. Then she smiles.

Even though it's almost dark out, we walk to the ShopRite together. There, under the fluorescent lights, we go through the meager selection of dyes. Spiced Auburn. Autumn Nutmeg. New Penny. Eternal Flame. That's the one that Annie chooses, holding the box, with the ridiculous, blow-dried model, tight against her chest. I'm not really sure that it's going to look good on her, with her fair skin and freckles. But she looks so hopeful as she counts out her change for the cashier that I don't want to say anything. I only stand there, my hand in her back pocket.

The sky is inky on the way home. We haven't had dinner and our stomachs are yowling and the trucks on the highway have lights that are too bright and too close. None of that matters except the way that it feels when we walk home together, our heads touching, our fingers both tangled around the thin white skin of the plastic bag.

Back at her house, she strips down to her bra and jeans. I wear crinkly gloves. The bathroom fills up with the scent of chemicals. I sing to her as I work the dye in, soft ballads from another century. The mixture looks like hot red blood against her hairline and behind her ears and in spots on the sink that we rush to wipe up.

"It burns," she says, wrinkling her nose and rubbing the heels of her hands into her eyes, but I can see when she drops her hands how she keeps catching sight of herself in the mirror and grinning, a secret smile. Like she is finally becoming herself.

When the timer on my phone goes off, I help her rinse her hair over the edge of the tub. The water runs bloody, then pink, like strawberry Kool-Aid. I keep a hand on her spine as I rinse and rinse and rinse but it never goes clear, even after we add a big squirt of conditioner. When we dry her hair on her mother's seafoam-green towels, it leaves pink splotches in the exact shape of her head.

In a way, the color is awful. Dark burgundy at the ends and almost petal pink at the roots. It's punk as fuck, and Annie is no punk. Just a nerd, really.

But in another way, at the same time, it is perfect; it is everything.

I run my fingers through the damp, unruly tangles. "Emperata Annit,"

I tell her. She looks at me, smiling sweetly. "Eyes like water. Hair like fire."

"Fists of fury," she says, kissing me, and my whole world smells like conditioner and peroxide.

"Girls?"

We break apart. There is Annie's mother, staring at us from the bathroom door. Neither of us had noticed the time, or heard her car coming up the driveway.

"Hi, Mom," she says, angling up her chin like she's spoiling for a fight. Even though her pale skin looks even paler now, somehow the pink brings out the gold tones in her eyes, which shine like a pair of chemical fires.

But her mother doesn't fight with her. She just lifts a hand to her mouth. "You look so grown-up," Mrs. **[Redacted]** says.

And then she starts weeping, right there.

Annie and I look at each other, my frown mirroring hers. Because we both know what is going unsaid, the words her mother won't dare to speak.

EIGHTEEN

A FEW WEEKS LATER, DAD comes in while I'm packing for the Madrigals trip. He awkwardly hovers around for a few minutes, nodding and kind of mm-hmming at all my makeup and hair ties on my dresser until I throw a bunch of T-shirts into my duffel bag and level my gaze at him.

"What's up, Freddie?"

"You know I hate it when you call me that," he says, giving me a Dad look.

I grin at him. "But it's your name!"

"I'm Dad. I should be Dad. Or Daddy, or Papa. We're not supposed to be friends."

I push out my lower lip, doing my best not to laugh. "Are you saying we're not friends?"

My dad scowls at me.

"So, Freddie," I say, grinning. "Or Papa Freddie, if that's how you have to be. What do you want, anyway? Have you come to bring me more shoes?"

"Hmm. I think you have enough shoes." But he keeps milling around behind me, trying to catch my gaze in the mirror. Finally, he leans his weight against my dresser and gazes at me, stroking an invisible beard. "It's about Annie."

Oh God. I turn away, brushing my hair from my face. "What about her?"

"You know that your mom and I like her a lot."

"Yeah?" I ask carefully, but hopefully, too. Because I want them to like her. Super-duper badly.

"But we'd still need to meet her parents. Or her mom, at least."

Oh. That. I grab a fistful of underwear and stuff that into my bag, too. I don't want to talk about this, but I guess I have to. I'm no good at lying to my dad. I make all the same lying faces he does. "Well, okay. We can ask. But there's something you need to know."

I don't turn around to see my dad's expression, but I can imagine it: an emoticon of arched eyebrows and gritted teeth. He's bracing himself. I know it from the way his breath has gone shallow and pinched.

"Yeeeeah?" he prods.

I sigh. "Okay. Well. Annie is James's sister."

"James." Dad says the name flatly, like he doesn't understand.

"James **[Redacted]**. You know. My boyfriend. I mean, ex-boyfriend, I guess. From middle school."

I turn slowly, curious to see Dad's face. It's his I'm-pretending-to-be-cool-with-this face. God, he's such a shit actor. But then he kind of cringes, and the whole thing falls apart. "I know who James **[Redacted]** is. Was. I drove you to his funeral, remember?"

"Yeah," I say, and my voice comes out soft and kind of babyish. "Are you mad?"

"What would I have to be mad about?" he asks, and it sounds like he's really asking, but I honestly don't know. I haven't done anything wrong. I haven't hurt anyone and I haven't lied even if I didn't tell the whole truth, not right away. Anyway, I'm not sure what to tell him. I shrug.

Dad comes and sits on the bed, rubbing his face with his palms for a minute, a tangled mess of visible anxiety. I sit awkwardly beside him.

"I'm not mad," he says.

"Okay, good," I tell him.

"But I'm not thrilled, either."

"Okay?"

He taps his leg on the carpet, all jangly. Lets out a breath, like he's trying to steady himself. Then he looks at me. I used to wish I looked more like him, especially when the other kids teased me, when the teachers stumbled over my name. I don't anymore. I like myself, my wild, thick black hair and my name. Anyway, it's not just the way we look that ties us together. It's his worry for me, and his love. His concern, creasing the space between his eyebrows.

"I hated when they kept calling you down to the police station like you were some kind of criminal."

I look down at my hands, my chipped nail polish. "I know. I hated it, too."

I remember the way the interrogation room smelled. I remember the way my parents' lawyer breathed, and the sound of pens clicking as they asked me question upon question, questions I had answered before, every question a new trap, and the way my mind raced and my heart pounded in my ear. I remember thinking of music: the songs James and I had listened to together, like the Manic Street Preachers, who he loved, an obsession I never really understood. And I thought about the songs we never got around to playing for each other. I remember "Help Me, Rhonda" screeching in my head.

It echoes through my mind now.

"I know his parents had something to do with that," he said. "His father looked so sanctimonious during the news interviews. You got this feeling that they were looking for a key to explain how their sweet little baby went wrong, and you fit what they wanted well enough. They wanted you to be the bad girl, you know? And you used to wear so much black. And all that eyeliner. I *know* it was just clothing. I never cared—but other parents did. The [**Redacted**]s did. Maybe we should have taught you—"

"No, Dad," I tell him fiercely. "You always made me feel accepted. That meant the world to me. They're *jerks* if they care that I wore a lot of black eyeliner. I mean, they *are* jerks. Annie says so. James did, too."

"Maybe I could have spared you some pain, though," he says wistfully. "I just didn't want you to get hurt and I know you did, anyway."

"Not your fault," I say again. But he sighs.

"I don't want you to get hurt this time around, either."

I look down at my hands again. My dad doesn't understand. He can't. Annie isn't James, and she's not her parents, either. *Yes*, what they did hurt me. But—

"She's nothing like them," I tell him.

My father is watching me carefully. "You're young. It's easy to think—"

"Dad!" I cry suddenly, surprising even myself. "Annie is wonderful. She really is. She makes me feel . . ." I trail off, because there's no way I can explain it to him. How when I'm with her, music and magic flow through me all at once. Life before her was ordinary, but now it's full of something else—something like *potential*.

He puts his arm around my shoulder and pulls me close, kissing my hair. "I know, Vidya. That's the problem."

I'm still tucked in against him. Warm. Safe. "What?"

"You're sixteen. In love. There are a thousand tragic rock songs about this. It never ends well. You know, I was sixteen once, too."

"I know. I've seen the pictures," I tell him, grimacing and laughing a little. I have to laugh, because I don't want him to know how deep they slice into me, his words. I don't want to fall out of love with Annie. Sure, it's always happened before. Either my heart gets broken, or the other person's does.

Except for James, I guess. That's one way out of the whole thing. You could just vanish into thin air. Then there's no breaking, no tears, no bad poetry.

But Annie is *different*. We have plans. Not just this Madrigals trip, or her ritual, but after. We've started to talk about it in a vague, laughing way. How once she has James back, I'll go to school for music in the city, and she'll go to school for art, and we'll make amazing things and be amazing people together.

"Be careful," Dad says, kissing me again. I close my eyes, listening to his heart thump through his T-shirt. "Mom and I are here if you need us, but just be careful, okay?"

"Okay," I tell him, but I'm old enough to know that I'm lying. There's nothing careful about my relationship with Annie. It's messy and it's beautiful and it's magical. And because of that, I know that I can't promise him anything at all.

NINETEEN

THE BUS LEAVES AFTER SCHOOL on Friday for our first Madrigals trip. We're all excited, electricity bounding off us and sparking through the air. Mrs. Kepler tries to get us to practice, but nobody wants to. We're too busy shouting and flirting and harassing each other, a real bunch of animals.

Annie sits next to me, her wild flame hair thrown back in a ponytail, her eyes squirrelly. I want to kiss her neck and wriggle my hand down into her jeans, but she's not into that PDA stuff, not even under the cover of my wool peacoat. So instead I lean my head on her shoulder as Harper goads us into a game of MASH like a couple of third graders. Annie's answers are terrible. Her top pick is *Gillian Anderson*, who, sure, can still get it, but random? Not that I can talk. I'm going to live in a swank beach house with Brian Wilson and our nine children. Annie's face flames almost as bright as her hair at that.

"But he's even older than Gillian Anderson," she says, and then she adds, "And he's got a cock."

Harper thinks that's hilarious. "I like this one, Vee," she tells me. "Keep her around, okay?"

You could paint the sky red with Annie's blushing.

The competition is at a state college a few counties away and begins as soon as we get off the bus. We file right into the mostly empty auditorium. Mrs. Kepler has to tap on the music stand over and over again to get us to warm up. I can see that the whole thing is wearing thin for her but it's hard to care—I'm sixteen and happy, damn it. Even when we kinda bomb our first song, it doesn't bother me too much until I see Southton High School get up there, dressed in head-to-toe period costumes, blowing us out of the water.

"Damn," Annie says. "Well, we suck."

And even though I think I love her, I hate her right then for wearing her heart on her sleeve, like she always does, and calling it like she sees it, like she always does, too.

Back at the motel after dinner that evening, Mrs. K reminds us that we have another competition early the next day, and the flat line of her lips is unamused. We check into our rooms, four to a suite, and bring our bags upstairs. I look at Annie, sprawled out in our double bed on her stomach, scribbling in her book, and I think, well, that's one of the plus sides of dating a girl. No need to sneak around, not really, like I would have with James or any other boy. I lie down next to her as she draws a strange, horned hare in her sketchbook.

"Tell me about this," I ask her. "It's beautiful."

She blushes almost instantly. I don't think Annie is used to anyone looking at her art this closely. I don't think she's used to anyone looking at *her* this closely. But it *is* beautiful. She's put down a soft layer of graphite, and then over that has begun to etch out individual pieces of fur with a mechanical pencil. It looks real, like you could reach out and touch it and feel the soft fur beneath. Instead, before she can answer, I reach out and touch the side of her face. Even though Harper's only a few feet away, we start to kiss before Annie can reconsider.

"Get a room, you two," Harper cracks. She's sharing a bed with Meg Demeran and isn't too thrilled about it. We know from last year that Meg snores like a jet engine.

I pull away from Annie and stick my tongue out. "We already have one."

Some boys come knocking on the door, Davey Riener and Shepperd Anson, and Harper goes over, whispering to them. Annie is ignoring it, giving my neck little tender half bites. But my ears are pricked up.

". . . party . . . Southton . . ."

"What's up, Harp?" I call, squirming a little bit out of Annie's grasp so I can sit up at the edge of the bed.

Harper glances over her shoulder. "One of the Southton girls is having a room party. You guys want to come?"

Meg does, and I do, too. But I see Annie's face, how it's practically collapsed in on itself. I squeeze her hand.

"Come on," I tell her, "it'll be fun."

"I hate fun," she tells me, but she gets up anyway, her hand in my hand and gently trembling as we follow Meg and Harper and Davey and Shepperd down the hallway.

It's only an hour until lights-out, when Mrs. K will stick her head into our room and make sure that we're all asleep. But I know from last year's trips that an hour's plenty of time to get wasted. Harper's brought along her smuggled water bottle of vodka and one of the Southton kids gets out those little paper cups you find in the bathroom. Annie and I watch everyone take shots.

I don't drink tonight. I've told her how much I hate it. It would look two-faced to go back on that now, so we only sit together, Annie's arm draped over my shoulder, watching the rest of them get sloshed.

"Hey," one of the Southton girls, whose name is Akilah, says, staring at Annie. "Do I know you from somewhere?"

"I don't think so," she answers. Across the room, Shepperd mutters something, and you almost wouldn't notice except Harper snaps, "Watch it!"

"What's that?" Akilah asks. Shepperd blushes, like he didn't mean to get caught. He's not looking at me and he's not looking at Annie.

"I said you might have seen her on the news," he says, and everyone from our school snickers. Behind me, I feel Annie's body stiffen.

"The news?" Akilah asks, all innocence and light, and the other Southton kids are elbowing each other. I kind of want to die, for Annie's sake. I wish I could climb under one of the motel beds and count the springs popping through the mattress, something, anything, to distract myself from the heat of their eyes.

But Annie doesn't care about the heat of their eyes. Sometimes I don't think she cares about anything.

"My brother disappeared," she says firmly, like she's not even embarrassed. "Two years ago. Maybe you heard of him. James **[Redacted]**."

The laughing stops. The snickering and jostling and drinking stops. After a minute, Shepperd starts laughing nervously, until Harper elbows him in the ribs.

"Shit," says Akilah. "Of course. James **[Redacted]**. I was obsessed with that when I was younger. I used to stay up way too late reading about him on Wikipedia, wondering where he went. I was kind of going through a hard time back then. It felt like something that could have happened to any of us."

Her words kind of shimmer on the air. I see Annie's expression soften, like she's not used to anyone talking about James like he was just another sad *kid* like the rest of us. She's starting to relax beside me when Akilah holds out a bathroom cup of vodka.

"Here."

She offers Annie the cup, but Annie shakes her head. "No, I don't drink," she says, even though she told me before that she does, sometimes. Wine at holidays, mostly.

"Smoke, then?" the girl asks. She goes over to her luggage and pulls out a plastic pencil case. Now it's my turn to go stiff and awkward, because I know what's going to happen and Annie doesn't, not yet, not really. We watch together as the girl begins to roll a lumpy little joint. "I was going to save this for later, when everyone else has gone to bed, but I think we should share it. You know, for absent friends."

She lights up. Everyone is watching, holding their breath as brown dragon fire curls its way out her nostrils. Maybe she senses that I'm the gateway to Annie, because she hands it to me next, and I take a small puff and hold my breath in. It's scratchy and painful in my throat.

"Here," I tell Annie, and I go to pass the joint to her, but she's still all stiff and awkward behind me, hardly breathing.

"I can't. I can't," she says, in a tiny, frantic voice.

"What?" I say.

Suddenly, just like that, Annie leaps to her feet.

"I can't!" she says, a little too loud, and then she heads for the motel room door. People are snickering again, but I know that they don't really find it funny. It's mostly embarrassing. I hand the joint off to someone and rush to follow her, catching the door just before it slams.

Annie's fast. She's already well down the hall.

"I can't. I can't," she says again as she slips into the stairwell. The lights around us buzz. "I took a vow, Vidya. I can't."

When she turns around, I realize that she's crying. She keeps wringing her hands like she's trying to take off some invisible ring.

"Okay," I tell her. I want to comfort her. No, that's not right. I want to tame her. She's shaking like a wild animal. "You don't have to. What you do with your lungs and your brain and your body are up to you."

She grimaces through tears. "Thanks, Mom," she says, voice heavy with sarcasm.

I laugh a little. I run my hand through my hair. "I was just trying to help," I tell her. And I realize I'm angry, too, whether at her or the situation, I can't be sure. "It's really not that bad, if you don't smoke it all the time. It can help you be creative . . . ," I trail off. This feels like it isn't going so well. "It's not a big deal. It's really not!"

"Whatever," she says, shaking her head. "Drugs. It's so ridiculous. Could you be more cliché, Vidya?"

That stings. I sit down on the stairs, not answering her for a long time. Annie finally notices my expression, which must say everything about how much that hurt.

"Sorry," she says. Her face is still teary when she exhales, hard. "I'm just scared."

"Of smoking?"

"Of the whole thing," she says. She cracks her knuckles. I flinch at the noise. "I caught Jamie smoking pot in the woods once. I knew that was the beginning of the end for him. He was slipping away from me, and I couldn't stop it. And then I really lost him—"

Her voice chokes in her throat. I hold out my hand. After a moment's pause, she takes it and sits on the stairwell beside me.

"I can't imagine what it's like to have a brother," I tell her, "much less to lose one."

She laughs at that, but it's not a funny kind of laughter. "It sucks."

"Yeah," I agree. My thoughts are turning over and over in my mind. I'm groping through the darkness for the right words, channeling my mother again. When I stroke Annie's hand, it's with the same even pressure with which my mom touches me.

"Pot didn't take your brother away," I tell her.

She sniffles. Nods. "I know. It's just . . . we made a promise to each other when we were little kids."

"When I was a kid," I start, smiling, "I swore I would never have sex. It just sounded revolting."

"I'm glad you changed your mind," she says faintly, then turns to plant a kiss just behind my ear. I lean into it. "But I'm still not sure," she murmurs against my neck.

I nod. "It's up to you," I tell her. And then I add, "No one will be mad at you if you don't. I won't be mad at you."

"But they *laughed* at me," she says. I grimace.

"Fuck 'em," I tell her. She cracks a small smile.

We stay there for a moment in the bright stairwell, breathing together, hardly moving. Then, with a sigh, Annie stands up and offers me her hand.

"Okay," she says. "I'll give it a shot."

I stare at her, numb for a moment. Shocked. It's not the answer I expected from her. I don't think it was the answer Annie expected from herself, either. She laughs a little—at me, at herself, I'm not sure which.

"Come on," she says.

I take her hand and together, we head back into the crowded motel room.

We're in bed when our motel room door opens, and for a moment all I can see is the sinister shape of Mrs. Kepler's head as she counts us. Her bun almost looks like a second smaller skull on top of her skull. I hold my breath until my chest aches and it's not until the door closes and the world is dark again that I take a long, jagged gasp.

"You're alive," Annie reminds me, and she's kissing me, her mouth wet and soft and supple, and I'm not afraid anymore, I'm only leaning into her in the pitch-black blackness. She's leaning back and kissing me, saying between kisses, "You're here. You're not dead, Vidya. You're alive."

Sensations wash over me: cold and pleasure and dark and we're kissing and we shouldn't be doing this here, with Meg snoring in the bed across the room and Harper probably eyes wide open and listening, but we do it anyway, I touch her, and her body feels like something, and then I realize with a grin in the darkness: she feels like *hot*.

After, we lie together and my heart pounds up in the darkness. I'm sure everyone can hear it, Harper and Meg and most of all Annie, my blood pulsing, my breath heavy and dull but then I hear Annie next to me. When I look over, I can make out the shape of her by the light of the red blink blinking smoke detector. At first I think she's crying again and my heart beats for her, but she's not. She's curled up in bed, her hands tucked under her chin, and by the light of the smoke detector, she's laughing, like someone just told her the funniest joke.

"What is it, darling?" I ask, because I'm stoned and suddenly it doesn't feel ridiculous to call her my darling, because that's what she is.

"Oh, nothing. It's just—it's just—" More laughter, and now Meg snorts and chokes and sits up, then hisses at us from across the motel room.

"SHH!"

I put a hand over Annie's mouth. She laughs into it, until finally her breath calms and she's just panting up into the darkness. When she looks at me, I can see that her eyes are wide open, like it might as well be daylight in that dark, dark motel room, and she's smiling, still.

"What is it?" I whisper, my mouth very close to her ear.

She looks at me, smiling and blinking, all brightness and day, and as if it's the happiest thing, the sanest thing, she whispers, "It was never me. It was always Jamie."

"What?" I whisper back.

"Every single idea I ever had, every law, every vow, every mountain we climbed, every river we named, it was Jamie. I was just the archivist. I was only the archivist."

My mouth is very, very serious in the darkness, a flat line. "I don't understand."

"I was the archivist, Vidya. Even of you. I didn't dream you up. He did. You were his idea first."

She's laughing again, howling into the dark.

"Would you keep it down?" Meg asks, and Annie clutches the pillow to her face and tries to calm her breath, but she can't, and I can't, either, not anymore, the tears in the darkness streaming down my face, but I can't tell you why I cry them.

TWENTY

I'M QUIET ON THE BUS ride home. But then, almost everyone is quiet—exhausted or hungover or both. Annie's got her head on my shoulder. She's drawing something. Her hands never seem to stop moving. When I glance over, I see that she's sketched out the bones and body of a hare, sliced open by a familiar knife that sits in the shadowed underbrush. The blood she's drawing is dark, heavy hatch-marked lines of graphite against the paper. The whole scene is beautiful and disgusting, all at once.

I know how that hare feels. But I don't tell Annie.

When the bus lets us off in the high school parking lot, both of our mothers are waiting in their cars. Annie grabs me, and I let her, right there, in front of our moms, in front of everybody, and I let her kiss me long and deep to prove to myself that everything is okay.

It's not.

"You must have had a nice weekend," my mom says when I hop in the car and slam the car door behind me.

"It sucked," I say gravely. "We lost."

"Hmm," my mom says. "Have you been practicing?"

No, of course I haven't. I've been preoccupied lately.

"As much as we ever practice," I tell her with a shrug, which I know is a cop-out. I've always worked harder at music than Harper and the rest of them, even when it was just me and James and Neal Harriman, making up crappy songs in Neal's basement. It never really seemed like *work* to me before. But Annie's distracted me from that. Made it seem like real things— piano, Madrigals, Brian Wilson—aren't half as important as the things that are going on inside her head. I start to fiddle with the radio so that I won't have to explain myself. Mom's looking at me sidelong, her mouth wry.

"You know, Vidya," she says as we head out of the parking lot. "It's time we started visiting colleges. Have you looked at the spreadsheet I made for you?"

I glower at her. "I'm not *going* to college. I'm going to music school. You must have been talking to Naniji again," I grumble.

It's mean, and I know it is. Mom's not wrong, anyway. I *should* be thinking about that stuff, and not just in the vague, fantastic way that I think about it when I'm with Annie. This is my real, actual life—not some fantasy novel.

Mom takes my brattiness in stride, though. She just rolls her eyes and lets out a little sigh. "Oh, Vidya," she says gently.

For some reason, that's the worst thing she could possibly say to me. I scrunch down low in the seat and try to make myself invisible.

So. Here's the problem: I love Annie, and I know I love her, but so many things about her make my heart feel sick in my chest.

Alone in my room that night, when I should be practicing piano for the recital that's coming up, or doing trigonometry homework, or looking at that stupid college spreadsheet my mother made me, I split a piece of note-book paper down the middle.

On one side, I write down the things I love about her. Freckles. Laughter. Boldness. The way she makes me feel like I could do anything. The way she makes me feel like I'm a character in a book.

I scratch out that last one. I put it on the other side, with a question mark after it. On the side with the things I don't like about her. Her family scares and confuses me. I'm not sure what's real and what's make-believe with her. I want Gumlea to be a game. The way James spoke of it, it was nothing more than a fairy tale told on boring family car trips. But Annie makes me feel uncertain. I don't think it's real. It's not. It can't be real. But she might think it's real, and she's lying to her psychologist about that, and that scares me, too.

And then there's James. The shadow we can never outrun. He's with us when we're kissing and when she's telling me about the fall of Gumlea's king. He's with us when I hold her hand, my fingers circling her knuckles, and I find myself thinking of James, and of how she feels like him.

I don't like how good that feels, how being with her has brought him back from the dead. Some spirits are better left buried, and I don't believe in spirits anyway. I'd moved on, before I moved on to his sister. And now I'm stuck.

And *Annie's* stuck. That's the worst part, isn't it? It's not just that he's a shadow I'll never outrun. Someday, I'll move away from this town. Go to the city. Finally start a band. What will Annie do? Sit here and wait for her brother to come back. I think about her artwork, how her hands are always all silvery from pencil dust, how she's *always* drawing, always coming up with these amazing scenes that are like something out of another universe. I think about how nobody ever seems to notice them except me. I think about how even Annie shrugs them off, like they're not important.

Like *she's* not important.

I tear the notebook page into tiny pieces and let them shower down into my trash can along with the stray hair from my hairbrush and a note from Keira that I found in my desk drawer last week and finally, belatedly threw away.

I trudge through the week, acting like it's nothing that I'm making lists like these—that I'm having *doubts* like these. I kiss Annie and leave my hand on her leg at lunch and tell myself what matters is how I *feel*. And in the moment, most moments, I feel good. Mostly.

But sometimes—at Madrigals, when I'm trying to sing and her eyes are shining out at me from across the risers full of love and magic—it doesn't feel good at all.

She calls me up a few nights later. It's a Saturday, and I've been in my room for hours, trying to write her a song, failing. I didn't expect her to call tonight. She should be at her dad's. She never calls on Saturday nights. But her voice is ragged, like she's been crying for a while.

"Mom says she's selling the house."

"What?" I ask. Horrors flash through my mind. I wonder where they'll be moving to. I always said I didn't want a long-distance relationship, but that was before Annie, before I felt her soft hip against my belly.

"I can't believe she's doing this, Vidya. I can't lose Gumlea. If we lose the house, we'll never see him again. This'll be it for Jamie coming back to us, and she doesn't even care. He's gone. Gone."

"Where are you? Are you at your dad's?"

"No. I'm at our house. Her house. God, I can't believe this. She won't even talk to me about it. She says there's nothing to talk about."

"Can you hold on a minute?"

"Yeah."

I go to Mom and Dad's room, where they're both up reading, their toes touching over the sheets.

"Can Annie come over tonight? I think she had a fight with her mom."

Dad looks at Mom. They nod together.

I put my phone under my ear. "If your mom can give you a ride, you should come over. Spend the night. Get out of there. Get some air."

There's a long pause. Annie sniffles.

"Okay, yeah. I'd like that. Sure. See you soon."

She hangs up. I hesitate for a minute, forgetting that I'm still standing in my parents' doorway like a little kid who swears she's just seen a monster under her bed.

"Everything okay, sweetie?" Mom asks. I force a smile.

"Yeah, sure," I tell her. But we all see right through it. Of that, I'm certain.

An hour later, Annie is sitting on my bedroom floor. She's taken off her sneakers and left them in a pile by my bedroom door, and she's clutching an overstuffed backpack to her chest. Her face looks wet, but I'm not sure if it's from tears or from the rain outside. It's one of those cold autumn nights that is basically winter. Her hair looks black, plastered to her face.

"I can't believe she didn't talk to you about this first," I tell her. "I mean, you grew up in that house, right?"

Annie clutches her backpack tighter and nods, sniffling. It's clear now that she *has* been crying. For hours, probably. "They bought it six months before Jamie was born," she says, her voice ragged. "Mom and Dad had rented for years before that but—but my mom was pregnant, and they wanted us to have stability, they said. Like, to live in a normal house. Like a normal family. Like we've ever been a normal family. It's such bullshit."

She rubs her fist against her eyes. I'm sighing as I sit down beside her.

"I mean," I say, "I can understand why she'd want to leave now. With the divorce and everything . . ." I trail off carefully. I'm talking *around* the issue of James, mostly because I'm afraid of what she'll say if I mention his name. "But you're fifteen. You're not some little kid. She should have talked to you about it first. It's—it's not *respectful*."

Maybe it's a ridiculous idea, that Annie's mom would respect her like my parents respect me. But they do. Even when they're being strict with me about something, I understand it's because they have my best interests at heart. Maybe that's why I can't imagine how I'd feel if they sold our *house* without talking about it first. They'd never pull the rug out from under me like that—ever.

"Respectful," Annie says with a snort. "She called up Dad and demanded he bring me home early and didn't even tell him why. He drops me off and there's the 'For Sale' sign outside and the Realtor sitting in there with Mom, having tea. When I tried to talk to her about it, Mom told me we couldn't discuss it now because there was *company* over."

"That's bullshit," I say. "Total and utter bullshit."

"Totally," she agrees. "When the old lady saw how pissed I was, she went to the bathroom. And that's when Mom said she *couldn't* tell me before, because she knew I wouldn't be *reasonable* about it."

"It's not like she even gave you a chance to be reasonable!" I protest, which, okay, feels a little ridiculous because if there's one word I would never, ever apply to Annie, it's *reasonable*. For a bunch of reasons, too many to count.

But Annie just says, "Right?" and kind of laughs softly, despite herself.

"You'll be okay," I tell her, taking her cold hand in mine. It feels clammy and halfway dead. "We'll get through this together."

306

She squeezes my fingers. "You don't know how much that means to me," she tells me, then puts her head on my shoulder. I tell myself that maybe it's true. We will get through this together. We'll write romantic emails and texts and the distance will feel like nothing in the scheme of things.

"Where do you think she'll be moving?" I ask her in a soft voice. Annie shrugs.

"Does it matter? I don't know. Probably Westchester, to be closer to her sister. Westchester. Ugh."

I laugh a little. It's a very Annie response. Of *course* she would hate Westchester. When I've imagined a future for Annie, it's either in the city or somewhere off in the middle of nowhere. Alaska or something. She looks at me, laughing a little, too. And then we're kissing. Her whole body feels wet and cool and her touch send shivers through me. She puts her cold hands against my stomach, under my T-shirt. I'm covered in goose bumps then, but I don't care. I wish we could be together like this forever. Kissing and touching, our bodies shivering together, setting off sparks.

The floor is hard under us but I don't even care. I think, *I'm going to make her forget the world is a terrible place*, and there, on my bedroom floor, I do—for a little while. Because after, I'm lying there with my head against her belly, my hair a dark tangle. She's not cold anymore. Our bodies feel almost the same. Warm and raw and bright. But then my gaze lands on her backpack, which has fallen, half-unzipped, on my bedroom floor.

There's the knife. That stupid knife, the one I chose so carefully, thinking it would be somehow romantic. But of course, the knife had nothing to do with us, not to Annie. It was *his* profile she drew on the side of the handle, facing her own. Not mine.

There's other stuff in there, too. Her schoolbag is packed with sticks and leaves and long tangles of twine. I can see the ends of tapered candles, four or five of them. And who knows what else.

"What *is* that all?" I ask, sitting up. Annie sits upright, too. She's blushing slightly, reaching for the backpack.

"I figured," she begins, tugging the zipper open all the way and starting to unpack her supplies, "that we can't wait until solstice anymore. The house might be sold by then. I was thinking we could go tomorrow morning."

"Go?" For a minute, my mind is swimming. I tell myself that I have no idea what she's talking about, but the sad truth is, I do.

"To the woods, silly," she tells me breezily. She's setting the supplies out on my bedroom floor one by one, handling them gently, like they're delicate eggs. There's the candles, with wax so pale that it looks like dead flesh. There's a little baggie of ash tied with one of those plastic clips from a bread bag. A bundle of sage. And a skull—like an actual skull, it must be from a mouse or something, the bones so delicate that I worry Annie might crush it. She sets it gently on the carpet, too.

"This is what we'll need for the ritual," she says, putting the knife at the center of it all. And then she looks up to me, blushing brighter, and sheepishly adds, "And . . . I thought it might be easier if you could get some pot."

I tug my T-shirt down over my naked belly, sitting straighter. "What?"

"I know that Jamie liked to smoke it. Honestly, it was kind of an interesting experience, on the Madrigals trip. Smoking. I think I get it now. I feel like it might make it easier to speak to him if we get high. Like there are holes in the veil. . ." She frowns, like she knows her explanation doesn't really make sense. "Anyway, if you don't have any . . ."

"No, I mean. There's someone I could call." I bite my lip. I haven't talked to Neal Harriman's friend Steve in forever. He kind of creeps me out, honestly, with his leering friends and the way they always elbowed each other, talking about me and the other kids. Neal and James thought they were cool, but I never did. Still, Annie's expression is laser focused. I can't say no to her. "I'll send him a text. My phone's downstairs."

Annie watches me leave my bedroom. I close the door so I don't have to look at her face. As I walk downstairs, my stomach feels like it's stuck somewhere in my pelvis. I can't decide if I'm worried, or afraid, or some other emotion, one I have no name for. I move through our dimly lit house. It's almost midnight. My phone's in the charging station, plugged in on the counter. But I stop at the doorway to the kitchen. Because Mom's there, washing dishes.

"Vidya," she says, glancing over her shoulder. "Do you girls need some snacks? I can fix you something."

Leave it to Mom to think of food at a time like this. Or at any time, really. I shake my head and grab my phone off the counter.

"No, we're good," I tell her, but when I turn on my phone, I just stare at it. Then I look up at my mom. "Actually, we're not good. I'm not good."

"Hmm?" she says, closing the dishwasher and turning toward me like she's been waiting for this. I feel myself cringe. I don't want to say it. I don't. It hurts to say it, but I'm clutching my phone so hard that my hands are white at the knuckles. But Mom is looking at me and waiting, so finally, finally, I puke out the truth.

"Annie scares me," I tell her.

She's frowning. "What do you mean?" she asks, and I hate that she doesn't even sound surprised and that she adds, "Vidya, has she *hurt* you?"

Has she? Well, no, not physically. Not in the way she thinks.

"No!" I say quickly, but then, because Annie is waiting, because Mom is waiting, too, the words all spill out. "She—she's obsessed with getting her brother back, somehow. She wants to do . . . this ritual? Like a Wiccan thing, kind of? She's up in my room with a mouse skull and this knife and some candles. She spent hours on this stuff. It's like how I used to go on and on about Middle-earth? Except she talks about this stuff like it's *real*. She lies to her parents about it and lies to her therapist about it, but it's not right, the way she talks about her brother like she can bring him back to life. Like we're not normal kids and like—"

I break off midsentence, holding my hands up against my face, pressing my phone against my cheek. I'm doing my best to hide from my mom's expression, which tells me she's taking my words very, *very* seriously.

"Oh God," I say through my hands. "I *like* her, like so, so much, but this whole thing—"

I want to tell her that it sounds nuts, but I can't quite bring myself to say it. It feels too mean. Especially when I know how it's hurting Annie, too, in a way. She could be making amazing art or telling amazing stories or joining the debate team or making playlists, but she's not. She's fixated on James instead. Dedicating her whole life to him, which feels to me like it's not any kind of life at all.

My mother just sighs. I'm bracing myself for it. Waiting.

"I knew she was trouble. With that brother, and those parents, and how they still won't meet us. I should have never allowed it. And then Daddy helping you to sneak around to see her. It's no good."

My hands are still up over my face. I moan into them.

"You knew about that?"

"Of course I did, Vidya. Did you think he wouldn't tell me? Your father can't *lie*. He's a terrible liar."

I pull my hands down. And despite the way it feels to have my mother notice how *bad* I've been, there's some relief in it. She's been watching out for me. Paying attention.

"He *is* a terrible liar," I say, and want to laugh, but it's clear from my mother's expression that this isn't a laughing matter.

"I went along with all this because he said you were *in love*. Like we were once in love. I know what it's like to have parents who don't approve. But Vidya—" she stops herself. I wince.

"Go ahead," I tell my mother. "Say it."

"Your father was *never* full of nonsense like this. He didn't distract me from school, or the people who mattered. He made me feel *safe*. Nanaji and Naniji came to this country to give me—and you—a better life than they had. They sacrificed everything. And this might not be the life they imagined, but our family loves and supports one another to do the right thing. Does Annie do this for you? Because you haven't been acting like yourself with her. You haven't been acting like the child I raised you to be."

I look down at my bare toes, biting my lip in the center. Haven't I? I love Annie. I want to help *her*. But mostly lately I feel invisible next to her. Because I'm not James. Because the story of James sucks all the other air out of the room. There isn't room for doing the right thing or the wrong thing with Annie. There's only Gumlea. Nothing else.

"Are you going to tell me to break up with her?" I ask, almost hoping she will. I pull down to look at the phone in my hand because I can't bring myself to look her in the eye.

"No. I'm only going to tell you to do what's *right*."

Guilt sinks into me like a fist into my belly. It's the worst thing she could have said. Because I know what's right. But I'm scared to do it.

"I know you care for her," my mother says when I don't say anything. "But on the night your father and I met, I knew that no matter what happened, he was going to help me be the best version of myself I could possibly be. Does Annie do that?"

I don't answer. Can't. My mother puts her hand on her cheek.

"Think about what I've said," she tells me. "I know you'll do the right thing."

And then she leaves. Like I didn't just tell her that the girl in my bedroom believes she can bring her dead brother back with magic and a little fireplace ash. Like I'm fully capable of handling this problem all by myself.

But am I?

I look at my phone again, then I put it back down on the counter. I go back upstairs. Annie's put her stuff away. She's crawled into my bed and is lying with her hands folded on top of the covers like a corpse. I climb in next to her.

"Did you call your guy?" she asks. I shrug and fake a yawn.

"Yeah, I sent him a text. We'll see if he answers."

"Thank you," she says, and it's only when she kisses me that I feel a strong undertow of guilt, pulling me out to sea.

TWENTY-ONE

WE DON'T FUCK THAT NIGHT, but I hold her, her head tucked beneath my chin, my hands against her rib cage. That night, mulling over what I'm going to do, I don't sleep at all. Meanwhile she's dead to the world, and when dawn comes, gray and feeble, I sit on the end of the bed with a cup of my mother's coffee and wait for her to wake.

"You're up early," she says when she finally stirs, sitting up to watch me. She's squinty and disheveled and so cute. I just want to lie myself down next to her and sleep forever, but I can't.

I gather my courage up around me like I might before a concert or a performance. I compose myself, making my face serious. "We need to talk."

Her face falls.

"Fuck," she says, sitting up straight in bed. "You couldn't get the weed?"

I laugh at that, a nervous giggly laugh, rubbing my fingertips over my brow and feeling the coffee steam back at me with every exhale. I can't believe her. She's so single-minded sometimes, so unaware of other people's feelings. Namely mine.

"God, Annie," I say, like I've suddenly found faith. "No. Seriously?"

Confusion furrows her brow. "What?"

To be fair, I've never talked to her this way. It's the way that she talks. Blunt, like my patience has all run out, if I ever had any patience at all. I'm usually gentle and accommodating, just like my mother. But I don't want to be gentle now. I need to be strong.

"No," I tell her. "God. I didn't even text the guy. I lied, okay? I can't help you with the ritual today."

Won't would be more accurate. *Don't want to* would be the truth. But *can't* will do well enough for now.

". . . Why not?" she asks. Her tone isn't accusatory at all. It's baffled, like she can't even imagine why I wouldn't want to stand in the woods and chant with her.

"Christ." More God stuff. I didn't know I had it in me. "Because it's not real. And it freaks me out. Annie, James is gone. He's dead. No amount of playing with knives or smoking pot in your backyard is going to bring him back. I like you so much, Annie, but—I can't do it."

I can't get sucked into this Gumlea stuff anymore. It's not good for me. I know it's not. Even worse, I know it's not good for *her*.

"I think you should tell your therapist what's going on with your mom," I tell her firmly. "She's there to help you. And you can—you can tell her about the ritual stuff, too. She'll know how to help you move on from it. You should be focusing on your art. Thinking about colleges . . ." I trail off. Annie's face is a twisted mask of horror. It's like I'm watching her heart shatter in slow motion. She flinches with every single word.

"Not James," I add, and I'm trying to speak gently, but from the way she grimaces I can tell that my words hurt her. Still, I go on and on. I tell myself I'm doing her a kindness. "You can't think about James anymore, or this ritual. You need to be thinking about yourself. That's why I can't help you with this. I'm sorry. I can't."

"But I need you," she tells me. Her chin is quivering. She's not quite on the verge of tears, but almost there. Desperate. When she says it, my heart lurches. But then she adds: "I can't do the ritual alone. I'm not a whole person, Vidya. I'm—"

"This is what I mean," I snap. Suddenly, I'm angry, like really, really pissed off. I stand up and go to my window, drawing in a few breaths. I can't be cruel to her, not after all we've been through, even if she thinks that I'm being cruel by saying it. "You're not half a person. You're a perfectly good person on your own. A beautiful person." I'm not looking at her. I'm gazing out the window at the neighbor's lawn, all littered with leaves. "I love you, Annie. But I can't make you whole. No one can. Not me. Not James. *You* have to do that."

There's an excruciating pause. I hope, maybe, that she's considering my words. That she'll give up everything that has to do with this crazy ritual thing, give up on James, and finally, for once, believe in herself. But instead, when her words come, they're sharp. Angry. All she says is "Fuck. Fuck."

I hear her get up and scramble around for her shoes and her bag.

"Where are you going?" I ask her.

"Where do you *think* I'm going?" she demands. "The door is closing, Vidya. Whether you're there with me or not—"

"You can't be serious," I say softly, but I see the look on her face and I know that it's true. She's going out there to the woods without me.

"He's not coming back," I try to tell her.

She's stuffed everything into her bag and thrown it over her shoulder. "I have to try," she says. "I have to—"

She puts a hand over her mouth, because what comes out then is a gasping sob. I take a step toward her, putting a hand on her shoulder. She shrinks away from my touch. She shakes me off like my hand is a fire poker and I've burned her. That's when it hits me: I can't help her with this. It's up to *her* to fix it, not me.

Which means it's over, doesn't it? If we can't work together, then we are fundamentally alone.

"Okay. I guess that's it, then. Goodbye, Annie," I tell her in a soft voice, and we both realize then what I'm really saying.

I hadn't *wanted* to break up with her. I promise you I hadn't. But I see now that there's no other road forward. I can't be with her and believe that she's a broken shell of a person without her brother. She can't be with me and let James go.

"Fuck!" she says one more time, and she lets the door slam shut behind her. I hear the rattle of her body on the stairwell, and her heavy sneakers on the front porch. I go to my bedroom window to watch her leave, but she doesn't look back at me as she streams down the sidewalk, her hair a blazing fire in the gray gray day. She either doesn't know or doesn't care that I'm watching her, or that my heart is breaking, too.

TWENTY-TWO

MY STOMACH IS A CHEWED-UP pile of dog crap. I don't eat all day, and when Mom brushes my hair out of my eyes, I flinch away from her touch.

"I don't want to talk about it," I tell her, and I hate how kindly her eyes regard me.

"Okay. I'm here if you need me," she reminds me. Even though I can tell she wants to kiss me, she doesn't. She's giving me my space.

I know I'm lucky. That's the worst part of it. When I go upstairs to my dad's office and he lets me hang out in there while he's grading papers, when he lets me take his old Epiphone Casino down from the wall and listens to me strum a few chords, he doesn't ask me any questions. He gives me my space, too. But his presence is safe and steady there, unwavering.

It's everything that Annie's never had.

I think about how her house used to feel at night. Empty and sharp, the angles from the lights jagged as knives. Her mom was hardly ever home, and when she was, they barely spoke to each other. Now I imagine Annie trudging around the woods alone, humming, chanting. Coming in from the cold to a lonely house with a "For Sale" sign on the curb. Maybe she puts on the TV just to fill up the silence. Maybe she puts on the playlists I've made her and cries. My parents don't even need to ask what happened; they take one look at my face and they *know*. But Annie? All she'd have to do is wipe away her tears after her mom comes in and fake a smile and her mom would have no idea. Because she doesn't *care*. Nobody cares about her. Not her mom or her dad or Elijah, not really. Not like I cared. And I did. Do.

But I don't call her. I can't. The things I said, I meant them. And I can't take them back now.

That night, around two in the morning, when I'm in bed not sleeping and not feeling anything except *dead* and *awful* and *suck*, my phone vibrates on my desk. I get up and go look at it, hoping it's Annie, hoping it's not.

Fuck. It's her.

Annie: Hey. Don't answer.

I don't. I hold the phone at arm's length, like it's a Fourth of July sparkler and it might burn me, like it's a snake, like it's a knife.

Annie: I tried the ritual. But it didn't work. So I got rid of everything. I went out into the woods and I buried the knife and the skull and everything. You can forget about it. Maybe you're right. Maybe there is no magic.

I still don't answer. I don't know what I'm supposed to do with all of this, whether it's supposed to change things between us, whether I'm supposed to take her back. But then my phone lights up again, and all my hopes are dashed.

Annie: And even if you're not right, I can't do it alone,

anyway. **That's the problem with Gumlea. It only**
works if there's two people. Otherwise it's just like
I'm talking to myself, and then what's the point?
Annie: I'm talking to myself right now, aren't I? Ugh. Fuck.

I imagine her face in my mind's eye, frustrated by her own slow, deliberate typing. She hardly ever keeps her phone charged. She's not good at pretending like she's the rest of us. Because she isn't.

Annie: I don't expect anything to be different. For us to be
together. I'm still a big weirdo, lost in my stupid stories. Same
as before. And you're beautiful. Amazing. Talented. Normal.
We are who we are, and you deserve someone who is nor-
mal, too, and who can love you like you should be loved.

I want to text her back: *You, too! You should be loved! You shouldn't bury*
yourself in this fucked-up bullshit just because your brother—
But what good would it do? None. No good at all. So I just stand there,
shivering in my underpants and T-shirt, crying and trembling and watching the messages roll in.

Annie: Anyway, I thought you should know. I thought it
would make you, I don't know. Happy or something.
Annie: I want you to be happy.
Annie: I'll see you in school tomorrow, but we don't have
to talk. Not tomorrow, not ever. Not unless you want to.
Annie: Good night.
Annie: I love you. I know I never said that before,

but I thought you should know that, too.

Annie: Okay. That's all. Good night.

I throw the phone back down on my desk like it's a live wire that's just zapped my arm. Then I cover my mouth with my hands. I cry and I cry into them, until I'm a soggy ball of tears on my bedroom floor.

I don't know I've fallen asleep until I wake up, my alarm blaring, my body aching at every joint and the pattern of the carpet pressed into my cheek. I don't know that I've slept until it's morning and everything is awful all over again.

TWENTY-THREE

I'LL SEE YOU IN SCHOOL tomorrow, Annie said, and when I get off the bus in the morning, my head full of cotton balls and my mouth dry as driftwood, I can't help but glance toward where I usually spot her, ambling off her bus.

But she isn't there.

And she's not in the hallway outside Mrs. Avery's first-period earth science class, and she's not tucked into her desk at the end of World History II. I duck my head down, pretending like I wasn't looking for her, but I can feel everybody's eyes on me as I slink off to class.

And I hear whispers, a low rustle, wherever I go. Even though she's absent, she must have told someone. Miranda Morganson, probably, who must have told everyone else. Now they're all talking about it, my name passing over a thousand pairs of lips, and not for anything good. I hurt her so bad she couldn't even come to school today. I was selfish. And now the rest of them are talking about it, that dyke who broke the other dyke's heart.

It's moments like these that I think that Annie was right about our little town. It's a shithole. I need to get out of here someday, escape to someplace where people are more open-minded and accepting and I can start fresh.

Not as the girl who dated the dead boy, or the girl who dated the dead boy's sister, but as *me*. Seeing how they look at me, how they whisper and murmur and elbow each other and then look away when I look back only solidifies my desire to get the fuck out of here. To escape.

I trudge through the lunch line, heap my tray with too much food that I know I'll never eat, chips and a sandwich and cookies and a brown carton of milk, then go to sit down with Harper and the emo boys. I can feel something pulling me toward the table where Annie used to sit with Miranda, an invisible string. But even though I'm exhausted, I'm strong, for a second or two. I don't look.

And yet when I sit down, everyone is watching me.

"What?" I ask.

Geoff, who has been in school with us since kindergarten and has loved me for at least half that long even though I pretend I don't know it, kind of looks hungry.

"I heard . . . ," he starts, and trails off.

"Yeah, well," I say wearily. "Don't get too excited."

They all stare at me, even Harper, kind of like I have two heads.

"Vee," Harper says, and she puts her hand on my wrist. "I figured Annie would have called you or something."

"What do you mean?" I ask, pulling away, rubbing my own hand like her touch burns. "We texted last night but nothing's changed. We're still broken up. Or whatever we are."

Even as I say it, they're still staring at me like they have no idea what I'm talking about. Like we're inhabiting entirely different worlds.

"You haven't heard?" Geoff asks. "It was all over the news this morning."

I blink. "What . . . ?"

Harper touches me again. This time I let her. "They found James. James **[Redacted]**. You know, Annie's brother. They found him. He's alive."

My brain is full of marbles. I can feel them rolling around in there, dizzily. I laugh, because it feels like the only thing I can do. "You're kidding, right?" I say.

But they all just stare at me.

That's when I grab my backpack and pull the zipper open. Even though Mr. Macklin is bound to catch me, I take out my phone, unlock it, and pull up the news.

Geoff's right. It's the first three headlines.

Missing boy, 16, recovered in Pennsylvania

Hudson Valley boy held captive for two years

*James M. **[Redacted]** returned to family*

When I look up from my phone, they're all watching me, waiting for my response.

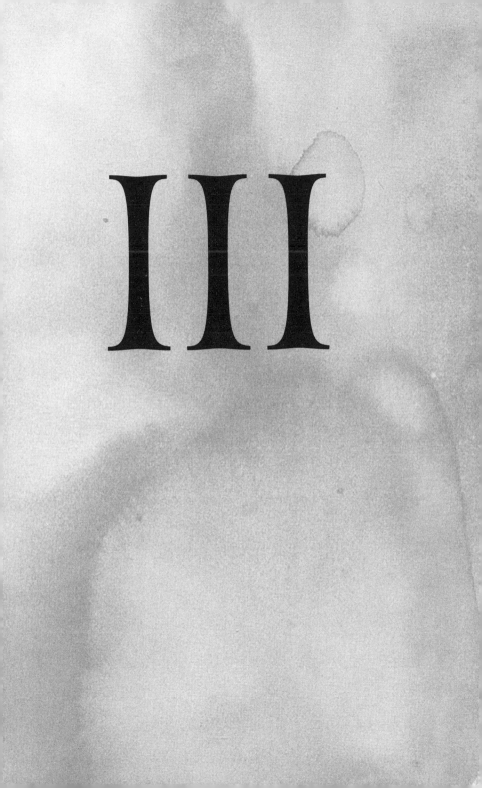

and i open up the fridge and what stares back at me is a six-
pack of cheerwine, plastic bottles, shining and sweating all red
red the color of sticky Sweet Blood and before i know it i run
off to the bathroom and i'm sick and i'm sick again because the
last time i drank that stuff was two years ago and i'll never forget the taste, too Sickly Sweet and Somehow Salty, how i still
licked my lips, happy i was finally going to get my stupid fucking drums, or what happened to me when i woke up later, how
He was on top of me and the mess in the bathroom After, this
bathroom, how i tried to clean it while He talked in a Sad Quiet
Voice about how i better not stain the linoleum with my blood

and lo! We have wandered all these years, mine hare & I. Across the
vast salt sea and over the ice floes of the North so we could scale the
mountain that should have been our home, the sanctuary of the Winter Watchers. But when we arrived, mine hare & I, we found the slopes
empty and cut slick by a hollow wind and only bones and the skins
of our friends. And so we gathered provisions, weapons, maps, furs,
ground tubers, drink skeins, and began our journey for the obsidian
tower and when we arrived nineteen moons later, we listened to the
sound of lonely ghost howls as we scaled the steps, mine hare & I. But
found no princess there, only in the topmost chamber a single bottle,
a single chalice, a wine the color of blood

and now i'm vomiting vomiting vomiting and in my mind's eye
it's red as cheerwine even though it's just normal puke, last
night's hot pockets and the bad coffee like He always makes in

the morning before He goes to work and i remind myself that
He hardly even touches me lately and haven't things been better, almost normal because He says he's been dating a woman
from work and He tells her that He's got a son and she has a
daughter, younger than me, and when He first told me that i
thought of Annie and how He used to yell *your sister can't help
you, she hasn't even looked for you* when i used to cry out for
her and i was nearly sick when He told me about His girlfriend
but i wasn't but if He's going out to buy fucking cheerwine i
know what's coming because i already got it and

and so we drink, first mine hare, her tongue gently darting out like
the mouth of the bottle is a salt lick. And then me, tasting her rabbity
breath around the bottle's lip and then the red sweet burn of the wine
as it courses through my body—down my veins and to the tips of
each toe, alighting a truth within me as it makes its journey: I am not
a Winter Watcher at all, nor the prince of this land as once I believed
myself to be. Instead, I am an interloper, a cunning thief of this world's
magic and it is time, at last, that I find my knife—lost in the sea many
moons ago—split open the sky with her blade and, finally, return
home. I have set out on this journey before. I have always failed. Now,
with the dark wine coursing through me, I am resolute. It is only later,
when I wake from my stupor, that I see that the body of mine hare has
gone cold beside me, dead

i flush and slump down in the bathroom, my hands pressed
over my eyes until i see a Thousand Stars and i could almost
cry but i don't, i'm only shaking and pressing my hands over my

eye sockets until i see Waves and then Lightning Bolts and then
Scattered Sand because i can't bring myself to look at myself in
the mirror if after everything i've done and everything He's put
me through He's going to do it again fuck fuck

and so I weep and rend my clothes and press my soggy face into her
scruff until I see a thousand stars. And I could almost vomit but I don't

sick again and then over, i'm brushing my teeth too hard until
my gums bleed, then rinsing them out with listerine, the yellow
kind, and it hurts and then i look in the fucking mirror

because what is there to do but pull myself together, sigh, and heft her
useless body down the stairs?

You're so handsome is what He used to say back when i first met
him in Neal's basement those first few times and even though He
was so much older it made me feel good to hear it but He hasn't
been saying it lately and He hasn't been touching me and let's face
it, i can't blame Him, my face is all pocked and then picked at and
then peeling and picked at again and my hair is greasy curls way
down my shoulders and He's always telling me to shower more
but fuck it what's the point and i'm wearing His clothes, still too
big on me, will probably always be too big on me, fuck

You're the half of me that's human is what she used to say and it made me
feel so good to hear it but lately hollow, as if I knew there was some
greater kingdom out there, waiting for me

i exhale hard and go and grab one of His cigarettes from the
kitchen table and sit outside on the concrete steps of the apartment complex and there's a lady there carrying her laundry to
the laundry room and i stub the cigarette out and pretend to
look embarrassed and she laughs and kind of lowers her eyes

    and now I exhale hard and dig, piling snow and soil atop her flesh.

Don't worry, she says, thinking she's a good citizen, *I won't
tell your dad.*

    Don't worry, I tell her, hanging my head low, *your life won't be in vain.*

and i smile and shrug and go inside even though my brain is
screaming *He's not my dad He's not my fucking dad He's not
old enough to be my dad are you people even paying fucking attention* but let's face it, they're not, because if they were
someone would have noticed something two years ago when He
came home with a brand-new fourteen-year-old son that He'd
magicked out of thin air, though okay, i think He told the land-
lady that His ex-wife had given Him custody if by "ex-wife" He
meant "my parents" and by "had given Him custody" He meant
"hadn't bothered to look for me much at all from what I could
tell"

(there was that one time i left a comment on their website thinking it would be a clue for them but the phone call i wanted and

the knock on the door never came and the facebook group and the hashtag campaign and the prayer requests from gram and poppy's church were all still there last time i checked but it's been more than a year because He changed the password on the desktop again because He says it will rot my brain but we both know the reason He really did it was because He was afraid i would say something, which i did, so there, asshole)

(Once I would have sworn that my hare kept me safe, that with her keen eyes I could see whole colors that the others could not see. I would have told you that I swore a vow, written in mine heart's blood on the day that I found her or she found me on the deck of a ship on the Brackish Sea, but now, trudging across the permafrost, doubts grow. Perhaps she was only a sweet distraction, meant to keep me from returning from the quaint, provincial land where I was born. . . .)

so i go inside and go to our bedroom, and go to my side of the bed and wedge my arm all the way down the wall past the cold clean target sheets and then feel all along the seam of the mattress until my finger hits It and i take out my Knife and stare at it for a long time thinking about the thing i've always been thinking about since i bought the Damned Thing on amazon, how i would do it, slicing His throat to ribbons or burying It in His belly, the softness of His belly and the hardness of the Knife, i'm staring at the Knife and shaking and thinking about it and remembering all the shit He's said to me about how i liked it and who He would tell and the fact that He's still so much bigger no matter how much i eat

I am lost and aimless again. This whole world is hollow, dead, and cold. At night I build a fire but the wood is too wet to make anything but smoke. My belly aches and I think, *I should have taken the hare's meat to keep me fed*, though the thought makes me sick a little. But I think she would have wanted it, her life for mine. Starving, cold, fingers numb, I wish I had my knife. Then I could whittle down a piece of damp wood into nothing, just to keep the blood warm in my hands. In the morning I wake on a bed of soil, not knowing I had slept and find my armor gone. I search everywhere, overturning every mossy stone, and I realize, I am being stripped of everything, I am unbecoming myself.

(i always thought by now i'd be taller, but i'm not, maybe it's because i'm always half-starving these days? He buys me everything i could ever ask for but fuck some days i think my stomach is a hole burnt straight through my body burning burning burning and i can't fill it and i can't put it out all i can do is eat and eat and when he comes home He's in one of His Black Moods because He can't afford this and He cries and i don't know if i'm supposed to comfort Him or what)

anyway, i don't have the stomach for violence like He said once: *You're a pacifist, I can tell*, when he was in one of His Thinking Moods After, the lights low and the windows open on a Summer Night and my legs bare and life feeling almost okay for a minute if i didn't think about the entire fucked-up context of it, the drugs in the bathroom and in my belly and the rope in

the nightstand drawer but i can't help myself, i can never help
myself because it's under everything: *i asked for this* and *fuck
it i want to go home*

> I walk into the afternoon, until the sun is a faint coin overhead and the
> ice begins to take on a glossy edge on every branch, not melting but
> shining, as though dipped in sugar. And the thought of food reminds
> me that I've had none again. I bend down, take a fistful of snow, let
> it melt on the heat of my palm and drink it down, my parched throat
> aching at each swallow, and then I look up and squint into the sun and
> realize I might die here, all alone in the empty world I made, as much
> > a prison as a sanctuary,

i put the Knife back where It was like i always do

> > when suddenly ahead, I see a rising column of smoke.

i could play video games or i could go for a walk, it's cold today
but not too cold, but I don't want to do any of that, i don't
want to do anything, that fucking cheerwine in the fridge and
my stomach pulsing like a Second Heart and when i go to sleep
it's with my pillow wadded up over my head but it doesn't kill
the screaming that rings in my ears, nothing ever fucking does

> I find new life inside myself, new heat, new heart, new blood. I run, my
> feet sinking into the snow, the smile frantic over my mouth, because
> smoke means *people*, smoke means *life*, smoke means *all is not lost.*

sometime in the afternoon i wake up and go to the fridge and look at those bottles again, i pick one up and the cap's loose, of course it is, so i put it back on the shelf and stare and then pick them up one by one, tighten the caps hard, shake as hard as i can

> In a forest of white pines, I find a hovel, built from rotting timber and vined in this endless winter by dry tendrils that look now like bones. The door is half off its hinges and open, just a gap, and I press my hand to splintered wood and push it in

it's the only thing i can think of doing, i'm not going to fucking *stab* Him, am i? in six plastic bottles shining with Blood Red Sap a thousand bubbles coalesce and break and my mouth is watering but i'm not going to be sick again i'm not i'm fucking not there are six plastic bottles, the closest thing i have to a Weapon because i'm too fucking weak All Soft in the Middle but maybe this will change something, if not for me, then for someone else

> and see a hunched, narrow figure sitting like a silhouette before the meager flames.

and i put them back in the fridge and i go and put the TV on and put my headphones on and play Left 4 Dead and the only thing in the world is the sound of zombies screaming as i bury a thousand bullets in their desiccated corpses

I creep closer, wishing, again, that I had my knife. But then I see the drawn, lined face underneath the steely hair. Annit, the Emperata, now grown old and tired, and her eyes are closed and she sleeps sitting up, and if it weren't for the rise and fall of her bone-thin breast, I'd wonder if she lived at all.

I sit beside her before the fire. I, too, sleep.

it's almost dark when the door clicks open and He comes home. i nod at Him without looking *hey* but then i catch His grinning bearded boy's face out of the corner of my eye, so fucking happy that my stomach sinks

I wake to the sound of pots jangling. The Emperata scurries about and in her movement she looks like a much younger woman—those familiar eyes lively and just a little bit dangerous, and as she notices that I'm awake she shoves a still-warm cookpot into my waiting hands.

My stomach snarls.

beautiful night! He says with a whistle, putting his keys on the table, and then i see why He's in this Bright Bright Mood— because there's this kid, this little kid, shaggy ten-dollar haircut and wearing a black patterned t-shirt with a flannel shirt over it and skinny jeans and black converses, this little kid ten or eleven, younger than me when i came here, and he follows Him into our apartment and he looks at me with his little kid face, a nervous smile lighting his lips and the little kid says

A feast! she tells me. I eat without thinking of the dangers of it—the abundant poisons of this place. I know that these are mistakes I have made before and will make again. I eat her gray gruel and drippy eggs and I could vomit, but I don't, and when my stomach seizes I only keep eating until it's quiet and I'm human again, the boy I once was and the man I'm becoming. I look at her, old now, and faded, as she sits down to polish her dented armor. *Sister*, I think, but she does not remember me, looking at me with eyes worn hard from a million battles. I want to ask her how I'll get home now. I want to ask her if she knows what happened to my knife. But she does not know me, not like she once did. Everything that has come and gone has changed us both, and we will never be the same.

hey

Hail and well met, traveler,

i take my headphones off

she says to me at last in a voice I hardly recognize.

bathroom's that way, He says, jerking his thumb to the door, and the kid bobs his head as a sort of thank-you and for a minute i see our apartment brightly drawn through his eyes: the posters peeling along the edges on the wall and the amazon boxes all crushed down in the recycling box in the corner and the xbox all the cords tucked away and the statues from anime movies on the shelves that i've put together on days He was at work, it all looks

so *proper* but kind of *wrong* like this is the house of some kids
pretending to be grown-ups which in a way i guess, it is

> *I don't know how to get home,* I tell her, and for a moment I wonder if rec-
> ognition sparks behind those familiar eyes. But she only shakes her head,
> and when her mouth opens again I see how many teeth she's missing
> now, so many teeth, so many crimes, so many tithes paid to an unjust
> King, and I see something tethered to her rope belt, a knife, surely not
> mine, but one much like mine, and that's when fear stabs at me

we are not Real People we are not Normal People

> that she isn't real this is a trap a trap a—

and the boy slips off to pee

> I dash out of the dark hovel, away.

He's standing by the kitchen table taking off His coat and i'm
on my feet in a flash

> My sister, my ghastly sister, ancient and shrunken, stumbles past her
> rough-hewn table but is on her feet, knife in hand, in a flash.

hey, i whisper, *what the fuck?*

> *Traveler,* she snarls, *what the fuck?*

What? He asks, smiling at me with his Yellow Coffee Teeth like i don't know what's going on. *He's my coworker's son. He's a little confused. He needs someone to talk to*

> She's following me through the forest of the white pines, but my boots are an echo of my racing heart as I dive deep into the mouth of a waiting cave and pull a trapdoor shut behind me.

Not you, i say, and i'm getting angry, *not fucking you*

> This isn't my sister, I tell myself, trembling in the mossy dark.

He looks bruised, his stupid round boy face with his stupid patchy beard, and i have never found Him attractive it was all about the way He spoke to me and looked at me and touched me and the way it made me feel

> Her footsteps make the wood overhead creak and groan.

Why not me? Why, have you ever wanted for anything? Sometimes He talks like that, like a Sacred Pilgrim or something, and it makes me want to hit Him but we both know i won't but i have a gotcha in my pocket, i've been saving it for a Long Time, *What about my fucking drum kit?* i ask Him, and He looks at me for a Long Time, considering me even as we hear the toilet flush in the bathroom *now*, He says, his voice very low, *remember what will happen if you don't behave. They'll all know that you asked for this. You came with me willingly.*

And all those moments we enjoyed ourselves together. You don't want your father to know about those, do you? Or your sister?

Traveler, she says in a singsong voice, and that's when I hear something strike the boards. It's only after I flinch back that I see it: the knife's blade burst through ancient wood. There is one last rustle of sound, a sigh. My heart is a bird and there are crows calling overhead and then she walks away and all that is left is their noisy silence.

once i swallowed his poison but now, in this moment, an impasse, Two Dogs, one fully grown and one nearly, snarling at one another, their hackles raised, and while once this den was big enough for Two Dogs, we both know i've outgrown it and now . . .

I crawl out of the cave, my hair laced with leaves.

the boy, ten or eleven, opens the bathroom door

She wasn't my sister. She was a trap, I assure myself, closing the trapdoor to examine

hey, thanks, the boy says, then he stands in the kitchen and offers me his hand almost like it's an After Thought but the nervous line of his smile tells me it's not, that i'm the one he's really wondering about and not Him, a thirtysomething man with a doughy Boy Face, *I'm Marco* i hesitate and in a moment that is too long for an outstretched hand i'm considering all of my names, James and Jamie and Michael and **[Redacted]** but what i tell him when i finally take his hand is, *i'm Jack*

Want something to drink, boys? He asks, too eager, and i don't answer but Marco nods and this kid is so skinny he looks like he could be starving and my own stomach growls but i don't answer and He gets the cheerwine out of the fridge and i'm holding my breath

When Jack came to live with me, He begins, handing Marco a bottle, *he'd never had cheerwine*

They don't make it in New York, i say, but then He shoots me a look, like i've said too much

That's where Jack lived with my sister, He says, which i guess is the Story Today, that i'm His nephew and of course it's a Story He's told Before, but one of, like, six, and i'm never sure what page we're supposed to be on and He reaches down and unscrews the cap and there's a short *fssssssszzzzzt!* and

there is a familiar knife hilt buried in the door, with the poorly drawn face of a boy and a girl and a bearded King and the ruby stone buried in the white bone and it's mine and it's mine, my drawing and my old weapon, my old friend. And I should have trusted her, because she kept it for me, and now the curved, strong blade has cleaved the wood but there's something else there, a pinned scrap of paper, and I bend

close, squinting, fixing my hand around the hilt, and see writing in

soda

my

explodes

sister's

everywhere

hand.

Oh crap, He says jovially, there's Blood Red Soda stains all
over His button-down and His stupid beard and even on His
glasses, Marco rushes forward to find our paper towels and
starts trying to sponge up the soda right from His shirt and He
is looking at the kid like a Hungry Wolf and suddenly i realize
who Marco reminds me of, it's Elijah, Elijah who was seven
when i left but must be nine now, Elijah whose paws were too
big for his body, my little brother my fucking Shadow my Soul
Elijah

Fewmets, I say to myself, tugging hard and hard again on my beloved
knife, until finally I fall backward, knife in hand, and the paper is free
and flying and reaching out, I must scramble to catch it. There. On

one side, equations. A name: Annie **[Redacted]**, period six. But there
is a shadow of something on the other side. Curling lines. Dark ink.

and panic grips my body, i could vomit again but i close my
mouth and swallow the bile down i won't i won't i need to be
here and Be Good for Something damn it

I turn it over and find one of my sister's maps. On the top, in her awful
calligraphy, *The Land of Gumlea*, and below, every creek and tree and
town and on the bottom, a shadowed line, the graphite crosshatched
and heavy. *The Veil*, my sister has written there in her loving hand

Maybe you should go get changed, i suggest to Him, and He
looks at me, a Question in His eyes, but i know how much He
hates to be dirty so He stands up again and unbuttons the top
button of his shirt

Might as well jump in the shower, He agrees, which was
exactly what i was hoping He'd say but i'm careful not to smile
too too wide. *Make yourself comfortable, boys*

and He disappears into the bathroom

and now I know where I must go.

but the water isn't running yet and i need to be careful. Marco
is still sopping the soda off the tabletop and he looks at me with
New Moon Eyes

Your uncle told me you like boys, he says and he's watching me, waiting for me to react, but i don't because there have been times when i liked boys and times when i liked girls and right now i tell myself it's mostly girls when He's at work and i'm jacking off alone, thinking of Vidya, her perfumey Wild Body a field i can wrap around myself like a blanket but this boy is waiting for something so i shrug

> I leave the cave behind, and I walk and I walk until there are no more pines, the snow biting and bright all around, I walk until I find a field blanketed white.

Yeah, i guess, i tell him, because i sense he wants help and maybe he really does need someone to talk to, maybe that's why he's here, maybe that's why i was so desperate to talk to Steve's Friend who was always hanging around with him, watching us boys like He could give us the Secret of the Universe, maybe we were Hungry Boys, wanting answers and someone to tuck us under their Wing and He had a fucking Wing all right, back then, making me feel like i was a man

> *Beggar's Graveyard,* I read off the map, and my eyes take in the dunes rippling beneath the snow, every hill and lump a body, and my mouth forms the Laws for Beggars: 1. Never borrow, always steal and 2. Don't get caught. I wonder if the King's justice was swift or if he cruelly lingered over the beggar children, plucking their eyes out, pulling out their teeth one by one, peeling their skin away. Once, I wondered what sort of King I'd be. No longer. My footfall crunches over snow, or bone, I'm not sure which.

I do, too, Marco says, *my dad would kill me if he knew*

It doesn't matter, I tell myself, *I'm leaving now . . .*

i'm holding my breath because the water still isn't running in
the bathroom and He is probably holding His breath, too, listening to us and waiting for Something to Happen and if He
thinks Something is Going to Happen between me and some
kid He's got another think coming

> but I still hold my breath as I pass through the field, ignoring how my
> boots sink deep, and I hold it tight until I see the edge of the town in
> the distance.

Hey, where do you sleep? Marco asks, peering past me to the
only bedroom and the one King-sized bed and my answer
comes without thinking because we've practiced this

> It's the first of many on the eastern edge of my sister's map, Old
> Town, where shadows rule, and I find on its outskirts an inn, candlelit
> and cozy. The door is open and my body, so, so tired.

On the sofa, and then, just as i say that, the water starts running,
a slow steady *hissssssssssssssssssss* and just as Marco is saying *cool*
i lower my voice and look at him with eyes made of Bone Flints

> *I need to stay. How much?* I tell the lad behind the counter and when he
> turns, my breath catches in my throat. He has flaxen hair, a pinched

face like a fox, and strong, curved muscles beneath his shirtsleeves, and I know those arms. I have slept in those arms.

We need to leave, now

No charge for Winter Watchers, m'lord, he says.

Marco laughs, a nervous laugh, squeaky, like a little kid

I laugh because it is absurd.

What are you talking about?

I'm no Winter Watcher. Don't you remember me?

We need to get out of here. If you stay . . . and for some reason i still can't bring myself to say it but then i look at the paper towel he's still holding wadded up in his hand, Wet Red with cheerwine and Something Else and i swallow hard and it's like the lump in my throat is a spiky horse chestnut *Look,* we need *to get out of here* now

I don't, m'lord. But I'll show you your room. He leads me to a windowless chamber, dark as a ship's cabin, and as he lights a candle for me i watch the familiar curve of his neck, which i have kissed, and think, How did we ever lose each other? But then he turns and a look of horror crosses his vulpine features.

No! and that's when i realize that Marco is a Wolf Pup himself because his lower lip trembles. *Look I don't know what's going on with you and your uncle but I'm not going with you*

> *M'lord, are you all right?* I feel a green wave wash over me and I realize that I've been ensorcelled. My body sways; he rushes forward, then catches me against his chest, exhaling: *No!*

He smells just like he always did and before the world goes black around me I taste his mouth on my mouth, kissing me and breathing me back to life

shit i hide my face in my hands and laugh-weep at him because he thinks i'm the one who is trying to Steal Him Away or but god the water is still running but for how much longer we need to go go go

and when I wake up I'm in the narrow bed in the narrow room, his lithe body tangled up in mine and mine all spent.

and just like that i have my answer, fist my hands, hold my head up high

> I feel the fine fur of his thighs, his chest's rise and fall. I feel my own intoxication. For strong, cunning boys and their strong, cunning bodies—a love I'd trade away, if I could, but I've never quite been able to work the spell out right.

Fine, i say, *stay but whateveryoufuckingdo don't you* dare *drink that soda*

What? nervous giggles. *Why?*

He put roofies in it

before Marco can answer me i turn and Walk Swift to the front door *Wait, what?* he's saying and in the bathroom i hear the tap squeal as He turns the water off and i don't look back at that little apartment but i don't have to, i know every single inch, the cracks in the plaster beneath the posters where i chipped away at the walls with my Knife when He was at work not for escape but for boredom and i remember every word in every book on the shelf the ones i wrote and the ones i read until the pages fell out and the curve of the blade of my Knife *fuck I'll have to leave my Knife* in my flesh or in my mind i know that there's a cobweb in the southwest corner of the bedroom and the way the light looks through the trees at every season and i will almost miss it but i also know what His arm feels like pressed across my back and the way the pills taste my own fear rising like bile and the guilt and all the Awful Things and when i look back i only look at Marco who watches me with Hard Eyes and does he even know what roofies are? Would Elijah? i don't fucking know

> *Our bodies enjoyed each other,* he says, and an icy chill cuts through me despite the warmth of that little room and his naked thighs beside me.

Drunkenly, I try to amble up from his warm arms, his warmer bed, and he's watching me with eyes like pools of melted honey and I'm pulling on my trousers, clumsily reaching for my shirt and fixing my leathers over my shoulders and stumbling around for my boots and trying to ignore the slithy hissing in my brain and the throbbing in my throat.

so i leave that world behind without a coat or a name and take off it's evening it's november and my breath is a cloud in front of me and the door slams behind me and i walk and walk and don't stop walking and then i think i hear someone calling out behind me *Jack? Jack!* and suddenly i'm not walking anymore i'm running between the apartment complexes but fuck i'll never make it to downtown this way not before he catches me and that's when i see a girl's bike, streamers on the handle-bars dark like Seaweed in Water, not chained but who needs to chain bicycles here? it's a safe neighborhood, just leaning against the brick of the building, and i know it's wrong and i know it's stealing but i can make reparations later because if something happens to Elijah i mean Marco i'll have bigger apologies to make

He watches me with puzzled eyes, his lips soft with sex, but I know what will happen again if I stay there, because it's happened before. So it's down the creaky stairs and out through the back kitchen and into the night. It's gray-black winter and it's cold and I walk off-kilter with one eye gone and I run into the streets of Old Town, beggars reaching out their spindly fingers toward me and I shake them away, rushing through the city, my steps loping, and that's when the church bell rings and that's when I see it in the moonlight: the King's three-horned stag, one hoof lifted, and I know what he's doing here, and I know that I've lingered here, with these temptations, for too long. He's waiting to take me to the Veil.

i grip the handlebars the streamers tickling my wrists and it's been two years since i've ridden a bike but it's true what they say you know and if i wasn't so scared, my Heart throbbing on my Tongue, it would almost feel

I grip his gold coat, perfumed with pipe smoke and freedom, and I dig my heels into his ribs and he gives a cry like shattered glass and as we ride away I think, if I wasn't so terrified, this would almost be

e x h i l a r a t i n g

e x h i l a r a t i n g

i ride and i think He might be following me in that big Blue Truck of His and i remember the first time i sat with Him in it, my feet on the dash, i thought i was pulling Something over on Someone, probably my dad, because here was this Guy, a fucking adult, who treated me like one, too, and i remember all the texts we traded, talking about philosophy and sexuality and my stupid fucking Wet Dreams and *He* understood me and *He* thought it was ridiculous that i couldn't be in a band with my girlfriend because clearly i was talented even if He'd never heard me play before so when He said He'd drive me to Pennsylvania to get a drum kit from His brother and He'd have me back in a few hours and that we could lie and say i was at Neal's i thought it was a pretty good idea and He was always touching me a lot, like putting his Hand on my Knee and squeezing in a weird way but fuck part of me thought it felt good, to be touched, and another part thought, Steve's a pretty good guy and if he's okay with hanging around with this Guy well then it must be Okay and in the back of the car there was a bottle of soda *thirsty, James?* He asked me, it wasn't until later when i was two weeks sleep deprived and my body sore under the ropes and my body a Raw Weeping Thing that we came up with the Jack stuff because a Jack is Every Man and i could be Anybody

I ride for a long night and a day through towns and cities and over cobblestoned streets and there are children who lay flowers at our feet, ditch lilies and dandelions. Boys wave their diaphanous banners and women lift their skirts as we pass so I can see what's underneath but I don't lean in to touch their curling hair and I don't stop to write my name in anyone's book and I don't dismount, ever. I know what might come from lingering too close to human flesh, how I might give in to my baser proclivities. Finally we stop by a riverbank beneath a grove of pines. The air is different here, sharper and clearer, and I pull my sister's map from my pocket. I draw in a breath; it trembles within my lungs but the stag nudges me with his leathery nose, so I get back on, my movements still uncertain, close my eyes and brace myself for the ride and the future to come. Home, please, home. And the family that was lost to me, long, long ago.

(can you believe it was my suggestion?)

(Will they even remember me?)

that Blue Truck, not a dark blue but a Bright Clarion Blue shining like the Sky Right Now a Sky Right After Sunset and Before the Stars Come Out but now it feels like a Dark Cloud full of Lightning coming after me and i ride and i ride and that stupid girl's bike hugs the shoulder and goes faster than i thought was possible, my legs are burning and it starts to drizzle cool and miserable and my whole body is Smoke and Steam and Heat and i ride and i ride off the shoulder and downtown

I ride on and on and on through charming towns and bustling cities and fields of blue flowers growing straight up through the winter ice and as we go, people bow to us and shout my name. My true name, like they've always known it: James Michael [Redacted]. Because I am a hero. I am the one who will open the Veil. If only they knew that I have tried before and failed. If only they knew that there is softness in my heart, a sickness, a tender place I can't bear to show

because once i was sick and for some reason He didn't want me to stay home, i think He was worried i'd die and He took me with Him in that Blue Truck and i felt trapped and safe all at once sitting in the parking lot under a blanket and i'd looked out the window at the Rite Aid and then saw across the street—a police station, just like that—and i was staring and staring and thinking about getting out but then He opened

the door and handed me some Robitussin and it was over, the
chance, my chance, my moment to leave

and i pedal faster and faster and faster wondering if the map
i've drawn in my mind is wrong, the map i've drawn in all those
notebooks He never looks in because He doesn't care what i
think until i catch the bright light of the Rite Aid and i skid to
a stop and an SUV almost hits me but i hang a left and there's
the police station and i drop the bike on the sidewalk and go
racing up the stairs

       until at the edge of an old tangled wood I spy a strange silhouette,
       jagged and black against a cliff face. I nudge the stag thataway and he
       trots over on his golden hooves, closer and closer until I see a massive
       sword plunged into the rock and skewered on its blade a boy, intes-
       tines draining down the mountainside. His hair is a matted tangle of
       brain and maggots and black black blood and the stag wheels back and
       so do I. That's when I realize that the naked trees clinging to the rock
       are not trees at all but more swords and more boys

and i am shocked that it's quiet inside, like Dead Silent, and the
silence is loud and screeching under the faint humdrum buzz of
the fluorescent lights when i step forward my shoes squeak on
the tile floor and His sweatshirt is soaked through with rain,
my hair stuck to the side of my face and my neck and i step
forward s l o w l y and my hands are shaking and my nose is
running so i wipe it on His sleeve

and I am shocked into silence, and the whole world is dead dead silence
all around except for the golden bells of the stag's hooves as we make
our way up the mountain now s l o w l y and my hands are shaking
and my mouth is full of bile so I spit it out.

there's a man, a cop, sitting behind a glass wall which is hazy
with scratches and he's on his phone and doesn't see me at first
until my shoes squeak again and then he looks up and he sees
me but i have to wonder what he sees: dirty boy with dirty
hair and zits, clothes soaked through and starving, it's gotta
be some Oliver Twist shit to him *Can I help you, son?* he asks,
which feels like a question from a movie so i stand in front of
the counter, it's god damned cold in there, and i'm shaking and
shaking

He killed them, says the stag, and I didn't even know he could speak and
the air is so thin that my lungs feel empty and I'm shaking and shaking

i say, *Excuse me, but something bad is going to happen, if it
hasn't already* in a voice that sounds kind of ten instead of sixteen

I say, *It was a blood tithe. They said their vows. They agreed to it.*

he looks at me for a long time, considering

And I don't know why I'm defending Him but suddenly I'm breathless
in the thin air and the stag just snickers.

What do you mean?

they put me in the police chief's office, drape a fake wool blanket like one of those airline blankets but green over my shoulders and give me a cup of Bad Tea, the cheap lipton kind with a picture of a lemon on the tag but Strong and Bitter as chalk

> I have been a feral child and I have been a pirate and I have romanced slippery mermaids and dagger-clawed sirens and I have spilled my seed into Gumlea's brown earth and I have had a thousand knots tied around me and sometimes I feel like the ropes hold me still

every once in a while someone comes in and asks me another question about Him but otherwise they leave me alone in there and they're not telling me what's going on and it's like

Time

Stands

Still

> but now I dismount to stand beneath at the edge of the Veil, my courage gathering like a thunderhead over an empty wood, and I see that the blackness is not blackness at all but the tar-bright, writhing scales of the dragon that circles the world.

finally a cop who looks younger than me but is hiding it under
an ugly mustache comes in and sits down at the desk *Are you
the chief?* i ask and he stares at me, tapping his pen on the pad
on the desktop

> **Will you help me?** I ask the stag but he only taps his hooves against the
> sodden ground and shakes his heavy-branched head.

Nope

> **Nope.**

neither of us says anything until one of us does

> **Have they caught Him yet?**

he looks like he's considering something but then he decides
against it and shakes his head *No. They went back to the
apartment and found the boy alone, playing video games*

i can exhale at this, i can almost laugh, how often was i the Boy
Alone, playing video games? days and days and years

> **I slowly exhale at this, imagining the people on the other side.**

They think He drove off looking for you, the cop adds, and my
abdominal muscles clench at that and i grit my teeth and try

not to feel anything because the first thing i felt was *good, I'm not replaceable, then* and what the fuck Kind of Feeling is that

> *Do you think they're waiting for me?* I ask the stag, my abdominal muscles clenching at the sick hope that tumbles inside me because I want to think I'm good, beloved, the cherished son, that on my birthday my father bent low to kiss my wrinkled baby feet.

Can I talk to the kid? i ask, and the cop shakes his head *No. His parents came to get him already*

> *No. Your family has never looked for you.*

more clenching and more gritting

> **A knife twists inside me.**

Parents

> P a r e n t s

fuck i can't even think about that, about Dad with his five o'clock shadow by noon and Mom who couldn't resist him but it breaks me to think about them and the cop taps his pen again *We need to call your parents, too,* he says, and i knew it was coming but i didn't, *before we can question you, since you're a minor*

Fuck, i say, and without even thinking about it i'm burying my face in my hands because it's just like He said, they're going to know everything now, every Ugly Stupid Bit

the cop doesn't answer so i drop my hands between my knees and sit with my head hanging

Okay, i say, not looking up. *Their names are Marc and Shira* [Redacted] *and they live in Wiltwyck, NY*

> *Okay,* I say, staring at the moving scales, *I need to kill it. I need to kill it*
> *and then I can get back home—*

Do you have a number for them? he asks, and when i give him mom's cell phone he jots it down on a lime green post-it and tears it off

> *Stop talking about it and do it,* the stag says, gives his golden hoof one
> final stomp, and then takes off.

then he stands, doesn't say anything else to me, leaves me sitting there wincing down that Bad Tea and i'm waiting and i'm alone again and i'm waiting just like i've been waiting for two years for Him to come home and for Him to touch me again after work and for someone to find me i'm waiting i'm waiting and my stomach dips and i'm imagining mom's face as she tucks the phone against her chin and sweeps her hair out of her eyes and i'm wondering if she looks the same or if she's dyed her hair and i'm letting myself miss her for the first time in forever as i imagine the Slow Dawning Morning of *Ma'am, we've found your son*

> I step forward timorously, trembling, wondering how many times I've done this, wondering how many boys have tried this, gripping their knives tight, clad in chain maille armor. But I have no armor now, only my leathers, and as I walk closer I feel the words form on my tongue:
> *Dragon, I've come for you.*

once i was asleep in the bed of a truck with my wrists and ankles bound and once i was asleep on a bare mattress with my wrists and ankles bound but looser and once after the ropes were gone we bought sheets and He touched me under them and i was asleep after and my stomach hurt and once coming home from gram and poppy's i fell asleep and when i saw the headlights streaming down the highway i thought i'd Died and the lights were my Soul shooting off to Heaven once i was asleep on the sofa while the DVD menu played the long days tumbling together and once and only once i fell asleep at Neal's house with Vidya and when we peeled ourselves apart she saw she'd missed a dozen calls from her mom and she just calmly called her father who wasn't mad at all and who covered for her with her mom and i had to walk home in the Snow in the Middle of the Night hoping no one heard me when i came in and the only person who was up was Annie and she took one look at me and slammed her bedroom door, the scent of another girl on me like a piece of Scarlet Text

stitched to my coat and once and only once i went for a walk
my Only Freedom but when i got back my key wasn't in my
pocket and locked out i fell asleep on the concrete steps and
a neighbor came and shook me awake and said *do you need
to use the phone?* so i went into his apartment which was a
weird mirror of our apartment and my hands wouldn't stop
shaking as i dialed because it crossed my mind i could dial 911
but then he would know my father would know and i asked
for this and i brought it on myself so i called my "dad" instead
and let Him know i was locked out and once a ton of times
dozens of times hundreds of times Neal and i fell asleep our
arms around each other but then he didn't want to anymore
and i still did and once and only once i fell asleep on the hard
chairs in a police chief's office, a scratchy acrylic blanket over
my body and i slept and i slept everywhere and i slept always
until a hand tentative uncertain touched my shoulder and
startled me awake

Once I slipped my finger inside the slick body of a mermaid and I
didn't like it but I kept it in there anyway because I thought it would
bring me closer to enlightenment. Once I untangled burrs from the
fur of my hare and she licked my knees in deepest gratitude. Once
and only once I stumbled across a pink-throated Winter Watcher girl
whose steed was a tortoise the size of a small car and she was sitting on
the shore of a greeny lake gone gold in early autumn and she let me sit
beside her on the walkway and our thighs touched warmly and it was
more thrilling than kissing or even getting laid and she just laughed
with her mouth open to the sunlight and my hare cuddled herself

around her turtle's craggy shell. Once and only once I was unfaithful to my princess in the tower when I stroked the white flesh of a young boy whose teeth were sharpened to ruby-dotted points and he panted like a feral dog. When he was done I said *please keep this a secret from Annit* so he crossed his tree house room and plucked one of the Daddy Longlegs from the dew-dotted cobwebs in the corner, a creature as big as my head, and he stomped it beneath his bare dirt-brown foot and then crushed the body into a powder. Once I knelt beside him and washed the dust down with wine and we prayed to hide our secret from the moon and once, dozens of times, hundreds of times I kissed a feral boy and fell asleep sweaty and warm beside him and I love him still but he never did love me, not even once. Once and only once I passed through the body of a dragon, her hot throat closing around me, my body squeezed inside her, my clothes disintegrating in the acid of her belly until I was belched free on the forest floor, naked, damp, and born anew.

a police officer, they're all running together

Son, apparently i am everyone's son, *your dad is here*

my dad my dad my dad my dad

it's dark in the office and i don't wanna go because if my dad is here then he must know what Happened to me all the Things i Did the Camera and the Videos, His crimes, but mine, too, and this will ruin me but it will ruin my dad worse my stomach is some kind of Raw Weeping Thing, my organs are a Mushy

Jumble as i get up and rub the sleep from my eyes taking my
time because my dad my dad my dad

It's dark in the forest and I don't know where I am, whether I'm
here or if I'm there. The dragon is gone and I am nothing, wearing
no clothes and carrying no weapons and my nakedness is small and
wrinkled in the cold and I am not a man and I am not brave. I'm only
a boy with a sickness inside him, a quartz in his navel that is fractured
and cracked because He He He

i follow the cop down the hall

I drag myself forward through the forest.

and there is a man at the end of it, standing by the desk, and the
light through the windows behind him is New and Gray and
soon it will be morning but november no birds singing not for
me and not for my dad and i wonder where Elijah is and where
Annie is and where my mom my mom my mom is, he's alone, his
shoulders saggy in one of his button-downs, and i see him before
he sees me and i wonder if I'll touch him, offer my hand to him,
and if he'll shake it or he'll be too disgusted, he's lost weight he's
a little more gray but it's him it's him it's my dad and he knows
everything and he is saying something to another cop but the
one who is leading me says *sir* and my dad my dad my dad turns

There is nothing here. It is a tangle of forest in November. No birds.
No snow. Only naked wild raspberry vines and garbage. There is no

magic. I am dead inside. Somewhere, somewhere, He has won already from His throne at the top of a dead world. I drag myself forward, trying to keep the warm light of home in my mind ahead, but my body is heavier than the heaviest weight. I'm a boy and He has won and I'm nothing now and this forest will go on forever because I've done this before.

I've made this journey before.

and i'm in his arms before i can even think about it, he's folding me into his arms and we're the Exact Same Height now but it doesn't feel different, he still smells like Black Coffee and Soil like he's been working in the garden out back like ten minutes ago but that can't be true he must have driven the whole way here, Hours and Hours, and he's holding me and holding me and i'm not letting go

But I think I see a shadow up ahead and I drag my heavy body faster now, because I know I need to meet him, this boyish shadow, this pale shadow, standing still in the middle of an empty forest, wearing blue jeans and a hooded sweatshirt that's warmer and softer than the inside of his girlfriend's body and I'm naked and cold in this empty wood, except for him, that boy, that selfish prince, and as I reach him, I see the knife in his hands. My knife. And I hear myself calling his name out through the forest: *Jamie.*

he takes over, puts a coat over my shoulders, doesn't look into my eyes when he speaks and he tells me that we're supposed to go to the hospital first and i ask why and he doesn't say the words Rape Kit but he finally looks at me and those words are in his mind and caught at the back of his throat, i can almost hear them and he says the lawyer, his lawyer, Don Muselmaan, do i remember him? will be here by lunchtime because the police need to ask me a few questions but first we have to go to the hospital for the Rape Kit that my dad won't Dare to Name

he's clutching his keys in his hand and he leads me out to the parking lot and i feel nervous because He could be Anywhere and because my dad knows All of It, he has to, but as we walk out to the parking lot i can't stop Wondering Something and we stop outside a black sedan i've never seen before and that's when I ask him

        He sneers at me, this puggish boy, his face aflame with freckles.

Where's mom?

        You're late.

he stares at me and his eyes go On and On, his hands Big and Strong on the roof of the car as he considers but now my hands are just as Big as his

        He stares at me and his eyes go on and on.

She's on her way.

that's all he'll tell me so we get in the car, it's Clean and it's Empty, like dad's cars always are (mom's cars are always a mess) and we drive to the hospital in silence and i want to say something and need to say something like *crap, I missed you, dad* but that seems wrong because i chose this it's my fault but then we drive down my old street—this town's so small—and the complex is at the end of the block and i almost can't breathe but then i see something, lights flashing in the Early Morning and dad slows down because the whole street is clogged with cop cars, he starts doing a k-turn, and i don't know whether i'm supposed to tell him this is where i lived and where this Guy took my Clothes Off while I was Sleeping and then put a camera on me and told me He'd send it to my parents if i didn't keep doing What He Said and it's Awful it felt Awful and what feels Worse were the days when it was just the Two of Us and it didn't feel as Awful because the World isn't simple dad like you told me it was

I want to tell him to leave me alone. That this is over now. That I'm going home at last. But I can't move my lips. And he's sneering at me and he's staring at me and his hands are shaking with the knife inside them, pointing out toward me, and suddenly, he screams, *I'm going to fucking kill you!* And I'm laughing, suddenly, laughing, naked in that ugly naked November wood. Because I was him once, and I saw this coming. This moment in the far-flung future when I would be filled with hatred for what I knew I'd always been, small and weak and exposed, and I had tried so many times to snuff out this moment, to stop it from coming, but it only ever led me here. Over and over again.

and i'm arguing with him in my head even though neither of us
has said a word

> *What are you doing?* he says. *Why are you laughing? Stop laughing at me!*

anyway, one of the cops waves him down the road and we turn
the corner instead and the lights are fading in the mirrors and
the moment is over

> Now he is a fury of nails and teeth and knife. Now my body is a wil-
> low bough bending. Now he bashes knee to groin, skull to skull. Now
> everything is black.

at the hospital, they're waiting for us, they take us to a room
marked off with a Little Curtain and the nurse who takes my
blood pressure won't look at me and my dad won't look at me
and Everyone Knows Everyone Knows and then she leaves and
my dad asks me in a Low Voice *Can I pray?*

> He's got heavy boots he bought from the witch store downtown with
> his girlfriend who would make him the man he wanted to be. He's got
> heavy boots and they're falling on my ribs, my belly, and he's scream-
> ing, tiny flecks of spittle flying everywhere:

Um, is my answer, *um*.

> *I hate you*, he says, *I hate you*.

which my dad takes as a Yes. he gets down on his knees and closes his eyes and is murmuring to himself and i'm watching and my eyes look like an Emoji of Shock because last I heard dad was what he called an Easter Atheist but there he is, hands clenched and praying, and i can't help but wonder what else i've missed if this has happened and my dad has become a quote unquote Man of Faith because he always kind of laughed at mom and her jewstuff *you don't even believe in that, shira* and she'd say *whatever marc I'm culturally Jewish*

I don't fight back. Even if I could, I wouldn't. I have seen time stretch out like a ribbon, how every turn and tangle could lead me only here.

now dad is on his knees Swaying and Whispering and i remember the time i went to Neal's church and the time i read a book on Buddhism and i asked Vidya to take me to her grandparents' temple but she told me that would be weird because she'd never even gone before and i remember wondering what i believed in and all the prayers i said when i was waiting for Him to come home from work in that locked apartment in the first days weeks months year before He said i could be trusted with a Key and i remember how i just stopped thinking about All of That about Anything because it hurt too much to think

He'll exhaust himself soon. I'm sure of it. I know, because I've been him, too.

the doctor comes in, interrupting dad's prayer, and he stands and Dusts off his Knees and shakes her hand and then she looks at me, mouth pressed together like she feels sorry for me and then they start the exam and i don't want to talk about What Happens After That

> The weight of his boots grows heavier. He collapses, his thin, clothed body over my emaciated, naked body. He's still holding the knife between his hands. I see then that he hasn't used it yet. I reach out my tired hand and touch my hand to his. I feel the knife.

we wait and dad is telling me about his lawyer who is a Really Great Guy and the doctor comes and goes and comes again and we wait some more and then the curtain parts and there is mom a Rush of Sandalwood in the Air and her hair has gray at the roots now and i don't remember so many crow's-feet but it doesn't matter *You're fucking here*, she says, and she clutches me to her, crying all over the place, and i'm only wearing a Thin Paper Robe and even as she holds me i hold the paper closed over my body like it Hides Something only Everyone Knows even my mother but she doesn't care because she holds me and holds me, *Here you fucking are*

> *Fucking do it already*, he says, but my hand isn't moving and his hand isn't moving because I realize now that *this* is the Veil, the black place inside you that forms a hard line. It is the thing you never could do, that you never *were* going to do, anyway.

almost as soon as she pulls away from me the Fighting Begins

I called Don Muselmaan

What? I don't want him talking to that leech

The police want to question him tomorrow. Don said—

I don't care what Don said. He's my son, too!

like there was ever any question but i'd forgotten about this, the
Charge in the Air when they're together and fighting, like they
were Dead the rest of the time and this was their way of Loving
One Another and i'm almost glad to hear it but it also makes
my breath catch at the base of my throat because i'd forgotten
i'd forgotten i'd forgotten everything about how awful this feels
and my hands are shaking, i pull on my jeans, the boxers still
tied up inside them

> I haven't killed him. He hasn't killed me. He falls back against the
> leaves, crying like a baby, and I'm crying, too, but quieter, the tears
> streaming down my face. Soon I will wake in the ocean. Soon I will
> wake in the mermaids' lagoon. Soon I will wake in a pirate's lair, the
> ropes splintering my wrists. Soon I will wake in a tower alone and find
> mine hare beside me, dead. There is no magic here. Only two stupid
> boys on the same pointless quest.

i need to get some air, i tell them, and they stare at me in shock
maybe it's because i didn't stop to ask for permission because
I'm not fourteen anymore because i have spent two years now
coming and going and never asking because i didn't have to ask

because He knew i would always circle back to him again, a
Dog on a Rusted Chain

> I've made a fool of myself. Or he's made a fool of me. Maybe we've
> been fools, both, all along.

But I just got here, mom says but dad shakes his head *Let him*,
he tells her at the same time i say *i'll be right back*

neither of them says anything as i walk out into the aisle of
identical curtained rooms my paper gown tucked inside my
pants like a shirt and my feet bare it's november but i think here
the air conditioner is always running and it smells like Death
i know because I have lived in a place that smelled like Death
for two years but still i'm wondering, can i really go home to
this? to them? fighting about me like i'm not even there and
then slamming their bedroom door to make up to one another
like we kids don't even know what's going on we'll just turn the
volume up on the TV and ignore it

> I know from the way that he sobs that he's still disgusted by me. And
> in truth? My hand on my knife, still, I'm disgusted by him, too.

maybe i can go live with gram and poppy if they're not dead
yet, I go past the nurses' station, nodding to the people who
have seen the Inside of my Body like it's No Big Deal, anything
can be normal if you act like it is even if the breath is still shallow in my chest and my hands cold and shaking shaking

There's nothing to do. No one to kill. Nowhere to go. No Veil to
pierce. And I think I'll never be gone from this place, looking up into
the empty steel sky.

i walk out into a hall and i don't know what i'm looking for,
Fresh Air, or maybe Light, and at the end of the hall is a vending
machine and i realize it's been like twelve hours since i last ate
aside from that Bad Tea, some pop-tarts before i puked them
all up and my stomach is snarling at me and i walk toward it,
fishing through my pocket for some change, counting it out,
a rubber-banded roll of clean bills and some quarters, nineteen dollars, seventy-five cents and i can get some cheetos and
a vitaminwater and maybe some nuts or something and i'm
glad i have His money and don't have to ask dad for the money
because he'd probably tell me to get Something Reasonable
like some crackers and a water but i want to Eat, i could Eat
the Whole World right now only there is a redheaded woman
standing at the machine in front of me, not facing me, and she's
taking her fucking time, like she's trying to crack the rosetta
stone of it, finally tapping out the numbers with her fingers and
she's getting cheetos and a vitaminwater and i guess she's more
of a girl, really, in some jeans and an old leather jacket, her hair
kind of scraggly and Bright Red and when she turns around,
her food clutched to her chest it doesn't even take me a minute
to realize those are my eyes she's looking at me through, that
white line of teeth, unapologetic and unapologetically hers

But then but then but then the sky is pierced by a blade, scalloped
edges glinting in the sunlight, and the trees fall away in ribbons and

the world seems to wilt and there is darkness behind it, like someone has torn a hole out of reality itself and the tears are gone and the boy trembling beside me in the earth is gone and the knife is gone and from the dark gaping maw climbs a half-grown woman, flame-haired, slouching beneath a leather jacket, and she holds a knife in her hand, not my knife—*her* knife—and every cell in my body cries *sister* and she dusts the mud off her jeans, an apology in her eyes as she reaches out a hand for me.

Jamie? she says, and i stand there, not moving, not moving out of her way, shaking and shaking and shaking

Jamie? she says, and I stand there, not moving, not moving a single slender inch, shaking and shaking and shaking,

Annie, I say.

Annie, I say.

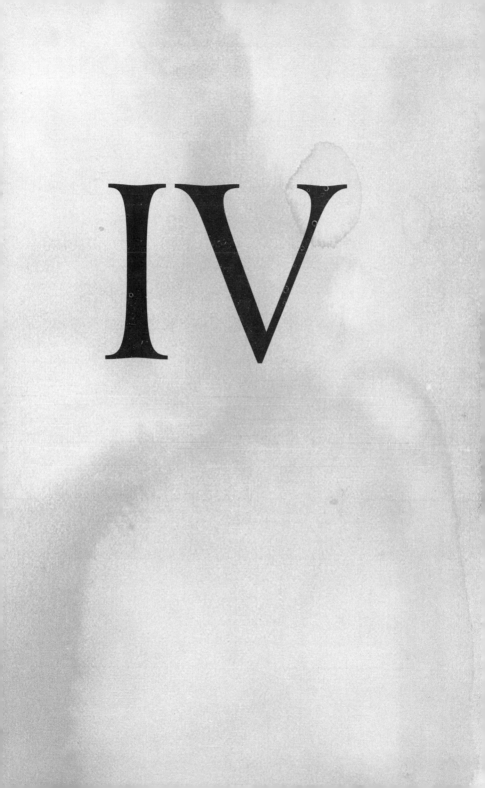

IV

29

THE VILLAGE BELOW WAS BLANKETED in a crust of early winter snow. Every chimney breathed mouthfuls of smoke into a firmament of endless gray. The boy on the mountain, whose name was James, imagined the lives in the houses, warm and sweet and easy. There would be bakers and coopers and candlestick makers, greengrocers donning their aprons for their long days of work. He had never looked at them with the dread or contempt his sister had, and now whatever quaint fascination he'd once felt had only intensified. It was as if there were a magnet inside him, drawing him closer. If only he could be one of them. If only he could be ordinary.

And then, crouching naked in the snow, James thought: Why not?

If there was to be a blood tithe, if there was to be a sacrifice, he had already paid it a thousandfold. He had spilled his blood and had it spilled for him, in a ship and in a roundhouse and in a castle, in a pickup truck and in a clean basement apartment, in his mother's bathroom and in a hospital room, too. He had seen himself ritualistically arranged, laid bare for all to see. He had given himself. And what had he gotten in return?

A fantasy. And only that.

James, who was now nearly a man, started down the cliffside, his feet burning in the snow. He had been called once, and maybe in another lifetime, in another world, he would have answered it, rising against black magic again and again and again. But for now he turned his back on Gumlea, on magic, on all of it. He went to the bottom of the mountain. He closed his book.

❧

Jamie was back. It should have been magical. I'd been the faithful one, keeping home and hearth warm and waiting for him. I'd been Penelope at her loom, unraveling my day's work over and over again. I'd believed, even when no one else had, even when the whole world had told me, *Let him go. He's dead.* Our reunion should have been a revelation, proof of a higher power—that a million forces coalesced upon the two of us in something resembling what ordinary people called "fate."

Instead, my brother returned, and in doing so he destroyed all magic in his wake.

Jamie had never been to Gumlea. It was just like my therapist had said: the kingdom was nothing more than an escapist creation meant to comfort myself in a time of turmoil, a story I would have certainly outgrown naturally had my brother never disappeared. There was no Annit. No Ijah. There were no pirates. No kings. There were no mermaids or dragon towers or phoenixes rising from the ashes, their bright plumage covered in flames. Now the fantasy had been *poufed* in favor of a new, ugly reality.

Kidnapped. My brother had been kidnapped. And kept in a first-story apartment, a place without curtains in the windows and, after the first year, a place where the door was rarely kept locked.

After he returned, I tried to ask what had happened to him only once. His first weekend home, we found ourselves standing in the kitchen together late at night. I couldn't sleep, and apparently, neither could he. As he riffled through the refrigerator, I gathered my courage. Maybe it would be a kindness, to let him know he could trust me. To remind him that I was there.

"Um, Jamie," I said, and then amended my sentence: "James."

He stood up, holding a carton of strawberries in hand.

"Yeah?" he said, a little harder than I thought he might. "What?"

I flinched. "Well," I told him. "I just want to say, if you ever want to talk, I'm h—"

My brother sighed. He looked down at the strawberries like they were very important, and very interesting.

"I know you're here, Annie," he said. "But I don't think you want to hear about it. Okay?"

I nodded a little, nervously.

"Okay," I told him, and watched as he opened the carton of strawberries.

"These are gross," he said. "Doesn't Mom ever clean out the fridge? I guess some things never change."

He chucked them into the garbage and walked off, without another word.

The thing is, Jamie was right. I *didn't* want to hear his story. Not in his own words. Not in his own voice. It was too horrible. It hurt too much. It was bad enough that I'd buried him once, that I'd lost him the way I had. But now, in the wake of his return, I'd lost Gumlea, too. I felt foolish, in the aftermath, that I'd ever believed that he'd gone to the Island of Feral Children. I'd been childish and naive, like a kid who believes in Santa Claus well into middle school. I told myself that it made sense at the time. For some reason. I tried, as my therapist encouraged me, to be kind to myself. But hearing Jamie tell me—in his own words—what had happened to him would mean admitting exactly how wrong I'd been. So I never asked about it again, and the silence between us became a widening chasm.

The funny thing is that I didn't have to ask, because the human mind is remarkably good at assembling a whole story from a few scattered pieces. I learned this lesson from my brother, and it's something I've carried with me since. You don't ever have to give someone your entire life story. A few words will suffice, and your audience will fill in the rest.

My brother would never return to school—his therapist said that the setting was too triggering for him. The school district would send tutors, retired teachers who left stacks of worksheets on the coffee table with the expectation that most would go undone. But even though Jamie got respite from high school, I didn't. I saw the soft, concerned looks on the teachers' faces, heard the whispers that continued to rush around me, unabated, everywhere I went.

Pedo. Captive. Stockholm syndrome. Creeper. Fag.

I put together the story myself from the things that were said and also from the things that weren't. I knew how bad it was from the way that Gram and Poppy looked at Jamie, like he might crumble to dust at any moment, from the way that even the supermarket cashiers regarded him, as if to say, *I remember you from the news.* I began to tuck away names, turns of phrase, images I saw on the internet that I'd never wanted to see. I didn't need to read a long-form article about my brother to learn the ugly truth, and I definitely didn't ask Jamie where had had been for two G-d damned years. I didn't have to.

I knew.

His name was Kevin Rapp-Palmer. He was thirty-two when he first met my brother in Neal Harriman's basement. He was a friend of a friend. A friend of Neal's older brother's drug dealer, actually, kind of quiet and well dressed for a guy who worked in the appliance section of Best Buy, and innocuous, though he'd never dated anyone and everyone thought it was weird and nobody held back in telling him so. He was from western Pennsylvania and moving back that way soon, and when they all got stoned that first night, Kevin talked about Nietzsche and my brother sat on the sofa next to him, thirteen and quietly impressed. He had never met a grown-up who cared about philosophy before, not really. Our mother said she did but didn't really have the mind for it, not like my brother. Before he left, Kevin gave Jamie his phone number. I can imagine how Calvin Harriman would have made a joke that maybe Kevin was going to take my brother out on a date, and can imagine that Neal would have slugged Calvin in the arm for that. I see these things sharply, as though they happened, though I never asked Jamie if what I imagined was true.

I think they must have texted one another over the months that followed, through eighth grade and Kevin's work transfer. I think Jamie must have told him about Vidya, about falling in love, about Dad and the drum kit Dad hadn't let him buy and the band he desperately wanted to start with his new girlfriend and his best friend. I think Kevin must have made him promises. Late at night, my brother's phone buzzing on the nightstand. I think Kevin must have told him he knew some guy who could sell him some drums, and he'd help my brother. I think Jamie must have been grateful.

I can almost imagine the way admiration and gratitude shone in my brother's eyes the day he skipped class and climbed into Kevin's truck, his backpack slung over one shoulder, not suspecting a thing as they drove onto the thruway. After an hour or so, Kevin offered him a soda. My brother drank. My brother started to feel woozy. The kids at school whispered about how he'd been *tied up* and I knew that Kevin must have pulled over on a side street while my brother slept and bound him with climbing rope and then, a few miles later, abandoned my brother's backpack in a rest stop after plunging his phone into a toilet.

Kevin put him in the bed of the truck, where there would be no risk of the other drivers seeing the boy sleeping in the passenger's seat, his hands bound in his lap. Then Kevin got back in the truck and began to drive.

Six months of terror. That's what I heard it called on the news before I could rush to change the channel. And it must have begun with this: waking up in the bed of a pickup truck, unable to move and half unable to breathe, the wind rushing over his body as Kevin drove and drove and drove.

My brother was hardly allowed to sleep in the early days. Kevin would wake him up in the middle of the night, after one hour or two hours or twenty minutes or ten minutes of sleep. He touched him. Took pictures of him. Told him he loved him and that if he ever tried to escape, our dad would see those photographs and know what kind of boy my brother *truly* was. There was manipulation and fear, and Jamie at the center of it. He was a boy at first, but then he got taller, strong. Still, he was scared. He didn't want my dad to know, or Elijah, or Mom. And even though he suspected he couldn't hide a thing from me, he didn't want me to know, either.

I knew that my brother could have left. Not at first, but later. He could roam the neighborhood most days, once Kevin was convinced that Jamie was good and obedient and would not call the police. And Jamie didn't run, to the police or anyone else. My brother stayed. They told people they were a father and son, or cousins, or friends. And if anyone they met suspected the truth, those people must have pushed it out of their minds. Kevin Rapp-Palmer was a good guy. He was fastidious, and he talked about books and film and video games and had a kind face even if he looked at you too intently when you spoke. He was a little creepy, maybe.

But harmless.

30

The night Jamie first came home, his dark hair was shaggy down his shoulders. He wore cheap clothes Mom had bought from a Walmart on the long drive back to New York State, a T-shirt with a surfing dog on it and a pair of navy sweatpants with a white tie at the waist. Jamie stood in our dim living room, staring at the cobwebs and Mom's schoolbooks spread out across the coffee table and the candy wrappers I'd forgotten to throw out that were scattered across the couch cushions.

"I saw the 'For Sale' sign out front," he said. Mom laughed nervously in the doorway, fussing with her keys. She waved her hand, dismissing him. Maybe we weren't moving at all. Maybe my brother's return had changed the future. Maybe we were all staying here now that he was back and everything was fixed.

It had been so long since I stood beside him that it was jarring in that moment: his unmistakable magic. It almost hurt, like staring directly into an eclipse. But it was sweet, too. Childish, like Christmas. Jamie was back! I wanted to throw my arms around him, holding him close. I wanted to sneak off to the woods with him and have him tell me all his secrets. But having Jamie back was like catching a powdery-winged cabbage moth between your hands. You didn't want to move too quickly. You didn't want to crush him.

"We're taking it off the market. I'll call the Realtor tomorrow. Now that you're back—"

"Still, it looks different," he said, his gaze hazy—like he didn't even know how his presence shifted the air around us, giving it a new electricity. My brother, the ghost, back from the dead. "It's changed."

Beside him, Elijah scoffed. He was becoming surly, like Jamie once had. "That's because Dad moved out," he said, which Jamie knew already, but his shoulders sagged to hear it.

I felt a stab in my heart. He was disappointed by us. We'd failed him, somehow, by moving on, by changing. I guess he expected us to all stay frozen in his absence, preserved in amber for all eternity as we had been on the day he got in some man's truck and drove right out of our lives. And I'd *tried* not to change. I hadn't wanted to leave the Island of Feral Children, or to give up everything we'd always believed. Didn't he understand everything I'd sacrificed for him? Friends. Normality. Vidya. Didn't he understand that I'd never given up *hope*?

But still, I'd made my betrayals, too. Rolling my eyes at his poetry. Telling Vidya that she should have been mine instead. Being so, so angry at him right before he disappeared . . .

I looked down, scared that if our eyes met, he would somehow learn the whole story—every ugly bit.

Mom crossed the room to put her hand on his shoulder. He leaned into her touch.

"I kept your room for you," she said. "It's just like you left it."

I braced myself. Because the room wasn't just like he left it. The drawing he'd done of Vidya was gone, and I was the one who had given it away.

But now, in this moment, I was safe. Jamie was clearly exhausted. He licked his lips, which were chapped and pale, and nodded. Then he went up the stairs alone and slammed the door behind him. If he noticed now that the drawing of Vidya was gone—slipped inside her pocket on the night of our shared birthday, the night I'd first drawn her to me and drowned in the scent of her skin—he never said a word to me about it.

He was quiet that first night. We were, too. I cooked dinner with Mom, moving in a silent choreography around the kitchen while Elijah sprawled out on the couch playing video games.

"We're really going to keep the house?" I finally asked as I scraped the vegetables into the pan. I'd begged her before, tears streaming down my cheeks. Now I picked my words carefully, though part of me suspected that it didn't really matter to her how I spoke or what I said. Not when Jamie was back, alone, upstairs.

"We don't want to do anything that will disrupt his life more than necessary. Not after what happened. We need to be stable for him. We'll be the strong ones." She pressed her lips into a smile.

I stared at her, my eyes wild and wide. Being strong for Jamie now? She had *no idea* what I'd sacrificed for him. Everything I'd done, or hadn't done, had been meant to bring him back home. When I left Vidya's house and tromped out into the woods alone, it had been *his* name on my lips. *Jamie Jamie Jamie*, I chanted, standing on one foot until I fell over, until I'd let out a ragged sob. I'd taken that knife—that stupid, stupid knife—and hugged it to my chest, trying to will him to come back to me. Then I'd buried it with my bare hands, until the hard-packed soil under my nails made my fingers ache. My mother hadn't known about any of it. She hadn't known how long I'd been strong for him. Not just that night, but for two years before that.

For my entire life before that, too.

That night, I felt the heavy weight of my phone in my pocket. I thought about texting Vidya, telling her the whole crazy story. Jamie was back, but it was nothing like I'd thought it would be. Maybe we would laugh about it, how my magic had worked, in a way, but it had been a black magic, a broken magic. Maybe she would have gently pointed out how it was obvious—to her, to me—how it was *finally* time for me to move on.

But how could I? My brother was here, sleeping upstairs. He'd experienced unimaginable horrors. And that wasn't all. *What your son did was very, very brave,* the nurse at the desk had said when we'd gone to pick Jamie up from the hospital. Mom had nodded, but she didn't look surprised. Of course she expected Jamie to do amazing things, even now. We all did. Jamie had been hurt, and now Jamie was a hero. If there was any time to think about myself, then *this* moment, this night, surely was not it. Not wanting to risk the temptation, I didn't take out my phone until hours later, when I figured it would be dead anyway. I didn't text Vidya. I didn't text anyone. I waited.

Jamie didn't wake up for dinner. He slept right through it. Mom went in to check and said that he looked peaceful, though there was doubt in her voice. She'd lingered so long in his room that her food went cold. Elijah and I exchanged wordless glances and got up to clear our plates.

31

He was quiet that first night, and the whole first week. But soon the bad nights started. My counselor had warned me to expect them, but I couldn't anticipate the terror of waking up for the first time in our usually silent house to the ear-shattering sound of my brother's screams.

"Don't touch me! Don't touch me! I'll fucking kill you!"

My own heart pounded as I stumbled out of my bedroom and into the hall. Mom had already turned on the light and thrown open Jamie's bedroom door. Elijah was at Dad's that night; no one had been able to convince Jamie to go there yet. He wanted to be home, he said. His real home. His *actual* home.

So I watched alone in the yellow light of the hallway as my mother crawled into my brother's bed and cradled his too-big body to her chest.

"I'm here, baby," she said, rocking him, even though he wasn't a baby. He wasn't even a boy anymore. His big man hands were cupped over his face, and he screamed once more into them. Mom rocked him, her lips against the crown of his head, tears streaming down her cheeks.

Feeling exhausted and off-kilter, I stumbled back into my pitch-black room. Jamie's sobs had died down, but his barky breath still came now and again through the thin walls. My heart raced. I reached up and touched the ancient drawings that hung above my bed.

"What did he *do* to you?" I whispered, and my stomach clenched for some reason at giving that thought voice. But of course I knew what had happened. Rape. He had been raped. The worst sort of crime against the best sort of person. I felt the smooth, soft grain of the paper beneath my hands, wondering how I'd never guessed at this, how I'd never imagined it. I'd known Jamie better than anyone. I'd once thought that we shared the same soul, the same heart. Obviously, I'd been wrong. What's worse, people had *said* it. I'd seen them whispering to each other at school or on the bus. I thought about the girl who had given me that joint at the Madrigals trip after admitting that she stayed up all night sometimes reading theories about my brother's disappearance on Wikipedia.

Some people think some guy in a van got him, she'd said after we smoked, when our heads had started to get hazy and our mouths had filled up with cotton. *Offered him a ride and then drove him out to the middle of nowhere. Like something out of one of those eighties movies about kids gone wrong.*

Back then, I'd only scowled at her. Derisive.

You have no idea what you're talking about, I'd said. I had been *so sure* that I knew where Jamie had gone. He was in Gumlea. The pirate had him. The pirate with hooks for hands, with his filmy eyes. The pirate had sung him sea shanties, smoothing down Jamie's hair and then tying endless knots in my brother's ropes. The pirate had been sick, yes. Perverted? Possibly. But rape? That hadn't entered the equation. I had never even considered it. There was no rape in *Gumlea.*

There was only silence now coming from my brother's room. After a long stretch of time—maybe minutes, maybe hours—I heard Mom get up and close the door and go to her own bedroom, satisfied that my brother was asleep.

But I didn't sleep at all that night, or most nights after. On most nights, my stomach was too queasy. I'd be on edge, waiting for Jamie's next nightmare, waiting for the screaming to begin. On the nights when I would finally succumb to sleep myself, I'd have nightmares of my own. The things that had happened to Jamie. Or, more often, the things that hadn't: the pirate, spilling his grog over my brother's bare skin, whistling ancient, tuneless songs. Pressing his lips to my brother's shoulder blades, drawing his hooks down the curve of my brother's back.

It was bad enough that I'd lost Vidya and Gumlea. Now I was supposed to face the real world, where everyone knew that my older brother had become a traumatized mess. If I could have buried the truth beneath a thousand pounds of concrete, I would have. But there was no escaping it.

Soon enough, I had to return to school. In a way, it reminded me of how my days had felt right after Jamie's disappearance. All eyes were on me, but none of the kids knew what to say. A few of the teachers tried. At the start of lunch the day I went back, Mr. Macklin, the gym teacher, called me over. He reached out his hand. I awkwardly reached mine out. Then he put a hand over and under mine, like the world's clammiest sandwich.

"I'm so glad your brother came back," he said. "I always remembered how talented he was at running. I prayed for him all the time."

I frowned, pulling my hand away. I never knew what to say to that kind of thing. Maybe Elijah or my dad would have appreciated the sentiment, but over the last few years I'd stopped praying for his return in any language but the languages of Gumlea. I'd said so many prayers, and they'd never done anything to get my brother back. And while I still went through the motions, my body unwilling to let the prayers go even if my heart had, the lack of answers had begun to make my faith waver. I wanted to ask Him why He'd returned my brother to me so changed when I'd always been faithful. But you can't have a *real* conversation with G-d. He never answered, so eventually, I quit asking.

"Um," I said, "yeah, thanks." Then I quickly retreated into the cafeteria. My eyes were down on the linoleum tiles. I didn't want to risk seeing Vidya or her friends. Instead, I just slid into what had once been my regular seat, at a table alone in the corner with Miranda, and buried my face in my hands.

Maybe under normal circumstances, she would have laughed. Or maybe asked me where I'd been for weeks, when I'd been obsessed with my first girlfriend. Maybe under normal circumstances she would have been annoyed at me for only coming back to our friendship now that the relationship with Vidya was over. But these were not normal circumstances.

"You all right?" she asked, not carefully or delicately like anyone else might have done, but like she actually *really* cared. I dropped my hands and looked at her. My friend. My oldest friend. Freckles on her nose. Her pixie cut all cowlicked. And her thin eyebrows, knitted up in worry for me.

"It's been a month," I said. She smiled vaguely and offered me some chips out of her snack-sized bag of Doritos.

"An entire month?" she asked.

I fished one out, loudly crunching. And laughed, despite myself. "An *entire* month," I told her. "Two, even. First I bury my brother, then

I finally get a girlfriend, then Mom says she's going to sell the house, then me and Vidya call it quits and then—"

"Your brother comes back from the dead?" she offered.

I shook my head. Snorted. Laughed again. "Yeah, you could say that."

Miranda paused, watching me for a moment. "Did you talk to him about what happened?" she asked, and for a moment, I thought she meant what had happened to *him*. To Jamie. I grimaced, and the horror must have been evident on my face, because then she added, "I mean, did you tell him about you and Vidya?"

She was looking past me, to where I knew Vidya was probably sitting. I wanted to look, too. But I couldn't let myself. If I looked at her, I knew I'd want to go back to her. To sit next to her and hold hands under the lunch table. To take solace in the smoothness of her skin, to let her whisper comforting words directly into the snail shell of my ear. And I couldn't. Not now. Magic was gone, dashed against the rocks *finally*—just like Vidya had wanted—but Jamie's return meant a reunion with Vidya was a nonstarter.

"G-d no," I said. "Not yet. We haven't really had time to talk. . . ."

"You don't have to, you know," Miranda said quickly, like she'd been thinking about this for a while.

I arched an eyebrow, reaching for another chip. "What do you mean?"

"You don't have to tell him that you and Vidya were together. I'm sure he has other things on his mind right now, but even after he . . . whatever, starts to get better. If I were him, I wouldn't want to know about it. It'd be one thing if you were still together. But you're not, right?"

I couldn't help it then. I turned around, looking right toward Vidya's table. It seemed like she and Harper Walton were cracking up over something, like they were having a swell old time. But then my eyes caught Vidya's, and her face fell. She started crumpling up her lunch and got up to leave. It hurt, to see her run away like that. But it's not as if I didn't expect it.

I turned back around. "We are definitely not together," I told Miranda.

She nodded. "Then skip it. Don't tell him, if you don't want to. Why make a complicated situation even more complicated? Even back before your brother disappeared . . ." She trailed off.

"What?"

"He was always kind of a jerk to you," she said. "You were always so *nice* and I know you told him everything but I don't know if he really appreciated that. He just kind of did what he wanted, right? And the thing is, that's fine. He's your brother, not your best friend. You can be supportive of him without, I don't know."

"What?"

"Without, like, peeling your skin off and opening your guts for him every time you talk. It's okay to be different people. Even now."

She went to take a Dorito, but I'd eaten the last one. She sighed, but not at me.

"*Especially* now," she added.

As the days and then weeks passed, my brother quietly revised himself. Mom took him to get a haircut, and to the mall in Poughkeepsie for a new wardrobe, which fit him better than the hand-me-downs from the folks at Dad's church. She took him to the dermatologist. And to see a new therapist, every single day. Not my therapist, but one who specialized in people with more complex trauma, like veterans with PTSD, shooting victims who had barely survived—and kids like my brother. While the rest of us went to school or work, my brother talked about his disappearance in a brightly lit office downtown five days a week. At least, I assume that's what they talked about. Jamie didn't offer anything to me, and I could never find the words to ask.

Actually, Jamie and I didn't talk to each other at all. I didn't even know where to begin. Sometimes I'd be doing homework or watching TV in the living room, and he'd float on over like a ghost. He'd sit in the easy chair—the one he used to spend hours draped across, reading—and he'd laugh too loudly at the terrible sitcom punch lines.

"That's funny, right?" he asked one night, not for the first time.

I tapped the cap of my pen against my notebook. "Yeah," I said. I examined his features. I had liked his hair better long, actually. Even if his skin was getting better. He looked too wholesome now. Too much like Dad. "Funny."

The corner of his mouth twitched. "You can change it if you want," he said. He went to hand me the remote, but I waved my hand.

"No, it's okay," I told him. "I have like a million proofs to do. I should probably go work upstairs."

Jamie looked at the remote like it might contain some sort of answer. Like it was a key. Or a knife. "Suit yourself" is what he said.

I carried my things up the stairs to my room and closed the door behind me. And then I took my notebook and hurled it at the wall, and kicked my garbage can over, too. I didn't know what was wrong with me, couldn't understand. I was supposed to be helping my brother get better. I was supposed to *support* him, like Mom had said. Like I always had, in a million tiny ways over the course of my entire life. But I couldn't even talk to him. Every time I opened my mouth, all I could think about were the things I couldn't say. Gumlea. Vidya. The night in the woods. And what else was there to talk about, really? His years spent in Pennsylvania, playing video games while his rapist went to work? His upcoming court date? The GED our father wanted him to get, if he could ever be bothered to study? He didn't know me anymore, and I didn't know him.

I sighed and started picking up my snack wrappers and pencil shavings from the floor. In that moment, brief and fleeting, I knew that I couldn't do anything to help Jamie. I couldn't even help myself.

32

Not everyone was so afraid to talk about what had happened to Jamie. Mom discussed it openly at dinner; she said that Jamie's therapist had advised her that it was best to normalize the experience. Still, his eyes were closed off and shadowed when Mom rattled on about, as she had begun to call it, "The Thing That Happened." You could almost hear the capital letters there. It reminded me of how Jamie and I had once spoken of Gumlea, with its Laws and Vows and Kings—only much, much worse.

Mostly, she talked about the upcoming court case. She'd finally conceded to using Dad's lawyer, who was giving them a fair price, at least, for such a high-profile crime. Don Muselmaan, she'd tell us, had said that it was important Jamie look sympathetic in the public eye. The defenses in other, similar cases—and there were only a few—had focused on how troubled the boys had been. How they had sought out adult influence, almost as if to say they'd been asking for it. My brother grunted at that, but the grimace that passed over his features was small and so quick as to almost be imperceptible. Mom didn't notice. She just talked about how handsome Jamie would look in a new suit, and how maybe he should cut his sideburns off, too.

"Don has a new strategy," she told us, spearing her fork into our kale salad. We'd had over two years of frozen dinners, and that's when she remembered dinner at all. Now Mom had signed us up for a CSA and bought a new blender so that she could make the two of them green smoothies for breakfast. It was as if she were waking up, coming back to life now that Jamie had returned. "We're hiring a media team. I don't know why we didn't sooner—I've been fielding calls left and right."

It was true. She'd finally disconnected our house line because of how much it would ring through dinner.

"Don suggested a media special," she continued. "One of those nightly news programs. He's not sure which yet. But he had a title. *The Lost Boy Returns.*"

"Like Peter Pan?" I asked, and I glanced at Jamie. I thought of how my brother had once looked in my imagination, clutching a knife in his hand, his shoulders weighed down by furs. Like Peter Pan, yes. But better.

Jamie glanced at me. Another quick glance, one Mom would never catch. "Sounds good," he said. "If it gets that fucker locked up, I'll do whatever it takes."

"Hey!" Mom said, wincing at his language, but my brother didn't even bother shrugging. He was sixteen years old, more of a grown-up than we'd ever thought he would be. Mom cursed all the time. Why shouldn't Jamie?

"What?" he said calmly, serving himself more salad. "You want him locked up, too, right?"

Mom scoffed. "Of course I do, Jamie," she said. The nickname didn't seem to bother him anymore. Not much did, except for what had happened.

"Great," my brother said. "*The Lost Boy Returns*, it is."

The special was to be filmed in the city, in an NBC studio in Manhattan. At one point, I was invited to participate. Muselmaan said it would be useful to show the impact on the entire family, but I didn't like the idea of the camera staring at me, scrutinizing me. And what could I have possibly talked about? How I believed Jamie wasn't dead, because he'd found a way into the fantasy world we'd invented when we were little kids? How I'd picked up my brother's girlfriend in his absence, like she was some sort of hand-me-down? I still hadn't told Jamie about any of that. So I begged off, claiming that I had to study for my upcoming midterms. It wasn't entirely fabricated, but it wasn't precisely honest, either. Still, nobody pushed. I think Mom and Jamie both knew that I was the last person who would help his likability in the public eye, even if Muselmaan couldn't have known that. Jamie had cleaned himself up, but I was still who I was. Messy, angry, awkward, always saying the wrong thing. Just *wrong*.

Once it was decided, my mother declared that they would make a special trip out of it, just the two of them. Her and Jamie. They would take the train to the city, book a hotel room. Maybe they would show some family photos on the special, and they had me sign a release for it, just in case. I scribbled my name on the contract, glad to be left out. I was eager for a few days alone in our house to pretend that the whole enterprise didn't exist.

For three days, I got silence, blissful silence, for the first time since Jamie came home. I felt guilty, how much of a relief it was. I

finished a painting I'd been working on in my room, flowers droop-
ing in a bowl of water. I studied. I listened to NPR. I texted Miranda
photos of my lunch. I enjoyed my solitude, my loneliness, ignoring
that strange tug I felt in the back of my mind. Somewhere, under hot
lights, my brother was secretly miserable. I knew without knowing,
just like I'd once known that he was alive. But I told myself it was
imaginary. I'd been wrong about how he felt before, after all.

The special aired a few weeks later. Mom made big plans to order
take-out food from the Indian place in Elting—butter chicken and
garlic naan, Jamie's favorite. She even bought us a bottle of sparkling
cider.

I took one look at the sweating bottle on the counter and asked if I
could go to Miranda's house instead.

"The whole thing feels like none of my business," I told Mom.

"What are you talking about?" she said. "It's your brother's *life*."

But before I could respond, Jamie stepped into the kitchen. He
picked up the bottle and looked at it, as if it contained something stronger than Martinelli's, something worth studying.

"It's okay with me," he said. "Annie doesn't have to watch it."

We both turned to stare at him, but Jamie only stared back.

"What?" he said.

That night, I sat on Miranda's floor, painting Warcraft figurines with
her. We never played the game, but she liked the way that they looked
on her bookshelf. It was funny, how much comfort I was taking in
spending time with her again. Though we'd nearly stopped talking
during the few passionate weeks of Vidya, we had picked up right where
we left off—hanging out, doing nothing of much importance together.

Now she held one of the diminutive knights in front of her face. "You don't want to watch it, even a little bit?" she asked.

I shook my head in a fevered sort of way, and then was quiet for a minute, watching her brushwork. Her hand was ridiculously steady. I was painting as much as I ever did at home—landscapes and still lifes now, nothing with people in it, nothing that told a story. Since Jamie had returned, I'd started to convince myself that my art was empty, meaningless. But no matter how carefully I tried to record real life, my strokes were sloppy, broad and expressive. Miranda was capable of a different kind of art. She made her own chain maille, tiny links she bent together by hand one by one.

"We don't talk about it," I said softly. "We never talk about it. I feel like if he wanted me to know . . . he would tell me, wouldn't he?"

Miranda looked at me, and I could see her eyes refocus from the figurine onto my own face. It made her look a little off-kilter for a moment, like we were sitting in entirely different rooms, in entirely different worlds.

"Maybe," she said. "Maybe it's too hard to talk about."

"It's *private*," I said, more firmly this time. "He's doing this because the lawyer says he has to. But I think, given the option, he wouldn't even talk about it to anyone. I mean, why would he?"

"Because . . . ," she began. But then she shook her head, like she was shaking away a thought. "Yeah, you're right."

The corner of my mouth twitched up. It wasn't exactly a smile, but it ended the conversation, anyway.

"Do you want a snack?" she asked. And if Miranda had been any-one else, she might have given me a meaningful look, or pressed me to talk about how it all *felt*. But I was already getting enough of that from my therapist and from Mom and from Dad and the world at large. Miranda was my best friend for a reason.

"Sure," I said.

She nodded and hopped up off her bedroom floor. "Sure. Chips or pretzels?"

"Pretzels," I said.

33

Jamie went to Dad's apartment once and only once, about a month after he returned. When he saw the pullout sofa and the dim, cramped bookshelves and the moving boxes still in the corner, never fully unpacked, he rushed off to the bathroom and slammed the door behind him. Elijah, Dad, and I could hear the vomiting sounds from the other side of the wood, but it would be a few minutes before Dad went over and knocked his knuckles against the painted surface.

"You okay, kiddo?"

After a few more minutes of retching, and then the *whoosh* of a flush, Jamie cracked the door open. His face was waxy and bathed in sweat.

"I can't stay here," he said. "I'm sorry. I can't. I can't."

Dad pressed his lips together, but what was he going to say? He only nodded.

The next week, for the first time in years, I didn't go to my father's apartment on a Saturday night. Instead, he and Elijah came to us. Mom was nervous. She skipped her Friday class and spent the whole night scrubbing our house from top to bottom, cleaning hair from behind the toilet, vacuuming the drapes.

"Come on, kids, you could help me out a little," she shouted down the hall, though it was clear by *kids* she meant *Annie*. My brother's domain was his room and only his room. His therapist had told Mom not to push him. He hadn't had rules or chores in captivity. It would take time for him to learn to live like a normal person again.

It wasn't something that needed a response. I turned up the music on my laptop, hoping to drown out everything that was happening around me.

At dinner, Dad's smile was strained at the edges. He'd brought our mother flowers from ShopRite, carnations that stayed crisp and new in the winter air. Once, this kind of sharp, clear weather made me think about the Winter Watchers. Now I stared out the closed French doors in our dining room and dreamed of being *anywhere* else.

Still, Mom asked me to light the Shabbat candles and Dad said grace over the loaf of bread she'd made, the first time she'd turned on the breadmaker since before Jamie disappeared. It was all so very *domestic*.

They chattered and clanked forks against their plates and Dad kept pouring more wine and toasting to my brother's return. Just a few weeks before Jamie had come back, he'd finally introduced me and Elijah to his girlfriend from church. Now there was no mention of *Debbie*. I should have felt happy, but it all felt fake. The only comfort, I told myself as I cleared the plates alone and the rest of them watched TV in the living room (Elijah wedged between my parents, Jamie sitting off from them on the floor, his expression unreadable to me) was that Dad wasn't staying. He'd go back to his own space before the night was over, and I could pretend this all was an unpleasant dream.

Later, when I sat in my room sketching, Jamie's shadow darkened my door for a moment. He seemed to watch me for a while, silent, thinking. I felt his presence there as much as I saw it. Once, I wouldn't have said anything to him. I wouldn't have needed to.

But now I turned. "What is it?"

My brother flinched, like my movement was too quick for him. "Do you think they'll get back together?" he asked.

I shrugged. "Who knows," I said. I flashed my hand through the air. "You know how the two of them are."

My brother chewed on his lip, peeling the skin away. He was always doing stuff like that. Picking his skin, which was clearer now. Biting his cuticles. He'd done it before, too, but it was worse than ever. Mom said it was because of the trauma.

"But they fight *all the time*."

I frowned. What Jamie was saying was true, sure. But it was also ancient history. They'd been broken up for two years, and while they sometimes bickered about custody agreements or lawyers, things were nothing like they used to be between them. Of course, Jamie didn't know that. That happened sometimes with him. He'd say something, and I'd suddenly remember that he was missing whole huge chunks of time.

"That doesn't mean they're not crazy about each other," I said, and for some reason, explaining it to Jamie made it all a little easier to digest. Maybe they *would* get back together. And even though I didn't want it, there wasn't much I could do about it, either. "Just because you hate someone's guts doesn't mean you don't love them, too."

Jamie was silent for a long moment. But then he made a strange noise. A snort of laughter, even though I didn't mean it to be funny. "Sure," he said, touching his hand to the door. "Whatever. Good night, Annie."

"Good night," I told him, trying not to frown, too, as I went back to my drawing.

34

Sometimes I wondered what it was like to be Jamie. Not the dark parts. I did my best to never let my mind touch that. But the rest of it. I wondered what it was like to sit around all day at home in his sweatpants, doing worksheets for school during what should have been his junior year. His tutors had him read Steinbeck novels, slim and important, and write five-paragraph essays summarizing them. No analysis. No thought. Once my brother had written poetry. Composed songs. Read philosophy. Now he watched TV and slept. My mother was good to him. Dad, when he was around, was kind. But he didn't have a life, not really. Even Eli seemed to avoid him. I think it was too much for him, too, what had happened to Jamie.

As the months rolled on, I still didn't know how to talk to him about it, about anything. Every time I tried, my heart would start to pound and I'd feel my fear take over. And I felt something else besides fear, something that was even harder to talk about. Anger. I'd look at him and feel resentment begin to squeeze my stomach. It terrified me, how angry I felt at him. I'd frantically tried to deny that anger, which I'd been carrying with me all this time, for years and years and years. I had no right to be angry. I knew that.

But I was anyway.

One night, when I was up late painting, I heard Jamie's bedroom door quietly creak open—and then heard his weight on the stairs. I could hear the back door opening. He was going somewhere.

I should have let him go. He was sixteen now. For years, he'd been coming and going as he pleased, and his therapist had said we shouldn't push him if he felt the need to wander. It had been a coping mechanism, she'd said, in a time of immense difficulty, and would likely be a comfort for him now. But for some reason, against my better judgment, against all practical advice, I put down my brush, stuffed my feet into my sneakers, and followed him out into the yard.

"Jamie," I called, in a hushed voice.

He was nearly at the creek. Even in the darkness, I could see him rolling his eyes at me. "You're supposed to be asleep," he said.

I shrugged. "So are you."

For a moment, my brother looked out toward the dark woods. Then he sighed. It was early spring; his breath fogged the air. He'd been home for six months, but we were strangers still.

"Fine," he said. "Come on. But you need to promise me you won't tell Mom."

"Of course I won't," I told him. "When do I tell her anything?"

He was quiet. I wondered, for a moment, if he'd even ever realized how different my relationship with our mother was from his relationship with our mother. We'd grown up in the same family, but we might as well have lived on different planets.

In silence, we launched ourselves over the creek together. Of course, we didn't turn around or slip into Gumlea. If I'd been wondering if it was officially dead for both of us, I had my answer.

But our bodies knew the way, without stumbling, with no map. Before we knew it, we had reached the pirate's sloop—the picnic table that some other boys, long-grown, had graffitied. There was a small fire blazing in the circle of rocks before it. And sitting there on the table itself was Neal Harriman, wearing a denim jacket, with a collection of shining bottles near his hip. He must have been home from his fancy private school for spring break. He'd hardly changed. Short, with pale hair and a pinched face like a fox. He'd tried to grow a mustache to cover it, but in the dancing light of the fire, I recognized him immediately.

"Annie," he said in surprise, and then he glanced at my brother, who only shrugged.

"She insisted on coming with me," he said.

Jamie went over to the table and grabbed a bottle. The liquor inside was bright pink, the color of a melted strawberry Popsicle. He opened it and started to down it, though it was already half drunk.

Neal glanced at me, his lip curling. I tried to understand what my brother had seen in him over all these years. I tried to understand what my brother saw in him now. I came up empty.

"Yeah, but remember last time?" he said.

I felt anger spark inside me. But before I could say anything, my brother did.

"She was a kid then," he said faintly, but he was looking at me like he wasn't quite sure. At last, as if it prove it to himself, he offered me the bottle. I looked at it sweating in his hand. I was fifteen, and I'd smoked pot once, but I'd never been drunk before. Still, I felt the sudden, urgent need to prove that I belonged there, too. If not to Jamie, then at least to myself.

I went and grabbed the bottle, not breaking eye contact as I drank. It tasted like a juice box. Strawberry Hill, the name on the label said, which sounded like the name some kids might come up with. Like the name of someplace in Gumlea.

The wine sloshed around in my belly, warm and too sweet. As the alcohol worked its way through me, I watched Neal crouch before the fire, poking it.

"I can't believe you still hang out with *Neal*," I blurted. "He never even told the cops about—"

My brother cut me off before I could say Kevin Rapp-Palmer's name.

"That's between the two of us," he said, his voice low and a little husky, like he was holding something in. A secret. Well, not much of one. It was the same thing I'd heard him say to Mom and the lawyer, that Neal Harriman wasn't at fault, that he didn't want him dragged into the whole mess. Mom hadn't understood his loyalty. I hadn't, either. Now Neal didn't even turn to look at me. He was too occupied by the fire. I took another swig, felt my anger swell, then die. Neal's fire sucked. The wood was wet and steaming. The flames were weak. Once, as a tiny child, I'd dreamed about the things that happened in the woods at night. I'd imagined teenaged parties like brightly painted bacchanals. Now it seemed impossibly ordinary. A poorly built fire, and a teenaged boy poking at it with a stick.

I could build a better fire, I thought, and then, suddenly, I felt inspired to do just that. I took another thick slug of wine and put the bottle back down on the table beside my brother. Then I shouldered past Neal.

"Watch it," Neal said to me, but I ignored him as I started to add bigger and better fuel, snapping off the sticks in my hand. Behind me,

I heard Neal go to my brother and murmur something.

"What's that?" I called back, looking at them. The fire sparked and danced in Jamie's eyes, but he didn't say anything. Instead, Neal spoke for him.

"I said, *How much trouble do you think you'll get in if she goes home wasted tonight?*" Neal's smile was jagged. Dangerous. He was poking me. Picking on me. He didn't want me here, and I could feel it. I looked at Jamie, waiting to see if he'd say anything. But he didn't.

Once, twice, I blew into the fire, watching the flames lick the kindling before it caught. Then I sat back on my heels. "I don't think you have to worry about that," I told them. "Mom doesn't care what I do. She never has. All she cares about is Jamie."

Finally, a response from my brother. He rolled his eyes. "We don't have to do this tonight, Annie," he said.

I frowned. "Do what?"

"I know you hate me. You said so already."

It was like a punch to my gut. I'd never said I hated Jamie. Had I felt it once or twice, in my anger and my grief? Of course I had. What sibling doesn't? But I *loved* him, too, and I'd never *expressed* anything but love for him. I'd been careful. I'd been supportive. I'd never let any thick, dark feelings out.

Now, dizzy with wine, I stood up straight, shaking my head. "I don't know what you're talking about."

"'Just because you hate someone's guts doesn't mean you don't love them, too.' You said it. Don't pretend like I didn't know what you meant. I'm not *stupid*."

"I know you're not stupid. I was talking about Mom and Dad—"

Jamie waved a hand through the air at me and drank down the last long breath of the wine. "Like hell you were," my brother said, scowling as he wiped his mouth against his sleeve. "I know how you feel about me. You can't even stand to be in the same room as me most of the time. We never talk, not like we used to—"

"Oh, come on," I said, rolling my eyes now, too. "'Like we used to.' Like we were even friends anymore when you left."

"He didn't leave," Neal cut in. "He was *kidnapped*—"

But Jamie wasn't listening to whatever it was Neal was saying, and I wasn't, either. We were talking to each other. Finally. Now my brother's words came swift and cutting.

"That was *your choice*," he said. "Didn't I try to come out here with you? To pretend that things were normal?"

I scowled, trying to remember the last time I had met him in the woods. Me and Jamie, locked in battle. Him screaming, *Fight me, Annie*. The fear and rage in his eyes when I refused. But the hurt, too. Sure, that had happened. I couldn't deny that it had. But it wasn't like he said. It was a lot more complicated than that.

"They *weren't* normal," I said fiercely—but my voice was tight when I said it. I was near tears already. "You can't pretend that they were normal. Do you know what it felt like to be me, Jamie? Everyone was always so worried about you—"

"Jeez, Annie," Neal interrupted me again, his words tromping right over mine, "how selfish can you get? After everything that's happened to him?"

But Neal didn't matter, not right now. He wasn't me, and he wasn't Jamie, and I wasn't about to start pretending that he was. "I mean before that," I said, slowly shaking my head. "For our whole lives before that. You were the golden child, Jamie. And I was no one."

"That's not true," Jamie murmured.

"Damn it." I looked down at the kindling in my hands. And in a flood of frustration, I snapped it between my two fists and chucked it into the flames. "It *is* true. Do you know what our mother said to me when I came out to her? When I brought my first girlfriend home? Not *I love you, sweetie* or *It's okay, I've always known.* Nothing. She said nothing. Like it didn't even matter to her. Even when you were dead, all of our lives revolved around *you.*"

There. I'd said it. Selfish and terrible and ugly, the truth hung in the spring air. The fire crackled. Neal, his eyes wide, grabbed another waiting bottle off the picnic table, and drank.

But my gaze was on Jamie. He was looking at me like his heart was breaking. Like I was breaking his heart.

"You mattered to me," he said, in a terrible, soft voice. "I thought about you every single day."

As he said the words, I knew they were true. I could tell from the look in his eyes, which were welling with tears. But even without his tears, I knew it was true anyway. My brother had thought about me on every ugly morning upon waking, and on every even uglier night. I knew it now because I'd known it then.

Still, I also knew it was false. And as much as it hurt him, and as much as it hurt me to say it, I needed him to hear it. Right then, right there, in the sacred space we'd once shared.

"Maybe you thought about your *idea* of me," I told him. "But you hardly know me. You haven't known a thing about me in years."

Jamie was crying now. I was, too. It felt, in that moment, like we were irreparably broken. That we would never be whole. Not because of what was done to Jamie, but because of some deeper wound, one we'd acquired years before. One that had been with us since the beginning, along with the better, brighter magic.

Neal, beside him, could have scowled. He could have said something cruel and cutting or thrown a rock at me in some desperate attempt to help. He didn't. He only held out the bottle to me. I climbed up on the picnic table beside Jamie and drank.

"It wasn't easy to be me, either," Jamie said softly, trembling beside me as the wine—this one flavored like those artificial peach rings we used to buy at the dollar store—somehow failed to make me feel any better. "Everyone watching me all the time like the whole world might break if I ever did the wrong thing. Do you think I wanted that? Even now, with Mom? If I screw up this court case, and he goes free, it's over—" His breath caught.

I squeezed my eyes shut. "I know," I whispered, because I did. I'd never wanted to *be* Jamie. I'd only ever wanted to not be me. "I know it was bad for you, too. I know it's bad for you now."

"Okay," my brother said. He wiped his face against his sleeve again, but I don't know that it really helped.

We were quiet for a long time in front of the fire, the three of us, watching the flames dance. Everything felt cold and empty and wrong. But then I noticed how Jamie was looking down at his hands in front of him. They were broad now, a man's hands. He seemed to be puzzling over something. Fitting pieces together.

"Wait," he said slowly, as a realization dawned on him. "You had a girlfriend? When? Who?"

I felt my stomach seize. For a moment, I said nothing. On Jamie's other side, Neal let out spluttered laughter. I realized then that Neal *must* have known about me and Vidya. He was Miranda's cousin. Our town was small. Word got around.

"Shit, Annie," he said, still laughing. "You haven't told him?"

I looked away from the fire and turned to face my brother. Took one last swig, swallowed, and, shaking, drew in a breath.

35

I'd memorized every inch of my therapist's office: the carpet that could never decide if it was brown or gray, the big wicker basket of fidget toys on the floor, the cheap prints of ferns and wild lettuces framed on the wall. The single window to the outside world had thick tinted glass. The trees beyond always looked like they were being glimpsed through cloud cover, even on the brightest days. I'd watch them tremble, brown on darker brown, and pet the arm of the sofa and contemplate speaking. Some days I didn't.

Some days—this day—I did.

"So you told your brother," my therapist said. Her name was Kit—a child's name, a doll's name. She was a vaguely hippieish woman in her midforties with narrow wrists and large glasses. Sometimes I thought she was amazing. Sometimes I couldn't stand her. Most days, like today, I settled on a sort of benign indifference.

"Yup," I said, the consonant popping on my lips. "I told him."

"How did that feel for you?" she asked, which was how she often phrased things. Not *How did it go?* or *What did he say?* but *How did that feel?*

"Awful," I said quickly, truthfully. I ran my thumbnail up and down the corduroy wales of the sofa. I was always truthful with Kit now, no matter how uncomfortable it felt. After all, now that I knew there was no Gumlea, what use was there in lying? I'd like to think it had opened a floodgate between us, this new, radical honesty.

But I'm not sure she'd even noticed. She still pushed her glasses up her nose with her forefinger, took notes in her pad, and regarded me with a knitted brow. Our essential interactions remained unchanged.

"Was he upset?" she asked mildly.

I closed my eyes. Nodded. I could feel an echo of his grief and his anger, even now. Or at least, I could feel what I had imagined to be his grief and his anger. Because honestly? Jamie hadn't said a thing. He'd sat there, listening silently to the whole damned story about how I'd stolen his girlfriend—how I'd *loved* her, how I'd thought she'd loved me—and then he got up and left. I'd stumbled after him through the forest, half drunk, leaving Neal to polish off those stolen bottles without us. But when Jamie got to the house, to his room, he only shut his door behind him. He didn't even slam it. Just closed it, quietly, calmly, and then I heard the lock slide into place.

It had been four days, and we hadn't spoken since. In a way, it wasn't really a change from how we spent our days before. I hadn't been lying when I'd said we weren't friends; what did it matter if we *still* weren't? But it was different now. Changed. Before, I'd felt a crack in his wall. A slender beam of light shining through. Now he'd put every rock back into place. There was no light. No hope.

"It's good you were honest with him," Kit Hendricks was saying. "That must have been very difficult. Without honesty—"

"I wish I hadn't said it," I said quickly, because I couldn't stand to hear my therapist talk about how, someday, maybe, me and Jamie could be healed. I didn't want to hope for it. Not when everything felt so hopeless. "In fact, I wish—"

I stopped abruptly, holding my hands over my eyes. Didn't want to say it. Couldn't.

"You know, Annie," Kit said, "I'm here for *you*. Not your mother or your father or your brother. Aside from the a few things I'd be obligated to share, legally . . ."

Silence stretched out between us. We both knew what she meant. She'd made that very clear when this all started. If I was a danger to myself or others, she'd have to tell my parents. I told her that was ridiculous, knife or no knife. It hadn't been a lie.

"Otherwise," Kit said, "what you say in this office stays between us."

"It doesn't," I said wistfully. "If I say it, he'll know."

"You know that's not true."

It was, but it didn't matter. Kit Hendricks was here for me. Why did I come for forty-five minutes twice a week if it wasn't for some variation on catharsis? I no longer had the magic of Gumlea to set myself free, but I had this tiny sliver of space in a life that often had nothing to do with me. I let a breath of air bubble my cheeks for a second, then blew it out, and all my ugly feelings with it.

"I wish he hadn't come back."

She pushed her glasses up her nose. "It must have been hard for you to see him again."

I petted the sofa, then switched to playing with the frayed denim around the hole in my favorite jeans. Kit reached down into her basket of fidget objects and handed me a Jacob's ladder toy. I curled my fingers around the wood squares, then flopped the pieces over themselves. Clack click clack.

"It's not that. It's not seeing him. It's not *him*." Clickety clack click. "I mean. Okay. That sucks, too. I can't look at him without thinking about what happened to him, and—"

"That's very common," she said, which was something she'd told me before.

"I know," I said. Clack clack. "Secondary trauma. You hear enough about something awful and it's almost like it happened to you. Okay, sure. But it's not just that. It's the rest of it, too. It's my *life*."

"Oh?" she said again, which was her standard line.

"When he left, my whole life fell apart. But lately it felt like it was finally becoming something. At school, and with Vidya. I felt like a normal person, or nearly one. Maybe my brother was dead, but I was still alive, you know? I was moving on. Now . . ." Clack clack. Click.

"Now the prodigal son has returned and your calf has been led to slaughter."

From the faint smile on her lips, I suspected that she'd been saving that line for a long time. I didn't understand the reference, but I shrugged. "It's all different now. Again. Mom takes a leave of absence from school and all anyone can talk about is the trial and Dad's coming over once a week for family dinners just to be near Jamie and we're supposed to think it's amazing." Clack. "But I don't. They're all *home* all the time. I miss the peace and quiet. I miss—"

It suddenly occurred to me precisely what I was saying. I missed the quiet. When my brother wasn't home all day, every day. When he was being held captive in another state, raped nightly. I tossed the fidget toy back into the basket and held my hands over my face again.

"It's okay," Kit said, "to have complicated feelings right now."

"No it's not. There's no room for my feelings here."

By *here*, I didn't mean this office, of course. This room existed for nothing *but* my feelings. But outside, in the world beyond, everything belonged to him. And maybe the real problem wasn't that it belonged to him *now*. It was that the whole world always had, stretching back forever, even before I was born.

"Home is hard," Kit agreed. "But maybe it's time for you to find somewhere else for your feelings. School or girls or art or friendship. You've become close with Miranda again, haven't you?"

I had, and I felt good about it. But there was just as much guilt there as there was joy. Because I'd been the one to let things fizzle in the first place, too distracted by the prospect of the black-haired princess to notice the friend who had been standing, stalwart and steady, by my side all this time.

"Yeah," I said. "But I can't rely on her to be everything for me. Or any girl, really. Sometimes I think that was the problem with Vidya. I expected her to *save* me, and Jamie, too. And nobody can do that. We're a mess. All of us."

"I don't know about that," she said. I darted my eyes up. Usually, she accepted what I said with a sort of polite blankness. But here she was, disagreeing with me. Politely, of course. Pushing her glasses up her nose.

"What do you mean?" I demanded, trying not to let my anger flare white-hot inside of me.

"Well," she began, "from everything you've told me, it seems that your brother *did* save himself. He walked out of that apartment on his own two feet and went right to the police. It took him time, but he did it."

I studied her face, the fine lines at the corners of her eyes and circling her mouth. I wanted to hate her. Who was she to tell me anything about my brother? But she was right. And I'd buried my head in the sand. I hadn't wanted to face what had happened to Jamie, which meant that I missed his strength, too.

My brother had been kidnapped, but he'd saved himself. And if he was capable of saving himself from *that*, wasn't I capable of clawing myself out of *this*, too?

How? I wondered. *Damn it, how?*

My heart pounded in my ears. I pointed to the clock over the door with one finger, arching my eyebrow at my therapist.

"Time's up," I told her.

We still had two minutes left, but Kit only smiled at me. "Sure," she said.

36

I'd finally said the words I thought might break the world. Yet somehow, the world kept turning. That night, I ate dinner with Mom and Jamie, and if he knew what I'd been saying about him, he didn't say a word about it. Didn't even let it show on his face, which was the same blank mask it always was. I did my best to look impenetrable, too.

"You teenagers," Mom said, "make such thrilling dinner companions."

No one laughed. It really wasn't funny.

After dinner, I did the dishes, then went up into my room to hide away from the world, like I always did. Put on an old playlist Vidya had made me, but somehow, the chords now rang hollow. Telling Jamie about Vidya hadn't ushered in a new era of peace. And telling my therapist how much I resented him hadn't helped, either. If anything, I felt even worse than I had before, like my bones were rattling around an empty cage of skin.

That night, I set my homework aside. I was the perfect student—honor roll, even—but it had never done me much good. Poppy had stopped sending me checks for my grades sometime after Jamie had disappeared. And our parents never said a word to me about my report cards; it was just assumed that I'd get a merit scholarship to the SUNY down the road, like it was assumed that a fledgling bird would one day fly. My classes weren't interesting, anyway. I didn't care about them. But I'd done well at them because I *could* and Jamie couldn't. What was the use in it now?

I'd spent my whole life defining myself against Jamie. When he was amazing, I was mediocre. When he was gone, I was there. The truth was, now that he was back—now that I was no longer Annie **[Redacted]**, the dead kid's kid sister—I had no idea *who* I was.

I picked up one of my paintbrushes from the cluttered floor, stuck it in my mouth, chewing on it. And then without thinking at all, I went and got my paints. It was the only thing I'd ever taken solace in—the only thing I'd ever let myself take solace in. Once, I'd created weird artwork of Gumlea. Portraits. Maps. Paintings of princes. Kings. Since Jamie returned, I'd been painting still lifes, fruit that rotted in my room until it attracted flies and Mom screamed. But I knew, if I was honest with myself, that I had better art inside me. Bigger art. I set out a canvas, began smushing oils around. At first, I was aimless, laying out colors without meaning, just to feel the brush against the taut surface, just to see cerulean against umber. I heard the words in my mind, heard the poetry in them, but wouldn't let myself feel that. Poetry belonged to Jamie, and right now, I needed something that was mine alone. I grabbed a palette knife and scraped the canvas clean. I started over. With a pencil this time. Working slowly, and more deliberately, too.

Cliché, maybe. But I sketched out a person. A freckle-faced girl with snarls in her hair. She wasn't an empress, or a knight. She was just a suburban kid who burned too quick in the sun. But she had her own sort of magic, didn't she?

I only stopped sketching when the heel of my hand was covered in graphite. By then, it was almost one, and on a school night, too, but I didn't care. No one did. Not Mom. Not Dad. Not Jamie.

So I picked up my pencil again, and began to draw.

I have always been a single-minded person. First it was Jamie, then Gumlea, then Vidya that occupied every single cell in my brain. Now I abruptly abandoned everything again in favor of something new: art. I finally dropped out of field hockey, a sport that I'd never really liked or cared about, anyway. I'd already long quit Madrigals. My paintings, which had previously only seemed like dabblings, stretched across bigger and bigger canvases as I tried to make a record of what I saw. I didn't paint my brother, or hares, or stags, or dragons, and certainly not knives. Those were illusions. Instead I mostly painted myself. My feet, with my bony toes, which I'd always hated. My hands. The faint scar on my upper lip from a fall I'd taken at the pool as a kid. I thought I could somehow freeze time, stop myself from whatever it was that we were barreling toward.

It didn't work. Junior year ticked away, and Miranda got a boyfriend, and sometimes we'd hang out in the parking lot of the Thai restaurant where he worked, arguing about which Doctor we liked best. Elijah failed math, and Mom was so angry that she was beside herself, and demanded he move back to her house for the rest of the school year. The world was shifting, changing, too fast for me to pin down. I finally stopped redyeing my hair. But I could look back at my paintings of when my hair had been red and pretend that not a single day had passed at all.

And when I painted, I didn't have to think about the boy sleeping late in the next room. How we didn't talk anymore. How we didn't even try. Sometimes I'd hear his weight creak the floorboards in the hallway or sense the pressure of his eyes on me, watching me as I painted. What did he think of me? Did he think I was talented, or a hack? Full of myself? Did he think anything about me at all?

He never told me. I never asked.

Eleventh grade puttered to a conclusion, what should have been my brother's senior year of high school. While his former classmates were getting their licenses and bragging about their college acceptances in the hall, Jamie quietly got his GED and started working in the produce department of the ShopRite. He grew his sideburns back out, and Mom argued with him about it, but the trial had taken so long at that point that she couldn't really tell him not to anymore. I stayed out of it. My grades were good, though I got my first handful of Bs. Miranda and her boyfriend and I started a weekly gaming group, and I'd sit with a sketch pad while the boys would argue about video games and I didn't kiss anyone and I tried to tell myself that it all was fine.

But I missed my brother. And more, worse, I missed Vidya.

I considered talking to her on more than one occasion. Once, between classes, I had to go to my locker to get my copy of *Germinal* and I saw her standing at the end of the hallway with Harper, chatting about some bulletin board they were decorating. I felt the potential there for connection. She even looked up at me for a moment, smiling just a little. But what would I ever say to her?

I loved you, but I was too crazy then, and I'm better now but it's too late or *Hi, my brother came home and I told him about us and he still hasn't forgiven me but would you like to get together sometime and catch up?* Or *I'm sorry I invited you to my imaginary nonexistent kingdom in the woods and I hope you didn't tell anyone about it because it's embarrassing even though it was my whole damned life once and are you seeing anyone these days?*

I knew I couldn't say that. I knew I couldn't say anything. So I snatched my paperback from the bottom of my locker and hustled off to class, pretending like I hadn't even seen her, or the way she had looked at me.

Our paths would only cross one last time before she graduated. It was the final week of eleventh grade, and all the seniors had been skipping out of our honors classes, leaving just a few juniors lingering behind. We heard rumors about lake trips and parties in the woods, but that part of high school was so out of reach for me and Miranda that it might as well have been mythical. Even on Cut Day, when as many juniors skipped as seniors, I came to class, and stayed late after school, too, to help Mrs. DeGrassio, the art teacher, clean out the supply closet. It was there that Vidya found me, her shadow cutting darkly down from the half-open door.

"Hey," she said.

When I turned, broken Conté crayons in hand, I almost couldn't believe it was her. But it was. Her hair was streaked lighter now, up in a sloppy summer ponytail. She was clutching a yearbook to her chest.

"Vidya," I said, and the name came out in a single whispered sylla-ble. It was embarrassing, actually. I turned away to hide how my cheeks were suddenly blazing red and started to sort the crayons by color in their boxes.

"Hey," she said again, and her voice was too full of hope for my liking. "Miranda told me I'd find you here. I hope you don't mind. I wanted to see you before . . ."

She trailed off, but we both knew what was contained in that ellipsis. Before she graduated. Before she moved away. Before she walked out of my town, my school, my life forever.

"I heard you're moving to the city," I said, still not looking at her. It hurt to look at her, the same way it hurt to look at the sun. "Julliard?"

"Mm-hmm," she answered, a little bit of excitement seeping into her voice. She was always so electrified when it came to music, and it was one of the things I loved about her. She understood what it was like to love something you couldn't see, something that could only be sensed in vibrations on the air.

"Congratulations," I said, but the word came out limp and wet and useless. I saw the expression on her face out of the corner of my eye, sad and a little bit deflated, and winced. "Sorry. I'm not good at goodbyes. Which is funny, because it feels like I've been making them—"

"No, it's okay," she said quickly, forcing a smile to light the corners of her mouth, cutting me off before we could talk about Jamie, which was probably for the best. "I just really wanted you to sign my yearbook. You were a part of my story when I was here. I want to be able to read this twenty years from now with my kids and get wistful, you know? And you . . ."

She trailed off again, but she didn't have to say a word. I understood. In a way, we'd been a missed opportunity, a regret. If only everything had been different. But it hadn't been. Jamie had come back and shattered that chance, and besides, I'd ruined it, anyway, with all my fantasy talk—my fixation on Gumlea. On him.

I sighed. Yearbooks seemed a little cliché to me—the kind of thing I would never have cared about under normal circumstances. But when I looked at her, she looked so *hopeful*, and my stomach dipped. I held out my hands.

"Sure," I told her.

She passed me the yearbook, and I sat down in the corner of the art room supply closet, rifling around for a moment through one of the drawers for a fine-point pen. I only found a .05, not a .07, but it would have to do. While she stood in the doorway, hands folded in front of her, watching in silence, I put Vidya's yearbook on my knees and started paging through it. It was already full of signatures. The endpapers were packed with well wishes for a good summer and a good time in college and people had drawn little hearts around her name and every single message seemed tender and honest and heartfelt and perfect. Inside my chest, my heart felt squeezed. There was nothing I could say that would be even close to sufficient.

I found my picture among the other eleventh graders. Anne "Annie" R. **[Redacted]**. Art Club. Honors Society. And nothing else. In the picture, my face looked pale and ghostlike and my eyes seemed more like punctuation than any functioning set of organs. I'd dyed my hair again right before school picture day in an attempt to look like a normal human being, but it hadn't worked. The color had come out too bright and too splotchy. I looked more like a malfunctioning stoplight.

I looked at the page for a moment longer. Then I started drawing on it. Over it, actually, digging the pen deep into the paper, letting the ink obscure the faces of all my classmates. It had been ages since I'd drawn anything fantastical, but the real world wasn't good enough for

Vidya. I'd wanted to give her magic once, to see how it felt to live on the other side of the Veil. My resolve firmed in my chest. I would draw her a dragon. The last dragon. The best dragon.

She watched as my pen marks eclipsed the entire page. The dragon was coiling her scaly body in on itself, twisting herself in knots. A pair of minuscule wings could be seen in one corner, and on the other side of the page there was a mouth, open and hungry and waiting. I drew gleaming teeth. I sketched an enormous eye. In the eye was a figure, a reflection. It was Vidya, as she looked to me now, a silhouette against a doorway. But I'm not sure that the girl in the dragon's eye would have been recognizable to anyone but me.

When I was finished, you wouldn't have even known that there were photos of students on that page. Only a dragon, smoke wafting from her nostrils. I signed the bottom. One word. Annie. Then I handed the book back to Vidya.

She grinned. Instantly, irrepressibly.

"Thank you," she said, hugging the yearbook to her chest. "It's perfect."

The expression on her face released a flock of birds in my belly. I looked down at the ground, letting my hair fall in front of my face. "Sure," I said. "No problem."

"Do you want me to walk you out to the late bus?" she asked, and for a minute, I could see it in my mind's eye. Maybe this would be the start of something, if only for a few weeks. A summer romance. Kissing Vidya. Curling up around her in the back seat of her car, smelling her hair.

But no. How could I? Jamie would find out, and it would hurt him, maybe worse than before. I couldn't do that to him. Not again. This, here, would be my punishment for what I'd done. I would not kiss Vidya. I would not kiss anybody.

"No," I said softly, and my voice sounded hoarse when I spoke. "No thanks. My mom is coming to pick me up."

"Oh," she said, and I knew how she felt about my mom from how she said it. "Okay. Have a good summer?"

It was a question that lingered on the air.

"You too" was all I said.

37

That summer was the trial. I wasn't home for it.

Instead, in late June, just a few weeks after school let out, I flew to Ohio with Miranda. Mom thought it was best that I was away for the trial anyway, and when the opportunity to go on a trip with Miranda came up, I took it. It was my first time on an airplane, and as the engines roared and the plane bobbed upward over a sky dotted with white-and-gold cumulus clouds, I imagined that I was shedding an old skin that didn't fit me anymore. I could be anyone when we touched ground. I didn't have to be Anne [Redacted], sister of James [Redacted]. I didn't even have to be Emperata Annit of Gumlea. I could call myself Elsinora if I wanted. I could call myself anything.

But it turned out that at Miranda's uncle's farm, I didn't need to call myself anything at all. It was an idle summer. We wore cotton sundresses and we fed the llamas and the chickens and walked aimlessly through the fields and the woods behind them, which were nothing like Gumlea. For one thing, it was miles and miles and miles to another farm. You never saw another person, much less their garbage. The woods were sweet and golden and sun kissed and that summer, so were we. We played spit late at night in the guest room at her uncle's house.

We read every trashy romance novel on her aunt's bookshelf. We tried to do a Dungeons & Dragons campaign with her cousins and failed miserably. We stole wine out of the liquor cabinet and drank until the room bucked and swayed like the hull of a ship and I told her stories I'd never told anyone but Vidya—about pirates and ropes and boats with grinning teeth.

"That's so fucked up, Annie," she said, giggling into her pillow. "Have you always been so fucked up?"

When she asked, it didn't feel like judgment. It felt like honesty. It felt like freedom. In the middle of nowhere Ohio, I no longer had to be ashamed, not even when I puked in her uncle's wicker wastebasket and we had to sneak it out to the trash in the middle of the night, hoping her uncle wouldn't hear our weight sagging the stairs.

I was strange. I'd always been strange. Fucked up, even. Not because of my brother's disappearance, or because of anything that had anything to do with my brother at all. No, it was in the way that I looked at the world, the mythology that formed the very fabric of my life. And the funny thing was, I didn't even care. I wasn't ashamed of it, not anymore. Actually, if anything, I missed it. I missed those pirates with their gangrenous limbs, the feral children tearing the bodies of fairies to dust. By the summer of my seventeenth year, I'd learned that the world itself was savage, too—and I was only one of the savage, strange creatures within it.

The next morning, my head pounding over breakfast (eggs, bacon, pancakes, heaps of yellow butter, and biscuits, too), Miranda's aunt handed me a letter.

"This came for you," she said. I didn't have cell reception out there. My mother said I should call on the landline once a week, but somehow, it never happened—and I never bothered checking my messages on the farm's sluggish Wi-Fi, either. But there it was, her jagged handwriting on that envelope. I tore it open, feeling my eyeballs pulse as I read the piece of folded legal paper.

Annie,

We won. Three life sentences. I've written you three emails but you haven't answered. Are you getting my messages? You should call your brother. He'd be glad to hear from you.

Yours,
Mom

"Can I be excused?" I asked. Miranda's aunt said of course I could. I wandered out the back door, barefoot, still in my pajamas. The screen door slammed behind me, but before I could walk out into the shifting hot cornfields, I heard it creak open behind me again.

"Annie, wait," Miranda said. I didn't stop, but soon she was by my side anyway, our knuckles touching as we walked.

"Aren't you going to ask me what's wrong?" I asked. My throat felt parched and dry with every word.

Miranda shrugged beside me. The truth was, she never asked. That was what I liked most about her. "I figure you would tell me if you wanted to."

I looked at her, her elfin features, her tiny mouth, her kind eyes. I would never love my friend the way I'd loved Vidya. It wasn't like that with us. But she was the closest thing I'd ever had to a sister. I hugged her. It was all that needed to be said.

"Do you need to use the phone?" she asked as I pulled away from her. I nodded and wiped away the tears. She gave my hands a squeeze. "I'll tell everyone to leave you alone," she said.

A few minutes later, I sat in her aunt and uncle's dim bedroom, the phone tucked under my chin. It took a few rings for Jamie to answer. When he did, his voice sounded distant, like he was living in a submarine in an ocean on the other side of the world. I guess, in a way, he was.

"Annie," he said softly. I gazed out the half-open window, watching the curtains stir.

"You won," I told him. "I got the letter. You won. You did it."

A long, crackling pause. And then a small snort of laughter. I couldn't tell if my brother was happy about it, not exactly.

"Yeah," he said dryly. "I did it."

Another pause. I ran a hand through my hair, unsure of what to say. "The Lost Boy Triumphant?" I finally offered, wondering if he could hear the capital letters around the phrase, like I was describing otherworldly heraldry.

Another snort. "Don't call me that," he said, but he didn't precisely sound mad about it, either. Mostly just tired. "I hated it when Muselmaan called me that. I'm not lost anymore, right? I can go back to being nobody again." Wherever Jamie was, in his room or on the back steps or somewhere else where our family couldn't hear, he smiled then, just a little. I could hear it in his voice. "If you have to call me anything, call me the Nameless Boy."

My stomach dipped, though I told myself it was just from the hangover. It was the first direct mention my brother had made of Gumlea since our fight in the woods that night with Neal. In a way, not talking about it had been like another sort of Vow. If we never mentioned it between us, neither one of us had to acknowledge how our magic was now broken.

But maybe it had always been broken, in a way. Because when I closed my eyes, I tried to see my brother as he had described himself way back then. As a Nameless Boy. Taking bits and parts from other places in Gumlea, the people and places I had loved. The Feral Children. The Winter Watchers. The Pirates. None of them had belonged to Jamie. He'd never had anything of his own.

"But, Jamie," I said softly at last. "You might not be lost, but you're not *nobody*, either."

A sharp silence. Finally, Jamie sighed. "I have to go," he said. "Celebratory dinner tonight. Mom's opening a bottle of champagne."

I winced. I'd made a mistake. Said too much. Hurt him again, without meaning to.

"Okay," I said limply. "Drink a glass for me."

"Will do," my brother said, and he hung up the phone.

I was quiet and unsettled that afternoon, through lunch and our afternoon walk in the woods. I didn't know how to tell Miranda what had transpired on the phone. So I figured it was easier to say nothing. That's what I'd been doing all along.

But then, just before dinner, Miranda called me up to the room we shared. She scrambled under the bed and came up with a box, then shoved it into my hands.

It was a watercolor set, brand-new.

"Seems like you needed a pick-me-up," she said. "So I ordered this for you. I know you've missed painting since we've been here."

I held it between my hands, turning over the tubes, almost tasting the names of the colors on my lips. Yellow ocher. Cerulean. Titanium white.

That evening, my headache mostly a memory, I sat on the front steps painting the fields before us while Miranda sat on the porch swing, reading a dog-eared fantasy novel she'd brought from home. We should have been doing summer reading, both of us. But Miranda didn't care for Charles Dickens, and all I wanted to do was paint. When I contemplated words, thoughts of Jamie seeped back in. He was free now, and I should have felt happy about it, but all I felt was a lump of uncertainty in my stomach for what would come next. For him. For me. So instead I painted, layering yellow on green on brown, watching the pigment leak into the water. There was a dark streak of trees in the distance, a summer storm bubbling on the horizon. I closed my eyes for a moment. I imagined. A shadow in the woods. It could have been a girl. It could have been a boy. I worked a dollop of paint into the corner.

"Ultramarine," I said softly. Miranda looked up at me.

"What?" she asked.

I shrugged. "It's nothing," I told her, but it was a lie. It wasn't nothing. It was a person, for sure.

I just wasn't sure who.

I kissed a girl that summer. Not Miranda. Not Vidya. Someone new. Her name was Reese and we met in the food tent at the state fair in Ohio. She had a rainbow key chain on her backpack and so I struck up a conversation with her and her friends. Miranda ended up going off with one of the boys Reese was with, a gangly emo kid with long dyed hair. She and her boyfriend had broken up before the trip, and she was eager to be free. So Reese and I stayed behind while they rode the Ferris wheel. We sat on a park bench, our knees angled together. She was wearing a tank top that showed a patch of freckles that were almost in the shape of a continent. I wanted to touch them. I wanted to be touched. She told me about her parents, who she hated, and she told me about school, which she hated, too. Her voice was low and husky. I don't think she was used to flirting with girls. As she talked, she played with the rainbow key chain.

"How about you?"

"I'm not interesting," I told her, and even though I was lying through my teeth, it felt good to say it. "I'm normal."

She squinted into the sunlight at me, the bridge of her nose wrinkling. I could see how the color of her eyes through her thick lashes was more complex than I initially thought—a blue speckled hazel like a stone you crack open to reveal a geode inside. I wanted to kiss her, but it felt risky there, surrounded by strangers, felt wrong. So I grabbed her hand and dragged her off toward the Ferris wheel. Miranda and the emo boy were getting off just as we were getting on. Her expression was wild and breathless. She smiled to let me know she was okay, that it was safe. That we could be safe up there, in the sky, all by ourselves. Reese was sweet, helping me up into the basket, her touch warm and eager. We both knew what was coming. The sky overhead was endless, thick with humidity. When we started kissing at the top, it felt like my lungs and mouth and lips were full of water. She tasted good. She tasted like nothing. I held her thick, soft waist in my hands, feeling the heat of her body through that tank top, drawing her close. I would never see her again, even though she texted me late at night sometimes, all about her parents, her life, nothing of consequence.

38

I came home so sunburned that my skin peeled off in sheets. My luggage was full of paintings, wrinkly pages of watercolor paper. I gave one to Mom. It was Miranda's uncle's barn, a sunset lit blue-purple behind it. There was another figure in the woods. My paintings were full of people, if you knew where to look. My mother didn't know where to look. Still, she hung it up on her office wall.

"This is good. This is really good," she said. "The art department at SUNY is really well ranked, you know. You need to start thinking about your application."

My mother had decided that I'd go to the college in the next town over without ever discussing it with me. I guess it seemed like the natural conclusion to all this, the whole family back together, forever. We'd never really talked about it; the truth was, I avoided even *thinking* about it. But when Mom brought it up that day, when my skin was still pink and crispy from the sun, when my bag wasn't even half unpacked, I let the idea of it sink down into me.

She wouldn't want me to live in the dorms. Our house was so close. It would be an enormous waste of money. No, no, she would expect me to commute. Gram and Poppy were talking about selling me their old car, and for a moment, in Mom's office, I saw it in my mind's eye. Driving back and forth down the same roads I'd always known—the same tangled woods that I'd once imagined were Gumlea looking dark and faint beyond them.

Miranda had already visited two dozen colleges by then. Her parents were helping her fill out the applications. Not a single one was local. Wherever she went, it was going to be a world away. When I imagined the future, it was a big, ugly, empty gap. Yawning and black. The kind of thing that would swallow me up.

"Sure, Mom," I said quickly, not wanting to let her see how unmoored I felt. I turned and shuffled down the hall, feeling cold despite the way my own skin was warm now, from the inside.

I went into the living room and slumped down on the sofa. Jamie was already there, stretched out in his old familiar chair. He was watching some bad sci-fi show, and he didn't even look up when I came in. I looked at him for a moment. He was wearing his work shirt from ShopRite, a little rumply and unwashed, the name tag hanging off-kilter from his pocket. *James.*

This wasn't a future I'd ever imagined for my brother. It wasn't a bad one, in the scheme of things—he was happy enough with his job, with smoking pot in the woods with Neal Harriman when Neal was home from his fancy school. Jamie seemed content enough most days to veg out watching TV when he wasn't sitting silently at the dinner table with our parents. But I felt it then, a deep and echoing sense of loss.

He was supposed to go to college someday, like Mom and Dad had done. He was supposed to move away and do brilliant things—beautiful things. He was supposed to be a writer or a philosopher, something fascinating, something that our mother could brag about at parties. He was supposed to lead the way for me, so I would know how to get out, too.

But we were stuck here, both of us. Jamie wasn't going anywhere, and so I couldn't go anywhere, either.

"This show sucks," he told me, and he tossed me the remote. "Here, you pick something."

I picked up the remote and just held it for a moment. Then, sighing, I changed the channel.

You'd think that after everything that had happened, Jamie would have been a celebrity. And sure, there were a few strange internet forums where posters discussed his current and former mental state, why he'd stayed and whether it was all the result of being insufficiently loved by our mother. We knew because occasionally she would stumble across them in her insomniac web searching, and because she'd come down to breakfast, dark bags behind her eyes, slamming the coffeepot and the cereal dishes down in front of us.

"It's none of their business! I'd like to see how *their* mothers treated them!"

Jamie and I would exchange looks, but neither of us would say anything. There was no room for anyone but Mom's anger at our dining room table.

Of course, we were meant to be left alone—Jamie had been under-age during the time of his capture, so our last name was left out of newspaper articles and the TV special. The Wikipedia entry on him was deleted a dozen times, though anyone who had been following our story from the beginning could have connected the dots. At first, people did, still interested in the teenaged boy who had vanished and then reappeared again, inches taller and spotted with acne. But once the trial concluded and Kevin Rapp-Palmer was locked away for three lifetimes without parole, the media seemed to decide that Jamie was boring. Occasionally, a boy would disappear, and we'd get a phone call from a reporter asking if he would like to sit down for an interview. But Mom fielded those calls and usually ended up shouting into the receiver about our right to a private life. Jamie was just a normal teenager, she'd say to me, talking right over the television. I turned up the volume.

Never mind that Jamie's life was smaller than it should have been. Mornings watching *The Price Is Right*, then off to work on a second-hand bicycle he got on Craigslist. Setting vegetables out under the misters, arranging them just so. Flirting with the slender, gap-toothed girl in the bakery, the one he eventually took out on a date. She came to the door for him that night. Blushing, speaking in low, awkward tones, he introduced her as Shelley.

"Can you believe it?" Mom asked after they left, lowering her voice even though they were already gone in Shelley's Subaru. It was one of the nights that Dad was visiting, and he was being careful. He avoided Mom's gaze and shrugged.

"She seems nice enough," Dad said. "Polite."

"Are you going to tell me she's a nice Christian girl, Dave?" But Mom was smiling when she said it. They always smiled at one another now, all teeth and gentleness.

Dad said, "I'm glad he's found someone."

"Thank G-d for small miracles," Mom agreed, driving a fork through her chicken chow mein.

That was when Elijah spoke up, his voice creaky and wry. "I think she seems like a fucking idiot."

Dad said, "Eli!"

But me and Mom just looked at each other. Because the truth was, we agreed with him.

So life moved on, as it always did. I'd learned that a long time ago when I tried to hold on to my baby teeth and lost every single one instead. It didn't matter how many offerings you served up to some invisible G-d or King. There was no stopping time, or Saturday dinners with Dad, or the SATs, or any of it. Mom got her master's, and we held balloons for her as she walked across the stage. We went out to eat and Dad stayed late with a bottle of champagne and was there in the morning, too, and life was changing again, shifting, but not in the way that I wanted, and there was nothing I could do to stop it.

"What'll we do if they get back together?" Elijah asked me one Saturday night as I scraped the plates and he stacked them into the dishwasher.

It was the same question Jamie had asked me a year before. And really, my perspective hadn't changed.

"I don't know," I said, speaking carefully. Jamie had already gone up to his room to call Shelley, but my parents were watching TV together in the living room. Holding hands. I wasn't sure if they could hear me. I wasn't sure if I wanted them to hear. "Be happy for them?"

My little brother, who was taller than me now, let out a snort. He didn't care if anyone heard or not, but then he'd always been subject to different rules than I had. "It's a mess when they're together. Mom won't let me go to church—"

"You'll have to stand up to her. Isn't that what *faith* means?"

"Oh, like you kept going to shul?"

I frowned. It was complicated, Eli knew it was, but then maybe it wasn't. Maybe I had too many excuses, maybe . . .

"He'll move out if Dad moves in, you know," my little brother added in a low voice. "He told me."

At that news I almost dropped one of the dinner plates.

I told myself in the moment that I wasn't surprised by the fact that Jamie might leave, not really. I told myself that the only shock was that they'd been talking about this—like friends. Like brothers. Like family.

But the truth was that I had never, ever expected him to leave. Not now. Not when I had already decided—or had it decided for me—that I was staying, too.

"Don't be ridiculous," I said quickly. "Where would he go?"

"I dunno," Eli said, snatching the plate from me. "Somewhere. Anywhere. He'll go live with his idiot girlfriend. He's seventeen. He can do whatever he wants. I think that's his plan, anyway. He says he doesn't want to live with the two of them together. He says he can't deal with it. All that fighting."

I frowned, recalling the night Jamie and I had talked about it. I'd tried to tell myself that he was being ridiculous. Whatever had happened between Mom and Dad was between them. The rest of us just went with it. But was that true?

Because Dad had always been hard on Jamie, right from the start. Screaming at him, telling him to get his head out of the clouds. Back then, Mom had defended Jamie. They argued about religion and lawyers. But Jamie was the one thing they'd ever really, truly *fought* about. I thought about Jamie's expression that night in the woods with Neal, how he cried. *It wasn't easy to be me, either.*

"Yeah," I told Elijah with a sigh. There was nothing else to say, really. Nothing else that could be done about it. Eli grabbed for the Cascade and squirted a gleaming orange pile of it into the dishwasher before slamming the door shut.

"I guess it doesn't really matter to you either way," he told me bitterly as I turned the dishwasher on. "I mean, you're not *actually* going to SUNY like Mom wants you to, right?"

There was hurt in his voice, but an accusation, too. I stared at him. I hadn't even let myself contemplate it. But in that moment, I realized that Elijah was right. I didn't have to go to SUNY just because Mom had decided it. I could leave. In fact, I needed to leave. I felt it suddenly, urgently, frantically. Undeniably. Like a thousand mosquito bites on your bare legs on a summer night—the irrepressible urge to *move*. No matter what Mom thought about keeping our family together, frozen like a set of pinned butterflies under glass, I was about to fly away. Because time kept moving and changing, and we couldn't stay this way forever. Especially if Jamie already had plans to move on.

"Come on," I said softly, and something in my voice almost broke. "Let's go watch TV."

Eli rolled his eyes at me, and then stormed out of the kitchen.

39

There are moments in your life that are passageways, cracks in a rocky wall, a thin beam of light guiding you up and up and out. And there are other moments that are like doorways that close in your face, firmly and abruptly. As winter of my senior year began, I began, in a scramble, to at last think about college. One day at the end of art class, I finally gathered up my nerves. The art teacher, Mrs. DeGrassio, was kind enough to me—though she never seemed particularly interested in my paintings. Once she'd stood over a self-portrait I'd done and told me, frowning, that she thought I was limiting myself. I hadn't known what to say to that. I'd been trying my hardest to create something honest, but there were so many things I never let myself feel, say, or do. I couldn't paint dragons all the time, like the one I'd drawn for Vidya. Sure, they made me happy, but they belonged to a different Annie, one who had died a long, long time ago. If they even belonged to her at all, and not to a version of my brother who was also, equally dead.

Still, Mrs. DeGrassio knew I was talented. So I'd hoped she would help. I approached her slowly. She was busy on her potter's wheel, her sleeves pushed up around her elbows, talking to some other student about the right way to work the clay. She was a ceramicist, primarily. She made vases, bowls. Which I thought was ironic, in a way—how was she any less limited than I was?

Maybe we didn't like each other. Maybe that's all there was to it.

"Excuse me?" I said softly. At first, she ignored me when I spoke. So I spoke louder the second time.

"Mrs. D. I really need your help with my portfolio," I said. I hated making myself vulnerable like that, but it felt like I had no choice. "My mom wants me to go to SUNY but I want to go away. . . ."

Get away, is what I meant. Ever since Elijah had mentioned it, my brain was busy with the promise of *freedom*, whatever that meant. What would it feel like to be in a whole new place, to be somewhere—someone—new? It would be like Ohio but better, dorming somewhere, surrounded by other kids who also weren't carrying the weight of their former lives.

"SUNY has a great art program,," Mrs. DeGrassio said. She didn't look me in the eye when she spoke, just kept her gaze on her own hands, slick with red clay.

"I know it is. But I want to go—"

"Annie," she said, hands still on the wheel, but she finally looked up at me when she said it. "If you wanted to go to art school, then you should have been working on your portfolio for at least a *year*. You could have signed up for an independent study with me. Do you know how much work is involved? You've already missed half of the portfolio review days. I'm sorry, but no."

As she spoke, I felt like the center of my body was slowly unraveling; my hope drifted far out to sea.

"But . . . I need *help*," I said once more, hating how weak I sounded, how desperate. For so long, I'd told myself that I needed no one and nothing, that I could pull myself out of this long, deep hole myself. I tried to imagine life at SUNY. Walking around those same familiar paths, the ones where me and Jamie had ridden scooters as kids. Running into Vidya's dad between classes. Hearing the whispers follow me, like they always had, and then returning to my old bed every night, the same old room, the same house. Even in the bright art room, the smell of crayons and wet earth all around me, I felt the walls closing in.

"I'm sorry," she said again, though she wasn't sorry and we both knew it. "I can't help you."

I rushed from the art room before the tears could start.

So, I didn't apply to art school. Mrs. DeGrassio didn't want to help me. But that didn't mean I couldn't crawl my way out of Wiltwyck, didn't mean I couldn't find an ally or two anyway. In the end, it was my therapist, of all people, who suggested Hampden to me. Well, not only Hampden. In fact, two days after I cried to her about how I could never go to art school, she came into our session with a whole stack of college brochures to places like St. John's and Evergreen, programs without grades or classes, a gleam lighting her dark eyes.

"You should find someplace *different*," she told me, and I could tell from her energy that she'd been waiting a long time to tell me this. "Some place that can synthesize your unique perspective into something that can be of use to the greater world."

I didn't want to tell her that I had no idea what she was talking about, so I pursed my lips, pretending to look uninterested in the brochures as I riffled through them. Then I stopped. There was Hampden, its logo, a coiling griffin, printed on the cover of the brochure. The other colleges featured gaggles of teenagers of every race grinning frenetically at one another, as though they were trying to prove something. Not Hampden. Pictured instead were two women standing in front of a painted mural. An enormous world tree had sprouted on the bricks behind them. There were mermaids swirling in the ether behind their heads. Neither one was smiling. Neither one had anything to prove. They weren't traditionally pretty—one was thick as a Venus of Willendorf; the other had acne-scarred skin and gauged ears and an eyebrow ring. But it didn't look like they cared that they weren't pretty the same way that other girls were pretty. They looked happy to be themselves. Happy to be different.

I touched the glossy paper and tried to chase away the thoughts that were pushing just below the surface of my mind.

Winter Watcher girls.

"What do you know about this school?" I asked, holding the brochure aloft.

I had the forms ready to go. The copies of my transcripts. The letters of recommendation. The application fee, saved from my birthday money. The essay I'd written on Hampden's motto: *Knowledge Is Insufficient.* I was ready, except I wasn't ready, because I needed my parents' financial information and social security numbers for the financial aid application. And the weeks were ticking by.

All through the holidays, I felt like a hollow shell of myself. The application deadline—January 15—loomed over me as I tried to find a way to raise the issue with my mother and failed, over and over again. At our annual Christmas movie matinee, while Jamie was at his girlfriend's and Dad and Eli were gone to some church service, and at our dim sum dinner after, I turned myself inside out trying to think of how to tell her, missing and missing my chance. A few days later, she sat next to me on the sofa, the laptop between us, and she told me what to write on my SUNY application. She even dictated an essay to me on the hardships I'd experienced, how I'd missed my brother through his disappearance and celebrated his return. I did what she said because I couldn't think of a way out of it. I was scared, I think, of how she'd react, and for good reason. Her unhappiness always loomed so much larger than my own.

For years, it had been easier to keep my head down to keep the peace. But now, as I hit send on the application to a school I never wanted to attend, breaking that peace had gained a new kind of urgency. Still, I'd trained myself too well. I'd taught myself that silence was a balm that could soothe any wound. So I kept my tongue tucked into my cheek, and now couldn't, for the life of me, figure out how to untuck it.

The first morning of the New Year was bright, the light clean and blue through my window. I rose, like I always did, pausing outside Jamie's door to listen to his steady breath. It was reassuring that he was still there, and real, too, and not some kind of illusion, even if we hardly ever spoke. I'd just heard a snore catch in his throat when footsteps shifted the floorboards on the stairwell. I drifted toward them, feeling outside myself.

There was Dad, wearing Mom's robe, halfway down the stairs already when he looked up over his shoulder at me. If this was supposed to be weird, Dad spending the night after the ball drop and champagne and toasts over Jamie's transfer to the meat department at work and my incipient attendance at the school down the road, he didn't acknowledge it.

"I was going to make some pancakes," he said. "Want to give me a hand?"

I hated pancakes, but I just nodded, feeling lost again, empty again.

I followed him down the stairs.

My father whistled as he assembled the ingredients. He set them out on the counter one by one. Slowly, I stirred the batter, until all the lumps went smooth. And then I just kept stirring.

"Dad?" I began.

He didn't eye me nervously like Mom might, didn't act as though every word was weighty and important. He was too busy dripping oil onto the griddle, watching the steam rise. "Mmm?"

"I . . ." I took a breath, and it caught raggedly in my chest. "I don't want to go to SUNY next year. There's another college. Hampden, in Massachusetts . . ."

I trailed off. I waited for my dad to say something, anything. I waited for him to tell me it wasn't possible. That he couldn't help me, the way Mrs. DeGrassio hadn't been able to help me. That I was on my own, like I always was, or worse: that he wanted me to stay right where I was for the rest of my G-d damned life.

Instead, he turned, calmly holding a hand out. I handed him the bowl of batter and watched him stand over the griddle, contemplating the steam. He wasn't looking at me when he answered, but one eyebrow was lifted, just a smidge.

"Tell me what you need, Annie," he said. Then he poured the batter down against the hot surface. It sizzled and popped.

"I'll need your financial info. Mom's, too. I need you to tell Mom. I need you to convince her that it's okay for me to—"

"Okay for you to what?"

I turned, bracing myself, half expecting to see my mother standing in the doorway, her mouth a thin line that had almost vanished with disapproval. But it wasn't Mom at all. It was Jamie, his dark hair tousled. Sleepy. Wearing boxers and a sweatshirt, the same things I always slept in. A shadow of me now, not the other way around.

"For me to leave," I said softly. "For me to go away to college."

Jamie stared at me. Blinked. Moved toward the coffeepot, which was noisily percolating. He drank coffee endlessly now, as if he was incapable of staying awake or even upright without it. He poured himself a cup, took a sip. I realized I was holding my spine straight, waiting for something. Part of me wanted him to express disapproval, I think. To beg me to stay. He'd had to fight so hard to get back to me, and now here I was, itching to go anyway.

But he only shrugged.

"Who cares what Mom says? You should go where you want. Wherever that is."

And then he shrugged again.

I stared at him, his words sinking in. Maybe they stung a little bit, but I couldn't hold it against him, could I? We weren't friends anymore. We were barely even housemates. He'd left me once, but now we were both leaving each other, and it was almost a mutual decision, a natural development. The truth was, neither of us had fought for one another in a very long time.

But at least I had Jamie's support. I told myself that it was *something*. I told myself that it was enough.

"Thanks, Jamie," I said.

He nodded stoutly, just as Dad let out a hiss.

"Burned the first one," he said as he scraped the griddle clean and started over. "The first one is just a practice pancake, anyway."

He smiled at us. Faintly, my brother and I both smiled back.

After the pancakes that sat like a rock in my stomach, after the coffee and sour orange juice and my older brother drifting off for his weekend work shift and my younger brother hiding in his room to do homework and talk to his church friends online, Dad dropped the bomb on my mother. I was cleaning the breakfast dishes, scraping each one clean, trying to pretend like I wasn't listening when I was actually, most definitely listening.

"She doesn't want to live at home," my dad was telling her. "She wants to go away to school. She found one she likes, Hampden. Kit Hendricks said—"

"Oh, she found one she '*likes*,'" my mom said, circling the word *likes* with air quotes, rolling her eyes. "Even if she applies, she might not get in. What if she doesn't? Then what?"

"What do you mean, 'then what'? Then she'll go to SUNY, or to somewhere else. We can have her apply to safety schools. Other SUNYs, schools in the city. It's not an issue. Anyway, her grades are amazing."

My stomach felt twisted in two ways around the greasy batter and butter and syrup. For one thing, it felt good to have *one* of my parents acknowledge that I'd done well in school. "Gifted" like my brother had been or not, all those years of keeping my head down and working hard had paid off. Sure, my grades had slipped a little in the last year or two. But my GPA was still solid, and in all honors classes. Not that grades were supposed to matter when it came to a school like *Hampden*.

But the other feeling was heavier, worse. Mom didn't think I could do it, didn't think I should. She was mocking me and my choices. Maybe if I were Jamie, she'd take what *I* wanted seriously. Whether it was a haircut or a bicycle or a job or a girlfriend, what Jamie did mattered. We discussed his choices as a family, mulling over them together. She just wasn't invested in me in the same way. Never had been. Never would be.

"She needs to stay here," she shot back. "We need to give Jamie *stability*. After everything he's been through—"

"You can't seriously expect our other children to stay frozen in time, Shira. She's about to be an *adult*. She needs to have a life outside Wiltwyck. Outside—"

"Don't say it, Marc."

But my dad said it anyway, and I'd love him forever for it.

"You—we—*all* need to let her have a life outside of Jamie."

Silence. I looked at both of them through the kitchen doorway. My dad's expression was flat. Firm. Unreadable. But not Mom's. It was like something was collapsing inside her. And even though I was glad that he'd said it, I kind of wanted him to take it back. I'd never wanted to hurt my mom. All this time, through Jamie's reappearance and disappearance, through his troubled adolescence, through the golden days of his youth, I'd only ever wanted to make her happy. But somehow, through time that stretched back and back and back, it seemed I never could.

"I don't have to go anywhere," I said softly, putting the last plate, finally, in the dishwasher. "I'll stay here. I'll go to SUNY."

"Good," my mom said. And when Dad didn't answer, she added: "See?"

But my dad shook his head. "It's not a question, Shira. She's applying."

And then he looked at me.

"Got that, kiddo?"

I nodded. Quickly, gratefully, before I could ruin it all for myself.

"Got it," I said.

40

Jamie had to work the day my family drove me through the mountains and the woodlands of western Massachusetts. He gave me a tight, wordless hug in the morning and told me we'd talk soon, though I knew it was a lie. We never talked, not really, nothing beyond *pass the peas* and *I think Dad slept over last night again*. What would we have to say to one another over the phone or in emails or texts? Nothing. But I appreciated the hug. Jamie didn't like touching people. It meant something that he was still willing to touch and be touched by me.

In his place, Mom, Dad, and Elijah drove me and all of my belongings to Hampden. The freshman dorm where I'd be living was in an ancient Victorian building that smelled of furniture polish, dust, and ramen soup. The extra-long twin bed that would be mine was covered in crinkly plastic.

"Cool," said Elijah, sitting on it, making the bedsprings creak. "Easy to clean if you puke. Or pee yourself, I guess."

"Eli," Dad warned, but my little brother only grinned.

My roommate was a hippie girl from Boston named Sophie. We got dinner in the dining hall that night, her family, mine, all of us. Her parents were unbearably stodgy, even worse than Dad. But Sophie had white-girl dreads and a nose piercing and, every time she spoke, my mom looked like she was holding back laughter.

"Yes, I'm sure studying abroad in India would be very *enlightening*," Mom said, her mouth quirking wryly. Sophie didn't notice the sarcasm, just kept talking about all the places she and her boyfriend planned to backpack that spring break. Her own parents just looked tired. Dad looked tired, too.

"Well," he said, sliding his slice of oversweetened pie away. "I think it's time we hit the road."

I walked them to their car, parked in a lot on the far end of campus. I hugged them goodbye, felt nothing. There were woods shouldering the highway, but I couldn't see anything in them. No potential. No magic. Not yet. When I walked back to the dorm, I kept my hands tucked into my pockets and my head down. It was strange to be so empty inside. I wasn't even afraid. Only hollow.

When I got back to the dorm, Sophie's parents were gone. She was unpacking a giant flat of bottled waters, trying to wedge as many as she could into her minifridge.

"Your parents seem sweet," she said. "You can tell they really love one another. Not like my parents, not since the divorce. They can hardly stand to be in the same room anymore."

"Actually, mine are separated," I said. I put my suitcase on my bed and started to unpack my clothes.

Sophie paused, looked at me with eyes like tepid water. "Oh," she said. "Is that hard for you?"

I could hear the unspoken implication: *her* parents' divorce had been hard for *her*. And she wanted to talk to me about it. She wanted to connect. She wanted us to be friends. And we were supposed to be, right? Roommates. It was meant to mean something. That's why I'd come here. To connect with people. To feel full of hope, alive again.

But I didn't know how to tell her the whole truth, the truth that we hadn't even touched on in our emails. I didn't know how to tell her about Jamie.

I bit my lip. "No," I said. "It's fine. They're probably going to get back together, but I don't care either way. Can I have a water?"

Sophie looked at me for a moment, her mouth open and soft. Then she handed me a bottle. "Sure," she said, and she turned away from me and blasted the music on her laptop. I'd said the wrong thing. I knew I had, but I didn't know how to fix it.

That night, I lay in my narrow bed staring up at the cracks in the ceiling. Sophie was still awake; I could tell from the way the plastic under her new sheets crinkled and creaked as she tossed and turned. I didn't toss and turn—I didn't even move. I kept trying to figure out how to tell her about my brother. Kept thinking about Jamie, too. I thought I would have escaped this feeling by crossing state lines and starting a new life. But I hadn't. The window AC unit that Sophie's parents had bought her from the Target in Hadley kept rattling in the frame. Outside, there was some forest, dark and lovely and deep. But it wasn't my forest, my Gumlea. And there were boys here, but none of them mine.

I thought I would have escaped that feeling by going away for school, but somehow, I'd just brought it with me. We were still alone together, no matter how many miles of highway stretched out between us.

It was like there was an invisible silver thread knotted through my stomach and elsewhere, as my brother slept, into his, too.

I turned over and forced myself to sleep.

41

There were no classes at Hampden. Instead, our coursework was composed of a hodgepodge of private tutorials and open workshops. That first semester, I discussed Descartes with a philosophy professor, read about the Milgram experiment with a rogue sociologist, and argued about Japanese cinema with a woman who I later learned had run the last video store in town for the past fifteen years. Because I didn't know how to talk to her otherwise, I picked up Sophie's regular pot habit, and often spent my nights in a haze getting lost around campus—or else shoveling food into my face in the dining hall, where they had every kind of cereal you could imagine, including the ones Mom had refused to buy me when I was a kid. I went to parties, but mostly stayed on the outside of things, watching. I felt like I was waiting for something, a slow doom building in my stomach, my skin goose pimply as I walked home at night across campus. But I wasn't sure what.

My professors didn't require us to write papers, and though some gave us the option, I never took them up on it. In my classes, my pen was always moving—but my notes never went anywhere. I wasn't sure how to get my thoughts to coalesce into anything meaningful. After all, I wasn't a writer. That had always been Jamie. My notebooks were full of delicious words. *Physical determinism. Leibniz. The best of all possible worlds. Obedience. Pareidolia. Pattern recognition.* And those words were joined by drawings: Skeletons. Bones. Animals. Woods. A knife, once or twice, though I quickly erased it. It all hinted at meaning but "meaning" still felt like it was beyond me. So many ideas, echoing inside my hollow skull.

Sophie, meanwhile, didn't bother with her tutorials. She had her boyfriend over nearly every night, and the room always stank of their cigarettes when I got back to it, even though she sprayed a pungent room spray over it to try to cover their smell.

"I just haven't found my narrative yet" was something she was fond of saying, while she tossed her dreadlocks over one shoulder and took another bong hit. Anywhere else, that comment would have been absurd. But we were all concerned about our narrative at Hampden. In our final year, our disparate studies were to culminate in a project that was supposed to encapsulate our experiences there. It seemed incomprehensible to me. I was too scattered. There was no common thread in my life—not one I was willing to pull at, at least.

Sophie, too, seemed to be threadless.

"Maybe you'd find it if you tried," I told her, wrestling the bong from her hands. She gave me a withering look. At first, she seemed to enjoy my company, but by the middle of the first semester, I could tell that her affection for me was growing thin. When she asked for a room change for next semester, it was both no surprise, and no great loss.

In the end, I shouldn't have worried about my narrative. It would find me, like it always did.

It started on a cold day in early November. I was coming back from the library, books tucked under my arm, my face buried in the scratchy synthetic fabric of my scarf, when I noticed a light flickering in a nearby barn. I knew there were classes in the outbuildings sometimes. Parties, too. Hampden was the kind of place where both parts of college life ran together.

I wandered in. There, at the center of it, a half dozen small, groaning space heaters painted directly on her, was a naked woman. She was posing in a crouch, as though she was looking at something on the floor. All around her was a ring of easels and students, drawing her in silence.

"What is this?" I asked someone, watching over his shoulder as he sketched her in charcoal. I'd known there were art classes at Hampden, but I'd avoided them so far. They reminded me too acutely of the life I might have had, had I gone to art school. But right now, I couldn't resist. The proportions he was drawing were all wrong, tits too full, stomach too narrow. I could have done it better.

"Life drawing," he said.

"Anyone can join?" I asked, which was a stupid question, because at Hampden, anyone could join anything.

"Yeah," he said. "You just have to kick in for her sitting fee."

I looked at her, considering. She had black hair, shorn close. Her dark skin looked almost purple in the dim barn light. I had the sudden urge to sit down and draw her, a flare of desire that was different from anything I had felt in years.

Winter Watcher, I thought, then shook the idea away. I'd come to Hampden looking for Winter Watcher girls, of course, but instead I'd mostly only found stoners and idle rich kids who talked about John

Cage and Andy Warhol like they were family friends. The kids I'd met so far weren't wild, like I was. They weren't anything, really. They were normal, just in different clothes.

I told myself that she was probably no different from the other girls. Still, her pose was dynamic. I wanted to draw her. Drawing would be easy. It always had been. It was the only way I could express myself without worrying about all the things I wasn't allowed to talk about. Jamie. What had happened to him. The way I always missed him. The magic I'd grown up with, which had proven itself to be false.

I turned and left that barn. But I returned the next week, cash in one hand, book of newsprint in the other. I put the money into the coffee can by the model's platform and set up my supplies by an easel.

I was disappointed when the model arrived and it was not the girl. Instead, it was a man, large-bellied and balding, draped in a ratty robe and wearing massive rings on both hands. When he undressed, I sighed. But I leaned forward anyway, taking the pen out from behind my ear.

It's a funny thing about bodies. Once you've seen enough of them, they're no longer scandalous. You begin to perceive the common threads between them, across gender, across age. The Y shape hidden inside the conch shell of an ear, or the strong tendons at the base of a skull. The way that flesh over a belly puckers. The vulnerability of armpits, of hands, of the soles of bare feet.

All that month, I drew bodies. When Thanksgiving break came, I decided I didn't want to go home and instead walked across the darkening campus to the barn to join the other stragglers who were orphaned that holiday. I sketched until my hands were black with charcoal and my fingers numb, whether from cold or from effort, I couldn't be sure.

It felt almost like a return. Once, in the woods, I had entered a sacred space where there was no doubt or angst or trouble. Here, that was true, too. There was only the work.

My mother was mad at me for staying away. She called me too often, then started emailing when I didn't return her calls right away. From the number of exclamation points in her emails I could tell that things were bad back in Wiltwyck again. And then, in early December, they came to a head. Mom called to warn me—called two dozen times to warn me. When I came home for Christmas break, Dad would be there. The entire time.

You'd think my mother would have been happy about it. They were in love again, deeper than the first time. But all she could talk about was Jamie.

"He moved in with that *girl*," she told me as I sat on my dorm bed in my nest of unmade blankets.

"Shelley," I told her. "They've been dating for almost two years."

"Barely a year," my mother said as I rolled my eyes toward the ceiling, counting the cracks. "He's too good for her."

I smiled wryly at that. She wasn't wrong, but Jamie said he was happy—who were we to argue with that? Hadn't he earned this small dose of peace?

"Jamie is complicated," I told her. And from her aghast silence, I knew that she knew I was right.

I heard a crackle on the other end, and then Mom added this: "He told me he's saving up money for a motorcycle. Can you believe that? He's going to kill himself. I know it. He doesn't care who will be hurt if we lose him again."

It was a gut punch, the thought of losing Jamie. But I couldn't give in to Mom's way of thinking. There was no good that would come from traveling down that long, dark path. The only thing we could do was march on, whether into darkness or light, I couldn't be sure.

I said all the things you're supposed to say during a phone call like that. I told Mom he was happy, that he was living his life, that he was an adult, that we should be happy for him. I told her that I was sure he'd be responsible, with Shelley and the bike and the apartment and everything else. I told her that I'd be home soon enough, and we'd all be together at Christmas, a family.

"On Christmas, your father wants us to go to *church*," she said, as if that was the worst thing of all.

"Okay, Mom," I said gently. I wasn't sure if the noise on the other end was laughter or tears. I hung up and left her like that, maybe laughing, maybe crying, and grabbed my portfolio, then rushed off toward the barn.

The model that night was a very old woman. Her knobby fingers were a challenge for the blue Crayola crayon that was quickly becoming my favorite medium. I tore through page after page of newsprint, each new drawing as bad as the last. And then I found a new page. Drew a skeleton. Maybe it belonged to the old woman. Maybe it belonged to someone else. Maybe it belonged to Jamie?

I saw it in my mind's eye—my brother as a boy, surrounded by wild, dappled light. He was up in the trees. In a tree house, on a long, sunny afternoon. His shirt was off. His chest was skinny and bare. He held something in his hands. Something leggy, delicate. A daddy longlegs, the kind we used to save from the backyard blow-up pool when we were kids. There was someone else beside him, someone in shadow. Another boy, his teeth filed down to points. I began to sketch it out, and then I stopped. It was all too familiar. Where had I seen this? It must have been a story we'd told to each other once. I looked at the face of the other boy there, didn't recognize him. Or maybe I did, and I didn't want to admit to myself what I'd drawn. I stopped, shaking, threw my crayon down on the easel's edge, and put my hands over my eyes. Nobody else noticed. They were too lost in their work.

I tore that page, crumpled it in my hands, then sat down and began to draw again, this time my eyes staying fixed on the old woman's kind, wrinkled face.

42

Christmas Day, after the presents were all unwrapped, and Jamie's girlfriend left to join her own family, and Dad and Eli went off to church, and Mom started washing the dishes too loudly in the kitchen, blasting Billie Holiday like her life depended on it, Jamie took me outside to look at his motorcycle. It was a cruiser, too big for his slight frame, and it had blue flames along the tank. That December was unseasonably warm, and the bike was bright and shining in the driveway, and when I touched the handlebar the rubber felt warm, too. I thought of Jamie's hare, smiled vaguely.

"Mom wants to murder you, you know," I said.

"Yeah," Jamie agreed. He was sitting in the curb, looking up at me, squinting past the sunlight. There was a question on his brow. I think he wanted to see that I approved.

"She's nice," I said, even though the words felt lame and insufficient. I started nodding, and Jamie nodded back.

"Thanks," he said. "That means a lot to me. I didn't think you liked her much."

I frowned. Then, with a laugh, I realized where the conversation had gone wrong.

"I meant the bike," I said. "Not Shelley."

"Oh." Jamie looked down between his motorcycle boots. They were still new, stiff and black. He laughed a little, too, but it was dry—self-deprecating. I went and sat beside him. My hip against his hip, our four boots all lined up in a row.

"Shelley's nice, too," I said firmly. "If you like her, I like her."

"She's good to me," he said. "I mean, what more can I ask for?"

I didn't say anything. I was waiting for Jamie to tell me.

"Hard, sometimes, though," he admitted. He blew out a stream of air. "That's why I bought this bike, I think. Shelley's not like me or you. I try to talk to her about books and stuff, and she gets mad at me. Tells me I'm trying to make her look stupid."

"Are you?"

Jamie only snorted. He didn't answer me, just went on. "Sometimes I feel like I just have to get out of that tiny apartment. That I just need to go, go, go. When I'm moving, it doesn't hurt to think so much. I don't have to worry about the things I'm not supposed to talk about. I can just fly."

He let one hand stream out above him, made a faint soaring noise with his lips. I watched him, squinting into the sunlight.

"It's your new Gumlea," I said. I was speaking without thinking, and Jamie turned to look at me in surprise. His eyes, so much like mine, were wide. Like he was relieved to finally talk about Gumlea. Maybe he was.

"Yeah," he said. "I guess it is."

We both looked at his motorcycle. I wondered to myself if he'd named it, or if it was as nameless as he thought he was himself.

"What's your Gumlea?" he asked.

"What?" I said. I couldn't look at him anymore, could only look down at the scuffed toes of *my* boots. Part of me couldn't believe we were talking about this. Finally. At long last. It felt like some kind of dream. I felt relieved, too, but I also felt terrified. Look what had happened the last time I'd been honest with Jamie. . . .

"Just what I said. What's your Gumlea? What do you do when you need to be all by yourself?"

"Mmm," I said slowly. "It used to be painting, or drawing, but lately—I don't know. It kind of hasn't been enough lately. Like no matter how hard I work, it's not coming out the way I imagined it."

"Yeah," my brother said, as though he already knew how I felt about art, though we'd never talked about it and he'd never really taken interest in anything I'd created. "You know, it's funny. I always thought that *Gumlea* would be your Gumlea. Like, forever."

"What?"

"Well, you know. You always loved it so much. Making up stories. It was an escape for me, but for you—"

"I wasn't the one making up stories," I said swiftly. "That was *you*. You were the storyteller. I was the archivist."

Jamie snorted. He stood up then and grabbed the helmet that dangled from one of the handlebars. It was kind of cheesy. Had blue flames on it, too, just like his bike.

"Yeah, I used to say that, but I don't know if it was ever true. Your ideas were the ones that stuck. Do you remember that story you made up about Annit and the harpy massacre? When you were, what, six? So fucking dark. Just completely gruesome. I was so jealous. Tried rewriting that one six or seven times, to prove to myself that I could tell it better. Don't think I ever did."

He fixed his helmet down on his head. Now it *really* hurt to look at him. Because I didn't believe him. I didn't know if a single thing he was saying was true.

"That was *your* story," I said. Through the narrow gap in the helmet, I could see my brother's frowning face.

"I think I'd know if something was my story or not," he said.

I had no idea what to say to that. I stared at him, frowning. Jamie sighed.

"Do you want to take a ride with me or not?" he asked.

I looked at the bike. I'd never ridden a motorcycle before. Part of me wanted to—but there was another part of me that felt distant and broken in that moment. Suddenly, fervently, I needed to be alone.

"No," I said quickly. "You go. I'll wait here for you."

My brother shrugged. "Suit yourself," he said, and tipped the visor of his helmet down.

I watched from the curb as he climbed on that bike and turned it on. The buzz and stutter seemed to vibrate right down into my guts. For a moment, this felt all too familiar. This was little sister stuff, letting my mouth form a slight smile as he revved the engine, stepped on the gas, and let loose the brake. From the curb, I watched as he sped off down our road. But I only saw that with half my vision.

With the other half, the inside eye, I saw the world as Jamie might see it, a blur of winter gray and yellow-white. I felt the thrum of the engine cut through me. I felt imaginary wings unfurling, and the world fell away as I took off through the sky.

43

I came home after break to an empty dorm room, one bed stripped naked in the center. The funny thing is, I felt more comfortable this way, with Sophie gone. I could have done anything with that room. Could have pushed the beds together or bunked them, could have strung up lights all over, could have hung my drawings of naked ladies on the walls. But I didn't. I let Sophie's absence remain clear and conspicuous and confined myself to half a room, as if that's all that I deserved, and maybe I thought that, deep down. After all, it's what I had resigned myself to, for a lifetime already.

Without Sophie there was no one to sit with at meals. I told myself I didn't care. I sat on the edges in the dining hall, doing my homework, spilling stir-fry over my books. After, I went and hid in the library just to avoid the echoing silence of my room. There was something comforting about the buzz of the lights, and the feel of the rough carpet beneath my feet. I'd go to the fiction section and pull out a novel at random and read it in one sitting. Fantasy mostly now. Stuff that reminded me of Vidya. Of Jamie. I started with Tolkien and Anthony and Jordan, authors I'd heard them talk about a long time ago. Yet whenever I put one of their books back on the shelf, I'd hear a voice in my head: *You could have written that better than him.* But I dismissed those thoughts. I wasn't a writer. And I'd given up on other worlds a long, long time ago.

Soon, I moved on. Found other voices. Women's voices. Jo Walton. Octavia Butler. Ursula Le Guin. Shirley Jackson. Margaret Atwood. Helen Oyeyemi. Joanna Russ. Kelly Link. Carmen Maria Machado. When I read *their* books, my body practically vibrated with pleasure. Sometimes I'd sneak them back to my dorm under my old smelly peacoat like they were delicious contraband just so I could read them over and over again.

January became February and suddenly the mild winter froze over and we were buried beneath three feet of snow. I spent most of my time either drawing or reading, and other than life drawing, I barely ever bothered going to class. I could feel how I was becoming stranger, more inwardly focused. I think other people could sense it, too. No one invited me to parties anymore. I sometimes stayed up at night texting Miranda, halfway across the country, but I didn't want to lean on her too heavily. She was busy with school, and with LARPing with her friends.

But then one night after life drawing, a boy who I'd seen there often—dark eyes, disheveled hair, Woody Allen glasses like a thousand other boys at Hampden—asked if I wanted to come to a party at his friend's apartment in town.

"I've been watching you draw," he told me. "You're really good."

As if that guaranteed that I'd be a good party companion? I bit my lip, chewing the chapped skin off it. The truth was, these days I was wary of anyone who was interested in me. I was used to being an outsider, a loner. It was a comfortable sort of solitude.

"Listen," I said. "I don't want to give you the wrong idea. I'm gay."

He laughed. "I am, too. I'm Petyr."

I guess it wasn't going to be that easy to dismiss him. Still, he had an easygoing smile, different from the guarded looks of most of the students on campus. I held out my hand, shook his. "Annie."

"Do you have a car?"

For some reason, in that moment I thought of Jamie's motorcycle, shining silver in the darkness of the night. I shook my head.

"Okay. I'll drive you. If you're down."

I shrugged, packing my pens into my bag. It wasn't as if I had anything better planned that night, other than tucking myself into my favorite chair in the back corner of the library with my best Thursday-night companion, Susanna Clarke. "Sure."

We crossed the frigid campus together, our breath a fog on the air in front of us. When we reached his old heap, he threw my portfolio in the trunk, then sat in the driver's seat to warm it up. He thawed his hands in front of the heater. I sat in the passenger's seat, rubbing my palms together.

"You cool?" he asked. I looked at him blankly for a moment, my face feeling as if it had been cracked wide open by the cold. Then I nodded.

He reached across me and pulled a baggie out of the glove box and rolled us a joint to share.

Through the falling snow, his little heap climbed the winding road, and the night was the blinding white of headlights against an infinite darkness. Petyr played some kind of loopy hippie music, and it took me a minute to realize that it was the Beach Boys. I laughed at that, and turned the stereo louder, and when his car almost spun on the ice, I didn't even care that we were about to die. *G-d only knows . . .* , I thought, but then my brain looped back on itself. G-d only knew *what*? But soon he swerved back onto the right side of the yellow dividing line, and the thought floated up into the endless night, and then disappeared.

It was almost midnight when we made it to the party, and the tiny apartment was already packed full of people. Petyr took my coat from me, and I stood there in the middle of it, watching people dance in one corner, and play some kind of card game with intricate invented rules in another, and two boys kissing on one of those plastic blow-up chairs, and the TV on and no one watching. I drifted through the rooms like a ghost, observing the tableaux, and finally found myself in an overcrowded bathroom as people passed around a bong that was taller than a small child. I took a hit, passed it, coughed, and everyone erupted in laughter. One sound cut above it, though. Laughter like bells, like music, or maybe I was just imagining it, maybe it was just the pot, but I saw a girl sitting on the closed toilet seat, her elbows on her knees. She was brown skinned and short haired and wearing a worn-out T-shirt and suspenders and cropped pants with leather saddle shoes underneath like she didn't even care about the weather and she was incredibly beautiful and I recognized her right away.

"I remember you," I said, craggy-voiced. "From life drawing."

Somebody whistled, but the girl just laughed. Time was slow, and I sensed the crowd parting like an ocean and then pushing us closer together like waves. I stood against the tile wall, close enough that her knees brushed mine.

"That means you've seen me naked. You have an unfair advantage."

"Do I?" I asked. Her eyes twinkled, but she didn't answer right away, so I added, "What got you into that line of work, anyway?"

Her smile went snaky, like she'd been waiting for that question. "It's not about sex, if that's what you're asking. Actually, for me, it's the opposite of sex. When I pose for a class, I'm using my body to make something more than what the world assumes about it. It's like, have you ever met a guy in a band and thought, *That asshole will probably write a terrible song about me later?*"

I grinned at her. In a way, it reminded me of something Vidya might say. She was always complaining about asshole guys in bands who thought she was somehow inherently less than them.

"Not personally," I told her, and it was true—asshole band guys had never paid any attention to me at all. "But yeah, I know what you mean."

"Well, this is different. This isn't having your story or your image stolen without your consent. This is about deciding the terms over your skin yourself. I get to say for once, *Put me in your art, but make it good or it's not worth a damned thing to either of us.* Plus," she added, "it pays better than a work study gig. Forty bucks an hour. Can't beat that."

I couldn't help it. I laughed. She was different than I expected. Better. Hard and bright and clever. She asked me, "What's your name, traveler?"

"Annie R. **[Redacted]**."

"Well, Annie R. **[Redacted]**. I'm Court."

"Is that your real name?" I felt my mouth smiling at her and saw her mouth smiling at me back.

"It's close enough."

Our conversation faded for a moment, and I could have lost her, but then I saw the picture on her shirt. It was a reproduction of a faded book cover. A little boy, feather in his cap, standing cocky in a window, while Wendy, John, and Michael looked on.

Peter Pan.

"What do you think Peter did after the Lost Boys went off to live in London?" I asked.

I saw her pupils shrink back and then flood her dark eyes. She was surprised. She looked down at her shirt as though she might find an answer there.

"That's an interesting question, Annie R. **[Redacted]**."

"You can just call me Annie."

She rolled her eyes a little. Laughed a little. "I know."

But I wasn't ready to drop the Peter Pan thing. The pot had made me bold, or stupid. I wasn't sure which. "But I mean, really. Hook was already dead. Did he and Tinker Bell just putz around Neverland for a few decades? Why didn't he come home sooner?" And then I blushed, because I felt like I had revealed something.

But Court was only faintly smiling at me. "You're a strange creature, aren't you?"

"Yeah, I guess," I said. I arched an eyebrow, studying her saddle shoes, her cropped pants. "And you're not?"

"I am," she said, like she was pleased to hear it. "But it usually takes people longer to notice."

"Not me," I told her. "But maybe we strange creatures can smell each other."

"For sure." She held out her wrist out to me, right under my nose. "What do you smell?"

I let my lips almost grace her skin. She smelled a little like old musty paperback novels, and a little like powdery scented deodorant.

"Weirdness," I said, and she giggled like a kid at that. I wasn't used to flirting so obviously, but I remembered what she'd said about life drawing. *This is about deciding the terms over your skin yourself.*

"Do you want to get out of here?" I asked her, then added, in case it wasn't clear, "Together?"

Her smile lit up the whole bathroom. She stood up, then offered her hand to me. She was taller than I was. Impossibly tall, a giantess.

"Come on," she said in a low voice. She took me to a back bedroom, and in a nest of coats that smelled like winter's chill, we kissed each other. And we didn't stop until it was morning.

We woke half-naked in the gray morning light, tucked beneath the heavy winter blanket. The coats were gone. I had a dim memory of people streaming in and out all night, blushing, apologizing, pulling their jackets out from under our tangled bodies. But I didn't feel embarrassed. Just spent, and maybe a little confused. There were books everywhere in this tiny back bedroom, shelves lining the walls and stacked in piles beneath them and spilled over every chair. And they weren't the kind of pretentious, important books you'd find in most dorm rooms at Hampden. No Plato. No Robert Anton Wilson. No Žižek. Nothing like that.

They were all children's books.

Alice. Narnia. Ann M. Martin and Louise Fitzhugh. E. Nesbit. E. B. White and Cynthia Voigt and dozens of Oz books and Beverly Cleary, too.

"Must be some kid's room . . ." I murmured. Buried beneath the blankets, Court giggled. When she poked her head out, I saw her brown eyes gleaming.

"They're yours?"

"I keep thinking of what you said last night about Peter Pan," she said as she stretched her arms luxuriously overhead. Her shirt was lost somewhere in the tangle of blankets. She only wore a soft, worn-out sports bra. I was wearing nothing but my undershorts.

"Yeah?" I said.

"Do you know about the real Peter Pan?"

I shook my head.

"He was an orphan. J. M. Barrie was a family friend who adopted him. But it wasn't like the movies, I don't think. He threw himself in front of a train eventually. One of his brothers got shot in the head during the war. Another drowned."

I winced.

"Then there was Christopher Robin Milne. You know, from *Winnie-the-Pooh*? He hated being a character in a book. He eventually gave his toys away. Said he didn't care about them. I don't think any children's book character just putzed around after the book ended. Not even Alice . . ."

I watched the light slip over her collarbones. "What about Alice?"

"She made it out okay, I guess. But Lewis Carroll had all those naked pictures of her. He wanted to marry her. Some people think he was a total pedo."

I stared at her. My heart was beating in my ears, too loudly. She turned to me, cupped my face in her hands, took in my trembling lips and chin.

"What? What did I say?"

44

Court and Petyr were best friends. Seniors, both of them, who had met the first week of school freshman year and been inseparable ever since. Now they were finishing up their capstone projects. Petyr's was a series of paintings of men in traditional pin-up poses. They were wry and winking and playful, had a sense of joy that my own paintings never had. Court, meanwhile, was working on a giant paper on the lives of the children behind the books. She said she didn't always want to moonlight as a life drawing model. She really wanted to be a children's librarian someday. It had been her only dream, from the time she was in diapers. I wondered what it was like to know yourself so well. When I showed her parts of myself, I had the feeling of being halfway unraveled.

When the three of us—a sort of trio now, a band, a team—would go to the diner together after life drawing, we drank too much black coffee and ordered off the children's menu, where the dishes were all named after ancient cartoon characters. I did my best to share what I could of myself. I couldn't tell them about Jamie, so I told them about Sophie, about Miranda, about my parents' separation and recent reunion. I told them about my high school, and the kids who drank in the woods, and how I'd pretty much never been invited. Petyr snorted at that, digging into his Donald Duck.

"I went to parties like those," he said. "Back when I was in high school and still pretending to be straight. Trust me. You weren't missing anything. A whole bunch of football players flirting with each other, mostly."

"And you never joined in?" Court asked, waggling her eyebrows.

"I can't deny that there were a few surreptitious underbrush hand jobs," Petyr said. Court grinned wickedly. I smiled, too, trying to hide how I was blushing a little. I wasn't used to being around people who spoke like this, and so openly. Other queer people. Who wore their queerness without hesitation or shame, like it was any other ordinary part of them.

Court had been born into this kind of openness. She'd been raised by a single dad who eventually started dating other men—and then married one. Her mother had made a reappearance in her midteens, and tried to take custody of her, making it clear that she thought Court's family life was "inappropriate." But Court had stood before a judge to make an impassioned defense of her two fathers. When I told her she was brave, she said she wasn't; she was just doing the sort of thing they would *always* do for her.

Her fathers were perfect. They were loving, supportive—they sent her lumpy care packages with T-shirts from the cruises they went on together now that they were empty nesters. I wondered what it was like to have home be a sanctuary, and not a thorny tangle. I'd wondered that before, with Vidya, but had never found an answer. Then my strange family had only ever been a liability. I wondered if that were true now, too.

That night, after we gorged ourselves on waffle fries, Court walked me back to the dorms, her freezing fingers tucked inside mine.

"You're holding back on me," she said out of the blue as we passed under a burning streetlamp that made the snowy path look bright white. "I know there are things you haven't told me about yourself."

I stopped in the path, turned to face her. Could feel how the frown had made a crease between my eyebrows. I couldn't deny it. I didn't know how to tell her about my brother, and so there was a huge chunk of my life that I was always talking around. It hadn't mattered with Vidya. She'd known all about Jamie. But it seemed like the sort of thing that might make this new, fragile romance heavier than it needed to be.

"Look," she said, "I just hope you didn't leave behind some stupid high school boyfriend—"

"Oh G-d no!" I couldn't hold back the look of horror on my face. "Do you really think I seem like the type to have a *boyfriend*?"

Court laughed, then sheepishly looked down at the toes of her shoes. She was wearing Converse sneakers, and I wondered if her feet were cold. I decided then that when we got back to my room, I'd help her take her shoes off and rub her feet until they were warm again.

"I don't know," she said. "People reinvent themselves. I really don't know you at all, Annie."

I blinked in surprise, but I supposed it was true. How could she know anything about me if she didn't know about Jamie? He was only someone I'd mentioned once or twice, in passing, dismissive. My older brother, who worked in a supermarket. It was the kind of thing that made the wealthy kids at Hampden uncomfortable to hear, so they never asked anything more about him. Now I winced to remember it. It was true, but it wasn't the whole truth. There were reasons that Jamie's life looked the way it did, and I'd been stepping around them.

How could I even begin to say it, though? *Something bad happened years ago. Not to me, but to someone I loved. But that's not even the worst part. The worst part was that I thought magic was real. And sometimes I wonder if it still is, but not in the way I thought. . . .*

"I don't know how to tell you about the things I'm not telling you," I admitted, letting my shoulders rise and fall. I'd tried already. Failed. It was too big. Too strange.

Court squinted up at the streetlight like it might hold the answer. "Maybe you can write it down," she said. "Maybe you can use a metaphor."

"A metaphor?"

"Yeah," she said, "You know, like Neverland wasn't just a magical land. It was also a place where J. M. Barrie could visit his brother who died as a kid."

The Lost Boy Returns, I thought. My frown deepened. "I'm not a writer," I told her.

She rolled her eyes at me. "What's a writer, anyway?" she said.

By the time Court's birthday came in late February, I'd taken what she said to heart. I thought I might give her the story as a gift. Sitting down at my laptop, I began to write a story about an old woman looking back on the brother she'd lost—even though he'd never died. It wasn't right, though. The words felt wrong. Plus, I wondered, in a way, if this were my story to tell at all.

I took long breaks from my story. I paced. I quit pacing and lay back in my bed, closing my eyes, and tried to imagine Jamie. I could almost see those long days at the grocery store, and fighting with Shelley over takeout, storming off on his motorcycle and riding into the silvery dark night. Forgetting his gloves again, and his hands getting so cold he worried about frostbite.

But that wasn't all of him. Something was missing, some lumincscent heart. A question. A gap. And so my words felt flat and joyless, empty. My brother had told me that I loved Gumlea once, and he wasn't wrong. But I didn't know how to find my way back to that love now. Not when there was still so much I didn't understand.

Finally, I gave up. I asked Petyr for a ride to the used bookstore instead, and we browsed the stacks in silence together, the spines of books staring out at me until I found the perfect one. It was an Edward Eager book, one I remembered stealing off Jamie's shelf when I was a kid. *Magic or Not?* it was called. On the flyleaf, I inscribed it for her, wondering if I was being too naked with my feelings, pressing forward anyway.

Not sure if you've read this one. It meant a lot to me once. Sometimes it feels like a question I'm still asking: Is there magic or not? Meeting you makes me think the answer is more likely yes than no.

Yours,
A

When she opened it and read the words I'd jotted on the front page, Court glowed.

"It's perfect," she said. "I've read *Half Magic* but never any of his other ones."

"This one is different," I told her. "This one is more like real life. The author is a character in it."

"Droste effect," she said, grinning. Later, I looked up the phrase, but in the moment, I only vaguely understood. Still, at least she was pleased. Maybe more than pleased. "I love it."

Court kissed the book like it was a Torah. Then she put it down on my dorm room bed and climbed over to me, kissing me, too.

"But you're the best birthday present," she told me, leaving kisses down my jaw, my throat. I had to admit that I felt the same about her. And it wasn't even my birthday.

That night, with Court tucked in against my shoulder, my phone buzzed. I groped around my nightstand for it, then found it, knowing somehow who it was even before I picked up my phone and looked.

Jamie.

"Hello?" I whispered. We never called each other, and we definitely never called each other at 2:17 a.m.

"Hey," he said. He sounded rushed, breathless. His voice was very low, like he was afraid of being heard. "You're awake."

"I wasn't," I hissed.

On the other end, my brother laughed. It sounded ragged. "I hope I didn't wake your girlfriend up," he told me, and that's when I sat up and pried myself out from under Court's sweaty, sweet body. Then I went to the bathroom I shared with my suitemate, turned on the light, and closed the door. I stared at myself in the mirror. My eyes were the same as always, and so were my freckles, but I noticed how I looked older now, a little less round around the jaw.

"How did you know about Court? Did Mom tell you I was dating someone?" I asked.

There was a long pause, a crackle. Finally, Jamie said, "Yeah."

"Cool," I said. I rolled my eyes. "Would have liked to have told you myself."

"You never tell me anything," he said, hurt in his voice, and I couldn't even argue against it because it was true.

"Why are you *calling*?" I said at last.

"Me and Shelley had a fight. She thinks—" There was a pause, an awful sniffle. I imagined my brother crying, like he had once cried as a little boy. Red-faced and raw, every feeling obvious on his boyish features. Of course, he was a man now. How many times had I seen our father cry, even after Jamie disappeared? Once? Maybe twice?

"Jamie," I said. "It's okay. You'll be okay."

Another long pause. Finally, I heard him exhale, crackly-voiced. "Okay," he said. "But I wanted to ask you how you—how you do it?"

"Do what?"

"Damn it. I—I mean, you're always yourself, Annie. You were never afraid to be yourself."

I was still staring at myself in that bathroom mirror, but in the strange light, and in light of my tiredness, it seemed like my flesh was almost starting to melt off. I could see the bones beneath my skin, the sinuses empty now—no baby teeth.

"That's not totally true," I told him. Thinking, *Still haven't found a way to tell my girlfriend about you yet.* "Anyway, it never seemed like there was much choice for me. I'm an open book, more or less. And you're . . . I don't know. You're a chameleon."

"Shape-shifter," he said, and let out a ragged laugh. "I can't—I just could never figure out how you weren't terrified to let the other kids and Mom and Dad and Gram and Poppy and everyone know how weird you are."

I winced. My brother wasn't wrong about that, in a way. But it wasn't something simple—wasn't something I was really proud of. Because it had made my life harder in a thousand different ways. With kids like Nina. With Vidya. Even with Jamie.

"Of course I was terrified," I said. "I'm always terrified."

A long pause. A laugh. "Really?"

I glanced toward the closed bathroom door, thinking of the beautiful girl waiting there, and everything I had not told her. Everything I would not tell her, until I was forced. It was too big, too scary. A dragon who could eat you whole and spit you out again.

"Really," I said. "Why do you think I always told so many fucked-up stories as a kid?"

"Because you were talented," he said, at the same time I said, "Because I was scared."

A laugh, mutual, but joyless. And then a strange, awkward silence stretching out after.

"What was your fight about, anyway?" I asked him at last.

Jamie got quiet for a long moment. When he answered, his voice was even lower than before. "Our future," he said. "She wants to get married. I told her I *can't* yet. I know I can't. Not until I clear things up with Dad."

"Dad?" I asked, feeling the deep crease between my eyebrows.

"I've been trying to call him," he said. "But I can't bring myself to do it. I sit there staring at the phone for hours but I just can't do it. She thinks I'm hiding something from her. Another woman, I think. But I told her that's not it. It's Dad. If I can't even tell *him* who I really am, how can I fucking marry *her*?"

He was rambling, practically incomprehensible. "What are you *talking* about?" I finally asked. But when he answered, something had shifted in his voice. His tone was flat. Dead.

"Nothing," he said. "It's nothing." He was shutting down again. Shutting me out. "Okay. I gotta go. Shelley just came home."

"Okay," I told him. There was a long silence, one where other siblings might tell each other that they loved one another. "Good night."

"You too," my brother said, and I hoped we both knew what the other meant.

45

Having Court beside me changed that February, and the cold weeks of March that marched on after. It could have been bleak and endless, white snow dunes piling up beside the dorm and then turning gray, the steam heat clicking in my empty bedroom like old bones. Instead, she was my fire, my internal heat. We hid in the library together, trading books. We flirted at the grocery store, making old women roll their eyes. Alone in my dorm together, she told me I could draw her so long as I made something worthwhile out of it. Then she twisted her long, limber body into positions that were absurd. When the timer on her phone went off, she came over to me, tucking her chin against my shoulder, and peered at what I'd done.

She challenged me. She told me my art was still missing something. "Your voice," she said, and I felt a fistful of tears rise in my throat then because I knew it was true. But I didn't know how to fix it. The words had always been Jamie's, or at least that's what I'd assumed when I was little. I didn't know how to untangle my story from his. I didn't know how to make my words *mine*.

For years, I'd been running away from him. And I told myself that he'd been running, too—from school, from our parents, from our previous lives. Isn't that what he'd told me that day on the motorcycle? That he just needed to keep moving. Maybe it was true, but I'd begun to suspect it was only a half-truth.

In March, just a fortnight before spring break, a boy by the name of Dylan Martin was found after being forced to live in a storage shed for three months. Dad called to tell me that Jamie was going to be on *20/20* to talk about what happened, his trauma and everything after.

"You should watch," he told me, though the tone of his voice suggested that he knew I wouldn't. But this time, I surprised myself, calling Court in the middle of the night the night before the special aired.

"I don't want to have phone sex," she whined, and I laughed through tears, because I'd been crying, thinking about my brother and everything he had been through and how I hadn't been there for him. I could hear her sit up in bed.

"Oh G-d," she said. "What's wrong?"

"I don't have a TV," I told her, and I knew that this would be a turning point and yet still found myself saying it anyway. After this, she would know the whole story, every ugly bit. "My brother's going to be on TV tomorrow and I don't even own one and I can't watch him."

"On TV?" There was a stretch of silent surprise. I didn't know how to explain to her that my produce manager brother was going to be on TV, that he'd been on TV before, so I just fell silent. After a beat, Court sighed. "Annie, Annie," she said. "My TV is your TV. Come over, baby."

So I did. The next morning I bundled myself up against the cold, wearing a scratchy hat and a scarf that I think had been Eli's before I stole it away for school, and Court picked me up outside the dorms. She took me back to her place, and she made us grilled cheese and canned tomato soup. It was the best thing I'd ever eaten, gooey and buttery and acidic and rich, and we bundled up together in her bed, the space heater pointed right at us, and watched my brother, small and strange on her flat screen.

"He looks nothing like you," she said, and it was true. At some point our features had diverged and now his face was more like Dad's, soft features and oddly pretty lips, whereas I was more like Mom these days with her high cheekbones and strong nose. It felt like a lifetime ago now that we used to feel like twins.

It didn't help that his hair had been slicked down with gel and they'd put a polo shirt on him. That had to be Dad's doing. The James M. [Redacted] Foundation was much more successful in their fund-raising efforts when my brother was presented as a good Christian boy, untouched by the darkness of his experiences.

Still, the darkness was there. Inherent. My brother was talking about how he'd lived in that little apartment with that little man, explaining that he'd presented himself as a son or a brother or a nephew to anyone who would have asked.

"But you weren't," said the interviewer, the lines of her face blurred by the camera's lens. "You were lovers."

My brother didn't hide his grimace. "We were never lovers," he said sternly. "There was absolutely nothing romantic about what happened between us. He was my rapist," my brother said. "He tortured me. He said he would hurt my family."

The interviewer paused, nodding. You could see that she knew she'd made a miscalculation. You couldn't just call someone's convicted rapist their lover—but the woman who was interviewing him wasn't quite ready to admit she was wrong.

"James, some questions have been raised about why you didn't go for help sooner—"

The corners of my brother's mouth were downturned. These were the questions he was always asked, the questions that everyone wanted answers to. Why hadn't he just left? Surely he could have done something, helped himself, walked away? He was a victim of course, and they always acknowledged that, but there was always hesitation in the way they talked about it. Shouldn't he have been a victim in the right way? Weren't heroes supposed to be faster, better, and braver, too?

"I was afraid," my brother said swiftly. "I was absolutely terrified. Until you've lived through that, you can't understand what it's like." But then I heard him say something strange: "In a situation like that, you have to carve out your own freedoms."

The interviewer didn't ask what Jamie meant by that. But I couldn't help but circle around the idea. Your own freedoms. Like the bike was to him now. Like Gumlea once had been for both of us. What had been his freedom in captivity?

The woman interviewing him didn't seem to wonder. Instead, she leaned forward and fixed her hand, which looked older than her face, on my brother's hand.

"James, do you have any thoughts you'd like to share with Dylan about how to move on from an experience like this?"

"Sure," he said. "You need family and you need faith. A community. I'm building my own family now. I just proposed to my girlfriend. She said yes."

My brother flushed at sharing this news, which was news to me. Or was it? I thought about our late-night phone call. Jamie's voice, shaking, when he told me they'd been discussing their future together.

I guess Jamie had worked out whatever it was he'd wanted to talk to our father about. Or else decided it didn't really matter. That seemed closer, truer. Our family wasn't very good at catharsis.

"You just have to look ahead," my brother continued. "Keep moving forward. Never back."

"Thank you, James," said the interviewer.

Court turned the television off. "Holy shit," she said, and the silence settled in thick between us. For a moment, I was terrified that it would swallow us up, the kind of silence that had enveloped me ever since Jamie had returned. But it didn't. After only a moment, the silence dissipated.

"Are you okay?" she asked me. "What am I saying? Of course you're not. That's so fucked up. I'm so sorry." When I didn't answer, she tucked me under her arms and drew me close. She ran her fingers through my hair.

"You've been carrying this for a long time, haven't you?" she asked. I nodded, pressing my damp face to her collarbones. Even in that moment, tucked inside her arms, I worried it was too much for her. Too heavy. Too big. Too weird.

But she just held me.

"I'm so sorry," she said. "I'm so sorry it happened to you."

Not to Jamie. To me. It had happened to me, too, I realized. And Court saw it, and saw how it hurt, even now.

"We were so close as kids," I whispered. "Mom used to say that you couldn't tell either of us a secret without the other knowing."

"You told each other everything?" she asked.

I laughed a little, through my tears. "We didn't have to. We would just know. Sometimes it felt like magic, but after Jamie disappeared, it started to feel like a curse."

"You must have missed him so much," she said, and her words were like a tender punch to my rib cage. Because, honestly? I hadn't.

"No, I—I didn't think he was gone. I thought—I thought he was talking to me, still, somehow, asking me to help him. But I couldn't. And then he came back, and he hadn't been at all where I thought he was, so I just . . . shut him out. I knew it wasn't fair of me, and I knew I was hurting him—"

"I bet it hurt you, too," she said. "To pretend like that part of your life hadn't even happened."

I nodded. I hadn't thought of it that way, even though of course she was right. "It did, but in the moment it hurt less than facing the truth."

We were quiet for a few minutes. The only sound was her heartbeat, her breath. And mine.

"Where did you think he was?" Court asked me finally. "You said he wasn't where you thought he was. Where'd you think he went?"

I winced, but I couldn't say it. Not just yet. I shook my head, burrowing deeper under the covers. Court still held me. Court didn't mind.

"That's okay, baby," she said, bringing her mouth close to my ear. "You'll get there soon. I know it."

I didn't feel so sure. But I decided, in that moment, to trust her anyway.

The next morning, I woke up early to make Court and her roommates breakfast. I filled the percolator with coffee grounds that looked like black crystals in the dim winter morning. I made toast from nutty, rough, cardboardy bread from the health food store. I fried bacon. Soon enough, Court came out of her room, looking disheveled and faint. She stood in the door for a while, watching me.

"You like taking care of people, don't you?" she asked.

I shrugged. "You're one to talk," I said, grinning. She grinned back but didn't deny it. "I took care of my little brother a lot after the abduction."

Abduction. Usually I wouldn't let myself even think the word. It was always *disappearance*. It was always *before he was gone*. But somehow watching my brother on that bad, overproduced television show had helped me be able to think those words, to wrap my mind around what had happened to Jamie, to me, to all of us.

"I keep thinking," she said as I peeled the bacon off the griddle and laid it out on a paper plate, "about what your brother said about moving on."

I felt the corner of my mouth quirk up. "It's a nice sound bite, but you shouldn't believe it. He was probably coached on what to say."

She cocked her head to the side, considering. "It didn't sound like a lie. He said he has faith. I didn't know you were religious."

I sat down with the plate of bacon and offered one to Court. She sat down, too, backward on her kitchen chair like she always did. She took one by the edges, delicately licking off the grease.

"That's the funny thing," I said. "Jamie isn't. At least not that I know of. We were raised Jewish, but I'm not sure he ever believed."

"Jewish, really?" Court glanced down at the bacon.

I laughed. "Okay, Jew-ish, maybe. But . . ." I stared at Court's thrift store plate, shiny with grease over the vintage floral pattern. There were dying leaves under it, wilting flowers, fruit gone to rot. It was the only plate like that. None of the other ones matched.

"But what?" she said.

"It meant something to me once. It got away from me, I guess. In high school. It felt weird going to shul alone, without—"

"Jamie?"

"Without anyone. My dad's super Christian now. My little brother, too. Who knows what Jamie *really* is. He might not know, either. Mom is—I don't know. She's flighty. It reminded her too much of him, so she didn't want to go anymore. So I stopped, too."

"You should go again. I'd go with you."

I glanced up at her, arching an eyebrow. "You're not . . . ?"

Court laughed and crunched down on the bacon. "No, I'm a Unitarian. It's all kind of the same, though, isn't it? At least that's what they taught us in my church. Anyway, if you wanted someone to go with you, I would. No big deal."

I smiled at her. Ate my bacon. Slurped my coffee, still black. It felt good to hear that. I don't know why, but it did.

"Sure, maybe," I said.

"Think about it" was Court's answer.

I did. That's how I ended up at the humanist synagogue, watching Court, a kippah on her head. It was strange to be at a new synagogue with new customs—no potluck after, but a candle lighting and Kaffeeklatsch with the rabbi, where he played a guitar and sang songs about the perseverance of our people. I felt too shy to introduce myself, but not Court. She went right over and shook his hand, then introduced me as her girlfriend. I felt grateful to her in a thousand different ways and wondered if the gratitude would ever end. After so long spending my life with my doors closed, they were swinging open, letting in small shafts of hope. After the service, we went to the diner and poured too much sugar in our coffees and laughed about it, giddy and overcaffeinated from our fingers to our toes.

I asked Court if she wanted me to go to church with her, something I thought I'd never do. I certainly hadn't been willing to go to church for my father. But Court was different. Still, she only smiled, and it seemed for a moment like there was a secret beneath her lips. "I really only ever go when I'm home, for Dad," she said. "I kind of have my own church these days."

That's how I ended up at Court's children's literature tutorial. She'd been talking to me about it for the entire time we'd been dating, suggesting I should come, but I'd danced around it—never really sure why. And now the weight of my excuses had evaporated. She'd done my thing. It was time I did hers.

There were five students and a professor in a drafty room in the library, arguing about subtext and paratext and metatext. I sat in the corner, sipping from a thermos of instant hot chocolate with a splash of rum in it, eyes wide and listening.

I'd never heard anyone talk about books this way before. They pulled them apart until there was nothing left but bones. They talked about how the books talked to each other. It reminded me of Gumlea, how the land had been littered with the stories that had been read to us at bedtime and that we'd seen on TV. At one point, the professor asked me what I thought, and all I could say, in a hushed, almost-reverent voice, was that I didn't know. Because I didn't. It was as if they were speaking a language I once had understood but had since forgotten.

After, as Court pulled on her duffle coat and yanked the hood up over her eyes, she kissed my cheek and said to me, "What'd you think?"

"It was amazing" was all I could say.

I felt like I was standing at the bottom of a great mountain, almost ready to begin my climb.

46

I dreamed I was back on the Island of Feral Children. The treetop village teetered, every bough creaking beneath. The homes were empty now, the children grown and gone on to lives of their own. Years and years ago they'd left sacrifices for me in their doorways, but the meat had been torn away by wild animals. Now all that was left were pelts, shivering on the wind, spotted with long-dried blood. They looked like flags. I walked through the breezeway, my face a scowl, breathing only through my mouth.

There was movement in the forest below. I crouched low, tracking it. The creature was huge, black as night, fur dotted silver like a million stars. A hare. And on her back, a boy, holding on tight with fisted hands. He cast his white face back, as though searching for something in the woods. I turned to look but didn't see anything. Only the birches, pale as bones.

Still, I felt his fear. Practically tasted it, sharp as blood on the air. *The King.*

No. That wasn't right at all. I peered through the branches, which had just begun to bud in the early spring. And saw something there. A flash of light against a golden crown.

The Queen.

When I looked back to the boy, he was gone.

I woke panting, my heart racing as though I'd been the one careening through the bright forest myself. Something was different, I realized. Something was wrong. I looked around my black room, my eyes finding the square digits of my clock: 3:57. I could hear Court's even breath droning on in the extra-long twin beside me, but it was no comfort, not tonight. Edgy and shaking, I pulled myself from the bed and began to pace back and forth across my room.

Once I read a story in a magazine about a man who had a neurological event on a golf course. He looked up at the sun, and something snapped inside him like a rubber band. He was always different after that, a whole new personality. I shivered as I padded back and forth across the tiny room. Something was wrong. Something was very, very wrong.

In the early hours of the morning, I acted without thinking. I sat down at my desk chair, closed my eyes, and reached out through the darkness.

Are you okay?

These were old paths, tangled and overgrown. But that didn't matter. My feet knew the way. As children, talking like this had been second nature. Some days, we'd tell jokes this way at the dinner table. Me in my high chair. Jamie in his booster seat. And we'd start giggling, both of us, out of nowhere—at the exact same time.

Still, it had been ages. No answer came back, not at first. I only had the sensation of wind rushing by, and his shock at my voice in his head, and his upset, and his worry. But in my mind's eye, still, I saw him—in the dark at the side of the road, slowing down his motorcycle, then stopping. Groping with his cold, numb hands—he'd forgotten his gloves *again*—for the phone that was in his pocket.

I opened my eyes. Lurched for the phone just as it started ringing.

"Jamie," I said, at the same time he said, "Annie."

Then there was a gap. A crackle. A moment of confusion. Dismay. Surprise. Finally, I sighed. He wasn't going to say it. I guess I had to.

"What happened to Mom?" I asked.

V

TWENTY-FOUR

COMING HOME TO WILTWYCK WOULDN'T be so bad if it weren't for running into people I used to know. My mom kept my room for me, even though she routinely threatens to turn it into an office. I can sleep on my old, comfortable bed and not a futon mattress whenever I want without worrying about my roommates having fuck buddies over in the middle of the day. I get to do my laundry for free, and Dad's always good for a glass of whiskey together and maybe a game of chess. It's kind of like a vacation from my ordinary life, so long as I don't try too hard to remember who I used to be. Like last time I came home right around the New Year, and Harper wanted to get together with Geoff Ryman and Asher Kent and I convinced myself it would be okay. But then we just ended up getting stoned out of an apple at Harper's grandparents' house and I had to sit there watching Geoff try to finger Harper on the shag carpet, both of them too blasted to even care that I was watching, like I hadn't known these people since kindergarten and it wasn't weird at all.

But it was weird. This wasn't who we were before, and I couldn't see why it was who we were supposed to be now, either. Did they really think it was all that interesting, hooking up with people we'd known forever? I couldn't understand how Harper could look at Geoff and see anything but the boy who had puked up strawberry Nesquik practically every day in third grade.

Since then, I've avoided leaving the house when I visit. I don't tag along with my dad to the Target and I don't go for long, rambling walks even when I can't sleep and I definitely don't go downtown, not to the witch store or anywhere else.

It's not the memories that get to me. It's the ghosts.

But you can't live like a total hermit. Not when you're a woman of childbearing age, apparently. Because this afternoon while my parents are at Uncle Jovan's visiting Naniji—without me, because I did my duty yesterday, taking them dinner and listening to Naniji's stories until I thought I'd fall asleep at the table—I take a long cozy nap and then wake up with a knife in my gut. My period arrives and I guess my mom must have gone through the change without even telling me, because there isn't a single tampon or pad in the house.

I stuff toilet paper in my underpants, throw on a hooded sweatshirt, hop in my Kia, and head to Kirky's. They've changed it since high school, added a sandwich bar and a crappy cappuccino machine, but mostly it's just like I remember, and the O.B.s are right where I remember them being, too. I fight the urge to stuff them in the pocket of my hoodie. Old shoplifting habits die hard, I guess, even when you haven't done it since middle school. But twenty seems too old to be lifting tampons, so I shuffle off to the counter with them instead, trying to kind of hide them behind my hand so that nobody sees. I don't know. It's still just embarrassing, even though I'd like to pretend it's not. Then I have to wait in line forever behind some trucker buying cigarettes. I consider buying gum, too. I try to pretend like I'm probably not bleeding all over my underwear. I'm looking at the ugly fluorescent lights and feeling obvious when I hear a voice behind me.

"Vidya?"

Inside, I'm cringing. I wonder who it's going to be and how much of my life I'm going to have to fill them in on before I can put in a God damned tampon. Will I have to tell them I dropped out of Julliard, that whole long sob story? Or can I just slink off to the dirty bathroom in the corner of the deli in peace?

But then I turn toward the front door and see a girl standing there. Her skin is bone white and kind of waxy, like she hasn't been sleeping lately. She's got a better haircut than she did last time I saw her, layered and kind of edgy, and her face has slimmed out. She looks more like her mom than she used to.

But her eyes. Her eyes are just like I remember them.

"Holy crap," I say, "Annie."

She smiles, and when she speaks, I hear that familiar swagger in her voice, like she owns Kirky's Deli and the town and maybe even the whole world.

"I guess it could be more awkward," she says. "I guess you could be buying condoms."

I duck back into the bathroom to *manage my situation*, as my mother might call it in polite company, then come out to find Annie waiting for me. She's leaning against the glass window, crushing a "Help Wanted" sign beneath her back, her peacoat bundled tight against her. She looks hot. Of course she does. I stand beside her for a minute, not sure of what to say. The March afternoon is gray and the sun is a glinting golden coin and the moment will be over soon, and I don't want that to happen.

"How have you been?" is what I end up asking, and I do my best not to cringe after I say it because it's so obviously not the right thing to ask, not with Annie. I should be asking her what she thinks about the Illuminati or something. I don't know. Something significant. Something fantastic. I always felt like I was a little too wispy compared to the weight of her. She laughs a little, and then blows her hot breath into her palms.

"I guess you haven't heard" is what she says. She's not looking at me. Those eyes are fixed out at the parking lot and the road ahead of us, headlights streaming by. Once I would have grabbed her hand and warmed it in my pocket. Once I would have held her jaw between my fingers and turned her eyes to meet mine, then kissed her, just to let her know I cared. Once I would have done a lot of things. but that was years ago. And I don't even know if she's single right now. I don't even know if she still dates girls.

"Heard what?" I ask instead.

She scuffs at the ground with her Palladiums, which don't seem warm enough for today, with the gray old dunes of snow piled up at the edge of the lot and the sunset cold and piercing out in front of us. Annie makes this expression that's grim and mysterious and shows teeth. But she doesn't answer. Instead she glances down into the plastic bag that's been hooked around her wrist since I got outside. I glance in. It's junk food. Hot Fries and Pringles and two bottles of Mountain Dew and a Butterfinger.

"You know," she says, "I was going to just eat this crap on the way back to the hospital, but do you want to go to the diner instead? I could use a break."

Hospital. Shit. It's gotta be serious. But it doesn't look like she wants to talk about it, not right now in the cold open air with the winter crows and truckers and entire planet listening. So I just stuff my hands down into my hoodie pockets, shrug, and say, "Sure."

TWENTY-FIVE

WE DRIVE THERE SEPARATELY, WHICH is probably for the best because if
we sat in the same car together I think my head would explode. Harper used
to say that the **[Redacted]**s were my catnip, and I think there was some
truth to it. Something about the cloudy, faraway look in Annie's eyes and
the deep pain beneath them that makes me just want to tear off her clothes,
or mine, whatever would be the fastest route to healing her. It's not healthy.
I'm not going to pretend that it is. So I'm glad to have like ten minutes to
myself in my car, the radio off and my hands steady at two and ten instead
of shaky and inappropriate when she's clearly going through some kind of
personal tragedy.

Still, I think as we get out of our cars outside the diner, *she looks damned
good in that peacoat.* She's filled out a little, looks less gangly than before.
And she seems to walk a little differently up the concrete diner steps, her
hand lightly gracing the rail as she goes. She was always confident, but now
she's self-possessed.

I bet she's dating someone, I think. *I bet she's in love.*

We get a booth for two beneath a giant taxidermized moose head. I've
always loved this diner, with its dark wood and Tiffany lamps and weird

dusty statues of bears in the corners. Annie slides her backpack in beside her and then promptly buries her nose in a menu.

"Do you think I can get away with ordering a kid's meal?" I ask. "The Popeye, or maybe the Big Bird?"

Annie smiles faintly, like she's thinking of something else. "Don't tell me. Let me guess: the Big Bird is chicken fingers."

"Nailed it," I say.

She laughs a little. But then she stops herself, like she isn't supposed to laugh right now. I wait until we put our drink orders in to ask.

"So . . . ?"

She looks at me, and it's like her eyes are boring into my soul. "My mom had a stroke," she says.

I wasn't expecting that. Not sure what I expected. Something with Jamie, maybe. But not that. I bring my hand up to my mouth.

"Oh God. Are you okay?"

She looks back down at the menu. The frown is deep between her eyebrows. "I'm fine" is what she says, but she isn't, I can tell. "They say she'll recover. After another surgery and PT."

"I'm so sorry. That must be terrifying," I tell her, and even though my voice is sympathetic, she slides her eyes away from me.

"Yeah."

I watch as a few tears dot the surface of her menu. I want to hold her hand and reassure her somehow that I'm here for her, that she's not alone. But before I can, the server appears, a middle-aged woman with pens stuck in her bun and a white nubbin of chewing gum visible between her teeth as she talks.

"What can I get for you girls?"

I'm about to tell her that we need another minute to decide when Annie answers. "Grilled cheese with bacon and tomato, please. And what are your soups?"

I look at her closely as the waitress rattles off the options: chicken matzo ball, beef barley, and tomato bisque, which is what Annie wants. If I hadn't seen it myself, I would have never known that Annie had just been crying.

When it's my turn to order, I try to train the question from my voice. I act like everything is normal, because that's what Annie wants. "Egg white omelet with broccoli and onion, please. Hold the toast."

Annie's looking at me as the waitress takes our menus away.

"What?"

"Egg white?"

"I'm on this health food kick. No gluten, no meat, no dairy, no egg yolks . . ." It feels wrong to be telling Annie about this, like I know she'll judge, and sure enough, her eyebrows are arched.

"What?" I say again. She shrugs. I think she's glad to be teasing me about my diet instead of talking about what's happening with her mom.

"It just sounds kind of disgusting. Sorry."

"It's fine," I tell her. It isn't, though, and silence settles between us like a throbbing heart spiked with nails, and I wonder why I'm here, and I wonder why I thought this would ever be anything but awkward and weird.

Then Annie sighs. "How's school?" she asks, in a tone that makes it clear she's only asking because she knows it's what she's supposed to say. To my surprise she actually perks up when I tell her the truth:

"I dunno. I dropped out."

Eyes wide, she leans forward. "Really?"

"Yeah, I started an internship at this recording studio my freshman year and it kind of took over my life. I'm a studio musician now."

She's grinning like a maniac, drumming her hands on the table. "That's terrific."

"It is?" I ask, uncertain, because usually people apologize to me when they find out I've dropped out of Juilliard. But Annie was never one for the usual responses to things, I guess.

"Yeah. You always wanted to be a band. Now you can be in, like, all of them."

I feel myself flush just a little bit at her enthusiasm. I'd forgotten this about Annie—how she'd often say the wrong thing, but, sometimes, exactly the right thing.

She's still drumming her hands now, excited for me. "What do you play?"

"Piano, mostly. Guitar or bass or ukulele, if they need it."

"Awesome. Totally awesome. You're so talented. You always were."

I grin. The waitress brings by our drinks, a root beer for Annie, a black coffee for me. Annie squashes her straw down onto the table and then drops beads of soda on the wrapper, and we watch together as it unfurls like a worm. I don't remember her being this kinetic as a teenager. She always seemed pretty placid. Now she seems restless, ready to take off at a moment's notice.

Her eyes dart up at me. "I always think of you when I hear the Beach Boys, you know. I'll be in the supermarket or at a party and I hear that fucker Brian Wilson and suddenly I'm fifteen again."

I cringe, taking a long slurp of my coffee.

"What, no longer a fan?"

"I mean, sure, they're talented. But their stuff always reminds me of high school. I was just so obsessed with them back then. I thought that because Brian Wilson was fucked up, then he must have had all the answers."

"And now?" Annie asks, chewing on her ice cubes.

"God only knows," I say. She grins at me. I grin back, then shrug. "Life's different now. Things are different. You know who I'm into lately? David Bowie. He and Iman were married for like thirty years. Stability. That's my jam."

"Weirdo," Annie says.

"Nah," I tell her. "Normie. And that's okay. That's the whole point."

Annie's looking at me oddly, her eyebrows knitted so closely together that they almost meet. "What if you were born Brian Wilson, though? What if your life is just kind of fucked up?"

"Can you transform yourself into David Bowie, you mean?" I ask, and Annie nods. For a second, there's an opportunity there. A vulnerable gap inside her, one I can fit inside, easily. I've always liked comforting her. And she always liked being comforted by me.

"I think it's just a matter of acting like you're David Bowie anyway. Doing what needs to be done, no matter what. Not getting lost in—"

"In all those Pet Sounds?" Annie asks, and flashes me a smile. Before I can answer, our food arrives. I watch as she breaks off half her melty grilled cheese sandwich and leaves it on a napkin between us.

"No pressure," she says, waving her fork toward my plate and the grayish-green lump of food on top of it. "But, you know, just in case."

As we eat, our conversation falls into a rhythm as comfortable as an old pair of jeans. She tells me about Hampden, where they have no classes or grades but plenty of drugs. I guess it shouldn't surprise me, the way she talks about pot like she invented it, but it does. I remember the things Harper said about Annie being a goody-goody—years and years ago now—and her blind, animal panic right before the only time we smoked. But time passes, and people change. Even people like Annie.

"How about you?" she asks. "Glamorous life in New York? Are you seeing anyone?"

Leave it to Annie to cut straight to the point. I'm picking the bacon out of the sandwich half she gave me, trying to look blasé about the whole thing.

"No. I'm testing singledom. I was dating a girl for a while. Priyanka . . ." I try to think of what I can say to Annie about Pri but come up blank. The truth is, no one really measured up after the **[Redacted]**s made mincemeat out of my heart. Pri was exciting, creative, dynamic—but she was no Annie.

"A nice Indian girl!" is what Annie says, her eyes lighting up. "Your grandparents must have been thrilled."

I study her face, trying to decide if she's making fun of me. But that's not the kind of person Annie is. She means it.

"Well, my grandfather passed away last year," I tell her. Her mouth twists sympathetically. "But yeah, my grandmother loved her."

Of course, it was kind of a train wreck otherwise. Still, I know that was my fault. Even after we'd both met each other's families, I could never commit, not fully. Pri knew it, saw it, how I always had one foot out the door. "Anyway, I'm happy being single these days. I know something will come along eventually, but I'm not in a hurry. How about you?"

I brace myself. And then she smiles, a slow, sly kind of smile, and my heart breaks just a little. "Yeah. I'm seeing someone. Her name's Court. She's . . ." and she trails off. In her silence is everything. The whole world.

"That's great," I say, genuinely, because I always thought Annie deserved to be loved—fully, wholeheartedly, in a way I had never been able to. I'm glad she's found that with Court, whoever that is. But the cheese is suddenly thick and sour on my tongue. I put the sandwich back down on the napkin and change the subject before Annie notices the hurt behind my eyes. "You know, I went back to Gumlea once. Senior year."

She puts her spoon back in her empty soup bowl with a clatter. "What?"

The betrayal is clear on her face. It's my turn to get all jittery. I speak too quickly, my words spilling over themselves. "I wanted to show it to Harper, that mountain you'd shown me. I'd been talking about it for years. We went in on the other side, near 32. I found the picnic table, but that was it. I couldn't find the mountain. Sometimes I wonder if I dreamed it."

The corner of Annie's mouth quirks up. "No, don't be stupid. It wasn't real. Gumlea was only a metaphor."

"But the mountain—"

"Hold on."

She turns away from me for a second, riffling through her backpack, her brown hair veiling her face. She finally pulls out a black ballpoint pen. Shoving her plates out of the way, she turns over her soup-stained menu. Then she starts to draw a map. Not of our world, at least no place that I recognize. Mountains on one side. Mountains on the other. And between them, a thick black line. A river.

"Jamie used to call it the River Endless. I know. It's a stupid name. He was always crap at names. He said we were born from that river. He said we return to it every night when we're asleep. And someday, when we die—"

"We wake up on the other side," I say faintly, watching as her hand, all stained with black ink, works. She looks at me and squints her eyes. I bet she's trying not to think about her mom.

"Yeah," she says. Then there's a long pause. Too long. "I shouldn't tell you this."

I lean forward across the table. "Why, because of James?"

"I guess. It's just . . . I used to wonder if Gumlea was real, but that felt crazy. Now I know that it's not. But the truth feels even crazier."

"What do you mean?"

"Gumlea was just a fantasy. Just kids' stuff. It was never anything more than that. But me and Jamie . . ."

I look at her quizzically. Her freckles are paler than they used to be, or maybe it's just the long, cold winter. Her lips are chapped. There's something haunted behind her eyes.

She turns away from me again, going through that bag of hers. She finally pulls out a notebook and throws it down on the table between us. "Jamie is going to move back home," she says. "To help Dad take care of Mom, when she can come home from the hospital. His fiancée was so pissed that she dumped him and wouldn't let him get his stuff. So he had me do it."

"So?"

"So there were all these boxes marked 'evidence.'"

"Stuff from the trial?"

Annie bites her lip. Nods. "This was his notebook. One of them, at least. There were like a dozen. From back when he was living with that guy, I guess."

She's suddenly uncertain, suddenly peeling dead, dry skin from off her lip and leaving a red patch behind. She still can't speak his name, the one on the news and all over the internet. Kevin Rapp-Palmer. The man who abducted James.

"And?" I prod.

She pushes the notebook toward me. It looks like a normal notebook, like something a high school student might carry. There are bad drawings of dragons on the front, and James's name in blocky script. I remember his handwriting, all those notes he used to pass me between classes. The song he'd written, which Annie had given to me, back when we both thought he was dead.

I open to the middle.

The boy struggled. He thrashed until his wrists bled from the rope burn. He kicked his body against the sweating flesh of the wall, the bed frame, the meager mattress. He tossed his thin bones and even thinner skin until he was dizzy and nauseated. Then he was still again, panting, his breath sounding just like the ocean beyond. In. Out. In. And out. Reminding him that he was still alive.

How much time passed? There was no telling in the mouth. Maybe hours. Maybe days. Maybe only twenty minutes. When footsteps sounded on the boards above, muffled and distant, every muscle in his body tightened. He couldn't let the pirate touch him.

"He always liked writing stories," I say faintly, trying to ignore the feeling that I am doing something wrong. This story is obviously about James and Kevin. Obviously.

But when I look at Annie, her eyes are wide and trembling. "It's not just a story," she says. "I *saw* that. I thought I was imagining it. I thought . . ."

She trails off, but it's okay. She doesn't need to finish. She thought she was going crazy, and so did everyone else. Even me.

"You grew up together. Telling stories. Of course you'd imagine similar situations—"

She reaches into her bag one last time, and when she throws something down on the table, it lands with a muffled thud on James's open notebook.

It's a knife. The knife I gave her, I think at first. With a white hilt and scalloped blade. But when I pick it up, I'm not so certain. The drawings don't look right. They look cruder.

"I thought you said you buried that," I tell her. Annie's teeth are gritted. She's close to tears again, and for some reason, I feel like crying, too.

"I did," she whispers, her words creaking out. "Vidya, I did."

I pick up the knife carefully. There's a hare drawn on one side in Sharpie, faded now in patchy spots. A King on the other, and a boy, and a girl. But they're ugly and strange, all wrong. I look at the notebook, the grotesque doodles in the margins. I think about what Annie has told me about school and life drawing, and the pictures she used to draw for me. All those beautiful pictures . . .

"I believe you," I tell her. I push the knife and the book back toward her. I can't stand to look at it all anymore. For some reason, the sight of them has turned my stomach. Maybe it's the cheese. I wonder if I'm going to be sick.

Annie looks at me with grim satisfaction. Then she puts her things— James's things—back in her bag.

"What did James say about this stuff?" I ask her at last. She sighs, a big, hollow sound.

"He said I could keep them if I wanted," she says. "He said he didn't need them anymore."

Her voice wavers when she says that. I feel my heart squeeze. "You could always do something with them," I offer. "Paint a picture. Write a book. Something."

Annie laughs, but it's dry and without humor. "People keep telling me that kind of stuff," she tells me. "You. Court. Even Jamie."

"Well," I say carefully, "we *know* you, Annie. All of us."

Her eyes flash up. There's a hint of emotion there that I can't quite read. "My whole life, everyone was always looking at him," she says at last. "Waiting for *him* to do something amazing."

I take a long, slow breath. Sigh. There's so much I never told Annie about her brother. It never seemed like my place to do it—and it doesn't now.

"He's got his own problems," I tell her simply, which is shorthand, maybe, but captures the general idea. "And you can't just waste your whole life waiting for him."

She looks down at the crusts of her sandwich. Picks one up. Nods. "Yeah," she says.

She chews on her crust. Shrugging, I pick up my fork and dig into the rest of my omelet.

TWENTY-SIX

I TRY TO PAY FOR our meal—after everything that Annie's been through, it only feels right—but she doesn't let me. All I can do is offer to cover the tip. We bundle ourselves up and head back out into the cold. For a second, we stand there staring at each other, a sort of "what next?" on our brows.

"You can come back to my parents' place," I tell her. "They're out. Maybe we could smoke a bowl, or . . ."

I think we both know what I'm asking, that last line that I'm tossing out into the sea. Her eyebrows lift, and there's a slight smile on the corners of her mouth, like I think she's glad to be asked. And we could. It would be so easy to fall into one another's arms, girlfriend or not. I know her mouth, the heat of her rib cage on me, and it wouldn't be like falling in love, not exactly, but it would feel good for a minute, and no one would ever know but us.

But she shakes her head, like I knew she would. "Nah. I have to get back to the hospital. Jamie will stay there all night if I don't, and Eli hates being there."

"Okay," I tell her, and nod. I go to offer her a hug. I don't know what I'm doing. My arms open, and she fits stiffly inside them. And the words spill out before I can even consider them. "I could come with you if you want.

You know, for support."

She pulls back, gazing at me in surprise. Honestly, I'm surprised, too. But I shouldn't be. I've always wanted to help her. To make her feel better. Deep down, I am definitely my mother's daughter.

"Sure," she says mildly. "I'd like that."

"Okay," I say, "I'll follow you." And then we get into our respective cars, and I follow her all the way to Kingston.

It's a cliché to say that hospitals smell like death. I don't know what death smells like. This hospital smells like stale air and warm pea soup. Annie is walking around like she owns the place, which I imagine is how she walks around everywhere, but my steps are small behind hers, uncertain. Because in the back of my head is a single frantic thought:

You shouldn't be here you shouldn't be here you should not be here.

But I'm here, streaming past the ugly hospital art. Everything is teal and pink and yellow and our footsteps echo on the floor and it's too hot in here, but I don't want to take my coat off, because I know I'm not going to stay for very long.

"Hey, E," Annie says to a boy sitting in a chair in the hall. It takes me a moment to realize who he is, all acne and lumpy curls and the faint hint of a mustache that he hasn't shaved yet. Elijah. He barely looks up from his phone as we pass, as we turn the corner into a room.

I stop short in the doorway at the sight in the bed. Wires and machines and a small body in them. Their mother is hooked up to a respirator, and though her eyes are open, she doesn't seem to notice we've come in.

"Mom," Annie says easily, like it's nothing, sitting on the side of the bed. "I'm here."

I just stand there.

There was a time when their mother had meant something else entirely to me. When I first heard about her, from James, it sounded like she was some kind of magical pixie—fun loving and irreverent in a way neither of my parents ever were. *She understands me* was what he'd told me, and I'd understood then, in the silences, what he meant. As much as I hated her later for everything she did to me, I always knew that James's mom understood him in a way his father never did.

But later, with Annie, things had grown more complicated. I could see how her intense focus on her son had rendered Annie invisible in their family. It wasn't that James could do no wrong and Annie always did the wrong thing. It was that she just didn't matter in the same way. Nothing did. No one did.

And I'd hated their mother for *that*, too.

Now the machines beep around her. Annie strokes her mother's fingers, trying to look brave—I think for me. I look down at the small, fragile woman who created both of them. The only two people I've ever let myself love. In that moment, I feel like my stomach is being torn in two. Like my heart is being torn in two. What am I even *doing* here?

"Who's this?" a deep voice says behind me. And I turn and see him then. Looking tired and faded but otherwise mostly the same. Marc. Annie's dad.

"Uh," I say softly, biting my lip. "I was just going."

It's not exactly true and wouldn't matter if it was, but it's the only thing I can think to say. Annie's eyes are on me. But I know suddenly, fiercely, that I do not belong here. This is a private moment. A family moment. And this is not my family.

"Okay," Annie says, and even though there is a question in her voice, I give my hand a small, silent wave.

Then I take off down the hall.

Down the elevator. Barely hearing the bad, piped-in music. Through another hallway, the carpet pattern like something terrifying—something out of *The Shining*. Past the gift shop, with its garish balloons and dull-eyed stuffed animals and the fake flowers by the door. I'm almost through the lobby when I see him, and the sight stops me dead in my tracks.

It's James.

I know, more or less, what he looks like, from that TV special that aired after he returned, which I watched with Harper in her room in horrified silence, and from my mom's reports. Mom's always telling me how she runs into him at the ShopRite, how once he helped her pick out a cantaloupe. She's always suggesting I go with her. I think she hopes it'll give me closure, seeing him. I'm always telling her that I don't need closure. What happened to me and James—and to James himself—happened a long time ago.

But seeing him in person is different. He's tall now. He's got this new presence that he never had as a kid. He's wearing a motorcycle jacket, open over his broad chest, and a soft gray T-shirt underneath it. He has side-burns. A shielded gaze. I used to think he looked just like Annie, but if I met him now, I don't think I'd even know they were related.

And he's not alone.

He's talking to a man in scrubs. A doctor, I think—or maybe a nurse? The man is shorter than James. Maybe shorter than me. He's got a round face and kind, open eyes, and I wonder for a minute if they're talking about Annie and James's mom, except the guy is smiling softly. He looks just so *happy* to be there, talking to James. I remember what that felt like, when I first met James, way back when we were in eighth grade. The magic of it. The intoxication.

And then the man leans forward and presses his cheek to James's cheek. Kissing him. But I would have known what was happening even without the kiss. I know because once, in ancient history, I lived it, too.

The man in scrubs walks off then, past me and down the hall. I'm just standing there as James turns back to watch him go. And sees me. Standing there. Watching.

Our eyes are locked. My eyes. James's. But I'm not really there in that hospital lobby. I'm in Neal Harriman's basement. It's the beginning of eighth grade. I don't know where Neal is or where his brother is, either. James and I have been dating for only a few weeks, and though we've kissed until our mouths are chapped, though we've slipped hands under clothing to caress and squeeze, the idea of crossing that threshold has seemed impossible, until this afternoon, when we find ourselves alone in Neal's basement, and suddenly, blushing, James procures a condom, and suddenly, blushing, I find myself consenting. It isn't sex. Not really. Only a few giggling, unsuccessful moments of full undress before we shiver back into our clothes and snuggle together on the crumby sectional, content to tell our friends that something has happened today, that now we are adults. We'll stay together for almost a year but never repeat this experiment, content with the magic we make with our hands and lips. Right now, some YouTube video is playing on their big TV, and his fingers are traipsing over my belly, just beneath the seam of my tank top. I feel self-conscious of the small dark hairs there, but they don't seem to bother James. He loves my body. He tells me that all the time. But he's had other loves. Boys. I know all about it, though he hasn't yet told another soul, and I haven't, either.

Today, though, I think, he's feeling brave.

"I'm going to do it," he says. "I'm going to tell my dad I'm bi."

I turn to look at him, smiling faintly. He's terrified, obviously, and I can understand it. The pressure his father puts on him—not that different from the pressure Naniji puts on my mom.

"Do you think it's worth it?" I ask him. "The risk?"

There's a long silence. The video keeps playing, the only sound.

"I read something," he says softly. "In the library. Kahlil Gibran. It was like some magic book. The passages seemed like spells."

"What did he say?"

"'Pain is the breaking of the shell that encloses your understanding.'"

He looks at me. I grimace. We giggle a little, both of us.

"Too emo for you?"

"Yeah," I tell him, and we're kissing again, like we're always kissing, a pair of innocent kids on Neal's sectional, our own magical kingdom at the heart of our world.

And now I'm twenty and I'm looking at him, remembering my disappointment back then when the conversation with his dad had never happened, how they had a big ridiculous argument about a drum kit instead. Now his eyes are soft and faintly trembling, and full of a new, raw love. I'm happy for him. I'm hopeful. I realize that this is an epilogue—overlong and unnecessary. And so I smile at him. And then I walk by him without a single word.

I'm in the parking garage when I realize that it's time to call up Priyanka and sing her that song I've been working on, the one that sounds like David Bowie. When the car door closes behind me, it's like a cord has been cut, and I'm free, I'm free, I'm free.

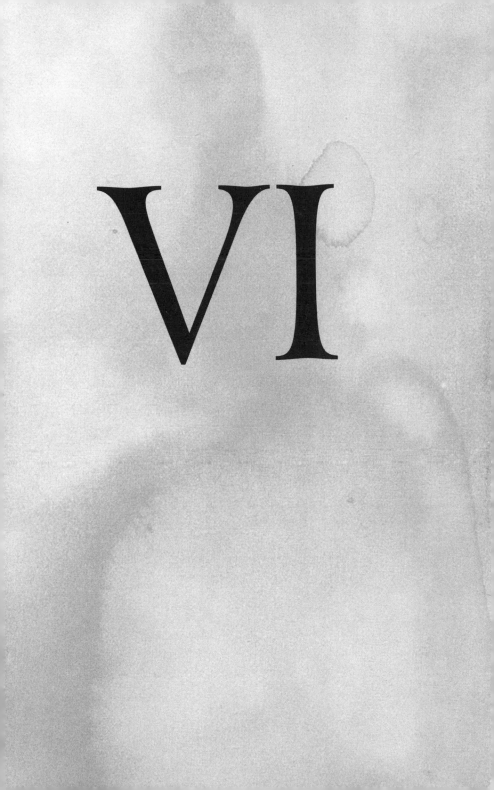

VI

and i wake up in the Black of Night with my heart marking out a Savage Drum Beat in my chest like i always wake up in the Black of Night for years now except the difference is that instead of waking up alone in my childhood bedroom or waking up alone in the bed i shared with a Coal-Hearted Girl i wake up in their bed their room their apartment and when i sit up panting my body slick with sweat they put a hand on the small of my back

and this time, when the pirates toss me overboard again, my body comes to rest on a stony shore. As I come to, I see how the dunes are marked with towers: one, two, a dozen more. Stones left by childish hands. I remember this place, this shore, this land, and the strange creatures who live here. Once, I was a child among them, telling myself I was not a child. Once I was a boy who claimed to be a prince. I see the shadows in the underbrush and know the feral children will soon come to claim me. I struggle against the ropes that bind me, hoping to free myself before they can carve my body out for supper. But the shadow who draws closer is no child at all but an adult, or nearly one, a luminescent beast with fine, curled hair and a trembling smile.

"Jay, are you okay?"

"Jay, are you okay?"

and i stumble to my feet giving my head a shake and i go down the hall to the bathroom and get myself a water and come back to sit at the foot of their bed to drink it while my heart still pounds out a Savage War Song, "Flashbacks," i say, and i shake my head again because always when i wake up in the dead of night i'm there for a moment in His bed in His apartment and it used to be that Shelley would scream at me for waking her but they are not Shelley and they are not Him either—they are someone new, a Brand New Luminescent Beast—and they only sit beside me and rest their head on my shoulder and in the darkness we wait for the memory to pass

They help me untie the ropes from my body. Our hands, working in synchronicity, in harmony, in chorus, and soon, I'm free from these ropes, sitting naked on a rocky shore and looking at this strange new creature, who looks at me with clear, kind eyes, and I realize that this is a new path, a new story, one that no one has written yet.

"I should head home soon," i say even as my head hits their pillow and Travis laughs a little and presses a hand against my cheek and kisses me because we met twelve days ago and already we have spent eleven nights together because when they are not at work and i am not at the hospital we are here talking in Low Tones to one another and doing nothing together and doing everything together and i'm not sure i've ever been In Love Before but i am most certainly and deliciously In Love Now

"There's something I'm supposed to do," I tell them, glancing at the hazy sunrise over this island like it holds an answer as precious as any

coin, and they take off their overdress to give to me. It billows out
around me in the warm island air.

"What am I going to do," i say softly, that question i've been
asking since that First Night when i got that Awful Call and
got to the hospital and there was this Luminescent Beast there
before me telling me what had happened to my mother because
i never expected one of the Worst Nights of My Life would also
be the Best and Travis lets out a sigh and kisses me again and
we're kissing for a moment for a long long moment and i think
this is not like what i shared with Neal when i was a child or
even Vidya this is not a Love that Lives in Darkness

"There's someone you can speak to," they say, smoothing the cloth
over my body, and I look into their eyes, anticipating their words
before they say them.

"About what?" they ask because we've talked about so many
things like how i'd like to go to college someday and read debord
or how my mother might heal and be changed and how my father
still confounds me and how there is a Jagged Line that connects
me to my sister even in the Worst of Times and how i was once
cruel to her and told her she was the archivist like she couldn't
even make her own stories when really we were Treasurers both i
mean it was right there in our name and we lived half our lives in
Other Places and squirreling the stories away for later which my
therapist says i might always do even if i never write them down
because for me these fantasies are a Coping Mechanism

"I've tried before," I tell them, willing them not to say her name. But
they shake their head.

"About my family," i tell them vaguely because i know i cannot
hide them anymore and i don't want to either

"You should try again," they urge me, and we look toward the jungle
in the distance, and the ramshackle, crooked houses that live within
it. I know that she's waiting for me in the tallest tree in the grandest
house on the whole damned island. The Emperata's got a quill pen
tucked behind her ear and her hands are stained with ink, and she's
waiting for me, still—like she's always been waiting.

"If I were you," they say carefully, "I would start with my sister."

Silence stretches out between us.

silence stretches out between us

ACROSS THE VAST SALT SEA

HEIR TO THE CRYSTAL THRONE, BOOK IV

By Anne M. James

CETUS BOOKS
NEW YORK

Cetus Books, Inc.
Beatrix Ian
Publisher
cetusbooks.com
Copyright © 2051 by Anne M. James
All Rights Reserved
Cover art by Petyr Murray
Cetus Books are distributed by Astomi Group (USA)

First printing, June 2051
4 5 6 7 8 9

Printed in the USA

For my brother,
for his help on this story
and every story.

PROLOGUE

ANNIT AND JAMIN watched their home burn.

It was the most beautiful thing they'd ever seen, the way the flames licked the redbrick walls like enormous tongues, turning the woodwork bright, then black. From their space beneath the wide front porch of Master Edon's house, they clutched hands and observed their belongings turn into a tower of gray. The twins had never been particularly materialistic, unlike their older sister, Corinth, but it still filled them with a fascinating mixture of excitement and dread to watch their toys, their beds, their father's work all go up in flames.

The townfolke did what they could to beat back the conflagration. They hauled bucket after bucket up from the creek's edge, until their hands were splintered and their faces black from smoke. It was all for naught. The home was meant to burn, and all the belongings inside it. Father and Corinth had barely escaped, eyes red and weeping and lungs full of acrid wind.

Thank the goddess Mother is already dead, said the twins, in their shared chorus of thought. Before she had caught the wasting disease, Mother had fallen off a ladder in the back larder. Only three steps, a freak accident, surely, for her bone had broken in four places and never quite mended right. She limped everywhere, loping steps, always trailing well behind her youngest children. She never would have made it out of the fire on time, had she not already died.

By the time the daylight had turned to purple gray, starless after the smoke, the fire had begun to die, too. The home was destroyed, though the townfolkes' work had saved the other finely built merchants' homes from burning. From the mud beneath the porch steps, the twins were unsure whether to be relieved or angry. After all, the other merchants were hardly any better than Father, with their fine clothes and their noses in the air. Or perhaps they were even worse. It had been Jin the Miller who had told their father to separate the children. "Not natural for a boy and girl to spend s'much time together," they'd heard him say when he had delivered Father's fine feathered hat to their parlor. Their father had grumbled, the frog in his throat twitching.

"Been together since the womb," he'd told Jin. But then the next morning, he pulled Jamin right out of bed at dawn, before Annit was even awake.

"Time for you to learn a trade, boy," he said. "Time for you to be useful."

When Annit had awoken, she was alone for the first time. She walked through the echoing hallways of their home, finding no one. It was only when she stepped into her father's workshop that she realized the reason for her solitude. There was Jamin, bending wires around a stone, his face a mask of concentration.

"Leave us, Annit," their father said without so much as lifting his head to see her. "Your woman's filth will interfere with our magic."

So Annit went to the creek. She walked through the forest. She tried to play hopscotch with the other girls, but they wouldn't let her. She tried to fill her day, but there was no filling it, not without Jamin.

Father's magic was a falsehood, anyway. Even Jamin said so.

That night when they tucked themselves in their straw bed together, Annit drew her brother close. Together, they made plans. Only Mother had ever suspected the power that the twins possessed—and once they'd had their way with her, she never spoke a word of it to Father.

"I don't want to hurt him," he said faintly.

"No one will get hurt," said Annit. "Besides, hasn't he hurt us? Separating us like he has?"

"He didn't *mean* to, though. He was only doing what the other merchants said he should."

"Still a cruelty."

They argued like that, round and round in circles, for hours. But in the end, Annit won—as she knew she would. After all, she and her brother had one heart, one soul. They wanted the same things, even if she was the only one who was ever brave enough to take them. At last, near dawn, he consented. Annit gripped his hands in hers and delineated her plan.

Two days later, the children, soot-covered and weary, crouched beneath the neighbor's porch as their home became a cinder. Their sister walked through the rubble, calling for them. They did not answer. Soon, they heard their father's voice yelling, too. Still, they uttered not a word, holding their breath together. When the night came on, deep and lovely and black as velvet, they finally crawled out, first Jamin, then Annit, just as they had from their mother's body thirteen years ago.

Annit watched as Jamin walked to the smoldering ruin that had been their home.

"What are you doing?" she asked in a whisper, worried they'd be found. But he didn't answer her at first. He only kicked through the soggy piles of detritus, searching. At last, he found an emerald, wrapped up with copper wire.

"Father said that this was a dragonstone," he told her. She watched as he hung it around his neck. "He said it would summon dragons."

"Father's a liar," she replied sourly. "Besides, what would you want with dragons?"

He looked at her, his eyes gone bright in the double moonlight. For a moment, she thought he resembled some sort of sharp-eyed hare.

"The same thing you want," he said. "Escape."

With that, her brother walked away from her, toward the forest's edge. She stood there, hands trembling at her sides. In that moment, she saw their future stretching out like a tangled ribbon. Perhaps it would be as she hoped, and they'd end at the same place. But in that moment she knew that the roads they chose to take them there would be very, very different. After all, she'd been the one to burn down their home. Jamin had been too afraid to light the wick. But not Annit.

Still, after a moment, his voice—as warm and familiar as her own voice inside her head—called out to her.

"Hey, are you coming?"

She hesitated only a moment before she went to join her brother, scrambling after him in the yawning darkness.

PHOEBE NORTH

is the critically acclaimed author of the novels *Starglass* and *Starbreak*. They were a Sustainable Arts Foundation finalist, and their short fiction and critical work has appeared in *Analog*, *Flash Fiction*, the *YA Review Network*, Umbrella Journal, and Strange Horizons, among others. Phoebe lives in the Hudson Valley, where they enjoy gardening, spending time with their family, and listening to music on outdated audio formats.

DRAMATIS PERSONAE

(Latin: "the Masks of the Drama")

Robert Foerster .... *the Boy in the Woods*

Jeffrey Krachun .... *the Runner*

Kenneth Kidd .... *the Scholar*

Sean Wills and Nathanial Merrill .... *the Queer Fellows*

Rachel Hartman .... *the Oracle*

Melissa Sarno .... *the First Reader*

Nova Ren Suma .... *the Mentor*

Stephanie Kuehn .... *the Wise Counsel*

Christine Heppermann .... *the Poet*

Jennifer Castle .... *the Gentlewoman*

Alysa Wishingrad .... *the Friend*

Anna Conlan, Elizabeth Brown,
and Sara Walton .... *Noble Countrywomen*

Erica Beckman .... *a Thaumaturge*

John Darnielle .... *a Lutist in the Court*

Tiara Kittrell .... *the Individual Friday*

Alexandra Rakaczki .... *a Shepherd*

Chris Kwon, Jenna Stempel-Lobell,
and Alison Donalty .... *Three Master Artists*

Shannon Cox .... *a Gifted Purveyor of Fine Volumes*

Jessica White .... *a Brilliant Tinker*

Alessandra Balzer and Donna Bray .... *Two Generous Gutenbergs*